Enid Blyton

Enid Blyton, who died in 1968, is one of the most popular and prolific children's authors of all time. She wrote over seven hundred books which have been translated into many languages throughout the world. She also found time to write numerous songs, poems, and plays, and ran magazines and clubs.

All eight titles in the Adventure series are also available individually from Macmillan Children's Books

The Circus of Adventure

The River of Adventure

Enid Blyton

MACMILLAN CHILDREN'S BOOKS

The Circus of Adventure
First published 1952 by Macmillan and Co Ltd
Revised edition published 1988 by Pan Books Ltd
The River of Adventure
First published 1955 by Macmillan and Co Ltd
Revised edition published 1988 by Pan Books Ltd

This double edition published 2002 by Macmillan Children's Books
a division of Macmillan Publishers Limited
20 New Wharf Road, London N1 9RR
Basingstoke and Oxford
www.panmacmillan.com

Associated companies throughout the world

ISBN 0 330 39838 5

5 7 9 8 6

A CIP catalogue record for this book is available from the British Library.

Printed and bound in Great Britain by
Mackays of Chatham plc, Chatham, Kent

The Circus of
Adventure

Contents

1

Home from school

The quiet house was quiet no longer! The four children were back from boarding-school, and were even now dragging in their trunks, shouting to one another. Kiki the parrot joined in the general excitement, of course, and screeched loudly.

'Aunt Allie! We're back!' yelled Jack. 'Be quiet, Kiki! I can't hear myself shout!'

'Mother! Where are you?' called Dinah. 'We're home again!'

Her mother appeared in a hurry, smiles all over her face. 'Dinah! Philip! I didn't expect you quite so soon. Well, Lucy-Ann, you've grown! And Philip, you look bursting with health!'

'I don't know why,' grinned Philip, giving Mrs Cunningham a big hug. 'The food at school is so frightful I never eat any of it!'

'Same old story!' said Mrs Cunningham, laughing. 'Hallo, Kiki! Say how do you do!'

'How do you do?' said the parrot, solemnly, and held out her left foot as if to shake hands.

'New trick,' said Jack. 'But wrong foot, old thing. Don't you know your left from your right yet?'

'Left, right, left, right, left, right,' said Kiki at once, and began marking time remarkably well. 'Left, right, left . . . '

'That's enough,' said Jack. He turned to Mrs Cunningham. 'How's Bill? Is he here, too?'

'He meant to be here to welcome you all,' said Mrs Cunningham, Bill's wife. 'But he had a sudden 'phone call this morning, took the car, and went racing off to London all in a hurry.'

The four children groaned. 'It isn't some job that's turned

9

up just as we're home for the Easter hols, is it?' said Lucy-Ann. 'Bill's always got some secret work to do just at the wrong time!'

'Well, I hope it isn't,' said Mrs Cunningham. 'I'm expecting him to telephone at any moment to say if he's going to be back tonight or not.'

'Mother! Shall we unpack down here and take our things up straight away?' called Dinah. 'Four trunks lying about the hall leave no room to move.'

'Yes. But leave two of the trunks downstairs when they're empty,' said her mother. 'We're going off on a holiday tomorrow, all of us together!'

This was news to the children. They clustered round Mrs Cunningham at once. 'You never said a word in your letters! Where are we going? Why didn't you tell us before?'

'Well, it was really Bill's idea, not mine,' said Mrs Cunningham. 'He just thought it would make a nice change. I was surprised myself when he arranged it.'

'Arranged it! And never said a word to us!' said Philip. 'I say – is anything up? It seems funny that Bill did it all of a sudden. Last time I saw him, when he came down to school to see us, he was talking about what we'd all do at *home* in the four weeks' Easter hols.'

'I don't really think there's anything *peculiar* about it,' said his mother. 'Bill gets these sudden ideas, you know.'

'Well – where are we all going to, then?' asked Jack, pushing Kiki off the sideboard, where she was trying to take the lid off the biscuit-jar.

'It's a place called Little Brockleton,' said Mrs Cunningham. 'Very quiet. In the middle of the country. Just the kind of place you all like. You can mess about in old things all day long.'

'Little *Brock*leton,' said Philip. 'Brock means badger. I wonder if there are badgers there. I've always wanted to study badgers. Lovely little bear-like beasts.'

'Well, *you*'ll be happy then,' said Dinah. 'I suppose that

means you'll be keeping a couple of badgers for pets before we know where we are! Ugh!'

'Badgers are very nice animals,' began Philip. 'Clean and most particular in their habits, and . . . '

Lucy-Ann gave a little squeal of laughter. 'Oh dear – they don't sound a *bit* like you then, Philip!'

'Don't interrupt like that and don't make silly remarks,' said Philip. 'I was saying, about badgers . . . '

But nobody wanted to listen. Jack had a question he wanted to ask. 'Are there any decent birds round about Little Brockleton?' he said. 'Where *is* it? By the sea?'

Jack was as mad as ever about birds. So long as he could do bird-watching of some kind he was happy. Mrs Cunningham laughed at him.

'You and your birds, Jack, and Philip and his badgers! I can't tell you anything about the birds there – the same ones as usual, I suppose. Now – what about these trunks? We'll unpack the lot; take the boys' trunks upstairs, and leave the girls' to take with us to Little Brockleton – they are not *quite* so hard-used as yours!'

'Can we have something to eat after we've unpacked?' asked Philip. 'I'm famished. The school food, you know, is so . . . '

'Yes – I've heard all that before, Philip,' said his mother. 'You'll have a fine lunch in half an hour – yes, your favourite – cold meat, salad, baked beans in tomato sauce, potatoes in their jackets, heaps of tomatoes . . . . '

'Oh, good!' said everyone at once, and Kiki hopped solemnly from one leg to another.

'Good!' she said. 'Good! Good morning, good night, good!'

The unpacking began. 'Kiki was dreadful in the train home,' said Jack, struggling with an armful of clothes, and dropping half of them. 'She got under the carriage seat to pick over some old toffee papers there, and such a nice old man got in. Kiki stuffed the toffee papers into the turn-up of

11

his trousers – you should just have seen his face when he bent down and saw them!'

'And then she began to bark like a dog,' said Lucy-Ann, with a giggle, 'and the poor old man leapt off his seat as if he'd been shot.' 'Bang-bang,' put in Kiki. 'Pop-pop. Pop goes the weasel. Wipe your feet and shut the door.'

'Oh, Kiki! It's nice to have you again with your silly talk,' said Mrs Cunningham, laughing. Kiki put up her crest and sidled over to her. She rubbed her head against Mrs Cunningham's hand like a cat.

'I always expect you to purr, Kiki, when you do that,' said Mrs Cunningham, scratching the parrot's head.

The unpacking was soon done. It was very simple really. Dirty clothes were pitched into the enormous linen-basket, the rest were pitched into drawers.

'Can't think why people ever make a fuss about packing or unpacking,' said Jack. 'Kiki, take your head out of my pocket. What's this sudden craze for toffees? Do you want to get your beak stuck so that you can't talk?'

Kiki took her head out of Jack's pocket, and screeched triumphantly. She had found a toffee. Now she would have a perfectly lovely time unwrapping the paper, talking to herself all the while.

'Well, that'll keep her quiet for a bit,' said Dinah, thankfully. 'Kiki's always so noisy when she's excited.'

'So are you,' said Philip at once. Dinah glared at him.

'Shut up, you two,' said Jack. 'No sparring on the first day of hols. Gosh, look at Lucy-Ann going up the stairs dropping a pair of socks on every step!'

The telephone bell rang. Mrs Cunningham ran to answer it. 'That will be Bill!' she said.

It was. There was a short conversation which consisted mostly of 'Yes. No. I see. I suppose so. No, of course not. Yes. Yes. No, Bill. Right. Yes, I'll explain. See you tonight then. Goodbye.'

'What's he say?' asked Lucy-Ann. 'Is he coming soon? I do want to see him.'

'Yes, he's coming this evening, about half-past five,' said Mrs Cunningham. The four children didn't think she looked very pleased. She opened her mouth to say something, hesitated, and then closed it again.

'Mother, what was it you said you'd explain?' said Philip at once. 'We heard you say, "Yes, I'll explain". Was it something you had to tell us? What is it?'

'Don't say it's anything horrid,' said Lucy-Ann. 'Bill *is* coming away with us, isn't he?'

'Oh yes,' said Mrs Cunningham. 'Well – I hope you won't mind, my dears – but he badly wants us to take someone else with us.'

'Who?' asked everyone at once, and they all looked so fierce that Mrs Cunningham was quite surprised;

'Not his old aunt?' said Dinah. 'Oh, Mother, don't say it's someone we've got to be on our best behaviour with all the time.'

'No, of course not,' said her mother. 'It's a small boy – the nephew of a friend of Bill's.'

'Do we know him? What's his name?' asked Jack.

'Bill didn't tell me his name,' said Mrs Cunningham.

'Why can't he go to his own home for the holidays?' asked Dinah in disgust. 'I don't like small boys. Why should *we* have to have him? He'll probably spoil everything for us!'

'Oh no he won't,' said Philip, at once. 'Small boys have to toe the line with us, don't they, Jack? We get enough of them and their fatheadedness at school – *we* know how to deal with them all right.'

'Yes, but why has he got to come to *us*?' persisted Dinah. 'Hasn't he got a home?'

'Oh yes – but he's a foreigner,' said her mother. 'He's been sent to school in England to have a good English education. I should imagine his family want him to have a few weeks in a British family now, and experience a little of our homelife. Also, I gather, there is some difficulty at his home at the moment – illness, I should think.'

'Oh well – we'll have to make the best of it,' said Lucy-

13

Ann, picturing a very little, homesick boy, and thinking that she would comfort him and make a fuss of him.

'We'll park him with you, then, Lucy-Ann,' said Dinah, who didn't like small boys at all, or small girls either. 'You can wheel him about in a pram and put him to bed at night!'

'Don't be silly, Dinah. He won't be as small as that!' said her mother. 'Now – have you finished? It's almost lunch-time, so go and wash your hands, and brush your hair.'

'Wash your hands, brush your hair, wipe your feet, blow your nose,' shouted Kiki. 'Brush your hands, blow your feet, wipe your – your – your . . . '

'Yes – you've got a bit muddled, old thing,' said Jack, with a laugh. Kiki flew to his shoulder, and began to pull at Jack's ear lovingly. Then, as she heard the sound of the gong suddenly booming out, she gave a loud screech and flew into the dining room. She knew what *that* sound meant!

'Jack! Kiki will peck all the tomatoes if you don't keep an eye on her,' called Mrs Cunningham. 'Go after her, quickly!'

But there was no need to say that – everyone had rushed to the dining room at the first sound of the gong!

2

Arrival of Gustavus

The afternoon was spent in looking all over the house to see if any changes had been made, and in exploring the garden from end to end to see what flowers were out, what edible things there were (only lettuces, alas!) and to introduce Kiki to six new hens.

'There's a new carpet in the guest room,' said Lucy-Ann. 'But that's all the changes there are. I'm glad. I don't like to come home and find anything changed. I suppose this small boy will sleep in the guest room, Aunt Allie?'

'Yes,' said Mrs Cunningham. 'I'm getting it ready in a minute or two. Go and join the others in the garden. You can pick a few daffodils, if you like – we want some in the hall.'

Lucy-Ann wandered off happily. The very first day of the holidays was always heavenly. All the first few days went slowly, and the thought of days and days of holiday ahead was one to dwell on contentedly almost every minute.

'Lucy-Ann! Come here! Kiki's having the time of her life!' called Jack. 'Look at her showing off in front of the new hens!'

Kiki was sitting on a post in the hen run. The six hens were gathered admiringly around her.

'Cluck-cluck-cluck,' they said to one another, and one stretched herself on tiptoe and flapped her wings as if trying to fly. Kiki put her head on one side, stretched herself on tiptoe too, spread her wings wide and took off. She sailed down to the surprised hens.

'Cluck-luck-luck, urrrrrrk!' she said, earnestly. 'Cluck-luck-luck, urrrrrrk!'

'Cluck-uck-uck, cluck!' said the hens, in admiration, and went nearer. One hen daringly pecked at one of the parrot's tail feathers.

This was insolence! Kiki danced round the alarmed hens, making a noise like an aeroplane in trouble. The hens took to their heels and fled into the hen house, almost tumbling over one another as they tried to squeeze in at the narrow doorway two at a time.

Kiki waddled after them, clucking again. Mrs Cunningham called from a window.

'Children! The hens will *never* lay us eggs if you let Kiki scare them.'

'Kiki's gone into the hen house – she'll probably sit in a nesting box and try to lay an egg like the hens!' called Jack. 'Come out, Kiki.'

Kiki came back and looked inquiringly out of the little

doorway. 'Polly put the kettle on,' she said, peaceably. 'cluck-luck-luck, *urrrrrk*!'

She flew to Jack's shoulder, and the hens looked at one another in relief. Was it safe to go out and wander round yet?

'There's the next-door cat,' said Dinah. 'Come to see what all the fuss is about, I expect! Hang on to Kiki, Jack.'

'Oh, she'll bark like a dog if the cat comes any nearer,' said Jack. 'Come on – let's see what the gardener has got in the greenhouse.'

It was a pleasant sunny afternoon, and the four really enjoyed themselves 'mooching about' as Jack called it. They all longed for Bill to arrive. Then the family would be complete – except, of course, that it would have one too many, if he really brought the unexpected boy with him!

'I'm going to watch at the gate for Bill,' announced Lucy-Ann after tea.

'We all will,' said Philip. 'Good old Bill! What luck for us that he's not on one of his hush-hush jobs just now, and can come away with us!'

They went to hang over the front gate together. Kiki kept putting her crest up and down excitedly. She knew quite well that Bill was coming.

'Bill! Pay the bill!' she kept saying. 'Where's Bill? Pop goes Bill!'

'You're a silly-billy,' said Lucy-Ann, stroking the parrot's soft neck. 'That's what you are!'

'*That's* an idiotic thing to call her,' said Dinah. 'Just as we're expecting Bill! She'll screech out "Silly-Billy" to him now, I bet you she will!'

'Silly-Billy, Billy-Silly!' shouted Kiki. She always loved words that sounded the same. Jack tapped her on the head.

'No, Kiki, stop it. Look, here's a car coming. Perhaps it's Bill's'.

But it wasn't. As it went by, Kiki hooted loudly – parp-parp-parp – exactly like a car.

16

The driver was astonished. He could see no car in sight. He sounded his horn, thinking there must be a hidden corner somewhere.

And then Lucy-Ann gave a squeal. '*Here's* Bill!' she said. 'A big black car, very sleek and shiny! Bill, Bill!'

She was right. It *was* Bill's car. It drew up at the front gate, and Bill's jolly face grinned at them as he looked out of the window. Somebody sat beside him. Was it the boy?

Bill opened the door and leapt out. The four children pounced on him. 'Bill! Good old Bill! How are you, Bill?'

'Silly-Billy!' screeched a voice.

'Ah – good evening, Kiki,' said Bill, as the parrot landed full on his shoulder. 'Still the same rude old bird. Aha! You want me at home to teach you a few manners!'

Kiki cackled like an excited hen. 'Now then – don't you lay eggs down my neck!' said Bill. 'What are you cackling about? Where's your mother, Dinah?'

'There she is,' said Dinah, as Mrs Cunningham came running to the gate. Bill was about to call to her when an extremely loud cough came from the car – a cough that was meant to be noticed.

'Oh – I completely forgot for the moment,' said Bill. 'I've brought a visitor. Did you tell them, Allie?'

'Yes, I did,' said Mrs Cunningham. 'Where is he? Oh, in the car. Bring him out, Bill.'

'Come on out,' said Bill, and in the midst of a dead silence the owner of the loud cough slid out of the car in as dignified a manner as he could.

Everyone stared at him. He was about eleven, and certainly very foreign-looking. His blue-black hair was curly and rather longer than usual. His eyes were as black as his hair, and he had thicker lashes than either of the girls. And he certainly had magnificent manners.

He went to Mrs Cunningham, and took the hand she held out to him. But instead of shaking it he bowed over it and touched it with his lips. Mrs Cunningham couldn't help

17

smiling. The four children stared in amusement.

'My thanks to you, dear lady,' he said, in a very foreign accent.

'That's all right,' said Mrs Cunningham. 'Have you had any tea?'

But before the boy chose to answer this question he had to make a further display of manners. He went to Dinah, and before she knew what he meant to do, he took her hand and bent over it. She gave a squeal and snatched it away.

'Don't!' she said. Lucy-Ann put her hands firmly behind her back. She didn't want them kissed either. What an extraordinary boy!

'Gus, old fellow – we just shake hands, you know,' said Bill, trying to hide his amusement at the sight of the two girls' indignant faces. 'Er – this is Gustavus Barmilevo, Allie. He will be with us for the next few weeks, as his uncle has asked me to keep an eye on him.'

Gustavus Barmilevo bowed very low, but did not attempt any more hand-kissing. Bill introduced the rest.

'Dinah – Lucy-Ann – Jack – and Philip. I – er – hope you'll soon all be good friends.'

The two boys shook hands with Gus, eyeing him with much disfavour. Goodness! Were they to put up with this little foreigner all the holidays?

Gus did a funny little bow each time he shook hands. 'Plizzed to mit you,' he said. 'What is zis bird? How you call it?'

'It's a Kiki-bird,' said Jack, solemnly. 'Gus, meet Kiki. Kiki, meet Gus!'

Kiki held out her left foot as usual, to shake hands. Gus looked extremely surprised, but his manners remained perfect. He held out his hand to Kiki's foot. Unfortunately Kiki dug her talons into his fingers, and he gave a loud yell.

'What a noise, what a noise!' said Kiki, severely. 'Wipe your feet and blow your nose. Fetch the doctor!'

'My finger's blidding,' said the boy, with tears in his voice. 'It blids, look.'

'Fetch the doctor, Polly's got a cold, fetch the doctor,' chanted Kiki, enjoying herself. The boy suddenly realized that it was the parrot who was talking. He forgot his 'blidding' and stared at Kiki in amazement.

'It spiks!' he announced in awe. 'It spiks. It spiks words. It sees my blidding finger, and spiks to fetch the doctor. I never haf seen a Kiki-bird before.'

'Come along in, and I'll put a bit of bandage on your finger,' said Mrs Cunningham, getting tired of all this.

'Yes. It blids,' said Gus, mournfully, watching a minute drop of blood fall to the ground. He looked as if he was going to cry. Then he said a most extraordinary thing.

'This bird,' he said, looking at Kiki suddenly, 'the bird – it must be in a cage. I order it.'

'Don't be a fathead,' said Jack, after a moment's silence of astonishment. 'Come on, Aunt Allie – let's go indoors. Gus might "blid" to death!'

This was a most alarming thought, and Gus rushed into the house at once. The others followed slowly. What an extraordinary boy!

'Bit dippy,' said Dinah in a low voice, and they all nodded. Bill's voice hailed them.

'Hey! What about a spot of help with the luggage?'

'Oh, Bill. Sorry, we weren't thinking,' said Jack, and ran back at once. 'Gus rather took our breath away. What nationality is he?'

'Oh, he's a bit of a mixture, I think,' said Bill. 'Don't bother him about his family or his home, or he'll probably burst into tears. Sorry to inflict him on you like this. He'll be better when he's shaken down a bit. I believe he got on quite all right at the English school he was at. Anyway – I'll take him off your hands as much as I can, I promise you, as it's *my* friend who asked me to keep an eye on him!'

'We'll help, Bill,' said Lucy-Ann. 'I expect he's shy. Oh dear – I was so afraid he'd kiss my hand! What *would* the girls at school say?'

'Well, I should hardly think they'd know anything about

it,' said Bill. 'You take that bag, Jack – and you that box, Philip. Well – it's nice to see you all home again! And Kiki, too, you old rascal. How *dare* you call me Silly-Billy?'

'Pop goes Billy, pop goes Billy!' screeched Kiki in delight, and flew down to his shoulder to nibble his ear. 'Pop-pop-pop!'

3
Gussy and Kiki

There really wasn't very much time that evening to get to know Gustavus Barmilevo. As they were all going off again the next day there was packing to do, and all kinds of arguments arose as to what was or was not to be taken.

Gustavus was bewildered by the noise of so many people talking at once. He sat staring at them all, nursing his bandaged finger. Kiki absolutely fascinated him. He watched her continually, but would not allow her near him.

As soon as she came near, he flapped his hands at her as if she was a hen. 'Go off!' he cried. 'Clear away!'

'He's as muddled as Kiki sometimes gets,' said Jack, with a grin. 'Kiki can't make him out. Now, where did I put that book? Aunt Allie, did I pack that big book?'

'You did,' said Aunt Allie. 'And I have unpacked it. For the third time, Jack, you are NOT going to take a score of books about birds. Two is more than enough, so make your choice.'

'You're so hardhearted,' groaned Jack. 'Well, I suppose you will allow me to take my field glasses? In fact, if they don't go, I shan't go either.'

'You can carry those round your neck,' said Mrs Cunningham. 'Do try and remember that there will be seven of us in the car and all the luggage, too. We really must take the least luggage possible. Kiki, bring that string back. KIKI! Jack, if you don't stop Kiki running off with absolutely everything I put down for a moment, I shall go mad.'

'Where is the cage?' suddenly demanded Gustavus, in a commanding voice. 'Put him in the cage.'

'She's a her, not a him,' said Jack, 'and stop talking about cages. No ordering about, please!'

Gustavus apparently did not follow this, but he resented Jack's firm voice. He sat up stiffly.

'This bird iss – iss – wicket!' he said. 'Not good. Wicket. I will not haf him wizzout a cage.'

'Now, Jack, now!' said Mrs Cunningham warningly, as she saw Jack's furious face. 'He's not used to Kiki yet. Or to our ways. Give him a chance to settle down. Don't take any notice of him. Gustavus, the bird is not wicked. She is good. Sit still and be quiet.'

'Where is the cage?' repeated Gustavus, in a most maddening manner. 'A beeg, BEEG cage. For a wicket bird.'

Jack went over to him and spoke slowly and loudly with his face close to the surprised boy's.

'I have a beeg, BEEG cage,' he said, most dramatically. 'But I keep it for small, annoying boys. I will bring it for you, Gus. If you want a beeg, BEEG cage you shall have it for yourself. You shall sit in it and be safe from that wicket, wicket bird.'

To Jack's enormous surprise Gustavus burst into tears! All four children looked at him aghast. How *could* a boy of eleven be so incredibly upset? Even Lucy-Ann was shocked. Mrs Cunningham hurried over to him.

'He's tired out,' she said to the others. 'It's all strange to him here, and he's never seen a parrot like Kiki before. Nor have any of us, come to that! Cheer up, Gustavus. Jack didn't mean what he said, of course.'

'I jolly well did,' began Jack. 'Kiki's old cage is enormous and . . .'

Mrs Cunningham firmly led the weeping Gus from the

21

room. The others stared at one another in complete disgust.

'Well! To think we've got to put up with *that* these hols!' began Jack. 'All I can say is that I'm going to take him firmly in hand – and he won't enjoy it one bit!'

'I'll take him in hand, too,' said Dinah, quite fiercely. 'Who does he think he is – laying down the law about Kiki and a cage! Oh, Jack – I do wish you'd got that old cage and brought it in. I'd have loved to see Gustavus's face.'

'Poor old Gussy!' said Lucy-Ann. 'Wouldn't he have howled! Poor Gussy!'

'Gussy!' said Kiki, at once. 'Fussy-Gussy! Fussy-Gussy!'

Everyone laughed. 'You've hit if off again,' said Philip to Kiki. 'Fussy – that's exactly what we'll have to put up with – fuss and grumbles and silliness all the time. Why didn't his parents bring up their kid properly? Fussy-Gussy! We shall get jolly tired of him.'

'Fussy-Gussy!' screamed Kiki, dancing to and fro, to and fro on her big feet. 'Wipe your feet, Gussy!'

'Dry your eye, you mean,' said Philip. 'I hope Gussy's not going to burst into tears *too* often. I think I'll borrow one of Mother's afternoon teacloths and take it with me to offer him every time he looks like bursting into tears.'

Mrs Cunningham came back, and overheard this. 'I think you're being a bit unkind,' she said. 'He may seem a bit of a nuisance, I admit – but it must be rather nerve-racking for him to be plunged into the midst of a company like this when he doesn't speak the language properly, and everyone laughs at him. I think you should play fair and give him a chance.'

'All right, Mother,' said Philip. 'All the same – it isn't like Bill to thrust someone like Gussy on us at a moment's notice, just at the beginning of the hols.'

'Well, you see,' said his mother, 'it's like this. Bill was saddled with this youngster – and he knew you wouldn't like having him. So he suggested to me that he should go off with him alone somewhere. I couldn't bear that, because a holiday without Bill would be horrid – and so we thought it would be best if Gustavus came with us all, and we tried to put up with him. It's either that or going without both Gussy *and* Bill.'

'I see,' said Philip. 'Well, I'd rather put up with Gussy than have no Bill.'

'That's what *I* thought,' said his mother. 'So don't make Bill feel too bad about it, will you? He's quite likely to vanish with Gussy for the rest of the holidays if you make too much fuss. All the same – I think you can quite safely help young Gustavus to join in. That won't do him any harm at all. He seems frightened and shy to me.'

'We'll soon show him exactly where he stands,' said Jack. 'But I really can't think how Bill was soft enough to take him on. Where's Gustavus now?'

'I've popped him into bed with a book', said Mrs Cunningham. 'There's such a lot of things to do this evening and I really felt I couldn't cope with upsets and bickerings the very first day you were home – so I thought everyone would be happier if he was in bed.'

'How right you were!' said Jack. 'Well, now dear Gussy is safely out of the way, let's get on with things. I suppose you don't want any help with the supper, Aunt Allie?'

'I imagine that's a roundabout way of saying you are hungry again?' said Aunt Allie. 'All right – the girls can see to supper. You boys come and help me finish packing the greatest number of things into the smallest possible bags! I'm leaving behind practically everything belonging to Gustavus – he's got the most *ridiculous* things – pyjamas made of real silk, for instance! And monograms on everything.'

'He must have gone through an awful lot of teasing at school then,' said Philip. 'I'm surprised they didn't have his hair cut. Most girls would envy him all that long curly hair.

Couldn't we get his hair cut, Mother?'

'Possibly,' said his mother. 'Let's not talk about him any more.'

The packing was finished by supper time. Mrs Cunningham was determined not to take more than a change of clothes for everyone: shirts, jerseys, blazers and macs. Once more she had to take Jack's enormous book on birds from where he had hidden it yet again under some shirts in a suitcase. She looked at him in exasperation.

He grinned back amiably. 'Oh, sorry, Aunt Allie! You don't mean to say it's got itself packed again!'

'I'm *locking* the cases now,' said Aunt Allie, with determination. 'Really, Jack, I sometimes feel you want a good spanking!'

Supper was a hilarious meal. Gustavus, having a tray of food in bed, listened rather enviously. He was tired, and glad to be in bed – but it did sound very jolly downstairs. He didn't somehow feel that he had made a very good impression, though. That bird – it was that 'wicket' bird who had made things go wrong. When he got Kiki alone he would slap her hard – biff!

Gustavus brought his hand down smartly as he pictured himself slapping Kiki. The tray jerked and his lemonade spilt over the traycloth. There – that was thinking of Kiki again. He was so engrossed in trying to mop up the mess he had made that he didn't notice someone rather small sidling in at the door.

It was the parrot, come to find out where Gustavus was. Kiki's sharp eyes had missed him at supper time. Then where was he? Upstairs?

Kiki went under the bed and explored the slippers and boxes there. She pecked at one of the boxes, trying to get off the lid. She loved taking off lids.

Gustavus heard the noise. What was it? He looked round the room.

Peck-peck-peck! The lid wouldn't come off. 'Who's

there? Who iss it?' said Gustavus, in an anxious voice.

Kiki debated what noise to make. She had a grand store of noises of all kinds. There was the screech of a railway train going through a tunnel. No — that would bring Mrs Cunningham upstairs, and she would be angry. There was the lawn mower — a most successful noise, but also not very popular indoors.

And there was quite a variety of coughs — little short hacking coughs — deep hollow ones — and sneezes. What about a sneeze?

Kiki gave one of her most realistic sneezes. A – WOOOOOSH-OO!' It sounded very peculiar indeed, coming from under the bed.

Gussy was petrified. A sneeze — and such an enormous one — and under the bed! **WHO** was under the bed? Someone lying in wait for him? He began to tremble, and the lemonade spilt again.

Kiki began to cough — a deep, hollow cough, mournful and slow. Gustavus moaned. Who was it *coughing* under his bed now? He didn't dare to get out and see. He was sure that whoever was there would catch hold of his ankles as soon as his feet appeared on the floor.

Kiki next did a very fine growl, and poor Gussy shivered so much in fright that his tray nearly slid off the bed altogether. He just clutched it in time. But a plate fell off, hit one of shoes standing nearby and rolled slowly under the bed.

Now it was Kiki's turn to be surprised. She hopped out of the way and glared at the plate, which flattened itself and lay still.

'Help! Help!' suddenly yelled Gussy, finding his voice at last. 'Someone's under my bed. Help! Help!'

Bill was up in a trice, striding over to Gustavus. 'What is it? Quick, tell me.'

'Under the bed,' said Gussy, weakly, and Bill bent down to look. There was nobody there. Kiki had decided that the joke was over, and was now safely inside the nearby wardrobe, her head on one side, listening.

'You mustn't imagine things, old chap,' Bill was saying kindly. 'There's nobody under the bed – and never was. Nobody at all! I'll take your tray and you can settle down to sleep!'

4

Off to Little Brockleton

Next day was bright and sunny, with big piled up clouds racing over the April sky.

'Like puffs of cotton wool,' said Dinah. 'I hope it's going to be like this all the hols.'

'I'm going to get the car,' said Bill. 'When I hoot I shall expect you all to be ready. Allie, you can sit in front with me, and Lucy-Ann must squeeze there too, somehow. The other four can go at the back. Luggage in the boot. And if anyone wants to be dumped on the road and left to walk, he or she has only got to behave badly, and I'll dump them with pleasure.'

'I really believe you would too, Bill,' said Lucy-Ann.

'Oh, not a doubt of it,' said Bill, putting on such a grim face that poor Gussy was really alarmed. He made up his mind that he would behave superlatively well, and he immediately put on his finest manners. He opened doors for everyone. He bowed. He tried to take whatever Mrs Cunningham was carrying, and carry it for her. When he got into anyone's way, which he did almost every minute, he sprang aside, bowed, and said:

'Excuse, plizz. I pollygize.'

'Polly put the kettle on,' said Kiki, at once. 'Polly, Polly – Polly-gize.' Then she went off into an alarming cackle of laughter.

'How's your finger, Gus?' asked Jack, politely.

'It has stopped blidding,' said Gus.

'Well, I warn you – don't try and play tricks with old Kiki,' said Jack, 'or she'll go for you – make you blid again – much, much blid!'

'Ah, wicket,' said Gus. 'I think that bird is not nice.'

'I bet Kiki thinks the same of you!' said Jack. 'You're standing in my way. You'd better move unless you want this suitcase biffing you in the middle.'

'Excuse, plizz. I pollygize,' said Gussy, hurriedly, and skipped out of the way.

At last everything was ready. Mrs Cunningham's cleaner came to see them off, promising to lock up after them, and come in every day to clean and dust. Bill was hooting loudly. Gussy was so terribly afraid of being left behind that he shot down the front path at top speed.

Bill, Mrs Cunningham and Lucy-Ann squeezed themselves into the long front seat. The other four got into the back. Gussy shrank back when he saw that Kiki was going with them, apparently on Jack's shoulder, next to him.

Kiki made a noise like a cork being pulled out of a bottle – POP! Gussy jumped.

Kiki cackled, and then popped another cork. 'POP! Pop goes the weasel. Gussy. Fussy-Gussy, Gussy-Fussy. POP!'

'What do you think you're doing, Gussy?' said Jack, seeing the boy slipping from the seat down to the floor.

'Excuse, plizz. I pollygize. The Kiki-bird, he spits in my ear – he goes POP!' explained Gussy, from his seat on the floor.

Everyone roared. 'Don't be an ass, Gussy,' said Jack. 'Come on up to the seat. Squeeze in at the other end if you like, next to Dinah. But I warn you – Kiki will wander all over the car when she's tired of sitting on my shoulder.'

'Blow your nose,' said Kiki sternly, looking down at the surprised Gussy.

'All ready, behind?' called Bill, putting in the clutch. He

pressed down the accelerator, the engine roared a little and the car moved off down the road.

'Heavy load we've got,' said Bill. 'What a family! This car is going to grunt and groan up every hill!'

It did, though it was a powerful car, and one that Bill used in his work. It swallowed up the miles easily, and Mrs Cunningham was pleased to think they would arrive at their destination before dark.

'What is the name of the place we are going to, Aunt Allie?' asked Lucy-Ann. 'Oh yes, I remember – Little Brockleton. Are we having a cottage, or what?'

'Yes,' said Aunt Allie. 'It's called Quarry Cottage, because an old quarry is nearby. It's about a mile from the village, and I believe only a farmhouse is near. We can get eggs and butter and milk and bread from there, which is lucky.'

'I shall ask about badgers as soon as I get there,' said Philip, from the back. 'I wish I could get a young badger. I've heard they make wonderful pets.'

'There! I knew you'd start hunting out pets of some kind,' said Dinah. 'We never can have a holiday without your bringing in mice or birds or insects or even worse creatures.'

'I've been thinking of studying *spiders* these hols,' said Philip, seriously. 'Amazing creatures, spiders. Those great big ones, with hairy legs, are . . . '

Dinah shivered at once. 'Let's change the subject,' she said. 'I don't know why, but whenever anyone even *mentions* spiders I seem to feel one crawling down my back.'

'Oh, gosh – don't say my spider's escaped!' said Philip at once, and pretended to look through his pockets. Gussy watched him in alarm. He didn't like spiders either.

Dinah gave a small shriek. 'Don't be mean, Philip – please, please. You haven't *really* got a big spider, have you?'

'Philip!' called his mother warningly. 'You'll be dumped in the road. Remember what Bill said.'

'All right. I haven't got a spider,' said Philip, regretfully.

'You can sit in safety, Di. I say, Gus, aren't you uncomfortable down there, on the floor, among our feet? I keep forgetting you're there. I hope I haven't wiped my feet on you yet.'

'That is not a nice thing to spik,' said Gussy, with dignity. 'I will be angry to have your feets wiped on me.'

'Let's play a game,' said Jack, seeing an argument developing. 'We'll look out for black dogs – white cats – piebald horses – red bicycles – and ice cream vans. The one who is last to reach a hundred must stop at the next ice cream van and buy ices for us all!'

This sounded exciting to Gussy. He scrambled up from the floor at once, and squeezed himself beside Dinah. Bill and Mrs Cunningham heaved a sigh of relief. Now there would be quite a bit of peace – everyone would be looking out and counting hard.

Gussy was not at all good at this game. He missed any amount of black dogs and white cats, and kept counting ordinary horses instead of piebald ones. He looked very miserable when he was told that he couldn't put all the brown and white horses he had seen into his score.

'He's going to cry!' said Philip. 'Wait, Gus, wait. Take my hanky.'

And he pulled out one of the kitchen tablecloths, which he had neatly purloined just before coming away, in spite of his mother's threats.

Gussy found the tablecloth pushed into his hands. He looked at in astonishment – and then he began to laugh!

'Ha ha! Ho ho! This is cloth, not hanky! I will not weep in this. I will laugh!'

'Good for you, Gussy!' said Jack, giving him a pat on the back. 'Laugh away. We like that!'

It was quite a surprise to everyone to find that Gussy could actually laugh at a joke against himself. They began to think he might not be so bad after all. He stopped playing the counting game after that, but displayed even more surprising behaviour at the end of the game.

Lucy-Ann was last to reach a hundred. She felt in her little purse for her money, knowing that she must buy ice creams for everyone, because she had lost the game.

'Please, Bill, will you stop at the next ice cream van?' she said. So Bill obligingly stopped.

But before Lucy-Ann could get out, Gussy had opened the door at the back, shot out and raced to the ice cream van. 'Seven, plizz,' he said.

'Wait! *I* lost, not you!' shouted Lucy-Ann, half indignant. Then she stared. Gussy had taken a wallet out of his pocket – a wallet, not a purse! And from it he took a wad of notes – good gracious, however many had he got? He peeled off the top one and gave it to the ice cream man, who was as surprised as anyone else.

'You come into a fortune, mate?' asked the ice cream man. 'Or is your dad a millionaire?'

Gussy didn't understand. He took his change and put it into his pocket. Then he carried the ice creams back to the car, and handed round one each, beaming all over his face.

'Thanks, Gus,' said Bill, accepting his. 'But look here, old chap – you can't carry all that money about with you, you know.'

'I can,' said Gussy. 'All the term I had it here in my pocket. It is my pocket money, I think. They said I could have pocket money.'

'Hm, yes. But a hundred pounds or so in notes is hardly *pocket* money,' began Bill. 'Yes, yes – I know you kept it in your *pocket*, but real pocket money is – is – oh, you explain, boys.'

It proved to be very difficult to explain that all those pound notes were not pocket money merely because Gussy kept them *in* his pocket. 'You ought to have handed them in at your school,' said Philip.

'They said I could have pocket money,' said Gussy, obstinately. 'My uncle gave it to me. It is mine.'

'Your people must be jolly rich,' said Jack. 'I bet even Bill doesn't wander round with as many notes as that. Is Gus a millionaire or something, Bill?'

'Well – his people *are* well off,' said Bill. He slipped in the clutch again and the car slid off. 'All the same, he'll have to hand over those notes to me. He'll be robbed sooner or later.'

'He's going to cry,' reported Dinah.. 'Philip, quick – where's that tablecloth?'

'I am not going to weep,' said Gussy, with dignity. 'I am going to be sick. Always I am sick in a car. I was yesterday. Plizz, Mr Cunningham, may I be sick?'

'Good gracious!' said Bill, stopping very suddenly indeed. 'Get out of the car, then, quick! Push him out, Dinah. Why, oh, why did I let him have that ice cream? He told me yesterday he was always carsick.'

Mrs Cunningham got out to comfort poor Gussy, who was now green in the face. 'He *would* be carsick!' said Dinah. 'Just the kind of thing he'd have – carsickness.'

'He can't help it,' said Lucy-Ann. 'Anyway, it's all over now. He looks fine.'

'Plizz, I am better,' announced Gussy, climbing back in the car.

'Keep the cloth,' said Philip, pushing it at him. 'It might come in useful if you feel ill again.'

'Everyone ready?' called Bill. 'Well, off we go again. We'll stop for lunch at one o'clock, and then we'll be at Little Brockleton by tea time, I hope. Gussy, yell if you feel queer again.'

'I am only sick once,' said Gussy. 'Plizz, I have lost my ice cream. Will you stop for another?'

'I will not,' said Bill, firmly. 'You're not having any more ice creams in the car. Doesn't anyone want a nap? It would be so nice for me to drive in peace and quietness! Well next stop, lunch!'

5

Quarry Cottage

Little Brockleton was a dear little village. The car ran through it, scattering hens and a line of quacking ducks. Bill stopped at a little post office.

'Must just send off a message,' he said. 'Won't be a minute. Then we'll go and call at the farmhouse to ask the way to Quarry Cottage, and to pick up eggs and things, and order milk.'

He reappeared again after a moment. The children knew that Bill had to report where he was each day, because urgent jobs might come his way at any moment — secret tasks that only he could do.

They went off to the farmhouse. The farmer's wife was delighted to see them. 'Now, you come away in,' she said. 'I've been expecting you this last half-hour, and I've got tea for you. You won't find anything ready at the cottage, I know, and a good tea will help you along.'

'That's very kind of you,' said Mrs Cunningham, grate-fully. 'My goodness — what a spread!'

It certainly was. It wasn't an ordinary afternoon tea, it was a high tea. A fresh ham, glistening pink. A veal and ham pie smothered in green parsley, like the ham. Yellow butter in glass dishes. A blue jug of thick yellow cream. Honey. Home-made strawberry jam. Hot scones. A large fruitcake as black as a plum pudding inside. Egg sandwiches. Tea, cocoa and creamy milk.

'I'm absolutely determined to live on a farm when I'm grown up,' said Jack, looking approvingly at all the food on the big round table. 'I never saw such food as farm houses have. I say, isn't this smashing?'

Gussy felt glad that Mrs Cunningham had insisted that he

should eat very little at lunch time. He felt sure he had an appetite three times bigger than anyone else's.

'What will you have?' asked the farmer's wife, kindly, seeing his hungry look.

'I will have some – some pig meat,' said Gussy. 'And some pie meat with it. And I will have some cream with it, and . . .'

'He's a little comedian isn't he?' said the farmer's wife, with a laugh. 'Pig meat! Does he mean ham? And surely he'll be sick if I pour cream over it all?'

'Cut him a little ham, if you will,' said Mrs Cunningham. 'No pie. He can't possibly eat both. And of course not the cream!'

'I have ordered my meal,' said Gustavus, in a very haughty voice, staring at the surprised farmer's wife. 'I will have what I say. Plizz,' he added as an afterthought.

'Shut up, Gus,' said Bill. 'You'll do as you're told. You're forgetting yourself.'

'I have not forgot myself,' said Gus, puzzled. 'I have remembered myself, and I want . . .'

'Shut up,' said Bill, and Gus shut up.

The others grinned. It was nice to see Bill squashing Gussy. Gussy was very angry. He glared at Bill, and seemed about to say something. But Bill looked across at him, and he didn't say it. Bill winked at the others, and they winked back.

'Fussy-Gussy,' remarked Kiki, from Jack's left shoulder. 'Ding-dong-bell, Gussy's in the well.'

'Pussy's in the well, not Gussy,' corrected Jack. 'Oh, you pest – you've nabbed a strawberry out of the jam!'

The farmer's wife took Kiki in her stride, and was not unduly surprised at her, nor annoyed. 'My old aunt had a parrot once,' she said. 'One like yours here. She didn't talk as well as yours though.'

'Is she alive?' asked Jack, thinking that it would be fun to put the two parrots together and see them eyeing one another. What kind of conversation would they have?

'Is who alive? My aunt or her parrot?' asked the famer's wife, pouring out cups of creamy milk. 'The parrot's dead. It was supposed to be over a hundred years old when it died. My old aunt is still alive, though. There she is, sitting by the fire over in the corner. She's my great-aunt really, and *she'll* be more than a hundred if she lives another ten years.'

The five children stared in awe at the old woman in the corner. She looked rather like a witch to them, but her eyes were faded blue, instead of green. She smiled a dim smile at them, and then bent her white head to her knitting again.

'She's a real worry sometimes,' said the farmer's wife. 'She wanders round and falls about, you know. And the doctor's off on a week's holiday soon, and what I shall do if old Aunt Naomi falls and hurts herself then, I don't know! There's no neighbours near but you – and you're a good bit away!'

'You send a message to us if you want us at any time,' said Mrs Cunningham at once. 'I'll certainly come. I am quite good at first-aid and nursing. So don't worry about the doctor going. Send a message if you want us.'

'Ah, yes – I could do that,' said the farmer's wife. 'Thank you kindly. Now – who wants a bit of that fruitcake? It's good, though I shouldn't say it, seeing that I made it myself.'

'If I eat any more I shan't be able to move a step,' said Bill, at last. 'Will you kindly make up your minds to finish, you kids? We'll get along to Quarry Cottage, and settle in. Did you manage to send a someone in to clean up the place for us, Mrs Ellis?'

'Oh yes,' said the farmer's wife. 'And she took eggs, milk, a pie, some home-made cheese, ham and butter and new bread for you. Oh yes, and a side of bacon. You won't do too badly down there! Come along to me when you want anything. I hope you have a good, restful holiday.'

They left the cosy farmhouse reluctantly. Jack eyed Gussy suspiciously, as the got into the car. 'You look a bit green,' he said. 'Sure you'll be all right in the car?'

'He'll be all right,' said Mrs Cunningham, hurriedly. 'It's not very far – he'll be *quite* all right.'

'Wishful thinking, Aunt Allie!' said Jack. 'Kiki's very quiet. Kiki, *you've* made a pig of yourself too – a little pig, eating such a big tea!'

Kiki gave a big hiccup. Nobody ever knew if her hiccups were real or put on. Mrs Cunningham always felt quite certain that they were put on.

'Kiki!' said Jack, severely. 'Manners, manners!'

'Pardon,' said Kiki. Gussy stared at her in amazement. It was surprising enough for a parrot to hiccup, but even more surprising that she should apologize! He quite forgot to feel sick because of his astonishment at Kiki.

Down a winding lane – up a little hill – down another lane whose hedges were so high that the children felt they were in a green tunnel. Round a sharp bend, and then there was Quarry Cottage, standing a little way back from the lane.

It was a pretty place, its garden full of primroses, wall-flowers and daffodils. The people who owned it had gone to the South of France for a holiday, and had been pleased to let it to Bill.

The windows were rather small, as they always are in old cottages. The door was stout, made of oak darkened by the years, and was protected by a small porch, thatched with straw like the sloping roof of the cottage.

'A thatched cottage – how lovely!' said Lucy-Ann. 'I don't know why, but thatched houses always look as if they belong to fairy-tales, not to real life. It's a dear little place.'

They went up the path. Bill had the key and unlocked the door. In they all went, exclaiming over everything.

'I need hardly remind you that this house, and everything in it, belongs to someone else,' said Mrs Cunningham. 'So that we'll have to be extra careful – but as you will probably be out of doors most of the day you won't have time to do *much* damage!'

'We shouldn't anyway,' said Jack. 'Not with Bill here ready to jump on us!'

The cottage was just as pretty inside as out, and very cosy and comfortable. The three boys had a big attic, the two girls had a small bedroom over the sitting room, and Bill and his wife had a larger one next to it.

The larder was full of food! Mrs Ellis, the farmer's wife, had certainly remembered them generously. Mrs Cunningham heaved a sigh of relief as she looked at the ham and bacon, eggs and milk. Housekeeping was not going to be the nightmare she had expected!

'You two girls unpack everything,' she said. 'We've not brought much with us, so it won't take you long. Arrange the boys' things in the big chest in their room – there's enough room for the clothes of all three there.'

'I cannot slip with others,' announced Gustavus, coming down the stairs into the hall, where the girls and Mrs Cunningham were undoing the suitcases. 'Never have I slipt with others.'

'What are you talking about?' said Dinah. 'Nobody wants you to slip. Why should you?'

'He means *sleep*,' said Lucy-Ann. 'Don't you, Gussy?'

'It is what I said,' said Gussy. 'I may not slip with others. At school I slipt by myself. Here I will slip by myself also. It iss the rule of my family.'

'Well, it isn't the rule here,' said Dinah. 'Get off those shirts, Gus. And don't be an ass. There are only three bedrooms, anyway.'

'What's the argument?' said Bill, coming in after putting the car into a shed, and seeing Gussy's frowning face.

'It's Gus,' said Dinah, piling her arms full of clothes. 'He's just announced he wants to sleep by himself. Says it's the rule of his family. Who does he think he is? A prince?'

Gussy opened his mouth to reply, and Bill hurriedly interrupted what he was going to say. 'Gus, you'll sleep with the two boys here. Understand?'

'I slip alone,' said Gus, obstinately. 'Never have I . . . '

'There's a tiny little box-room he could have,' said Dinah, suddenly, a gleam in her eye. 'I saw it just now, when I was upstairs. He could "slip" there. I'm sure he won't mind the dozens of colossal spiders there – ugh, they've all got hairy legs. And I heard a mouse – or it might have been a rat – scuttling behind the cistern – and . . . '

Gus looked horrified. 'No. I do not slip with spiders and mouses,' he said. 'But still it is not right that I should slip with Philip and Jack. And I will not slip with that wicket bird.'

'Come in here a minute, Gus,' said Bill, and he took the boy firmly by the shoulder, led him into the sitting room and shut the door. The two girls heard a murmur of voices, and looked at one another in surprise.

'Mother, what's all the fuss about?' said Dinah, puzzled. 'Why doesn't Bill put that silly young Gus in his place? If he's going to be high and mighty all the time, and give his orders, and act in such an idiotic way, we're all going to hate him.'

'Leave it to Bill,' said her mother, and then changed the subject. 'Take those things up, Dinah – and Lucy-Ann, put these things in my room, will you? Now, did I pack Bill's set of pipes, or didn't I?'

The girls went upstairs. 'Mother's as mysterious about Gus as Bill is,' said Dinah, crossly. 'Is there some mystery about him? Can he be Prince in disguise, or something?'

'What! A funny little boy like him!' said Lucy-Ann, in disgust. 'Of COURSE not!'

6

Mostly about Gussy

It was fun settling in at Quarry Cottage. Mrs Cunningham was pleased and happy. She hadn't been looking forward to a holiday for seven people, five of them children, knowing that she would have to do everything for them, and that perhaps the shopping would be difficult.

But it was easy. The village was not too far away, even for walking purposes. The farm-house was willing to supply a wonderful selection of good food. Mrs Gump, the tiny little charwoman, came every day, and was cheerful and hard-working. She also liked children, which was a great blessing.

She didn't like Gussy, though. 'He orders me about, that one,' she complained. 'He even wanted me to go upstairs and fetch his handkerchief for him, Mam. He's staying with you, isn't he? Well, I'm not going to be ordered about by anyone, specially not little nippers like that.'

Gussy was very difficult those first days. He didn't like this and he didn't like that. He complained if he was given a cracked plate. He absolutely refused to make his bed, though it was a rule in the house that everyone should make their own.

'I do not make beds,' he announced, in his haughtiest manner. 'Mrs Gump shall make my bed.'

'Mrs Gump shall not,' said Dinah, firmly. 'You go and make your own — and for goodness' sake don't make such a *fuss*, Gussy.'

'Fussy-Gussy, Fussy-Gussy!' chanted Kiki, in delight. 'Fussy-Gussy, Fussy . . . '

Gus caught up a book and flung it at Kiki. The bird dodged easily, sat on the back of a chair and cakled with laughter. Gus was just about to pick up another book when

38

he found himself on his back on the floor.

Dinah had put up with enough from Gussy. She had now lost her temper, and was showing him how well she could do it! She banged his head on the floor, and he yelled the place down.

Mrs Cunningham came in at once. 'Dinah! What are you thinking of? Get up at once. Go upstairs and stay there till I come to you.'

'He flung a book at Kiki,' panted Dinah, rising up red and angry. Gussy still lay on the floor, and the tears ran down his cheeks.

'Get up, Gussy,' said Mrs Cunningham. 'I'm just as cross with you as I am with Dinah. Go up to your room too, and stay there.'

'You cannot order me,' said Gussy, with as much dignity as he could manage through his tears. 'Send this girl back home. And that wicket bird.'

'GO TO YOUR ROOM!' said Mrs Cunningham in such a furious voice that Gussy leapt to his feet, tore up the stairs, went into his room, slammed the door and turned the key!

Bill came in. 'It's Gussy again,' said his wife. 'He's such a little *fathead*. I hope this is going to work out all right, Bill. I think we should have thought of some other idea. The others don't understand, you see. Can't we tell them?'

'I'll have a word with Gussy again,' said Bill. 'If he doesn't come to heel I'll take him away by myself – but I thought it would be so much safer if he was here with all of us.'

He went upstairs. Mrs Cunningham also went up to Dinah. Lucy-Ann was with her, arranging the clothes in the drawers. Dinah was very mutinous.

'It's all very well,' she said, when her mother scolded her, 'but why should Gussy spoil everything for us? He's always interfering, always ordering us about, always wanting the best of everything for himself – and fancy DARING to try and hurt Kiki!'

'I understand how you all feel,' said her mother. 'So does

Bill. But he's promised to keep an eye on Gussy for the next few weeks, and he must. I think perhaps it would be best if he took Gussy off somewhere, and left us here by ourselves.'

'Oh, *no*,' said Lucy-Ann at once. 'No, Aunt Allie! You've married him, and he belongs to us now. Please don't let him do that! Dinah, *say* something!'

'Well – I thought, I *could* put up with Gussy, rather than have Bill leave us,' said Dinah. 'But – but – oh dear, I *can't* promise not to go for Gussy. I don't think I'll be able to stop myself! And I can't possibly let Bill go away either.'

'Well, stay here by yourself for an hour and make up your mind,' said her mother, losing patience. 'Lucy-Ann, come downstairs with me.'

Nobody told Jack or Philip about Gussy flinging a book at Kiki. Kiki didn't forget though! She plagued the life out of poor Gussy! He never knew when she was under the table ready to tweak his toes at the end of his sandals. He never knew when she would hide in his bedroom and wait for him to come up. Then she would produce one of her extra-ordinary noises and send him downstairs in a panic at top speed!

'Well, if Bill didn't punish him – and I don't think he did – *Kiki's* doing it all right!' said Dinah to Lucy-Ann. 'Anyway, Gussy is certainly better. I wish he wasn't coming on the picnic with us today, though.'

A picnic had been arranged for everyone on Sugar-Loaf Hill. It was really the name that had attracted the children – Sugar-Loaf Hill! What a lovely name!

They set off together, Bill and the boys carrying the food in satchels on their backs. Gus had made a fuss, of course. He seemed to think that it was a great indignity to carry something on his back.

'Never haf I done this before,' he protested. 'In my country it is the – how do you call it? – donkeys who carry for us. Why do you not haf donkeys? I will not be a donkey.'

He was puzzled at the shouts of laughter that greeted this speech. 'Oh, Gus – you'll be the death of me,' said Jack. 'Do you mean to say you didn't *know* you were a donkey?'

'It is bad to call me that,' said Gussy, frowning. 'In my country you would . . .'

'Oh, gee-up, donkey, and stop fussing,' said Philip, giving Gussy a shove. 'Leave your satchel behind, if you like. No one will mind. It's got your lunch in, but nobody else's! We're carrying the girls' lunch, and Bill's got Mother's. You've only got your own.'

'So chuck it into the bushes, then you won't have to carry it like a donkey,' said Dinah, with a squeal of laughter. 'Go on, Gus!'

But Gus didn't. He thought better of it, and took the satchel of food on his back, though he looked extremely annoyed about it.

Sugar-Loaf Hill was just like its name – it was very like a sugar-loaf, cone shaped but flat at the top, and was covered with primroses, cowslips and dog-violets.

'We ought to be able to see quite a good way from the top,' said Jack, as they toiled up. It was a stiff pull up but at last they were at the top. A strong breeze blew round them, but the sun was hot, so it was very pleasant to feel the wind blowing by.

'I say! Gussy carried his lunch after all!' said Jack, pretending to be surprised. 'My word, I'm hungry.'

They all were. They ate every single thing they had brought, and Kiki had a good share, too, especially of the bananas. She loved holding a banana in one foot and biting big pieces off it.

Gussy sneezed. Kiki immediately sneezed too, a much bigger sneeze than Gussy's. Then Gussy sniffed, a little habit he had which annoyed Mrs Cunningham very much.

Kiki sniffed too. 'Stop it, Kiki, ' said Mrs Cunningham. 'One sniffer is quite enough.'

'Polly's got a cold,' said Kiki, and sniffed again, exactly like Gussy. Gussy took no notice but after a minute he suddenly sniffed again.

'Blow your nose!' shouted Kiki. 'Where's your hanky!

Gussy's got a cold, send for . . . '

'Be quiet, Kiki,' said Jack. 'Gussy, don't keep sniffing. If you do, you'll set Kiki off and she'll do nothing but sniff too.'

'I do not sniff,' said Gussy. 'That bird is wicket and too clever. It should have a cage.'

'Shut up, Gus,' said Bill, who was now leaning back, enjoying a pipe. 'Remember what I said to you.'

Gus apparently remembered. He subsided and lay back and closed his eyes. The others sat and looked at the view. It was marvellous, for they could see a great way off.

'That's the village over there,' said Philip, pointing. 'And there's the farmhouse. And you can just see the tops of the chimneys and a bit of one end of the thatched roof belonging to Quarry Cottage. In those trees, look.'

'And there's the road we came by — the main road,' said Jack. 'Where are my field glasses? Would you pass them, Di. Gosh, I can see miles with these. I can see the way the main road twists and turns; I can see the traffic on it — looking just as small as the toy cars we used to have, Philip. Have a look.'

Philip put the glasses to his eyes. They really were magnificent ones. He could see for miles, just as Jack had said. 'Yes — it's queer to see the cars and the lorries looking like toys, going along those ribbony roads,' said Philip. 'Now — there's a black car — rather like Bill's. I'm going to watch it and see how far I can follow it.'

The others lay back, half asleep, listening to Philip's voice. The sun was hot now, and they didn't feel inclined to go walking after such a big picnuc,

'Yes — it's on the main road still,' said Philip, staring through the glasses. 'There it goes — a good speed too. Jolly good speed. May be a police car, perhaps.'

'You can't tell a police car so far away,' said Jack. Bill looked up from his newspaper. He knew a lot about police cars!

'Tell me its number and I'll tell you if it's a police car,' he said. The boys laughed.

'That's clever of you, Bill,' said Jack, 'but you know jolly well you're safe — you can't possibly read the number at this distance. Still got the car, Philip?'

'Lost it for a bit,' said Philip. 'It's gone behind some buildings — no, there it is again. It's come to crossroads — it's gone across. Now it's stopped.'

Gussy gave a little snore which Kiki immediately copied. Philip went on his car story.

'A man got out — I think he must have gone back to look at the sign post. He's got into the car again. Yes, they missed their way, they're backing. Ah, I thought so — they've turned down the other road — the road that leads to our village.'

'You'll tell us it's at Quarry Cottage next,' said Jack, sleepily. 'You're making all this up now, I bet!'

'I've lost it again. No, here it comes,' said Philip, pleased. 'Yes, it's going through the village — down into the lane. It's stopped again. I think they're asking the way from someone — a labourer probably. Can't see from here. On they go again — and they've turned up the farm road! They're going to the farmhouse. Probably rich relations of Mrs Ellis.'

Bill put down his paper abruptly and reached out for the glasses. He focused them on the farmhouse and saw the car immediately — a big one, obviously expensive. He studied it intently for a minute and then handed back the glasses without a word.

'Do you know the car, Bill?' asked Jack, curiously, seeing Bill's expression.

'No,' said Bill. 'I don't. But — it just makes me think a bit, that's all. Sorry I can't tell you any more. I'll wander up to the farmhouse tonight and ask a few questions — then I'll know a bit more!'

7

A surprising announcement

Philip and Jack were more interested in the car, after Bill's remarks. They took it in turns to keep an eye on it, but it simply stayed where it was for twenty minutes, and then went away, taking the same route as it came.

'It's gone, Bill,' said Philip. 'I expect it was only some visitor. I say, look at Gussy! His mouth is wide open. Let's put something into it.'

'Let sleeping donkeys lie!' said Jack. 'And don't put ideas into Kiki's head! She'll hunt around for something now to pop into Gussy's mouth.'

Philip looked round at everyone. Only Bill and Jack were awake besides himself. He put his hand into his pocket and brought out something – something small and brown and pretty. It sat up on his hand.

'I say! You've got a dormouse! What a pet! said Jack. 'Don't let Dinah see it – she'll have a fit.'

'I got it on the way here,' said Philip. 'I saw it sitting on a branch and it let me pick it up.'

'It would!' said Jack, enviously. 'You've got some magic about you, Philip. I've never seen an animal yet that didn't come under your spell. Isn't he a pretty little fellow?'

'I've called him Snoozy,' said Philip, stroking the tiny creature, whose large black eyes shone like mirrors in his head. 'Dormice are very dozy, snoozy things. I must remember to buy some nuts from the grocer's next time we go to the village. Snoozy will like those. We won't tell Dinah. He'll live comfortably in my pocket. I've had dormice before – they're very tame.'

'How nice to keep putting your hand in your pocket and

feeling a furry dormouse there!' said Jack. 'Hallo – do I hear voices?'

The boys looked in the direction of the voices. They saw two men, obviously farm labourers, taking a path near the foot of the hill, talking together.

'I think I'll just scoot down and ask them if they know anything about badgers here,' said Philip. 'Coming, Jack?'

The two boys ran down the hill. The men heard them coming and looked round. 'Good afternoon,' panted Philip. 'Do you mind if I ask you a question or two? It's about badgers.'

'Badgers – what may they be?' said the younger man.

'Eee, man – you know badgers,' said the older man. 'Brocks, they be.'

'Oh, the brocks,' said the younger fellow. 'No, I don't know nothing about *them*. Never seed one in my life.'

'That's a-cause you sleeps in your bed every night!' said the other man, with a laugh. 'Brock, he comes out at night. I sees him many a time.'

'You're an old poacher, you are, Jeb,' said the younger man. 'Out at nights when honest folk are asleep. That's how you see the brocks!'

'Maybe, maybe,' said the older man, with a twinkle in his bright eyes. He turned to the boys. 'What are you wanting to know about the brocks?' he said.

'Well – I'd like to wach them,' said Philip at once. 'I'm keen on wild creatures – all kinds. I've not had much chance of seeing badgers, though. Where can I see them around here? We're at Quarry Cottage.'

'Ah, so that's where you be,' said the old man. 'Then you'll find old Brock not far away from you, little master. You may see him in the woods on the east side of the cottage – that's the most likely place – or you may see him down in the old quarry. I saw a badger's sett there – his den, you know – last year. I knew he had his hole down there by the big pile of earth he'd taken out of it.'

'Yes — that's right. He always does that,' said Philip, wishing he could get to know this old fellow. He felt sure that he would be able to tell him many tales. 'Well, thanks very much. We'll watch in both places.'

'There's owls in the quarry too,' said the old man. 'Little owls, and barn owls and tawnies. They go there for the rats and mice. I've heard them — the barn owls — screeching their heads off. Frighten the life out of you, they do!'

'I know,' said Jack, making up his mind at once that he would go and watch in the quarry. He liked owls very much. Perhaps he could get a young one and tame it. But he'd have to be careful not to let it see Snoozy the dormouse. That would be the end of Snoozy!

The boys walked off together, exploring the cone-shaped hill. A shout from above attracted their attention.

'Jack! Philip! We're going back in a minute. Are you coming with us, or do you want to follow sometime later?'

'We'll come now,' shouted Jack, and he and Philip began to climb up towards the others. They found Gussy awake but scowling. He spat something out of his mouth as they came up.

'Manners, manners!' said Jack, reprovingly.

'He says somebody popped bits of grass into his mouth,' said Dinah, with a giggle. 'So he keeps on spitting them out. Did *you* put them in, Jack?'

'No,' said Jack. 'And Philip didn't either.'

'There you are!' said Dinah, triumphantly, turning to the angry Gussy. 'Nobody put anything in your mouth when you were asleep. You're just making it all up. I bet you chewed a bit of grass yourself.'

'I did not,' said Gussy. 'It was a wicket thing to do. It nearly chocked me. I was chocked.'

'Choked, you mean,' said Lucy-Ann. 'Well, it's a mystery. Nobody did it — and yet you were nearly "chocked" with grass. Don't spit any more. You *can't* have any left in your mouth now.'

Jack and Philip threw a quick look at one another. They knew quite well who had played this trick on poor Gussy. Gussy saw the look and rounded on them. 'You know who did it! I saw you look!'

'All right. We know who did it,' said Jack. 'A jolly good trick too. We thought of doing it ourselves, you looked so silly with your mouth wide open, snoring.'

'I do not snore,' said Gussy. 'And tell me who did it.'

'Come on,' said Bill. 'I expect it was old Kiki. She's done it before – to me! Can't you see a joke, Gus?'

Gus suddenly exploded into his own language. He stood there, shaking his long hair back, his face scarlet, and a string of incomprehensible words coming from his mouth. Nobody understood a thing.

Kiki was intensely interested with this string of words she didn't understand. She sat herself on Jack's shoulder, near to the angry Gus, and listened intently. When he stopped for breath, she continued on her own.

'Gibberollydockeryblowykettlefussy-gussy,' she began, and poured out strings of nonsense into which she wove many of the words she knew, mixed up with ones she didn't! Everyone roared. It sounded exactly as if Kiki was talking to Gus in his own language.

Gus was silenced. He stared at Kiki, amazed. 'Does she spik English now?' he demanded. 'What does she spik?'

'She's spikking a lot of nonsense, bad bird!' said Jack. 'Be quiet, Kiki. Don't show off!'

Bill and Mrs Cunningham had already set off down the hill. The girls followed, giggling. Gus was annoying but he really did provide them with a lot of amusement.

Gus followed them at last, shaking back his long hair defiantly. He spat now and again as if he still had grass in his mouth, and Kiki copied him with joy, going off into cackles of laughter every now and again.

It was about half-past five when they got back to Quarry Cottage. 'If any of you want tea after that enormous lunch, will you please get yourself a glass of milk, and some biscuits?' said Mrs Cunningham. 'Or a bit of fruit cake if you feel real pangs of hunger?'

All the five children apparently felt real pangs, for they raided the larder and reduced the fruitcake to a mere fragment of itself. They also drank all the milk, much to Mrs Cunningham's dismay.

'Now we've none for your cocoa tonight or for breakfast tomorrow!' she said.

'I'll get some at the farm when I slip up this evening,' said Bill. 'It will be a good excuse to go up and ask a few questions.'

'Any mystery on?' enquired Dinah. 'I'm never sure about you, Bill! Even in the middle of a holiday I always wonder if you've got a hush-hush job on as well.'

'Mystery or not, Bill always keeps his eyes open!' said Philip. 'It's part of your job, isn't it, Bill?'

'Let's play a game,' said Dinah. 'Where are the cards? Let's play Racing Demon. Do you play it, Gus?'

'I play it,' said Gus. 'I played it at school last term. I am good with this game. Very good. I go as fast as this.'

He pretended to be putting cards down, and was so vigorous that his hair fell over his eyes. He pushed it back. He was always doing that, and it got on Dinah's nerves.

'Your long hair!' she said. 'It's always in the way.'

'Now don't start anything,' said Jack. 'A spark is enough to set him off. Talk about being touchy! Don't glare like that, Gus, you make me shake at the knees!'

'Poof!' said Gus, rudely.

'Poof!' said Kiki at once. 'Poof, poof, poof!'

'That'll do,' said Jack. 'One poofer is quite enough in the family. Got the cards, Di? Oh, good!'

They were soon sitting in a ring on the floor, playing Racing Demon. Kiki couldn't understand the game at all and wandered off into a corner because Jack wouldn't let her pick up any of the cards.

'Poof!' they heard her say to herself quietly. 'Poof!'

Surprisingly enough Gussy *was* good at Racing Demon. He was very deft with his cards, and very sharp to see which pile he could put them on. He got very excited, and panted loudly. His hair fell over his eyes, and he pushed it back. Jack calmly put a card on a pile that Gus was just about to put one on, and Gus exclaimed in annoyance.

'I was going to put mine there – but my hair fell over me!'

'Why do you *have* hair like that then?' said Dinah. 'It's really very long. Why don't you get it cut?'

'Yes, that's a good idea,' said Philip, putting a card down. 'We'll go into the village tomorrow and see if there's a barber. He'll cut it shorter for you, Gus. You'll get a crick in your neck, tossing your hair about like that!'

'Yes. Good idea! We'll have it cut tomorrow,' said Jack, grinning at Gus.

Gus surprised them. He flung down his cards, stood up, and went scarlet in the face. 'Short hair is for boys like *you*,' he said, scornfully. 'It is not for me. Never must I have my hair short. In my country always it is the custom for such boys as me to wear their hair long!'

'Such boys as you!' echoed Jack. 'What do you mean? You've got a very high opinion of yourself, my lad. You may come from a rich family, but you act like royalty, and it won't do. You're not a Prince, so don't try and act like one. It only makes you ridiculous.'

Gus drew himself up to his last inch. He threw back his hair once more. 'I *am* a Prince!' he said, dramatically. 'I am the Prince Aloysius Gramondie Racemolie Torquinel of Tauri-Hessia!'

8
Bill explains

There was a dead silence after this dramatic announcement. Nobody said a word, not even Kiki. They all stared in astonishment at Gus, not knowing whether to believe a word of what he had said.

Then his lips began to shake, and he tried to press them together firmly. Lucy-Ann was sure he wanted to cry again! 'I have broke my word!' suddenly wailed Gus. 'I am a Prince and I have broke my word!'

A voice came from behind them. It was Bill's.

'Yes, you have broken your word, Aloysius Gramondie Racemolie Torquinel. And your uncle told me you would *never* do that. How am I to keep you safe if you break your word?'

Bill came forward, his face stern. Everyone stared at him in alarm. Whatever was up?

'Bill – he's not *really* a Prince, is he?' said Jack.

'Believe it or not, he is,' said Bill. 'His uncle is the King of Tauri-Hessia.'

'Well! That explains his peculiar behaviour,' said Dinah. 'His ordering people about – and his high and mighty airs – and all his money and boasting.'

'And his long hair too,' said Bill. 'The Princes in his country never have their hair cut short as ours do. They wear it a certain length, as you see. It's bad luck on him, really, because he gets teased. Still, the boys at his school knew who he was and knew he couldn't help it, and he didn't have too bad a time.'

There was a pause while the four took a look at Prince Aloysius. He shook back his hair and Dinah groaned.

'I wish you wouldn't do that, Gussy. I can't call you Ally –

Ally-something or other. You'll have to go on being Gussy.'

'Oh, he must,' said Bill, at once. 'I gave him the name of Gustavus Barmilevo for a special reason. Things – rather serious things – are happening in his country at the moment, and it's essential that he should go under another name here.'

'What serious things are happening?' said Jack. 'Revolts or something?'

'Well, I'll tell you,' said Bill. 'His uncle is King, and as he has no children, Gussy is the heir to the throne. Now there are certain people in Tauri-Hessia who don't like his uncle or the firm way in which he governs the country. Incidentally he governs it very well, and our own Government thinks him a very sound ruler.'

'I can guess what's coming,' said Jack. 'Those who don't like the strong uncle think it would be a good thing to get a weak youngster, who'll have to do what they tell him, and put *him* on the throne. Then they can do as they like!'

'Exactly,' said Bill. 'And so they are on the look-out for Gussy here. If they can get hold of him and put *him* on the throne, he will have to do exactly what he's told. His uncle will be imprisoned or killed'.

'And Gussy knows all this, does he?' asked Philip.

'He knows all right!' said Bill. 'Everything was explained to him. He's fond of his uncle; he doesn't want to be used as a kind of pawn by his uncle's enemies – and so he was put in my keeping, and told to be merely a foreign schoolboy called Gustavus. And here he is.'

'I have broke my word to you,' said Gussy, sounding very doleful. 'Mr Bill, I ask you to pardon me.'

'Well, don't do it again, that's all,' said Bill. 'Nobody here is likely to give you away, fortunately – we are all your friends – or would like to be if only you'd behave yourself a bit better.'

'I behave better at once immediately,' said Gussy, emphatically.

'Hm. Well, we'll see,' said Bill, drily. 'It would help considerably if you could try to behave like the others so that if any stranger comes hanging round he'll think you are an ordinary schoolboy staying with friends. At present I think you're behaving rather stupidly, not like a Prince at all. In fact, if I were a Tauri-Hessian citizen, I'd be sorry to think I'd have *you* as King when you grew up.'

'Bill – is it the Tauri-Hessian Government or ours that has asked you to have charge of Gussy?' said Dinah.

'Both,' said Bill. 'It's important to both Governments that there should be a sound, strong ruler in Tauri-Hessia. I can't tell you why at present. I think it's possible that all this will blow over in a few weeks, and then Gussy can go back to school in safety. In the meantime, we've got to make the best of all this.'

'Yes. I see everything now,' said Dinah. 'You should have told us at first. Bill. We'd have understood better.'

'I had orders not to say a word except to your mother,' said Bill. 'She had to be in on this, of course. I took this cottage because it was well hidden and nobody would guess that Gussy would be here. And I thought if you all came too, he would be even better hidden – hidden in the midst of you, one of many, so to speak.'

'You're clever, Bill,' said Lucy-Ann, slipping her hand in his. 'We'll look after Gussy. We won't let him out of our sight. Gussy, we're your friends.'

'I thank you,' said Gussy, with a funny little bow. 'It is an honour.'

'That's the way to talk,' said Bill, and gave him a clap on the back. 'Now then, everyone – you've got to forget all about Aloysius Gramondie and Tauri-Hessia. Got that?'

'Yes, Bill,' said everyone. They looked rather solemn. It was peculiar to have serious and unusual problems suddenly presented to them candidly in the middle of a game of Racing Demon. The ordinary and the extraordinary didn't really mix. They turned with relief to their game again, as

Bill went out of the room to find his wife and tell her what had happened.

'*Look* what Kiki's been doing while we've been talking!' said Jack, in exasperation. 'Mixing up all the cards. Put down the ones you're holding, Kiki!'

'She's been playing a quiet little game by herself,' said Lucy-Ann, with a laugh. 'And she's holding two cards in her foot eactly as if she was waiting for her turn to go. Put them down, Kiki.'

'One, two, three, six, eight, four, one,' said Kiki, getting her numbers muddled up as usual. 'Three, four, buckle my shoe.'

'One, *two*, buckle my shoe,' said Lucy-Ann. 'Your memory's going, Kiki!'

Kiki gave a hiccup, as she often did when she thought she had made a mistake.

'Enough, Kiki,' said Jack. 'Anyone want another game?'

Nobody really felt like one after all the revelations Bill had made. They didn't like to discuss them in front of Gussy, though they were longing to talk about them.

Mrs Cunningham put her head in at the door. 'Bill's going up to the farm for milk. Anyone want to go with him? Not Gussy, he says.'

'I'll go,' said Lucy-Ann, scrambling up. 'I'd like a walk. You boys stay with Aunt Allie, and look after her.'

'Right,' said Jack, thinking it was just as well to do so, with prospective kidnappers and revolutionaries about, even although they might be as far away as Tauri-Hessia.

'I'll stay behind too,' said Dinah. 'I've got a blister on my foot.'

So Lucy-Ann went off happily with Bill. She liked getting him alone. He was always jolly and full of fun when they were all together, but Lucy-Ann thought he was even nicer alone. She slipped her hand through his arm, and they walked off in the dusk together.

'In case you want to say anything about Gussy, I'll just

warn you not to,' said Bill, in a low voice. 'I don't want the slightest suspicions to get about that he's not all he seems. It would be a very serious thing for him if he were forced to be King at his age.'

'I won't say anything,' said Lucy-Ann in a whisper. 'Let's talk about Jack.'

'You're always ready to talk about Jack, aren't you?' said Bill, amused. 'Well, I must say that Jack has got something I'd dearly like to have myself.'

'What's that? Kiki?' asked Lucy-Ann.

'No – a very nice little sister,' said Bill. 'It's good to see a brother and sister so fond of one another.'

'Well, our mother and father died when we were very young,' said Lucy-Ann, 'so we only had each other. But now we've got you and Aunt Allie, and we've got Philip and Dinah as well. We're lucky!'

'I'm lucky too,' said Bill. 'A nice ready-made family for me! Hark at the owls hooting round. What a collection of hoots!'

'That was the little owl,' said Lucy-Ann, who had been well trained in bird calls by Jack. 'That "tvit-tvit-tvit" noise. And that lovely long quavering hoot is the tawny owl.'

'And what in the world is *that*?' said Bill, suddenly startled by a loud screech near his head. Lucy-Ann laughed.

'The screech owl – the old barn owl!' she said. 'He does that to frighten the mice and the rats.'

'Well, he scared me too,' said Bill. 'Ah – is that the farmhouse looming up? It is. You come in with me, Lucy-Ann, and don't be surprised at my conversation with Mrs Ellis!'

They knocked at the door and went into the big, cosy kitchen. Although it was a warm night there was a fire in the chimney corner, and old Aunt Naomi sat there, knitting, huddled up in shawl.

Mrs Ellis hurried to meet them. 'Well, it's good to see you! And how are you getting on? Settled in nicely? That's right.

Now, what can I do for you? Sit you down, do!'

They sat down. Lucy-Ann found a rocking chair and began to rock to and fro. A big tabby came and jumped into her lap, settled down and went to sleep. Lucy-Ann felt quite honoured.

Mrs Ellis brought her a piece of cake, and she nibbled at it and listened lazily to Bill. He gave Mrs Ellis all the news first. Then he went on to talk about Quarry Cottage.

'It's a lovely, peaceful spot,' he said. 'I shouldn't think strangers ever come along here, do they, Mrs Ellis? Except people like ourselves who want to stay for a bit.'

'Now, it's funny you should say that,' said Mrs Ellis, 'because two strangers came to our farmhouse this very afternoon – in a lovely black car. Rather like yours, Mr Cunningham.'

'I suppose they lost their way,' said Bill. Although he spoke in his ordinary voice Lucy-Ann knew that he had pricked up his ears at once.

'No, they hadn't lost their way,' said Mrs Ellis. 'They'd been hunting round for a nice farmhouse to stay in for a few days – the man's wife has been ill, and simply longed to be in a quiet farmhouse, with good food. Somebody told him of our farm, and they came to inquire.'

'I see,' said Bill. 'And – er – did you say you would take them, Mrs Ellis?'

'I did,' said Mrs Ellis, 'though my husband scolded me for it. He says my kind heart runs away with me! Theyre coming tomorrow. They said their name was Jones – but it's my belief they're foreigners!'

'Foreigners,' said Bill, slowly. 'Yes – I had an idea you were going to say that!'

9

An afternoon out

Lucy-Ann stopped rocking the chair, and her heart sank into her shoes. Foreigners! Did that mean they were from Tauri-Hessia, or whatever the country was – and had they tracked down Gussy? Oh dear – surely, surely another adventure wasn't beginning! This had seemed as if it would be such a nice peaceful holiday.

'Blow!' whispered Lucy-Ann to the cat on her knee. 'Blow Gussy! Blow his uncle!'

Bill asked a few more cautious questions, but Mrs Ellis had nothing else to tell him of any interest. He got up, took the milk she had brought him from the dairy, and paid her. He thanked her, said good night, and out he and Lucy-Ann went, into the starry night.

'I fear – I very much fear – that somebody is on Gussy's track,' said Bill, in a half-whisper as they went along together. 'Now how could they have guessed he was with us? It's a pity he's so striking-looking, and so easily recognizable. I suppose someone must have spotted him with me, made enquiries about me – and as soon as they knew who I was, the rest would be easy. Hm! I don't like it very much.'

'Will you and Gussy have to disappear from here?' whispered Lucy-Ann, so softly that Bill could hardly hear. 'Please don't go away, Bill.'

'I'll have to discuss things with your aunt,' said Bill. 'Don't say a word to Gussy. He'll get the wind up properly, if I know anything about him. And on no account must any of you leave him alone anywhere – always keep him in your midst.'

'Yes, Bill,' said Lucy-Ann. 'Oh dear – I do wish those

people weren't going to the farm. Bill, they *might* be ordinary people, mightn't they? They haven't *got* to be enemies, have they?'

Bill squeezed Lucy-Ann's hand. 'No. I may be wrong. But I get hunches about these things, Lucy-Ann. And I've got a hunch this very minute. You needn't worry. I shan't let anything happen.'

'Well — so long as you're with us,' said Lucy-Ann. 'But please don't go away, Bill.'

'I won't,' said Bill. 'Not unless I take Gussy with me, which would really be the safest thing to do.'

They reached Quarry Cottage, and went in. Gussy and Dinah had gone to bed. Aunt Allie and the boys were still up, reading.

Bill put the milk in the larder and came back. He sat down and told the three of them what Mrs Ellis had said. Mrs Cunningham looked grave.

'How did they know he was down here?' she wondered. 'Oh, Bill — what shall we do now? Shall we leave here at once — all of us?'

'No. That would tell the enemy too much,' said Bill. 'I don't see that two people — a man and a woman — can do very much by themselves — I mean they can't fall on us and wrest Gussy away from our midst! As long as there are only the two of them we haven't much to fear — and Mrs Ellis will soon tell us if any more arrive. One of the boys can go up each day for milk, and get the latest news.'

'Right. We'll go on as we are then,' said his wife, and Lucy-Ann heaved a sigh of relief. 'You'll tell Gussy of course, Bill — put him on his guard? He's got to be very sensible now — keep with us all, not wander away — and I'm afraid the boys must fasten their window at night.'

'Blow!' said Jack, who hated a shut window at night. 'Kiki's enough of a sentinel, Aunt Allie. She would screech the place down if anyone came.'

'I'd feel safer with your window shut,' said his aunt. 'I think Kiki *would* screech. Still — I don't want to run any risks.'

Gussy was told the next morning, and so was Dinah. Philip was posted up by the farm to watch the new people arrive. They came in the same black car that Philip had seen through his field glasses the day before. It was long and low and large — and very expensive-looking.

'A Daimler,' said Philip. 'I bet that can get along! Now — can I spot what the visitors are like?'

There were two. One was a spruce, tall, lean man, wearing a very well cut suit, an eyeglass in one eye, and hair smoothly brushed back. The other was a woman — pretty, young and with a very foreign voice. The man spoke English well, but he was obviously a foreigner too.

He handed the woman out very carefully indeed. Then she leaned on his arm as they walked up the path to the farmhouse door. They went very slowly.

'Either she's been ill or she's pretending to be,' thought Philip. 'I'd better go back and tell Bill — and Gussy too. He may recognize them from my description.'

But Gussy didn't. He shook his head. 'No, I don't know them.'

'I wouldn't be surprised if they come along here sometime today,' said Bill. 'Just to have a snoop round. I feel sure they know I'm at this cottage — and that Gussy may be with you all on holiday!'

Bill was right. That afternoon, while Jack was bird-watching near the house, he heard the sound of voices. He peeped through the bushes. It must be the visitors from the farm! The man had an eyeglass in his eye, as Philip had described — and the woman was walking slowly, leaning on his arm.

Jack sped indoors by the back way. 'Bill! he called. 'They're coming. Where's Gussy? He could peep at them as they go by and see if he knows them!'

58

Gussy ran to a front window and hid behind the curtain, waiting. But the couple from the farm didn't go by! They turned in at the front gate and came right up to the cottage door. A sharp sound came on the afternoon air.

Rat-a-tatta-TAT!

Mrs Cunningham jumped. She was having a rest on her bed. Bill opened the door and went in.

'Allie! It's the couple from the farm What nerve to come right to the house! They obviously don't think that we suspect anything at all. Will you go down and open the door? I shan't appear – and Gussy mustn't either. The others can, of course.'

Bill went to tell Gussy to keep out of the way and Mrs Cunningham ran down the stairs to the front door, patting her hair tidy. She opened it.

Two people stood on the step, a man and a woman. The man raised his hat politely.

'Forgive this sudden visit,' he said, 'but my wife and I were taking a short walk, and she has begun to feel faint. A cup of water would help her, I think – if you would be so kind?'

'Oh – do come in,' said Mrs Cunningham, hoping that Gussy wouldn't come running down the stairs. 'I'll get some water.'

She took them into the little sitting-room. The woman sank down into a chair and closed her eyes.

'My wife has been ill,' said the man. 'I have brought her down to the farm for a few days – good air, and good food, you know – better than any hotel! But I should not have taken her so far on her first day.'

'I'm so sorry,' said Mrs Cunningham, playing her part as best she could. 'Dinah! Where are you? Get a jug of water and a glass, will you, dear?'

Dinah sped to the kitchen, and came back with a glass jug of ice-cold water, and a glass on a little tray. She put them down on the table and looked curiously at the couple. They looked back at her.

'And is this your daughter?' said the woman. 'What a nice child! Have you any other children?'

'Oh yes,' said Mrs Cunningham. 'Another of my own and two adopted ones. Fetch them, Dinah.'

Dinah went to fetch the others. They came in politely, Lucy-Ann, Philip and Jack. The woman screamed when she saw Kiki on Jack's shoulder.

'A parrot! Don't let it come near me, I beg of you!'

'Wipe your feet,' ordered Kiki. 'Shut the door. Grrrrrrrrr!'

The woman gave an exclamation in a foreign language, and said something to the man. He laughed.

'My wife says that people who come to visit you should have good manners, or your parrot will soon teach them,' he said. 'So these are your four children. But have you not a fifth?'

'No,' said Mrs Cunningham. 'Only these four belong to me.'

'I thought Mrs Ellis said there was another little boy,' said the woman, sipping the water.

Mrs Cunningham reached for the jug and refilled the woman's glass, hoping that she would not pursue the subject of the 'other little boy'. But the woman persisted.

'Perhaps you have a little boy *staying* with you?' she said, sweetly, smiling at Mrs Cunningham.

'Oh, I expect Mrs Ellis means Gussy,' said Mrs Cunningham. 'Little Gussy is staying for a while – till his family can take him home.'

'And may we not see the little Gussy?' said the woman. 'I love children. Do not leave this little Gussy out.'

'Anyone know where he is?' said Mrs Cunningham, in a voice that made the four children quite certain that she didn't want them to know. They didn't know, anyway! Gussy was at that moment in the wardrobe upstairs, where he had put himself straight away at the first sound of the knock on the door. Bill had thought he might as well stay there!

'I've no idea where Gus is,' said Jack. 'Doing something on his own, I expect. Do *you* know where he is, Philip?'

'No idea,' said Philip. 'Messing about somewhere, probably out in the woods.'

'Ah – he likes to wander about, does he?' said the man. 'Well – we may see him when we go back to the farm. Thank you, Madam, for being so kind to my wife. May I please give your four nice children something to buy ice creams with? And here is something for the little missing Gussy also.'

To the children's surprise he put down a five-pound note on the table in front of Mrs Cunningham. She pushed it back at once, quite horrified.

'Oh no – please! I couldn't hear of it. We only got you a glass of water. No, no – take this back. I couldn't possibly allow the children to have it.'

The man looked surprised and rather uncomfortable. He put the note back in his pocket. 'Just as you please,' he said. 'In *my* country it is only a courtesy to return a kindness.'

'What *is* your country, sir?' asked Jack, at once. 'Aha!' he thought. '*Now* we'll bring you out into the open.'

The man hesitated, and the woman gave him a quick glance. 'My country – oh, I come from Italy,' he said. 'A beautiful land. Come, my dear, we must go.'

He took his wife's arm and led her to the door, his eyes searching everywhere for the missing Gussy. He bowed to Mrs Cunningham and went down the path.

She called a sentence after him, and he turned. 'What do you say?' he said. 'I didn't understand.'

Mrs Cunningham repeated it. He looked puzzled, bowed again, and went out of the gate. He disappeared with his wife up the lane.

'Well, *he's* not from Italy!' said Mrs Cunningham. 'I called out to him in Italian to say that he was to give my best wishes to Mrs Ellis – and he didn't understand a *word*!'

10

An urgent call

Jack slipped out to make sure that the couple went back to the farm. He came back to report that they had and Bill held a conference at once. Gussy had been hauled with difficulty out of the wardrobe.

He had recognized the woman but not the man. 'She is Madame Tatiosa,' he said. 'The wife of the Prime Minister. I hate her! She is clever and sharp and cruel.'

'What — that pretty young woman!' said Mrs Cunningham in astonishment.

'Yes,' said Gussy, nodding his head vigorously. 'Once she was a spy for our country. My uncle told me. A very clever spy. And she married the Prime Minister, and tells him what to do.'

'Hm,' said Bill. 'And you didn't know the man, Gussy? Not that that matters. You've recognized one of them and so we know for certain that they're after you. I almost think we'd better clear out. I really don't know what to do for the best! I think I'd better take you and hand you over to the keepers in the Tower of London! You'd at least be safe there!'

'But you said, Bill, that if there were only two of them, the man and the woman, they couldn't very well do anything to Gussy,' said Jack. 'Why not let one of us keep watch each day to make sure no other car comes down to the farm — or no other visitor? I can easily go and spend the day at the farm, and watch — and Philip can watch the next day.'

'I think perhaps you're right,' said Bill, puffing at his pipe. 'Anyway — we'll stay put for the next two days, and wait for the enemy to make the next move. There's no doubt that they think Gussy's the boy they want. I expect Mrs Ellis has described him carefully to them – and he's easily described!'

'Yes – long hair, for one thing,' grinned Jack. 'Shall I nip along to the farm now, Bill, and keep watch for the rest of the day? I can go and ask for some butter or something, and then hang round, helping with a few jobs. I'd like that, anyway.'

'Right. You go,' said Bill, and Jack sped off with Kiki on his shoulder. The others got up to go for a walk, well away from the farm! 'Take your tea,' said Mrs Cunningham. 'Nobody will know where you are, if you go off for a walk, so nobody will be able to find you! You should be quite safe, Gussy!'

So Gussy, Philip and the two girls went off with a picnic basket. They walked for about two miles and then found a glade that was golden with polished celandines. They sat down, hot with their walk.

'This is heavenly,' said Lucy-Ann. 'I do love celandines. They look as if someone polished them every single morning. Jolly good workman he must be – he never misses a petal!'

Dinah gave a scream. 'Oh – what's that on your shoulder, Philip! Oh, it's a mouse!'

Philip's dormouse had decided that the pocket he lived in was getting too hot for his liking. So he had squeezed his way out, run up Philip's vest, and appeared through the opening of his collar. There he was now, sitting up on the boy's shoulder.

'Oh – a dormouse!' cried Lucy-Ann in delight. 'What's his name, Philip? Will he let me hold him?'

'His name is Snoozy and it suits him', said Philip. He felt in a pocket and brought out a nut. He gave it to Lucy-Ann. 'Here, take this, Offer it to him on the palm of your hand and he'll run over to you.'

Lucy-Ann balanced the nut on her palm and held it out to the tiny mouse, being careful not to move too quickly. The dormouse watched her hand coming close to Philip's shoulder, and his whiskers quivered as his nose twitched.

'He can smell the nut,' said Philip. 'Keep quite still, Lucy-Ann. There he goes! How do you like the feel of his tiny feet?'

'Oh, lovely!' said Lucy-Ann. 'Isn't he a *dear*, Philip. I wish I had one too.'

'I'll try and get you one,' said Philip.

But Dinah gave a squeal at once. 'No! She sleeps with me, and I'm not having mice in the bedroom.'

'But this is a *dor*mouse, not a housemouse,' said Lucy-Ann. 'It doesn't smell, or anything. It's just perfectly sweet.'

Snoozy nibbled daintily at the nut. A bit broke off and he took it into his front paws, sitting up just like a squirrel. He looked at Lucy-Ann out of his bright eyes.

'He's got such big black eyes that they really are like mirrorrs,' she said. 'I can see my own face, very tiny, in each of them.'

'*Can* you?' said Gussy, in surprise and put his face close to Lucy-Ann's to look into the big eyes of the dormouse. It fled at once, disappearing down Philip's neck at top speed.

'You moved too fast, Gussy,' said Lucy-Ann crossly. 'You *would* manage to startle him.'

'Excuse, pliss. I pollygize,' said Gussy. 'I beg your pardon, Lucy-Ann.'

'All right. But I do hope Snoozy will come back,' said Lucy-Ann, rather cross.

He peered out of Philip's neck once or twice, but he wouldn't come right out. 'He's not *abso*lutely tame yet,' explained Philip. 'I've not had him long enough. But he soon will be. He'll be coming out at meal times soon and nibbling his little nut on my bread-plate.'

'Not if I can help it,' said Dinah.

'Don't be silly,' said Philip. 'You simply don't *try* to like dormice. You . . . '

'Someone coming,' said Lucy-Ann, suddenly. Her sharp ears had caught the sound of voices.

'Get under the bush, Gussy,' ordered Philip. 'Go on, quick!'

Gussy vanished at once, and the bush closed over him. It was a pity it was a gorse bush, but Gussy didn't have time to think of prickles.

Two men came by, talking in the broad accent of the countryside. One was the man who had told Philip so much about badgers. He waved to him.

'It'll be a good night for badgers tonight!' he called. 'Moonlight – and that's what they like.'

'Come out, Gus,' said Philip, when the men had passed. 'False alarm.'

Gussy crawled out, scratched on face, hands and knees by the gorse prickles. He was very frightened.

'He blids,' said Dinah unkindly. 'Gus, you are blidding all over.'

'It's nothing much,' said Philip, taking out his handkerchief and scrubbing the drops of blood away here and there. 'Everyone gets pricked by gorse sooner or later. Cheer up, Gus. And for goodness' sake don't complain.'

'I don't like blidding,' said poor Gussy, in a woebegone voice. 'It makes me feel sick.'

'Well, be sick then,' said hard-hearted Dinah. 'But don't make a FUSS.'

Gussy made a valiant effort and swallowed hard. He didn't fuss after all. What a victory!

After they had eaten every crumb of their tea, they decided to go back. Philip wanted to have a look at the quarry on the way to see if he thought that badgers might really make that their haunt.

He wandered round the big deserted place, examining the hedges round for signs of a badger's sett. The girls and Gussy ran the few hundred yards that lay between the quarry and the cottage. Lucy-Ann thought they ought to, in case any enemy was lying in wait!

'Any news?' she asked, as they went indoors, panting.

'Has Jack come back from the farm yet?'

He hadn't. Nobody had any news at all, it seemed. Jack had none either, when he came.

'Not a soul came to the farm,' he said. 'And I didn't even see the man and the woman. They must have been in their room all the time. Once I heard a "ting" – as if somebody was using the telephone. It might have been them.'

'Can't tell,' said Bill. 'Well – I seem to have had a lazy day. I've got some papers to read and then I suppose it will be supper time. There's going to be a fine moon tonight!'

'Just right for badgers,' Philip whispered to Jack. 'Like to come out and see if we can find any?'

'Rather,' said Jack. 'We can slip out when the others are in bed. Gussy always sleeps so soundly, he'll never hear!'

Supper time came. Cold ham, a salad, junket and cream. 'Just the right kind of meal,' said Philip. 'Why can't we have this kind of food at school?'

'Don't let's start up the subject of school meals *again* Philip,' said his mother. 'You're yawning. Go to bed!'

'I think I will,' said Philip. 'Coming, Jack?'

Jack remembered that they had planned an outing in the moonlight, and he nodded. They might as well get a little sleep first. Gussy went up with them. The girls stayed down to finish their books and then went up too.

'I'll set my little alarm clock for eleven,' said Philip to Jack, in a low voice, not wanting Gussy to hear. 'I'll put it under my pillow and it won't wake anyone but me. Gosh, I'm sleepy.'

In ten minutes all the five children were fast asleep. Downstairs Bill and his wife sat listening to the radio. 'We'll hear the ten o'clock news and then go to bed,' said Bill.

But, just as the ten o'clock news was about to come on, there came a cautious tapping at the front door. Bill stiffened. Who was that? He looked at his wife, and she raised her eyebrows. Who could that be at this time of night?

Bill went quietly to the door. He didn't open it, but spoke with his mouth close to the crack.

'Who's there?'

'Oh, sir, Mrs Ellis has sent me down to beg you to come up to the farm,' said an anxious voice. 'It's her old aunt. She's fallen down and broken her hip. Can you come? Mrs Ellis is in such a way! She sent me to ask you, because the doctor's away.'

Bill opened the door. He saw a bent figure, wrapped round in a shawl. It must be Alice, the old woman who helped Mrs Ellis in the kitchen. 'Come in,' he said.

'No, sir, I'll be getting back,' said the old woman. 'You'll come, won't you?'

'Yes, we'll come,' said Bill. He shut the door and went back to tell his wife.

'It's a message from Mrs Ellis about the old aunt. Apparently she has fallen and broken her hip,' he said. 'Will you go, Allie? I'll take you there, of course, and then I must leave you and come back here, because of Gussy. But Mr Ellis will bring you back, unless you stay for the night.'

'Yes, I'd better go at once,' said Mrs Cunningham. 'Poor Mrs Ellis! Just what she was afraid might happen!'

She got her things on, and Bill and she went out of the door. 'It's not worth waking up the children and telling them,' he said. 'They're sound asleep. Anyway, I'll be back here in a few minutes' time.'

He shut the door quietly, made sure he had the key with him to open it when he came back, and then set off with his wife. What a wonderful moonlight night! Really, he would quite enjoy the walk!

11

Happenings in the night

The moonlight streamed down over the countryside as Bill and his wife set out. 'What a lovely night!' said Bill. 'As light as day, almost!'

They went up the tiny lane, hurrying as much as they could. 'I'll ask at the farm if Mr Ellis can bring you back,' Bill said, 'I won't stay even a minute. I'm worried about Gussy. I may get a glimpse of Madame Tatiosa and her companion – but I don't particularly want them to see *me*.'

They were passing a little copse of trees, a patch of dense black shadow in the surrounding moonlight. Bill and his wife walked by, not seeing a small movement in the shadows.

Then things happened very quickly indeed. Four shadows came from the copse of trees, running silently over the grass. Bill turned at a slight sound – but almost as he turned someone leapt on him and bore him to the ground.

Mrs Cunningham felt an arm round her, and a hand pressed over her mouth. She tried to scream, but only a small sound came from her.

'Don't struggle,' said a voice. 'And don't scream. We're not going to hurt you. We just want you out of the way for a short time.'

But Bill did struggle, of course. He knew what these men were after – Gussy! He groaned in anger at himself. This was a trick, of course! Old Aunt Naomi hadn't had a fall! There had been no real message from the farm. It was all a ruse to get them out of the house, so that it would be easy to kidnap Gussy.

Someone gagged his mouth by wrapping a cloth firmly round his face. He could hardly breathe! He wondered how his wife was getting on, but he could see and hear nothing. He stopped struggling when at last his arms were pinned behind him, and tied together with rope.

There was nothing he could do. It was four against two, and as they had been taken by surprise they were at a great disadvantage. Perhaps he would be able to undo the rope that bound him when his captors had gone to get Gussy. He might still prevent the kidnapping.

Mrs Cunningham was scared, and did her best to get away, but one man was quite sufficient to hold her and bind her hands and feet. She too was gagged so that she could not scream.

'We are sorry about this,' said a man's voice, quite politely. 'It is important to us to take the little Prince out of your hands. His country needs him. We shall not harm him in any way – and we have not harmed you either. We have merely put you to some inconvenience. Once we have the Prince one of us will come to untie you, if it is possible. If not – well, you will be found by some farm worker early in the morning.'

The men left Bill and his wife against a haystack, protected from the wind. One of them had gone through Bill's pockets first, and had taken out the key of the cottage.

Bill listened as the men went off. Were they gone? He rubbed his head against the ground trying to get off the cloth bound round his face. Was his wife all right?

He was furious with himself. To walk into a trap as easily as all that! The woman with the message must have been one of the gang, of course. No wonder she wouldn't come in. He should have been suspicious about that. An ordinary messenger would have waited for them and then walked to the farm in their company.

He remembered the 'ting' of the telephone that Jack said he had heard that afternoon. That must have been Madame Tatiosa or her companion telephoning to their headquarters to say that they knew where the Prince was, and requesting help to capture him. Another car must have come down that evening with other members of the gang. It all fitted in so well – but poor Bill saw the plot after it had been carried out, instead of before!

He wondered what was happening at Quarry Cottage. He believed the man who had said that he was not going to harm the little Prince. All they wanted to do was to depose his uncle and set Gussy up in his place. Poor Gussy! He would be made to do all that the gang wanted, and his life would be very miserable.

Nothing was happening just then at Quarry Cottage. All the five children were fast asleep, and so was Kiki. The window of the boys' bedroom was shut, as Bill had ordered – but of what use was that when the enemy had the key to the front door!

Time crept on – and eleven o'clock came. Philip's alarm clock went off under his pillow, whirring in a muffled way that woke him up with a jump. At first he didn't know what the noise was, then he remembered.

'Eleven o'clock!' he thought, and slid his hand under his pillow to stop the alarm ringing. He sat up. Moonlight poured into the room, and made everything silvery. Just the night for badgers!

He padded across the room and shook Jack. 'Wake up! Eleven o'clock!' he whispered, right into his ear. He did not mean to wake Gussy, and have him clamouring to go with them! But Gussy was very sound asleep indeed. The moonlight streamed on to his face, and showed up the long lock of hair that had fallen as usual over his forehead.

Kiki awoke as soon as the alarm went off. But she was used to muffled alarm clocks, and merely gave a little yawn, and stretched her wings. If the boys were going out, she was quite ready! Nothing would persuade her to be left behind.

The two boys dressed quickly in shorts, jerseys and rubber-soled shoes. They took a last glance at Gussy. His mouth was wide open again. Jack grinned as he remembered the bits of grass that Kiki had popped into it on Sugar-Loaf Hill.

They crept downstairs, pausing outside Bill's bedroom door to make sure all was quiet, and that Bill and his wife were asleep.

'Can't hear a thing,' whispered Jack. 'They must be *very* sound asleep! Not even a snore from Bill!'

This wasn't very surprising, of course, as Bill was at that moment struggling with his ropes as he lay in the shelter of the haystack.

'We'll go out the back way,' whispered Philip. 'The front door creaks a little. Don't bump into anything in the hall, for goodness' sake.'

Kiki was on Jack's shoulder, as quiet as the dormouse in Philip's pocket. She could always be depended on to keep silent when it was necessary. She knew quite well that the boys were trying not to be heard. She pecked Jack's ear affectionately, wondering what he was up to on this moon-light night.

The boys went out of the back door, and then stood still, debating which way to go.

'I think I'll come up to the little wood with you first,' said Jack. 'I might pop down to the quarry later, to hear the owls there, and see if I can watch them swooping on mice or rats.'

So they went silently to the wood on the east side of the cottage, making no noise in their rubber-soled shoes. They kept to the shadows of the hedges, afraid that someone might see them, even in this deserted spot. The moonlight was so very brilliant!

They came to the wood. Philip knew what type of place badgers would visit, and he led Jack to a hedge overshadow-ing a big bank.

This is the sort of place to wait about in,' he said. 'Let's squeeze into that bush there.'

They crouched down in the black shadows. An owl sud-denly hooted nearby, and Kiki at once hooted back, copying the long, quavering hoot exactly, and making Jack jump.

'Shut up, Kiki,' he whispered fiercely. 'You'll bring all the owls down on us with your hooting. Gosh, here comes the one you mimicked!'

An owl swooped by his head, and he ducked. So did Kiki! Kiki longed to hoot again. She loved puzzling any other bird.

She kept silent, half-sulky. The boys listened with their sharp ears, watching for any movement. Suddenly Jack gave Philip a nudge. A long, snake-like animal was hurrying by.

'Stoat,' whispered Philip in Jack's ear. 'And what's this? A hedgehog!'

The hedgehog was curious about the black shadows sitting under the bush. He came fearlessly up to investigate. Philip put out his hand slowly, and the hedgehog sniffed it over. Jack quite expected to see him climb on to Philip's knee! No creature was ever afraid of him.

But the hedgehog was hungry and he ran off to find the slugs he liked best. The boys thought he went along as if he was a little clockwork animal. They waited for the next night creature to appear.

And this time it was a badger! It really was. Philip drew in his breath sharply. He had hardly hoped to see one so soon. It was a biggish creature, with a curiously striped black and white face. It stood absolutely still in the moonlight, sniffing, wondering if it could smell a danger-smell – a smell of humans?

But the wind blew from the badger to the boys, and he could smell nothing. He could hardly be seen as he stood in the full moonlight, because the black and white stripes down his face were so exactly like the black and white shadows of this moonlit night.

'Perfect camouflage!' whispered Philip, and Jack nodded. Then he nudged Philip. Something else was coming.

'*Young* badgers!' thought Philip, in delight. 'A family party – yes, there's mother badger at the back. What a bit of luck!'

The young badgers were skittish little bear-like things. They began to play about, and the two boys watched their curious games, quite fascinated.

The little badgers began to bounce. They really *did* bounce, on all four legs, jumping up and down in the same place, looking like fat, furry balls. They bounced at one another! One knocked another over, but in a flash he turned a somersault, came up under the first badger and knocked *him* over!

This head-over-heels game seemed a favourite one, and the young badgers played it for some time. Then the parents gave a little call, and went off into the wood; the young ones stopped their game and followed.

Jack gave a little laugh. 'What an amusing sight! I've never seen animals play *that* game before! Do all badgers turn head-over-heels like that?'

'I've heard so,' said Philip. 'A keeper once told me that a grown badger will spring traps that way – he just turns himself head-over-heels on the trap, sets it off, and then takes the bait! All he loses is a few hairs off his back.'

An owl hooted again, some way off. It was a tawny owl calling. Then there was a screech from a barn owl. Kiki stirred on Jack's shoulders. She was longing to do a bit of hooting and screeching herself!

'I think I'll go back now,' said Philip, getting up. 'I'd like to stay and watch for a few more creatures to come by, but I'm afraid I shall fall alseep. You coming, Jack?'

'Well – I rather think I'll go and wander round that quarry a bit,' said Jack. 'I'd like to see what owls are there – and I'd like to give old Kiki the chance of calling them, to see if she really can bring them to her. I know she's longing to try. Aren't you, Kiki, old bird?'

Kiki muttered something into his ear, afraid of speaking out loud. Jack got up and stretched. 'Well, you get to bed, and I'll come when I'm ready' he said. 'I'll be about half an hour, I expect. Don't be surprised if you hear thousands of hoots in a little while, once Kiki gets going!'

Philip went back to the cottage, and Jack made his way to the quarry. Little did they guess what a shock they were both going to get in the next ten minutes!

12

Capture!

Philip made his way to the back door of the cottage, but just as he was about to go in, he stopped. What noise was that? It sounded like someone going to the front door – someone tiptoeing up the path, surely?

The boy hesitated. Could it be someone after Gussy? He'd better warn Bill then – go in and wake him. He tiptoed quietly through the back door, into the hall and up the stairs. He stopped at the top and looked back, hearing a small sound.

The front door was opening quietly, but with the little creak it always gave. Then a torch was flashed on and off very quickly. Yes – Somebody *was* getting in.

Philip yelled at the top of his voice. 'Bill! BILL! BILL! Wake up, Bill. There's someone getting in.'

He was standing just outside the girls' door as he yelled, and they woke up at once. Gracious! – who was shouting like that?

'Someone's getting in. Quick, Bill, quick!' shouted Philip again, wondering why there was no answering shout from Bill's room nearby.

The girls' door opened and Dinah looked out, scared. 'What is it? Who is it? Where's Bill?'

'Keep where you are,' said a voice suddenly, and a torch was flashed on to the three of them, for Lucy-Ann had now appeared, trembling.

Philip pushed the girls violently, and they almost fell into their bedroom. Then he rushed into Bill's room, yelling again. 'BILL! Do wake up!'

The moonlight showed him a completely empty bed – a bed not even slept in! Then where was Bill? And his mother – where was *she*? Philip was astounded.

Gussy was now awake, up in the attic bedroom. He sat up, bewildered. What was all this shouting? He suddenly noticed that Jack and Philip were not in their beds, and he leapt out of his, afraid.

Downstairs, in Bill's bedroom, Philip was still yelling. Bill *must* be somehwere about – but where? 'Bill! I say, BILL!'

A torch flashed into the room, and two figures loomed up by the door.

'You won't find Bill,' said a voice. 'Or his wife either. We've got them. And now we want the Prince Aloysius. We do not intend to harm him in any way – but he must come with us. His country needs him.'

'What have you done with my mother?' demanded Philip, fiercely. 'I'll get the police! What do you think you're doing, capturing people, and coming after the Prince! You can't do that kind of thing in Britain!'

'Oh yes, we can,' said the foreign voice, smoothly, and the man stepped into the moonlight. Philip saw that it was the man who had come with the woman that afternoon. Behind him were other people – how many? Philip wished that Jack was with him. One boy wasn't much against all these people. He didn't count Gussy as a boy!

One of the men behind called out something in a language that Philip didn't understand, and received a sharp order in return. There was the sound of feet on the stairs leading up to the attic bedroom. They were after Gussy, who had done quite the wrong thing, and had appeared at the top in the bright moonlight! He had been seen at once, of course.

Gussy fled into the bedroom, slammed the door and locked it. He leaned against it, trembling. Then he ran to the window. Could he get out?

No. Gussy was no climber, and although Jack and Philip would certainly have had a shot at clambering down the creeper, Gussy was afraid he might fall.

'Unlock this door!' cried a voice, but Gussy did not obey. Then two of the men flung themselves against it, and it broke down easily. They clambered over the broken panels and went to Gussy. He screamed.

One of the men bowed to him. 'Your Highness, we have not come to harm you. We have come to take you back to Tauri-Hessia to be crowned King in the place of your uncle. He is not liked, your uncle. The people want you instead.'

'It's a lie!' shouted Gussy, trembling. 'I've been told all about it. My uncle is too strong a ruler for you, and you want a boy instead who will do as he is told. I will not come!'

All this was said in his own language, so that the girls, listening fearfully in their room below, did not understand a word. Philip pushed by the men at the door of Bill's room and ran up to Gussy.

'Look here,' he said fiercely to the two men there. 'You know that the British Government *and* your own Government won't let you make Gussy King. You'll get into trouble with our Government, you know. You'll be clapped into prison either here or in your own country.'

The men, joined by the other two below, had a quick conference. Philip didn't understand a word. Then the tall man with the eyeglass bowed slightly to Philip.

'You too will come with us,' he said, 'and the other children as well. You will – er – be companions for our little Prince – and we do not think your Government will be *too* angry when they know we hold you also!'

'Oh! So you think you'll take us and make us a kind of hostage, do you?' said Philip, quite beside himself with rage. 'You think you can bargain with our Government just because you'll hold us prisoners! My word, you don't know the British people. You'll be sorry for this! Holding us to ransom! I never heard such a fatheaded idea in my life. You

76

aren't living in the Middle Ages, you know!'

The man heard him out to the end, quite politely. Then he made a motion with his hand, and two of the men pounced on Philip and Gussy and held them in such a vice-like grip that it was quite hopeless to get away.

'Run, you two run!' yelled Philip at the top of his voice, hoping that Dinah and Lucy-Ann would have the sense to rush into the woods and get away. But although they did manage to tear downstairs, they found a man in the hall, and he was quite able to hold the two kicking, yelling girls until yet another fellow came to his help.

Sharp orders were given by the man with the eyeglass, who seemed to be in command. One man detached himself and went upstairs. He came down with an assortment of clothes for the girls and Gussy, who was, of course, still in his beautiful silk pyjamas. The girls were in pyjamas and dressing gowns, but had no slippers on. The man was sent back to fetch shoes.

'Where's Bill?' said Lucy-Ann, with chattering teeth. 'I want Bill. What have they done with him? And where's Aunt Allie?'

'Don't be frightened,' said the man with the eyeglass, patting her. 'We shall treat you very kindly. We shall not hurt you. It will be nice for the little Prince Aloysius to have his friends with him. You will have a fine time in Tauri-Hessia.'

Lucy-Ann suddenly realized that Jack was missing. She looked round wildly for him. 'Where's Jack? What have you done with Jack?'

'Ah, yes — there was another boy. I remember now,' said the chief man. 'Where is he?'

'Out bird-watching,' said Philip, sullenly. His only hope now was that Jack would see and hear this disturbance and go to fetch help before they were all whisked away. He had given up struggling. What was the use? He would only get hurt, and he could see that if the girls were going to be captured, he certainly must go with them to look after them as best he could.

'Bird-watching! At this time of night!' said the man. 'What strange habits you Britishers have! We will not wait for this boy Jack. We do not need him.'

They opened the front door again, and pushed the four children out in front of them, holding their arms tightly.

'It is of no use to scream,' said the chief, still very politely. 'There is no one to hear you – and we should gag you if you did scream.'

'Philip – what shall we do?' asked Dinah, scarlet with rage at being captured like this.

'Nothing,' said Philip. 'Just – er – hope for the best.'

Dinah guessed what he meant. Perhaps even at this very minute Jack was bringing help!

Lucy-Ann stumbled along miserably in her dressing gown. She had been allowed to put on her shoes, and so had the others. She was worried about Bill and her aunt, and very *very* worried about Jack. Would she be taken off to Tauri-Hessia and have to leave Jack for months and months? Where *was* Jack?

Jack was down in the quarry with Kiki. He had found plenty of owls hooting and screeching there, for, as the old farm hand had said, it was a wonderful hunting place for owls of all kinds.

Kiki had been having the time of her life. She had hooted and screeched and twitted, and had brought a crowd of owls almost down to Jack's shoulders. One owl, a barn owl, had screeched deafeningly in his ear, and had struck him with a wing.

Jack decided that he was too easily seen where he stood. He must get under a bush somewhere, or else the next owl might scratch his face with a sharp talon or two!

He moved to the other side of the quarry and made his way to a big hedge there. As he drew near, the moonlight glinted on something under the hedge. Something that shone brightly. Jack stopped. What could it be?

He went cautiously forward, and saw that something dark and long and very big was under the tall hedge, as close to it as possible. The moonlight caught its polished surface here and there.

'Gosh! It's a car!' said Jack, in the greatest astonishment. 'A car exactly like the one the couple have at the farm — it must be the same one. What's it doing here?'

He went over to it. It was empty. Nobody was in it at all. The key had been taken out so that it could not be driven away.

'Has somebody parked it here to go and spy round Quarry Cottage?' wondered Jack. He went to the back of the car. It had an enormous luggage boot. Jack opened it and peered inside. It was empty except for an extra inner tube and a few tools.

Kiki hooted again, and an owl answered her. 'Be quiet now, Kiki,' said Jack. 'We've got to do a bit of spying. We'll creep back to Quarry Cottage and see if there's anyone snooping round there.'

But before he could do that, he heard the sound of foot-steps coming into the quarry, and he dived into some bushes.

The footsteps made quite a lot of noise, because there were eight people coming into the deserted quarry, where the car had been parked. Jack peered out of his bush and saw, to his great alarm, that Philip, Dinah, Lucy-Ann and Gussy were all being held very firmly indeed! He stared, bewildered, unable to think what to do.

Kiki suddenly screeched — but it was not an owl screech, it was a real parrot screech — and Philip recognized it at once. It was Kiki! Then Jack must be somewhere in the quarry still!

He gave a shout. 'They're taking us away! Tell Bill!'

The man holding him gave him a shove. 'You were told not to shout! What's the use of shouting here? There's no one to hear you!'

But there was, of course. There was Jack. But what was Jack to DO?

13

The extra passenger

Jack stared in distress at the four children being bundled into the car – Philip and Dinah at the back with three men, and Gussy and Lucy-Ann in front with the driver. What a crowd! If anyone saw the car going along with such a number of people in, surely it would be noticed and stopped?

'Yes, it would,' thought Jack, 'so that means they can't be going very far – they will arrive at their destination before daylight. Are they going to take them to some hiding place fairly near then? Why in the world have they got Philip and the girls as well as Gussy?'

Everyone was now in the car. The doors were shut as quietly as possible. The engine was started up – and just at that very moment Jack had an idea!

He ran, crouching, to the back of the car. He hadn't had time to shut the luggage boot properly when he had opened it to look inside. Could he get into it before the car drove off? It was such a fine big one.

The car began to move very slowly out of the quarry, bumping over rough places. Jack flung himself at the back of it, and clambered up on to the luggage boot. It swung right open, and Jack half-fell into it. Kiki was astounded, and flew off his shoulder at once. Jack stared at her anxiously. He dared not call her back.

But, as soon as she saw Jack settled in the boot, she flew down again, and found his shoulder. She talked solemnly into his ear, in a very low voice, trying to tell him in parrot language that she thought these goings-on were extremely peculiar, but that so long as Jack approved of them, she did too — and she was coming with him, even in this dark, smelly car boot!

Jack felt comforted to have her. He puzzled over everything. Where was Bill? And Aunt Allie? How was it these fellows had been able to get into Quarry Cottage so easily and capture every one? But what had they done with Bill! Was he lying knocked out in the cottage? Ought Jack to have gone to see, instead of climbing into the boot?

The car had now gathered speed and was going down country lanes very fast. It drew up once, at some dark little house, where a man came out. There was another car there and one of the men in the first car thankfully got out and went to the second car. This went on ahead, as if guiding the other. Jack was glad. He didn't want bright head lights behind him, showing him sitting in the boot!

'I ought to close the boot and shut myself in. But suppose I can't get it open again?' he thought. 'I simply *must* see what place they're taking the others to. If I can do that, I can soon raise the alarm, have the place surrounded, and everyone rescued! I hope no one sees me here.'

Another hour's run in the smooth-running powerful car — then it stopped. There was a sharp exchange of words, a light flashed, and a gate creaked open.

'Hallo! We're here already, wherever that may be!' thought Jack. 'Had I better get out now, while the car has stopped? Blow — it's too late. They're going on again.'

The car bumped over a dark field. And then suddenly a strange, extraordinarily loud noise started up not far ahead. Jack jumped violently, and Kiki gave a loud screech, which fortunately couldn't possibly be heard in the enormous noise going on.

81

'An aeroplane!' said Jack. 'So *that's* what they've planned. They're going off to Tauri-Hessia! They must be. And they'll hide Gussy somewhere till their plans are all ready, and the girls and Philip with him. Nobody will know where they are.'

He felt the car come to a stop with a bump. He crawled out of the boot at once, and ran to a big shape looming up nearby. It was a lorry. Jack crouched beside it, watching.

He saw an aeroplane not far off, its propellers whirring. It hadn't all its lights on yet, but men were round it with lamps. It was obviously soon going to take off.

What was this place? A private airfield? Jack had no idea at all. He watched all the passengers in the big black car tumbling out, one after the other. He thought he heard Lucy-Ann crying, and his heart sank. She would hate all this! She wasn't tough, like Dinah. Where would she be tomorrow?

Everyone was hurried towards the plane. Jack left his hiding place and hurried too. He had had another idea! Could he hide in the plane? He had hidden in the car, and no one had suspected it. Would there be any place to hide in the plane?

He thought of the planes he had flown in. The luggage-space would be the only place. There probably wouldn't be much there. It was a risk, but he'd take it. If he was discovered, well, at least he'd be with the others.

'But I *mustn't* be discovered!' he thought desperately. 'If I am I'll be hidden away somewhere too – and I simply *must* find out where the others are being taken, so that I can somehow get word to Bill.'

Kiki came to his help, quite unexpectedly. She didn't see why she shouldn't talk to the others, whose voices she had recognized as soon as she heard them getting out of the car. She left Jack's shoulder and flew towards Lucy-Ann.

'Pop goes the weasel!' she cried. 'God save the King! Send for the doctor!'

The four children in front turned round in utter amazement. 'Kiki! KIKI! How did *you* get here?'

The men pushing them forward stopped at once. They had no idea that Kiki was only a parrot, and had not even spotted her in the darkness. They thought she must be someone coming after the children, on the airfield, someone quite unexpected, who had followed them!

Orders were shouted. Lamps flashed here and there. Kiki was frightened and flew back to Jack.

'Wipe your feet!' she called, much to the amazement of the men with the lamps.

Jack ran round the other side of the lorry, for the men were coming too near him. Then he saw his chance. Everyone's attention was on the men who were searching the field with lamps. Nobody was watching the plane.

Jack ran to it in the darkness, stumbling as he went. Thank goodness the moon had conveniently gone behind a remarkably black cloud! He felt a drop of rain. Perhaps the moon wouldn't come out till he was safely in the plane.

He reached the plane, and thankfully saw the steps up to it. He ran up and found himself in the plane. No one was there. He groped his way to the back, where he hoped to find the luggage-space. He felt something that was shaped like a crate. Yes – this must be where they put the luggage! He felt round again, and came across a box. It had a lid, and he lifted it up, hoping that the box was empty.

It wasn't. It was full of something soft, that might be clothes, or material of some kind. It felt like silk. Jack pulled most of it out and stuffed in into a corner, behind the big crate.

Then he hurriedly got into the box and pulled the lid down. Only just in time! Kiki was with him, of course, silent and astonished. Jack had tapped her beak to tell her she must be absolutely quiet.

He heard the sound of voices and the noise of feet going up the steps into the plane. He heard shouts, and bangs and whirs. The propellers, which had stopped, were started up again, and the aeroplane shook violently.

The wheels bumped very slowly over the field and then the bumping stopped.

'We've taken off,' thought Jack, thankfully. 'And I'm here with the others, though they don't know it. Now will my luck hold? Shall I get to wherever they're going without being discovered? I do hope so! If only I can find out where they will be hidden, things will be easy.'

It was uncomfortable in the box, but as Jack had left some of the soft material at the bottom, at least he had something soft to crouch on. Kiki didn't like it at all. She grumbled in his ear, and then suddenly produced a tremendous sneeze.

It sounded very loud indeed to Jack. He sat as quiet as a mouse, waiting for someone to come and look round the luggage-space. But nobody did. The noise of the engines was too loud for Kiki's sneeze to be heard. It was a real sneeze, not a pretend one, and Kiki was just as surprised as Jack was when it came.

The children in the front of the plane talked in low voices, sure that the engines would drown what they were saying. It seemed queer to be sitting in a plane dressed in night clothes – all but Philip, of course.

'*Was* that Kiki we heard out on the field?' said Lucy-Ann. 'It must have been. I'm sure I heard "Pop goes the weasel"!'

'I believe it was,' said Philip. 'I wouldn't be surprised if old Jack hung on to that car somehow. After all, we know he was in that quarry – he probably saw what was happening, and managed to hang on behind somehwere.'

'I wish he was with us now,' sighed Lucy-Ann. 'I shan't like being without him. Where are we going, I wonder? To some horrid old castle – or perhaps a palace? Gussy, have you got a palace?'

'Yes,' said Gussy. 'But only a small one. We shan't go there, because the people know me. They would see me. I have heard these men talking, and they do not want me to be

84

seen yet. First they must deal with my uncle. I hope they will not kill him. He is nice, my uncle.'

'I sincerely hope they *won't* do anything of the sort,' said Philip. 'You'd *have* to be King then, Gussy. How I'd hate to be a King! Always having to be on my best behaviour, never to lose my temper or do a thing that was wrong or impolite, having to be nice to people I hated, and . . . '

'Why isn't your father King?' asked Dinah. 'Why are *you* the heir to the throne?'

'My father is dead,' said Gussy. 'There is only my mother, and in our country women are not allowed to rule. So one day I must be King. I shall like it.'

'Well – you like ordering people about, and showing off,' said Dinah. 'So I suppose it'll suit you. But I can't say you're my idea of a King. Oh dear – I wish this hadn't happened. All our Easter hols spoiled!'

'I hate all this,' said Lucy-Ann, dismally. 'I'm cold, and now I'm sleepy.'

'Cuddle up to me,' said Dinah. 'After all, it's the middle of the night, so we *ought* to feel sleepy. I do too. Let's go to sleep. It will make the night seem shorter.'

'I could go to sleep at once if I didn't keep thinking of Bill and Aunt Allie,' said Lucy-Ann, shutting her eyes, and getting close to Dinah for warmth. 'I keep on thinking about – about – I keep on . . . '

Philip smiled at Dinah over Lucy-Ann's head. She was asleep already, in spite of her 'thinking'. Poor Lucy-Ann – she fell into adventures as readily as the others, but she didn't enjoy them nearly so much!

Jack fell into an uncomfortable sleep too, in his box in the luggage-space. Kiki tucked her head under her wing and slept peacefully. The plane went on and on in the night, through a rain-storm, and then out into clear weather again, with a moon still bright in the sky.

None of the children saw that it was flying over the brilliant, moonlit sea. None of them gazed down to see the towns that looked like toy villages far below. The engines droned on and on, and the rhythm lulled the sleepers for mile upon mile.

And then the plane began to circle over a small airfield. It had arrived! Philip woke in a hurry and shook the girls. Gussy woke too and looked down from the window.

'Tauri-Hessia!' he said, proudly. 'My country, Tauri-Hessia!'

14

Jack is on his own

The sun was up, just above the horizon, when the plane landed gently on the runway. The sky was golden, and in the distance small whitewashed houses gleamed brightly.

Jack awoke when the engines stopped. He lifted up the lid of his box slightly, listening. Had they arrived? Then he heard Gussy's voice. 'Tauri-Hessia!'

'So we've arrived,' thought Jack. 'Now – what do I do next? It's daylight – though I should guess it's only just sunrise.'

The four children in front were hustled out. The little airfield was completely deserted except for a few mechanics. A large car stood waiting. The children were pushed into it without a moment's pause. Obviously they were to be hurried somewhere secret as fast as possible.

Jack got out of the box and made his way cautiously to a window. He saw the children just below, getting into a big car. The man with the eyeglass appeared to be in command, and gave an order to the chauffeur as he got in. The man was holding open the door and bowed. He saluted too, and repeated something after the man with the eyeglass.

'Borken!'

Then he got into the driving-seat and drove swiftly off the field to a large gate in the distance.

'Borken!' said Jack to himself. 'Now would that be the name of a place – or just a Hessian word for "Thank you" or something? Well – they've gone. Kiki, you and I are on our own in a strange land whose language we don't know. And we have only got a few English coins in our pocket – so what do you suppose is the best thing to do?'

'Send for the doctor,' said Kiki, putting up her crest and looking very wise. 'Send for the doctor. Put the kettle on.'

Jack went on looking out of the window. It seemed to him that everyone had walked off to a little wooden building at one end of the airfield – to get refreshments, perhaps? Jack felt that he would like some too!

He went cautiously into the other part of the plane. Not a soul was there. In fact, not a soul was to be seen anywhere, even on the field or in the distance.

'I think the time has come for us to go, Kiki,' said Jack. 'Ready for a sprint? I hardly think we'll get away without being noticed – but at any rate we'll have a good start, if the men have to come from that wooden building right over there.'

He went to the landing steps and ran down them. Then he sprinted at top speed across the field to the entrance. Nothing happened for a nimute or two, and then two men appeared at the door of the distant building. They shouted loudly, and then began to run after Jack.

But he had a wonderful start, and the men gave up almost at once, and returned to the building. 'Just a boy longing for a close look at an aeroplane!' they said to one another.

Jack ran out of the entrance and found himself on a wide, deserted road. No one was in sight. He could not even see any houses. This must be a very lonely airfield! He began to walk along the road, Kiki on his shoulder. He was very hungry indeed now.

'Why isn't anyone about?' he thought. 'Not a car to be

seen so I can't get a lift. I wonder where the others are by now? Wish I was with them!'

He suddenly remembered that it was very early in the morning. Of course no one would be about yet. The sun had only just risen. Possibly he might meet a workman or two soon.

He met a man cycling along the road after a while and held up his hand to stop him. The man put one foot on the road, and stopped his bicycle.

'Eglinoota?' he said. At least, that is what it sounded like to Jack. He looked astonished to see Kiki.

'I'm English,' said Jack, trying to speak slowly and clearly. 'Where is the police station?'

'Eglinoota?' said the man again, looking bewildered. 'Oota? Oota?'

'Parp-parp,' said Kiki, suddenly. 'Parp-parp!' It sounded exactly like the hooter of a car! Jack laughed.

'Did you think the man kept saying "hooter"?' he asked Kiki. 'Well, he wasn't. Goodness knows what he was saying! I wish I knew what "food" was in the Hessian language!'

'Powkepotoplink?' said the man, trying again. He pointed to the parrot. 'Powkepotoplink? Ai, ai!'

He suddenly took out a notebook and a pencil and began drawing something on a page. Jack wondered what it was. The man tore out the page and gave it to him.

The drawing looked like a small map showing various roads. There was something that looked like a pond also, and something else that looked like a church spire. At the bottom of the map the man had drawn what looked like a tent. He jabbed at it with his pencil.

'Powkepotoplink,' he said again, very loudly, as if that might help Jack to understand.

'Plink-plonk, plink-plonk,' said Kiki, at once, and went off into a cackle of laughter. The man looked at her in admiration. He undid a bag and took out a small sugared cake. He presented it to Kiki, who took it with her right foot, making a sudden clucking noise like a hen.

Jack looked at it with hungry eyes and the man noticed the look. He delved in his bag again and brought out an enormously thick sandwich with some kind of bright red meat in it. He presented this to Jack, who was thrilled.

'Thank you,' said the boy. 'Thank you very much.'

'Cheepalikkle,' said the man, incomprehensibly, and rode off, waving. Jack walked on, munching the huge sandwich. Kiki put out her parrot-tongue and licked the cake. She didn't like it and gave it to Jack. In return he gave her some of her favourite sunflower seeds, of which he always kept a supply in his pocket. She sat happily on his shoulder, cracking them.

Jack looked at the map. What did it mean? Why had that man drawn it? He must have thought there was some particular place Jack wanted to go to – but Jack himself didn't know of any place in Tauri-Hessia that he wanted to find, except the place where the others had gone. And that might be Borken and it might not. Borken might mean anything in this unknown Hessian language!

He walked on and on for miles, feeling much better for the sandwich. He decided that he must look for a police station if ever he came to the end of this wide, deserted road. It looked as if it had only been built to lead to the airfield! Except for the man on the bicycle he met nobody at all.

But at last he saw houses in the distance. Ah – he was coming to a village – no, a town, because as he came nearer he saw that it was far too big to be called a village.

'If I could just find somebody who spoke English, it would be such a help,' thought Jack. 'I could ask for a police station then, and get a telegram – or a cable – sent to Bill. I wish he'd come out here and help. I wonder what happened to him. I bet those fellows knocked him out.'

He came into the town and looked around him with interest. The shops were small and dark, the houses were whitewashed or pink-washed, and seemed to run to curls and squiggles and much decoration – rather 'fretworky', Jack decided. Curly roofs, squiggly bits of woodwork here and there, and windows whose sills were covered with decorated flower boxes.

The people looked like farmers and were dressed in bright, simple clothes. No woman wore a hat, but many wore shawls. The men wore rather tight trousers, and had some kind of sash round their waists. Their waistcoats were gaily embroidered, and somehow they reminded Jack of bull fighters though he didn't quite know why.

The children were very thin, and simply dressed. Even the little girls wore long, rather raggedy skirts, and the boys wore tight trousers like their fathers but had no embroidered waist-coats. Instead they had very bright red, blue or yellow shirts.

They soon saw Jack, and ran to him. The parrot fascinated them.

'Powke, powke!' they yelled, pointing at Kiki, who was delighted at being the centre of attention. She put up her crest and lowered it, and even did a little hoppitty dance on Jack's shoulder.

'Powke – that must mean parrot,' thought Jack. 'Hey, you kids – where's the police station?'

They didn't understand a word, of course. They followed Jack, talking together, still entertained by Kiki, who was showing off tremendously.

Then a small boy with a little wooden gun ran up. He pointed it at Jack, and shouted 'Pop-pop-pop!'

That was quite enough for Kiki. She stood up on her toes and shouted at the top of her voice. 'Pop! POP! BANG-BANG-BANG! Pop goes the weasel! Powke, powke, powke.'

There was an awed silence after this effort of Kiki's. Everyone stared, still trotting after Jack.

Kiki went off into one of her idiotic bouts of laughter, and the children all began to laugh too.

'Wipe your feet, blow your nose!' shouted Kiki, and then made a noise like an express train in a tunnel.

This made a tremendous impression. The children fell back a little, startled. But they soon caught up again, yelling. 'Powke, powke, powke', and soon the crowd was considerably bigger, and Jack began to feel like the Pied Piper of Hamelin with so many children following him.

Then an official-looking person stopped him at a crossroads, and addressed him quite sternly, pointing to the crowd that had now gathered round him. Jack didn't understand a word.

'I am English,' he said. 'English. You speak English? Yes? No?'

'Ha! Ingleeeeesh!' said the person, and took out a black notebook which immediately told Jack what he was. Of course – a Hessian policeman!

'You speak English?' said Jack, hopefully.

The policeman rattled off something at him, and held out his hand. He still had the notebook in the other one. Jack hadn't the faintest idea what he wanted. He shook his head, puzzled. The policeman grew annoyed. He slapped his hand with the notebook and shouted again.

Jack shook his head once more. Kiki shouted back at the policeman. 'Pop goes the weasel, put the kettle on, POP!'

All the children laughed. There were a good many grown-ups around now, watching. One suddenly put his hand into his pocket and drew out a worn, doubled-over card. He showed it to Jack, and made him understand that that was what the policeman was asking him for.

Jack saw that it was a kind of passport or identity card. He hadn't got one on him, of course, so once more he shook his head. Kiki shook hers, too, and the children roared.

The policeman shut his notebook with a snap and put his hand on Jack's shoulder. He fired a sentence at him in sharp Hessian and pushed him in front of him smartly.

'Now where do we go?' thought Jack. 'What a colourful

policeman – blue trousers, red shirt, blue sash, an imposing kind of flower-pot helmet – really!'

But he didn't think things were quite so happy when he saw where the policeman was taking him. There was no doubt about it at all. It was a police station, a small, square, whitewashed place, sober-looking and severe, with a good many more of stern-faced policemen standing about.

'Look here! You can't put *me* into prison!' cried Jack, struggling away. 'I've done nothing wrong! You let me go!'

15

The map comes in useful

Jack was pushed firmly into a small, square room with one bench in it against the wall. He was made to sit down on this, and the policeman went to report at a big, untidy desk. He spoke very quickly, and it all sounded like a lot of Double Dutch to Jack.

It did to Kiki too, and she sat on Jack's shoulder and sent out such a stream of unending nonsense that every policeman in the place stared in admiration.

Nobody was standing in Jack's way to the door. He looked at it. He thought he would make a dash for freedom, and try to get away from these awkward policemen. He was half-afraid he might be locked up for weeks. Perhaps they thought he was a beggar or a tramp? Perhaps it was a great crime not to have some kind of card to say who he was?

He saw his chance, when nobody was looking at him, and raced for the door. He was down the steps and into the street before a policeman stirred! He heard shouts behind him but he didn't look back. Down the dusty street he ran at top speed, turned a corner, ran down an alley, and came to a big door.

He ran inside and looked round. No one was there. A squawk attracted his attention, and made Kiki look round in interest. Jack saw a parrot in a cage, a very colourful one with blue and green and yellow feathers.

Kiki flew to the cage and stood on the top. She bent her head down and looked inside excitedly. Another parrot!

'How-do-you-do, how-do-you-do!' said Kiki. 'Good morning, good night! Pop goes the weasel!'

The other parrot gave another squawk. It seemed rather scared. Then Jack heard the sound of footsteps, and before he could move, a voice spoke – a gentle voice, soft and kind.

A girl stood there, aged about twelve. She was beautifully dressed in bright silks, and her long dark hair was woven in and out with bright ribbons. She stared at Jack in surprise.

'Eglinoota?' said the girl. 'Oota?'

Jack wished he knew what this 'oota' word meant. He really didn't know what to say. He pointed to the parrots and smiled cheerfully. 'Powke, powke!' he said. The girl looked at the two parrots and laughed.

Then, to his delight, she slowly spoke a few words in English. 'Where – you – go?' she said. 'You – English – yes?'

Jack fished out the bit of paper the man on the bicycle had drawn him. It would look as if he really *was* going somewhere, if he showed her that! She took it and nodded her head.

'Come,' she said, and took him to the door.

'Listen – do you know anyone who speaks English well?' asked Jack, eagerly. The girl didn't understand, though he reapeated it several times. Then she heard a voice from somewhere in the house, and she gave him a push, pointing down an alley, and then to the right. Jack thanked her, called Kiki and went out. He ran down the alley and came to the end. Then he turned to the right and went quickly along a narrow, dusty street with high walls each side.

He stopped at the end and looked at his map. He supposed he might as well follow it. Obviously the bicyclist must have had some reason for drawing it. It might lead somewhere useful!

In front of him was what would be, in England, a village green. But this green was parched and dusty, and three skinny hens wandered over it looking thoroughly miserable. At the side was a big round pond in which dozens of small children were paddling. Jack looked at his map again.

'Ah – the pond! Yes, I must be on the right road. I'll go down here, and see if I can spot the thing that looks like a church tower.'

He went on for some way without seeing anything like a church tower. At last he stopped a kindly-looking old woman and showed her the map. He pointed to the drawing that looked like a church.

She nodded her head at once. She took his arm and pointed across a field. There was a path there. It led upwards towards a hill. On the hill Jack saw a building with a great tower. He couldn't imagine what it was, unless it was a Tauri-Hessian church.

He went on again, over the field and up to the tower. He looked at the map again – it showed a winding road from the tower and this road led to the drawing on the map that looked rather like a tent. Jack looked up from the map and recognized the winding road, going down the other side of the hill on which the tower stood. But what could the tent-like drawing be?

An old man sat on a bench, dozing. Jack went cautiously up to him and sat down. The old man opened an eye, saw the parrot and sat up at once.

'Good. He's awake,' thought Jack, and pushed the map in front of him, pointing to the tent-like drawing, and trying to make the man understand that he wanted to get there.

'Ahhhh.' said the old fellow, in a hoarse voice. 'Pik-katioratyforg. Ahhhhhh!'

'Very helpful!' thought Jack. The old man got up and tottered a little way down the path. Then he pointed with his stick.

'Surkytalar,' he said. 'Surky.'

'Surky',' repeated Jack, and looked where he was pointing. Then he stared hard. He knew why the bicyclist had drawn the tent now! In a big field were crowds of tents and vans! It must be a circus of some kind – a travelling circus!

'Of course! Surky – he means circus,' thought Jack. 'It's a circus. That's why that fellow on the bike directed me there. He thought I wanted the circus – thought I was trying to make my way to it, because I'd got a talking parrot. Well, well, well! I've solved *that* puzzle!'

He thanked the old man and thought he might as well make his way to the circus. Somebody there might possibly speak English. Circus people knew all kinds of languages. Anyway they were usually kindly folk, they might give him a meal and help him a bit.

So Jack, suddenly feeling very hungry again, went down the long winding road to the field where the circus was.

It took him about half an hour to reach it and when he got there he saw that it was packing up to move on. The tents were being taken down, horses were being put into some of the vans and there was a great deal of shouting and noise.

Jack leaned over the gate. A boy came by, carrying a load of boxes that looked very heavy. As he passed, the pile toppled over, and he dropped about four of them. Jack leapt over the gate and went to help.

The boy was about his own age, swarthy and black-eyed. He grinned at Jack, and said something he couldn't understand. He said it again, in another language. Still Jack didn't understand.

'Merci beaucoup,' said the boy, trying again this time in French. Ah – Jack understood that!

'Ce n'est rien!' he answered. The boy looked at Kiki and rattled off something in French again, asking Jack if he was a circus boy and had come to ask for a job there.

Jack answered as best he could, for his French was not really very good. 'I should like a job,' said Jack, in French. 'Better still, I should like a meal!'

'Come with me then,' said the boy, again in French, and Jack followed him to a van. A woman sat there, peeling potatoes.

'Ma!' said the boy, in English. 'Here's a hungry kid. Got anything for him?'

Jack stared at the boy in astonishment. Why, he was speaking English! 'Hey!' said Jack, 'why didn't you speak English before? I'm English!'

'My Dad's English', said the boy, grinning. 'My Ma's Spanish. We don't mind what language we speak, really. We've picked them all up in our wanderings around. Ma, give this boy something to eat. Do you think he can get a job with us? Where do you want to go?' he asked Jack.

'Well – is there a place called Borken anywhere about?' asked Jack, hopefully.

'Borken! Yes, we're on the way there,' said the boy, and Jack felt suddenly cheerful. 'It's a big town, and outside there's the Castle of Borken on a hill.'

Jack drank all this in. A castle – would that be where the others had been taken? This *was* a bit of luck after all his set-backs. He would certainly go with this travelling circus if they would have him.

Ma gave him a meal. It was very rich and rather greasy, but Jack enjoyed it because he was so hungry. Then Ma said something commanding in Spanish and the boy nodded.

'Got to take you to the Boss,' he said. 'And let him look you over. Got anyone to speak for you? Anyone's name to give? The Boss will give you up to the police if you've run away from any kind of trouble.'

'No, I don't know anyone here who will speak for me,' said Jack, anxiously. 'I just want to get to Borken. I've got friends there.'

'Oh, well – maybe they'll speak for you,' said the boy. 'Look, my name's Pedro. What's yours?'

'Jack,' said Jack. He followed Pedro to a big motor caravan. Pedro rapped on the door, and a voice growled something from inside. They went in, and Jack saw a vast, enormously fat man sitting in a great chair. He had startlingly blue eyes, grey curly hair, and a beard that fell to his waist. He looked rather a terrifying kind of person.

'You speak for me, Pedro,' said Jack. 'I shan't be able to understand a word he says, unless he speaks English.'

'I spik the English,' said the old man, in his deep, growling voice. 'English boys are good boys. Where you come from?'

'Well – nowhere particularly,' said Jack, wondering what to say. 'Er – I've just been wandering about since I came to this country. But I'm hoping to meet my friends at Borken.'

The old man fired a question or two at Pedro. Pedro turned to Jack. 'He wants to know if you've ever been in trouble with the police?' he asked. This was awkward. Had he been in trouble with the Hessian police? Well, no, not really, Jack considered. So he shook his head.

'He wants to know if you'll make yourself useful here?' said Pedro. 'He can see you must be used to circuses because you're carrying a talking parrot around with you. He says that if we stop here and there on the road to Borken, you can put your parrot on show if you like, and earn a bit of money by making it talk. He says, make it talk now.'

Jack rubbed Kiki's soft neck. 'Talk, Kiki,' he said. 'Make a noise!'

Kiki was always ready to talk. She raised her crest and began unexpectedly to sing at the top of her voice. 'Humpty-dumpty sat on a wall, Humpty-dumpty fell down the well, ding-dong-ding-dong, pussy's in the well, Fussy-Gussy, ha ha, ha! Wipe your feet and shut the door, oh, you naughty boy, pop-pop-POP!'

Kiki ended with a loud sneeze and a hiccup which sent Pedro into fits of laughter. Kiki cackled too, and then went off into her express train performance, which drew people from all over the field at once.

'Ha! She is goot, fery, fery goot!' said the old man, laughing, which made him appear as if an earthquake was

97

shaking him. 'Yes – yes – you may come with us, boy.'

'I say! Your parrot's a wonder, isn't she?' said Pedro, as they walked back to his van. 'Would you like to sleep with me in my little van – look, the one behind Ma's? There'll be room for you if you don't mind a squash.'

Jack didn't mind at all! He would soon be on the way to Borken. Borken Castle! Would he find the others there? He'd get Bill over as soon as he could to rescue them – if only they were there!

16

With the circus

Jack liked Pedro very much. He was a born circus boy, with all their manners and ways, and he was sensitive enough to know that Jack did not want to talk about himself or what he was doing in Tauri-Hessia, wandering about with Kiki. So he asked him no questions, and Jack was very grateful.

He couldn't have told him the truth, and he didn't want to tell him lies! Perhaps when they were in Borken, and he knew Pedro better, he would be able to tell him a little – perhaps even get his help.

The circus went on the road that evening. The vans and lorries creaked out of the fields, and went clattering down the highway. It was a rough road, and the vans swayed about dangerously. Some of them had caged animals inside, and Jack watched them anxiously. What would happen if a van went over – would the animals escape? There were bears in one van, and two chimpanzees in another.

Kiki was a source of enormous amusement to everyone in the camp. Many of the circus folk could speak a broken English – enough to make themselves understood, anyway! They laughed at everything Kiki said. They brought her all kinds of titbits, and when they found that she was fond of tinned pineapple they raided the shops they passed, and bought tins of it!

Jack asked Pedro many questions. How far was Borken? Who owned the castle? Was it very old? Could anyone see over it?

Pedro laughed. 'Borken Castle – and the whole of Borken – and all the land we are passing through – is owned by the Count Paritolen. He lives at the castle, and as for letting anyone see over it – my word, they'd be clapped into a dungeon before they even got through the door!'

'He sounds rather fierce,' said Jack, gloomily. If the others had been taken to the Count's castle they wouldn't have a very nice time, with such a fierce captor!

'He's a very strong and determined fellow,' said Pedro. 'He hates the King, who is too strong for him. He'd like to make the young Prince Aloysius king – then he could rule the country himself, through the Prince, who would have to do as he was told.'

'I see,' said Jack, his heart sinking. What could he hope to do against a man like Count Paritolen?

'Is this Count the Prime Minister?' asked Jack, suddenly remembering what Gussy had said.

'No. His brother-in-law, Count Hartius, is Prime Minister,' said Pedro. 'They're both alike in hating the King – but Count Hartius is weak, where his brother-in-law is strong. It is his wife who rules him – a very clever woman, so they say – Madame Tatiosa.'

Jack listened to all this intently. He was beginning to have a clearer idea about things. How strange to be suddenly plunged into the middle of all this – to know the little Prince himself – to be so near the Castle of Borken, and to be on the land of Count Paritolen, who wanted to depose the King! It sounded like a tale in a book, a tale that had suddenly become real.

'How do you know all this, Pedro?' he asked.

'Oh, everyone in Tauri-Hessia knows it,' said Pedro. 'It may mean civil war, you see, and all the people fear that. If the King is deposed, and this young Prince is put in his place, the people will take sides and will be at one another's throats in no time – and circus people like us will have to get out of the country as quick as we can! So we keep our ears to the ground to find out what is going on.'

Jack was certain that he himself knew the latest news of all! He was sure that as yet no one in Tauri-Hessia knew that Prince Aloysius had been kidnapped from England, and was even now a prisoner in Borken Castle. But what was going to happen next? Would the plot take one step further, and news come out that the King had been killed – or put into prison?

Jack fell into deep thought – so deep that he didn't even hear Ma calling to him to come and eat. The boy suddenly felt that he had become a very important person in this plot – someone fortunately unknown to the plotters – but who might spoil the plot altogether if only he could manage to get into the castle.

'Penny for your thoughts!' said Pedro and gave him a punch. 'Wake up! You look very solemn. Anything on your mind?'

Jack shook himself, and smiled. Kiki had flown off his shoulder to Ma, who was fishing up some peculiar titbits for her from a big black pot.

'Polly put the kettle on,' said Kiki. She cocked her head on one side and looked at Ma. 'Bonnytageloota!'

Ma slapped her knees and laughed. She loved Kiki. She pointed to Kiki. 'She spik Hessian!' she called.

Jack was astonished. Now how in the world did Kiki manage to pick up the Hessian language? Really, she was a marvellous mimic. 'What does "Bonnytageloota" mean?' he asked.

'Top of the morning to you!' said Pedro, with a grin.

The circus stopped at a big village, and set up camp for

two days. Jack was busy then. He had to give Pedro a hand in all kinds of ways – putting up tents, pulling vans into place, setting up the benches in rows, running here and there for the 'Boss', whose name Jack never could manage to pronounce.

The circus folk approved of Jack. He was willing and quick, and he had good manners, which made him very popular with the women, who had got used to plain ways from the menfolk. Jack liked most of the circus people – they were kindly and generous, quick-tempered and cheerful – some were dirty and slovenly, too, not always very honest and sometimes lazy. They were good to Jack, and made him one of themselves at once.

They were a curious lot. There was Fank, with his three bears, one of the great draws of the show. The bears were all large, dark brown, and were natural clowns. They boxed, they knocked each other over, they lumbered round in a laughable dance, and they adored Fank, their trainer.

'Don't you go too near them, though,' Pedro warned him. 'They're treacherous. No one but Fank can manage them. Bad-tempered, bears are – have to be careful of them.'

The two chimpanzees were amusing fellows. They walked about hand in hand with their owner, a tiny woman called Madame Fifi. She wasn't much taller than they were! They really loved her.

Jack liked them very much, but soon found that they were dreadful pickpockets! They slipped their furry hands into his pockets without his knowing, and took his handkerchief, a notebook and two pencils.

Madame Fifi gave them back to him, with a laugh. She poured out something in French – or was it Spanish or Italian? She spoke so quickly that Jack couldn't even make out what language she was speaking. She saw that Jack didn't understand, and produced a few words of English.

'Bad boys!' said Madame Fifi, pointing a tiny finger at the chimpanzees, Feefo and Fum. 'Smack, smack, smack!'

There were Toni and Bingo the acrobats. Toni was a marvellous rope-walker, and raised a perfect storm of cheers and shouts when he performed on a wire rope high up in the big circus tent. He could do anything on it – run, jump, dance – even turn head over heels. Jack was always afraid he would fall.

'Why doesn't he have a safety net?' he asked Pedro. 'You know, he'd kill himself if he fell from that height!'

'Ask him!' said Pedro with a laugh. So Jack put the question to Toni, when the acrobat came across to talk to Pedro's mother. Toni was Spanish, but he understood English well, though he did not speak it fluently.

'Pah! Safftee net!' he said, in scorn. 'Onnly in Eengland is a safftee net put for me. I do not fall! I am Toni, the grrrrreat TONI!'

There was Tops, too, a clown whose great speciality was stilt-walking. It was absolutely amazing to see him stalk into the ring, as tall as a giant. He had big boots fitted on to the bottom of his stilts, and to most of the children in the audience he seemed a true giant, especially as he had a tremendous voice.

He had had a peculiar bicycle built for himself, very tall – and he could ride this when still on stilts. That brought the house down! Another thing that made everyone laugh till they cried was when someone in the ring wanted to talk to Tops. They brought in a long ladder and put it right up to his waist – then up the ladder somebody ran to talk to the clown at the top of it.

Tops was a funny little man in himself, always joking. His big voice didn't fit his small body. 'That's why he learnt stilt-walking,' Pedro told Jack. 'To be tall enough for his voice! That's what he always says, anyway.'

There was Hola, the sword-swallower. Jack watched him, shuddering. Hola could put a sword right down his throat up to the hilt! He would put back his head, and down would go the sword.

'I can understand his being able to swallow short daggers or knives,' said Jack. 'Well – not *swallow* them, exactly, but stick them right down his throat – but Pedro, HOW can he swallow that long, long sword of his? It's awful to see him. It makes me feel quite sick.'

Pedro laughed. 'I'll take you to Hola's van when he is in a good temper,' he said. 'He will show you how he does that.'

And one evening Jack had gone across to Hola's bright yellow van, and had been introduced to Hola himself, a tall, thin fellow with sad eyes. Pedro spoke to him in German, and Hola nodded and produced a small smile. He beckoned Jack into his van. In a big stand were all sizes of knives, daggers and swords. Jack pointed to a very long sword indeed.

Hola took it up. He put back his head, and down went the sword, down, down, down his throat right up to the hilt. It wasn't possible! How could a man do that?

Up came the sword again, and Hola took it out of his mouth and smiled, still with his sad expression. He handed the sword to Jack.

And then the boy understood how Hola could do such an extraordinary thing. The sword was collapsible! It could be made to slide into itself, so that it became only the length of a long dagger. By a most ingenious mechanism, worked by a knob in the handle, Hola could make the sword shorter and shorter as he swallowed it.

Jack was most relieved. He was allowed to press the little secret knob, and see how the pointed end of the sword slid upwards into the main part, making itself into a curious dagger.

The circus folk were certainly interesting to live with! Jack, couldn't help enjoying the strange, happy-go-lucky life, although he worried continually about Lucy-Ann and the others, and was impatient for the circus to go on to Borken. He was so afraid that he would be too late, if the circus was too long on the way.

'But I *must* stay with them,' he thought. 'It is the best possible hiding place for me. The police would certainly get me sooner or later if I wandered off on my own. But I WISH the circus would get on a bit faster. I simply *must* get to Borken soon, and do a bit of prowling round the castle on my own.'

17

Borken at last!

Kiki was a great success, not only with the circus folk, but with the people who came to visit it.

The Boss kept his word, and allowed Jack to show Kiki. Pedro helped him to make a little stand with a gilded perch set on a pole. Kiki was thrilled!

'I believe you think you're on a throne or something!' said Jack, grinning. 'Princess Kiki, the finest talking parrot in the world! Now – what about a song?'

Kiki was always ready to do anything if she could get claps and cheers and laughter. She really surpassed herself, and made Fank, the bear trainer, quite jealous because she drew such a lot of people to her little sideshow!

She sang lustily, and although she mixed up the rhymes and words she knew in a most ridiculous manner, the Tauri-Hessian folk didn't know that. They really thought she was singing a proper song.

Then she would always answer them if they said anything to her, though as they didn't speak English they had no idea what she was saying. Still – she answered at once, and usually went off into such a cackle of laughter afterwards that everyone roared too.

'Tikkopoolinwallyoo?' somebody would ask Kiki.

'Shut the door, fetch the doctor, Polly's got a cold!' Kiki

would answer at once. Even Jack had to grin at her, she enjoyed it all so much.

Her noises were the biggest attraction of all. Her sneezes and coughs and her sudden hiccups made the village people hold their sides and laugh till the tears fell down their cheeks. They were rather overawed by her express-train-roaring-through-a-tunnel imitation, and they didn't understand the lawn mower noise because they did not use them; but they really loved the way she clucked like a hen, grunted like Fank's bears, and barked like a dog.

Yes – Kiki was a great success. Jack felt that she was getting very spoilt by all this fuss – but she did bring in money to him, so that he could pay Pedro's mother for the food she gave him, and for letting him share Pedro's little van.

The rest of the money he tied carefully up in his handkerchief, thinking that it might come in very useful if he needed any in Borken. He kept his hand on it when Feefo and Fum the chimpanzees were anywhere about. They would pick his pocket if they could – and he would lose all his savings!

'We shall be in Borken tomorrow,' Pedro told him, as they got orders to pack up that evening. 'The Boss has got a pitch there – a good one too, at the bottom of the castle hill.'

Jack's heart leapt – ah, Borken at last. A whole week had already gone by, and he had been getting very worried indeed. Now perhaps he could get some news of the others. If only he could! Was Lucy-Ann all right? She would so hate being a prisoner in a castle.

They arrived in Borken the next evening. Jack first saw the castle from a long way off. It stood on a hill, and looked like something out of an old tale of King Arthur and his Knights. It was immensely strong, and had four sturdy towers, one at each corner.

'Borken Castle,' said Pedro, seeing it suddenly, as they came out of a thick wood, through which a rough road ran.

He pointed to the great hill. 'In that castle many a prisoner has been held – and never heard of again. The dungeons are . . . '

'Don't,' said Jack, fearfully. 'Don't tell me things like that.'

Pedro looked at him in surprise. 'What's the matter? Not scared of a castle, are you?'

'No,' said Jack. 'Er – whereabouts were prisoners kept? In a tower? Anywhere special?'

'Don't know,' said Pedro. 'We might have a stroll round it sometime – but we wouldn't be allowed to go too near it, you know.'

The circus camp settled itself in a sloping field just at the bottom of the castle hill. The townsfolk came streaming out to watch them set up camp. Evidently it was a great thing for them to have a travelling circus visiting Borken.

Children darted in and out, shouting and laughing. One small girl came running up to Pedro, calling out something excitedly. He swung her up into his arms, and she shrieked in delight. 'Pedro, Pedro, allapinotolyoota!'

Pedro replied in the same language. Then he turned to Jack, grinning with pleasure. 'My little cousin Hela,' he said. 'Her father married my aunt. He is a soldier in the Hessian army.' He turned and asked the excited Hela a few questions.

'Hela says her mother is with her father here – she is working as a maid in the castle for Madame Tatiosa, who is living at the castle now. And Hela lives in the castle too.'

This was news! Grand news! Now perhaps he would hear something about Lucy-Ann and the others. He stared at the small, lively Hela in excitement. But wait – wait – he mustn't give himself away. He mustn't blurt out questions without thinking. He frowned and tried to think what would be the best thing to ask.

'Pedro – has Madame Tatiosa any children?' he asked at last. 'Would she – er – would she like us to give a little show in the castle for them, do you think?'

'Madame Tatiosa has no children,' said Pedro. 'I can tell you that. If she had, she would try to make one of them king! She is a clever, dangerous woman, that one.'

Hela wanted to know what Jack had asked. She listened and then went right up to Pedro and whispered something in his ear, her eyes dancing. Then she put her finger to her mouth as if telling him not to talk of what she had said.

'Silly child!' said Pedro. 'You have been dreaming!'

'What did she say?' said Jack, impatient to hear everything that Hela said. To think she lived in the castle. Why — she might see the others every single day!

'Hela says that Madame Tatiosa must have adopted some children, because sometimes, when she goes with her mother to one of the towers, she hears children's voices,' said Pedro, laughing. 'And she says that no one but Madame Tatiosa and Count Paritolen go right into that tower. She says it is very mysterious, but that no one must know, because when she told her mother what she had heard, her mother threatened her with a sound whipping for making up stories.'

'I see,' said Jack. 'Does she know which tower this is? Could she show us from where we stand now?'

'You don't want to believe a word she says, Jack!' said Pedro. 'She is a babbler, a story-teller, our little Hela!'

'Ask her, all the same,' said Jack, in such an insistent voice that Pedro did what he asked. Hela gazed up at the great stone castle. She pointed to the tower on the south side.

'That one,' she said, in a half-whisper to Pedro, and Jack understood, although she used Hessian words. She put her finger on her lips again to make sure that Jack and Pedro understood that they mustn't give her away.

Jack took her to buy some sweets. He wished intensely that he could speak the language of the country, but although he had picked up quite a few words — though apparently not so many as Kiki had! — it was impossible to hold any sensible kind of conversation with Hela. He didn't know enough of her language.

She chattered away to him and he didn't understand a word. He bought her the sweets and she flung her arms round him and hugged him. Then she ran off at top speed to show the sweets to her friends.

The camp was soon ready. The circus was to open the following evening. Jack had been very busy indeed, and was tired. But he was determined, quite determined that he was going to prowl round the foot of the great castle that night. Should he ask Pedro to go with him? No – it might be awkward to have Pedro there, if he *did* manage to get into touch with Philip and the others. He would have to explain everything to Pedro, and he didn't quite know how the circus boy would take his news.

Ma called out something to Pedro as he and Jack went to her van to get their evening meal. Pedro listened, and looked grave.

'What's up?' asked Jack.

'It's Fank, the bear-trainer,' said Pedro. 'He's feeling ill again. The Boss is very worried.'

'Why?' asked Jack. 'It will only mean that the bears don't perform, won't it? Anyway, Fank may be better by tomorrow.'

'It's a great loss to the circus when a big attraction like Fank's bears is taken off,' said Pedro. 'But there's worse to it than that. No one can manage those bears but Fank. They get quite out of hand when he's ill – won't let their cage be cleaned out – won't eat – fight one another. Once they even broke down their cage and got out. Fank had to crawl out of his bed in his caravan and somehow get them back. But it nearly killed him!'

'Poor Fank,' said Jack. 'Well, let's hope he is all right again by tomorrow. I don't particularly want great bears like that breaking down their cage and wandering about the camp, I must say. Fank's a wonder with them – I've watched him. He teases them and plays with them – and they fawn round him like dogs!'

'Not many people can manage animals as Fank can,' said Pedro. 'He had lions once – and two tigers – trained them all by himself. Then he suddenly said they didn't like performing and sold them to a Zoo. And yet they were the best trained lions and tigers in the world!'

'And now he's got bears,' said Jack. 'He must love animals very much, and they must love him. There *are* other people like that, Pedro. I know a boy who can do anything with animals, too.' He was thinking of Philip, of course.

'Ever tried his hand with lions, or tigers or bears?' asked Pedro. 'No? I thought not! I bet *they* wouldn't eat out his hand. Cats and dogs and rats and mice and other creatures are easy to do what you like with – but not the big animals – the bears and the great cats!'

'No, I suppose not,' said Jack, thinking that Philip had never had the chance to work his magic on great creatures like those. 'Well – I hope Fank will be better tomorrow. *I* wouldn't like the job of cleaning out the bears' cage, I must say. I'd be afraid of their claws in my back the whole time!'

Jack did not go to sleep as quickly as he usually did, when he lay down on his mattress in Pedro's caravan. He didn't mean to. He was going to explore all round the foot of Borken Castle. He had bought a torch in the town that day. He didn't quite know what good he would do, wandering round in the dark – but it was the only thing he could think of. He had to do *some*thing!

He slid off the mattress as soon as he heard Pedro breathing deeply. He didn't want to wake him. He went out of the van, holding his clothes. He put them on in the darkness, and then, with the surprised Kiki on his shoulder, he set off to the castle hill.

If only he could speak to the others! If only he could make sure they were still all right!

18

Up to the castle!

Jack went stealthily out of the camp. All was quiet. There was no lamp or candle alight in any of the vans. The circus folk were tired out with setting up camp again, and had gone to bed early, in readiness for their grand opening the next day.

It was a starry night, with no moon, so there was not much light. It was not pitch dark, however, and Jack did not need to use his torch, once his eyes had got used to the darkness. The stars gave a faint light, just enough for him to avoid falling over anything.

He went up to the slope of the hill where the camp was placed. He came to a low castle wall. He shone his torch here and there, and found a place he thought he could climb, where the stones were rough and uneven.

His rubber shoes helped him a good deal. He wished he had rubber gloves on his hands, too, so that his fingers would not slip on the stones as he tried to grasp them!

He was over at last. He looked round cautiously, not daring to put on his torch. He seemed to be in a small courtyard. He strained his eyes. He could make out the great bulk of the castle easily. It rose up high, towering about him, solid and strong. He despaired of ever getting inside – or even of getting in touch with Philip and the others!

He crept quietly over the courtyard, stumbling now and again over an uneven stone. He suddenly walked into something that scared him tremendously, and made Kiki give a frightened squawk.

Something wrapped itself round his head! What was it? In a panic Jack tore at it, and ran forward. But something

110

flapped at him again, and covered his whole face. Desperately Jack switched his torch on and off for a moment, to see what was attacking him.

When he saw what it was, he gave a laugh of relief, and felt very silly. He had walked into a line of washing! A sheet had 'attacked' him, that was all — and the thing that had wrapped itself round his head was a jersey.

A jersey! Jack stopped. A jersey — such things were not worn in Tauri-Hessia. He stepped back and flashed his torch on again. Yes — it was either Lucy-Ann's or Dinah's. There was no doubt of it. So they definitely *were* there. Good, good, good! They were quite near him, somewhere. If only, only he could get to them.

He stood and considered. If the children were held in secret, then it was strange that their clothes should be washed and hung out on a line. People would see them and be surprised. Perhaps this courtyard was an enclosed space — a secret yard where nobody came, except possibly Madame Tatiosa. Would she wash the clothes though? She might, if she didn't want anyone to know about the children.

Perhaps Hela's mother was in the secret too? Perhaps *she* washed for the children, cooked their meals and so on? Somebody would have to do that.

There must be a way into the castle from this little yard — possibly a back way into the kitchen or wash-houses. Jack went towards the great walls of the castle and flashed his torch up and down. He would have to risk being seen by someone! He would never find out anything if he didn't use his torch now and again.

There was a small wash house there, as he had expected. He tried the door. It was locked. He shone his torch in at the window and saw coppers and pails and washing baskets. Yes, that was where the washing was done. What a pity the washerwoman had remembered to lock the door!

Jack looked at the little wash-house. It was built out from

the castle wall. He flashed his torch to the roof of the wash house – and then higher up. He saw something that made his heart jump in excitement!

There was a window not far above the wash house roof – and as far as Jack could see it had no glass in it at all! It was a very old, narrow window and might never have had any glass, he thought.

'Now, let me think carefully!' he said to himself. 'If I could get up on the wash house roof – and then up to that window – I'd be inside the castle at once, and could look for the others. But how can I get up to the roof? I really don't think I can climb it, though it isn't very high.'

He couldn't. It was just *too* high for him to jump and catch hold of the guttering to pull himself up. There was no pipe he could climb up, either. Nothing at all.

'A ladder,' thought Jack, desperately. 'If only I could find a ladder.'

He began to hunt round, feeling rather hopeless. Kiki sat still on his shoulder, puzzled. She knew she must not make a sound, but she longed to, especially when a bat came swooping near her.

Jack went carefully round the yard. It wasn't very big. He came to a small shed. It was not locked, only latched. He opened the door carefully, horrified at the squeak it made, and flashed his torch inside.

Wonder of wonders! There was a ladder there! Jack could hardly believe his eyes. He went over to it. It was very old, and some of its rungs were missing – but it might do. It just might do! Anyway, he would try it.

He pulled it out of the shed, upsetting a can of some sort as he did so. The noise echoed round the yard, sounding extraordinarily loud. Jack halted, holding his breath. He quite expected to see lights flashing up in every window.

But none came. Everything was still and dark. He heaved a sigh of relief. Perhaps nobody had heard the noise after all – or perhaps nobody slept on that side of the castle.

He carried the ladder over to the wash house. It was not

very heavy, because it wasn't very long. Still, it would be long enough, he was sure.

He set it up against the wash house. It reached almost to the roof. He flashed his torch at the rungs to make sure which were missing. Then he put his torch into his pocket, and with Kiki flying round his head in excitement, he began to climb.

It certainly was a very old ladder! One of the rungs he trod on almost gave way. He hurriedly missed it and put his foot up to the next. He was very thankful when at last he was at the top.

Now to pull himself on to the roof. He managed to get there with a scraped knee and sat panting. Now for the next step – to get to the window above, in the castle wall itself.

The roof of the wash house was flattish, and Jack was able to make his way on all fours. He came to the wall. He stood up cautiously, feeling it with his hands, and then used his torch again.

'Blow! The window's just too high for me to pull myself up,' thought Jack, in deep disappointment. 'I can reach the sill with my hands – but can't get enough hold to pull up my body.'

He wondered if he could use the old ladder again. He crawled back to it. He put his hand down and felt the top-most rung. Then he pulled hard. The ladder seemed a great deal heavier to pull up than it had been when he only carried it level. He tugged and tugged.

It was difficult to get it over the edge of the roof, but he managed it at last. He had to sit and hold the ladder by him for a while, because it had taken all his strength. He felt very pleased. Now he could put the ladder up to the window, and getting in would be child's play!

He managed to get the ladder to the castle wall, though it was a very dangerous business, and twice he nearly rolled off. But at last he was by the wall, and raised the ladder carefully. It was difficult to find a safe place to put it.

At last he thought he had got it as safe as he could manage.

Now to go up. He hoped that the ladder wouldn't suddenly slip as he was climbing it. That wouldn't be at all a pleasant thing to happen!

He climbed up as quickly as he could, his heart thumping. Would the ladder hold? He got right to the top, and was just clambering onto the window sill when the ladder slipped beneath him.

It slid sideways, fell on to the roof with an appalling noise and then crashed down into the courtyard. NOW there would be people waking up and coming to see what the noise was!

Jack pulled himself right through the window. As he had thought, it had no glass, and probably never had had. He jumped quietly down inside the window and crouched there, waiting.

He waited for three or four minutes, with Kiki nibbling his right ear, not making a sound. Then he stood up and stretched himself. He peered out of the window.

No – nobody was about. He could see no lantern or torch flashing, could hear no voices. This side of the castle *must* be uninhabited then, or surely someone would have heard such a tremendous noise!

Dare he flash his torch to see where he was? He waited another minute and then, hearing no sound, flicked his torch on quickly and off again. But he had seen enough in that second.

He was in a small room, piled with chairs and benches, set neatly on top of one another – nothing else was there at all.

'Just a storeroom for extra furniture,' thought Jack. 'Come along, Kiki – we must remember we've got to find some other way of getting out of the castle – we can't get out the way we came in! That ladder is certainly out of our reach!'

He went to the door and looked out into what seemed a corridor. Not a sound was to be heard. It was pitch dark here, so he flashed his torch on again. Yes – a long stone passage without even a carpet runner on it. No pictures about. No chairs. This certainly must be a part of the castle where nobody slept.

He went down the long corridor, his rubber shoes making no sound. He came to the end, where there was a window – a round one, with glass in it. He turned the corner and saw another long corridor, high-ceilinged, a little wider than the other, but still very bare.

Halfway down the corridor changed from bareness to comfort. A beautiful carpet ran down it, almost touching the walls each side. A big settee, covered in a golden damask, stood at one side. Great pictures hung on the walls.

'This is where I've got to be careful', thought Jack. 'There's even a lamp alight on that round table over there – a dim one, it's true – but still, enough for anyone to see me by!'

He went on. He passed an open door and looked cautiously inside. The light from another lamp just outside showed him what looked like a grand drawing-room. Tapestries hung all round the walls. Mirrors hung there too. A great carved table stood in the middle, its polished surface gleaming softly in the light of Jack's torch.

He went out into the passage again, and considered what to do. First – in which direction was the tower that Hela had said the children were in? He must go in that direction if he could puzzle it out. He would have to find stairs too and climb them.

He decided to go on down the corridor. He must come to stairs soon, leading up into a tower! He came to another door, wide open. He peeped inside. How grand this castle was! What magnificent furnishings it had!

The room must be a library. It had books from floor to ceiling. Goodness – had anyone ever read even a hundredth of them? Surely not!

A noise made Jack flick out his torch and stand absolutely still. It was a noise in the room he was standing in – the library. It came from behind him – a whirring, groaning noise. Kiki gave a small squawk. She was as startled as Jack. Whatever was it?

19

An adventure in the night

Whirrrrrr! Whirrrrrrrr!

'Ding-dong-ding-dong! Ding-dong-ding-dong! Ding-dong-ding-dong! Ding-dong-ding-dong! DONG, DONG, DONG, DONG, DONG, DONG, DONG, DONG, DONG, DONG, DONG, DONG!'

Jack sat down suddenly on a nearby chair, his heart thumping. It was only a clock chiming and striking! But what a start it gave him! Midnight – exactly midnight. Well – the people in the castle ought to be asleep, that was one thing to be glad of.

He got up and went back to the door. He went down the corridor again, and then, facing him round the next turning, he saw a great flight of stairs – a marble stairway, almost covered by a fine sweep of thick, beautifully patterned carpet.

'I suppose that leads down to the hall,' thought Jack. 'Down to the entrance. Well, that gives me a guide – let me see – if the front entrance is down there – then the tower I want should be a bit further on. Come on, Kiki – down the corridor again!'

And down the endless corridor went the two of them. It was lighted by lamps, and was too bright for Jack's liking. The doors he passed now were shut. Perhaps they were bedrooms. He certainly wasn't going to look in and see!

He came to a sturdy oak door set in the inside wall. He paused. The tower ought to be about here. Would that door lead up to it? It looked different from the other doors he had passed. He tried the handle gently. It was a thick ring of iron and as he turned it sideways the door opened.

Jack pushed it wide. Stone steps led upwards, lighted by a

dim lamp. He stood and debated with himself. Should he risk it and go up? Yes – he felt sure this was the way to the tower.

He tiptoed up and came to the top. He looked round in surprise. He was on another floor now, and the layout here was different from the one below. He was in what looked like a great hall, draped with magnificent curtains. A gallery overhung one end. There was a small platform at the other end, and on it stood music stands. The floor was highly polished, and Jack suddenly realized what the hall was.

'It's a ballroom!' he thought. 'My word – what grand dances they must hold here! But now I seem to have lost my way to the tower again. Perhaps there's another stair somewhere!'

He went round the ballroom. On the other side, behind some curtains, he came to a door. He opened it and found that it led to a kind of ante-chamber. Opening off this was a stone staircase – a spiral stair that wound upwards.

'This is the tower staircase!' thought Jack, excited. 'It must be. Hallo – what's that?'

He could hear the sound of nailed boots on stone! Quick as lightning he slid behind a nearby curtain. The footsteps came nearer, stamped, turned and went back again. How extraordinary!

Jack put his head carefully round the curtian. Going down a stone passage opposite was a soldier, gun on shoulder. He must be on guard – guarding the tower! He disappeared down the passage, his footsteps sounding farther and farther away till Jack could hear them no longer. Then back he came again to the foot of the tower stairway.

Stamp-stamp! The sentry turned round once more and marched into the passage. Jack watched him again. He was dressed in Hessian uniform, very smart and decorative. Jack had seen many of these soldiers while he had been with the circus. Perhaps this soldier was Hela's father?

He waited till the sound of footsteps had completely died

away again, then made a dart for the entrance to the spiral staircase. He ran up it swiftly, knowing that he had about half a minute before the return of the sentry.

Round and round wound the stairway, and at the top it grew so steep that Jack could no longer run up the steps, but had almost to climb!

He came to a little stone landing with a round window. A chest stood beneath the window, and an old chair stood beside it. Opposite Jack was a big, sturdy door, made of dark oak, and studded with great nails. He looked at it. Was Lucy-Ann behind that door? Dare he call her name?

He tiptoed to the door. He pushed. It was fast shut. He turned the great handle, but still it would not open. There was a keyhole there, but no key. He bent down to look through the keyhole, but could see nothing.

He could hear nothing either. Jack wished he knew what to do for the best. If he knocked on the door and called, he might find that the children were not there after all but that somebody else *was*. And the somebody might not be at all pleased to see him! Also, the sentry downstairs might hear him and come rushing up – and there was no way of escape up on this little landing!

And then he saw something in the light of his torch – something very surprising – something that told him for certain that the children *were* inside that room on the other side of the oak door!

A tiny creature had slipped under the wide space at the bottom of the door, and sat there, looking up at Jack with large black eyes.

'Philip's dormouse!' whispered Jack, and knelt down slowly. 'Snoozy! You *are* Snoozy, aren't you! You're Philip's dormouse! Then Philip *is* in there!'

The dormouse was very tame. It had lived for some time with four children who adored it, petted it and had never once frightened it. Even Dinah had fallen under its spell, and loved it, though she would not let it run all about her as the others did.

And now here it was, on Jack's hand, its whiskers twitching, its big eyes watching him and Kiki. Kiki looked at it in surprise, but made no attempt to hurt it.

'Did you hear me, outside the door!' whispered Jack. 'Did you leave Philip and come to see who the midnight visitor was? How can I wake Philip? Tell me!'

An owl hooted somewhere outside the castle. The dormouse leapt from Jack's hand in fright and scuttled under the door. The hoot of the owl gave Jack an idea. The sentry would take no notice of an owl's hoot – but if he, Jack, gave a hoot just under the crack of the door, it would certainly wake up Philip. It would sound far away to the sentry, but very near to Philip! Far far better than banging on the door, which was a noise that might echo down the stairs and make the sentry come bounding up!

Jack lay down on his tummy. He put his face to the door, and placed his hands together to blow through his thumbs and hoot like an owl. This was the way to make a quavering hoot, so like an owl's that no one, not even an owl, could tell the difference!

'Hoooo! Hoo-hoo-hoo-hoo!' hooted Jack, and the noise went under the door and into the room beyond.

Jack listened. Something creaked – was it a bed? Then a voice spoke – and it was Philip's!

'Gussy! Did you hear that owl? It might have been in the room!'

But Gussy, apparently, was asleep, for he made no answer. Jack got up and put his mouth to the door, trembling in his excitement.

'Philip! Philip!'

There was an astonished exclamation. Then Philip's voice came, amazed. 'Who's that? Who's calling me?'

'It's me – Jack! Come to the door!'

There was a pattering of feet the other side and then an excited breathing at the keyhole.

'Jack! Good gracious! How did you get here? Jack, how wonderful!'

'No time to tell you my story,' whispered Jack. 'Are you all all right? How's Lucy-Ann?'

'We're all well and cheerful,' said Philip. 'We flew here . . . '

'I know,' said Jack. 'Go on – what happened?'

'And we were taken here by car,' said Philip, his mouth close to the keyhole. 'And Gussy was sick, of course. Madame Tatiosa, who met us in the car, was furious with him. She's here, in the castle – and her brother too, Count Paritolen. We don't know what's happening, at all – have *you* heard? Gussy keeps worrying about his uncle.'

'His uncle is still safely on his throne as far as I know,' said Jack. 'But I expect they'll have a bust-up soon – everyone's expecting it. Then Gussy will find himself in the limelight!'

'Jack – can you rescue us, do you think?' asked Philip, hopefully. 'How did you get here? Gosh, I've been thinking you were miles away, at Quarry Cottage! And here you are, outside the door of our room. Pity it's locked!'

'Yes. If I only knew where the key was, it would be easy,' whispered Jack. 'Where does your window face? East or north?'

'North,' said Philip. 'It's just opposite a peculiar tower built all by itself – a bell-tower, with a bell in it. Gussy says it's an alarm-tower – the bell used to be rung when enemies were sighted in the old days. Our window is just opposite that. Now that we know you're here we'll keep looking out.'

'Give my love to Lucy-Ann,' said Jack. 'Is she in the same room as you?'

'No – the girls have another room,' said Philip. 'Look – let me go and wake them. They'd be so thrilled to speak to you.'

'All right,' said Jack, and then he stiffened. Footsteps! *Footsteps at the bottom of the spiral stairway.* 'Someone coming!' he whispered, hurriedly. 'Goodbye! I'll try and come again and we'll make plans.'

He stood up, and listened. Yes – that sentry was coming up the stairway. Had he heard anything? Jack looked round desperately. How could he possibly hide on this small landing? It was impossible.

The chest! He ran to it and flashed his torch on it. He lifted the lid. There was nothing inside except an old rug. He stepped inside the chest, Kiki fluttered in too, and Jack shut down the lid. Only just in time! A lantern flashed at the last turn of the stairs and the sentry came on to the landing. He held up the lantern and looked round. All was in order. He clumped downstairs again, his nailed boots making a great noise. Jack's heart slowed down and he heaved an enormous sigh. He got out of the chest and listened.

Philip's voice at the keyhole again made him jump. 'He's gone! He always comes up every hour. Jack – I never asked you. Have you got old Kiki?'

'Rather! She's been with me all the time,' said Jack, longing to tell Philip what a success Kiki was at the circus. But Philip didn't know about that either, of course. He didn't even know how Jack had got to Tauri-Hessia. What a lot there would be to tell him and the others!

Kiki began to whisper too. 'Blow your nose, shut the door, ding-dong-bell, Polly's got a cold. God save the King!'

Philip chuckled. 'It's good to hear her again. Shall I get the girls now?'

'No,' said Jack. 'I'd better go while it's safe. Goodbye, Philip.'

He went very quietly down the spiral stairway. He stood and listened. Where was the sentry? He must have gone down the passage again, on his regular beat. Jack slipped across the ante-room, and into the great ballroom.

He stood there for a moment, looking round the dimly lighted room. And then something caught his eye and he jumped.

On the far side was a great picture – and as Jack looked at it, it moved! It moved sideways across the wall, and behind it appeared a black hole.

Good gracious! Whatever was happening now?

121

20

The way out

A man's face suddenly appeared in the hole. Jack would not have been able to recognize it but for one thing – the man wore an eyeglass in one eye!

'The Count!' thought Jack. 'My word – what's he doing, popping up in secret places in the middle of the night?'

The man jumped down to the floor. A door at once opened near him and a woman came out. Jack recognized her, too. Madame Tatiosa, the pretty woman who had pretended to be ill at Quarry Cottage – the wife of the Prime Minister!

This was evidently a secret meeting between her and her brother. Where had he come from? Why was he so excited? The two of them spoke rapidly together and Madame Tatiosa seemed very pleased. She kissed her brother on both cheeks and patted him on the back.

'Her plans seem to be going well, whatever they are!' thought Jack. 'I bet it's something to do with the King. They've probably arranged to capture him soon. That means that Gussy will be hauled out of that room and made to sit on the throne. I don't like the look of Count Paritolen. He's a nasty bit of work – and it's quite plain he's been up to something tonight!'

The brother and sister, still talking excitedly, went into the room from which Madame Tatiosa had appeared. The door shut. Jack heard the clink of glasses. They were going to celebrate something, perhaps? Things were obviously moving.

Jack wished fervently that Bill was there with him. But Bill probably didn't even guess that the five of them were in Tauri-Hessia. He had no means of knowing that they had come over by plane. He was probably hunting for them all over the place in England!

Jack looked at the hole in the wall. Where did it lead to? He felt impelled to go and look at it. He could still hear clinking and talking in the room nearby. He ran across to the hole, clambered on a chair and looked inside. He could see nothing, so he felt for his torch.

Then he saw the door of the room opening! There was only one thing to do – he must tumble inside that hole and hope for the best!

So in went Jack, almost falling over himself in his hurry. He found that there were steps there, and he slid down them, landing with a bump at the bottom. He sat there and listened, full of alarm.

But it seemed as if the Count and his sister hadn't heard anything. He heard their voices in the distance. And then he heard something else! He heard a slight scraping noise, and the light that came into the hole where he was hiding was abruptly cut off.

'Gosh – the picture's gone back into place. I'm trapped!' said Jack, in alarm. He went up the steps and felt about at the back of the picture. The back was of stout wood, and fitted tightly over the hole. It wouldn't move even when he pushed it. He didn't like to do anything violent in case the Count heard him.

He put on his torch. He looked down the steps and saw a passage at the bottom. Well – it must lead to somewhere! It might even lead out of the castle! The only thing to do was to try it and see.

So Jack went down the steps again, and into a narrow little passage. He came to the conclusion that the passage must run just inside the walls of the room, at a little below the level of the floor. It went round at right angles quite suddenly – then there were more steps, very steep indeed.

Down them climbed Jack, thankful for his torch. It was very musty in the passage. He came to a place where there seemed to be a little light shining behind the left-hand wall. What was it?

Jack soon discovered! It was a small hole made in the wooden panelling there, and through it he could see into a dimly lit room – a room where people apparently met to discuss things, for there was a round table with chairs pulled up to it, and blotting pads and papers were set out neatly.

'Hm – a nice little spy hole,' thought Jack. 'well – on we go. Wherever does this lead to, Kiki?'

Kiki didn't know – she only knew she was getting rather tired of this trip. She clung to Jack's shoulder and grumbled in his ear.

The passage went downwards again, not by steps this time, but in a steep slope. Jack found himself in a much narrower, lower passage now – he had to bend his head down. Two people would have found it difficult to pass one another. Kiki protested, because the ceiling kept brushing the top of her head.

'I wish I knew where this is all leading to, Kiki,' said Jack. 'I don't like it any more than you do! Hallo – here's a cellar, or something!'

The passage suddenly ended in a round cellar-like place, full of old junk. The entrance to this was only a round hole, through which Jack climbed, glad he wasn't as fat as the old 'Boss' of the circus.

'Now where do we go from here?' he thought. He flashed his torch all round. Nothing much to see but junk. Then he flashed his torch on the ceiling above his head – it was only about two inches higher than he was.

'A trap door! *Surely* that's a trap door! If only I can open it!' thought Jack.

He pushed hard – and it opened! It swung right back and landed flat with a tremendous crash. It startled Jack horribly and made Kiki screech like a barn owl!

Nobody came rushing up. Nobody shouted 'Who's there?' Jack waited a minute and then clambered out. Where was he now? He began to feel he must be in a kind of nightmare, where nothing really led anywhere – only just on and on, steps, passages, holes, cellars, trapdoors – what next?

Again he shone his torch round. He was in a very tall, very narrow building of stone. Great ropes hung round him. He turned his torch upwards, and then he knew where he was!

'The bell tower! The tower that is just opposite Philip's room! That passage I've come down must be a secret way into the castle. Well – what a discovery!'

He went to the doorway of the bell tower. There was no door there, merely an archway. The place was apparently built just to hold the great bell and nothing else.

And then Jack discovered something that filled him with relief and joy. The bell tower was built *outside* the castle wall and not inside! He could run down the slope of the hill to the circus with nothing to prevent him – no walls to climb – no windows to jump from – there he was, outside the castle, walls and all.

'That's a bit of luck!' thought the boy. 'Come on, Kiki. We're out. Now we'll go back and get a bit of sleep!'

It wasn't long before Jack was creeping into Pedro's caravan. The floor creaked loudly, but Pedro did not awake. Jack stripped off his things, thinking hard.

He felt pleased. Lucy-Ann and the others were safe. They had come to no harm. They were safe as long as Gussy wasn't King – then they might be held as hostages if the British Government sided with the present King, and demanded that he be put back on the throne. Jack could quite well imagine that Count Paritolen and Madame Tatiosa would delight in threatening all kinds of dreadful things where the children were concerned, if the British Government made things too uncomfortable for them.

'The thing to do is to rescue them quickly before Gussy's uncle is captured and Gussy's put on the throne,' thought Jack. 'I really must try and get in touch with Bill. But it will be difficult, because probably the people in this part of the country are on the side of the Count – and if I try to get news through to Bill, I'll be captured myself!'

He fell asleep thinking of it all. He had had a night of real adventure and he was tired out. He didn't even wake when Mr Fank's bears created a great disturbance in the early morning, and tried to break their cage down!

Pedro told him about it at breakfast time. 'Nobody dares to go near them,' he said. 'They haven't come to fighting each other yet, but they will. And then they won't be any use in the circus.'

'Isn't Mr Fank better then?' asked Jack.

'No. Worse,' said Pedro. 'The Boss is really worried. Pity that friend of yours you told me about isn't anywhere near here. If he's as clever as you say, he might be able to quieten the bears and manage them!'

Pedro was joking, of course – but Jack sat up straight, and began considering the matter at once. He was sure that Philip *could* managed the bears, of course. Could he *possibly* tell Pedro where Philip was – and say that if Pedro would help him to rescue the children, Philip would try to do his best for the bears?

'What's the matter?' said Pedro, looking at him curiously. 'You seem excited about something.'

'Well – I *could* get hold of my friend, but only with help,' said Jack. 'He's – well, he's not really very far away.'

'Really? Why didn't you tell me?' said Pedro. 'Where is he?'

Jack hesitated. Could he trust Pedro? He asked him a question. 'Pedro – tell me truthfully – are you on anybody's side in this business about the King and the Prince Aloysius? I mean – what do you think about it?'

'Nothing,' said Pedro, promptly. 'I don't care which of them is King. Let them get on with it! The only thing I don't want is civil war here – we'd have to clear out of the country quickly then. Circuses and war don't go together! Why do you ask me that?'

'I might tell you later on,' said Jack, suddenly feeling that he had told Pedro too much. 'But I'll just say this – if I could get my friend here – with *his* friends too – we'd prevent civil war – Frank's bears would soon be under control and . . . '

'What rubbish you talk!' said Pedro, looking astonished. 'Stop pulling my leg. I don't believe a word of it.'

Jack said no more. But, as the day wore on, and Fank got no better, and the bears' behaviour got much worse, he felt inclined to tell Pedro a good deal more. It would be really marvellous if he could get Philip and the rest into the circus – what a wonderful hiding place for them all! Gussy would be too noticeable, of course. How could they disguise him?

'Of course! With that long hair of his and those thick eyelashes and big eyes, he could be dressed as a girl!' thought Jack. 'What a brainwave! I think I will tell Pedro everything. I'll tell him after the show tonight.'

The circus gave its first show at Borken that evening. It opened with the usual fanfare of trumpets and drums and the people of the town streamed up excitedly.

The bears, of course, were not on show, but otherwise everything went well. There was a good deal of grumbling from the townsfolk about the bears, because they had been well advertised, and some people demanded their money back.

'We must get those bears going somehow,' grumbled the Boss. 'We must pull Fank out of bed! We must get somebody else in. We must do this, we must do that! Where is Fank? Those bears will maul each other to death soon!'

After supper Jack spoke to Pedro. 'I want to tell you a lot of things,' he said. 'I want to get your help, Pedro. Will you listen? It is very important – very important indeed!'

'I am listening,' said Pedro, looking startled. 'Tell me all you want to. I will help you, Jack – I promise you that!'

21

A daring plan

'Where shall we go?' said Jack. 'In your van? Nobody can overhear us there, can they?'

They went inside the little van and shut the door. Pedro looked puzzled – what was all this about?

Jack began to tell him. He told him about Gussy staying with them at Quarry Cottage and how he turned out to be the Prince. Pedro's eyes almost fell out of his head at that! He told him of the kidnapping, and how he, Jack, had stowed away first at the back of the car, and then in the aeroplane, in order to follow the others.

'You're a wonder, you are!' said Pedro, staring at Jack in the greatest admiration. 'You're . . . '

Jack wouldn't let him say any more. He went on rapidly with his story, and brought it right up to date, telling Pedro of his adventure of the night before.

'I never heard anything like this in my life!' said Pedro, amazed. 'Why didn't you ask me to come with you? You knew I would. It was a dangerous thing you did, all by yourself.'

'Will – I'm used to adventures,' said Jack. 'I just had to find out about my sister, anyway – and the others too, of course. Now, Pedro – this is where I want your help. I MUST rescue the four of them before the King is kidnapped or killed, and Gussy is put on the throne. You see, if Gussy is missing, there wouldn't be much point in doing away with his uncle. They must have Gussy to put in his place, because they want a kid there, so that they can make him rule as they like. Count Paritolen and his sister, Madame Tatiosa, and the Prime Minister will be in power then. Do you understand?'

'Yes, I understand,' said Pedro. 'But I'm not used to seeing history happening before my eyes like this. I can't think it's real, somehow.'

'It *is* real,' said Jack, urgently. 'Very very real. And, Pedro, if we can get Philip here, in the circus, he could manage those bears as easily as Fank. I tell you, he's a wizard with animals — it doesn't matter what they are. Why, once, in an adventure we had, a crowd of Alsatian dogs chased us — we thought they were wolves, actually — and Philip turned them all into his friends as soon as they came up to him!'

Pedro listened to all this with a solemn face. He was much impressed. He had guessed, of course, that there was something unusual about Jack — but the story he had to tell was so extraordinary that he could hardly believe it all. He did believe it, though. He was sure that Jack would never lie about anything.

'Well — what do you want me to do?' he asked at last. 'I'll do anything, of course. But honestly, Jack, I don't see how we can rescue your four friends from the tower room of Borken Castle — locked in, with a sentry at the foot of the stairs! It's impossible!'

Jack sat and frowned. He was beginning to think it was impossible too. Plans had gone round and round in his head for hours — but none of them was any good.

He couldn't get in through that window over the wash house again, he was sure. The ladder would have been discovered by now, and taken away. Also — even if he did get in that way, how could he let Philip and the others out of that locked room? He didn't even know where the key was!

'And to go in the other way wouldn't be any good either,' he thought. 'Down that trap door and all through those passages — I'd only come up against the back of that big picture, and I've no idea how to make it move away from its place! And then again I'm no better off if I do — I still don't know where the key to that tower room is!'

Pedro sat and frowned too. To think that he and Jack

could perhaps save the starting-up of a horrible civil war – and they couldn't think of even one sensible thing to do!

'Jack,' he said at last. 'Do you mind if we tell someone else about this? My two best friends here are Toni and Bingo, the acrobats – they might be able to think of some plan. It's their job to think of good ideas!'

Jack looked doubtful. 'Would they give my secrets away, though?' he said. 'It's important that nobody else should know what we know – once the Count suspected that anyone was trying to rescue the four prisoners he holds, he would spirit them away somewhere else, and probably hurry his plans on so that we couldn't possibly stop them.'

'You needn't worry about Toni and Bingo,' said Pedro. 'They're the best pals I ever had, and ready for anything. This is the kind of job they'd jump at – it's right up their street. I'll go and fetch them now.'

He went off across the field, and Jack sat and worried. He wasn't happy about telling anyone else. Soon the van door opened and in came Pedro with Toni and Bingo. They didn't look in the least like acrobats, in their ordinary clothes. They were slim, lithe young men, with shocks of hair and cheerful faces.

'What for you want us?' said Toni, the rope-walker, in broken English. 'It is trouble with the Boss?'

'No,' said Pedro. 'Look here, Jack – shall I tell them? – I can speak to them in Italian, which they know best, and it'll be quicker.'

· 'Right,' said Jack, wishing that he could use half a dozen languages as easily as this much-travelled circus boy.

He didn't understand a word of what followed. Pedro spoke rapidly, using his hands excitedly just as all the Spaniards, French and Italian people did in the circus. Bingo and Toni listened, their eyes almost falling out of their heads. What a story!

Then they too began to chatter in excitement, and Jack could hardly contain himself in his impatience to find out what they were saying. Pedro turned to him at last, grinning broadly.

'I have told them everything,' he said. 'And it pleases them! They have an idea for rescue – a surprising idea, Jack – but a very very good one!'

'What?' asked Jack, thrilled. 'Not *too* impossible a one, I hope!'

'Shall I tell him?' said Pedro, turning to Toni, 'I can tell him more quickly than you.'

'Tell him,' said Toni, nodding his head.

'Well, said Pedro, 'they got the idea when I told them how you escaped out of that trap door in the tall bell tower. I told them it was exactly opposite the window of the tower room – and they said it would be easy to throw a rope across from the top of the tower, to the window!'

'Yes – but I don't see what good that would be,' said Jack, puzzled. 'I mean – the others couldn't get across it – they'd fall.'

'Listen!' said Pedro, 'you have seen the trapeze swings that Toni and Bingo use in their acrobatic tricks, haven't you? Well, those swings can be attached to the wire rope by pulley wheels, and run to and fro. Would your friends agree to sit on a swing in turn, and be pulled across, hanging from the wire rope? It would be easy!'

'Good gracious!' said Jack, startled. 'My word! What an idea! It's not workable!'

'Si, si! It is wukkable!' said Toni, excitedly. 'We go up the bell tower. We get rope across to your friends – I walk across – easy! I pull swing behind me, hanging on rope. I place each boy or girl safe on swing – and I run back on rope dragging swing by wire – one, two, three, four times, and everyone is safe! Good idea, no?'

'Is it *really* possible?' said Jack. 'It sounds very dangerous.'

'Ah, no, no – it is simple, this way,' said Toni. 'I do it all, I, Toni!'

131

Bingo nodded his head. He apparently agreed with Toni that it was a good and perfectly possible idea. It would certainly only have been thought of by wire walkers or acrobats, Jack was sure.

'And then, zis boy – how you call him – Feelip – he will take Fank's bears and make them good?' said Toni. 'Everybody plizzed!'

'Everybody pleased,' agreed Jack, getting excited too. After all – these acrobats were used to things of this kind. It seemed nothing to them – though to ordinary people it appeared to be a very dangerous and quite impossible feat.

'Tonight we go,' said Toni. 'We have all things ready. We tell the Boss – no?'

'No – not yet,' said Pedro, considering. 'And not very much, when we do tell him. Nothing about the Prince or anything like that – only just that we've got a friend of Jack's to help with the bears. I'll have to think up some way of explaining the other three – but I'm not worrying about that yet.'

Toni and Bingo went off to their van, talking nineteen to the dozen. This was evidently something they were going to enjoy very much!

Jack could hardly keep still now. He kept on and on thinking about Toni's plan. Would it be all right? Would Lucy-Ann be too afraid to swing across on a trapeze-perch, and be caught at the other end of the rope by Bingo? What about Gussy? His hair would stand on end! And yet what better way was there? There wasn't any other way at all!

The circus opened as usual, and again there were grumbles about the non-appearance of the bears. Fank tried to get up, but it was no use. He couldn't even stand. The bears, hearing the circus beginning, and the shouts of the side-shows, became restless and excited. They had allowed no one in their cage that day, not even to clean it, and their food had been hurriedly poked between the bars.

They wouldn't even eat that! It lay in their cage untouched. They padded up and down the floor, heads down, grunting and growling all the time.

The show was over at last, and the townsfolk went back to Borken, chattering and laughing. Jack helped Pedro to clear up the litter, pick up the fallen benches, and sweep the big circus ring.

'Thinking about tonight?' whispered Pedro. as he passed him. 'I bet Toni and Bingo are! I saw Toni taking one of the trapeze swings out to shorten the rope, so that he could use it tonight.'

They had a late supper, and then Ma yawned. 'Bed!' she said, and creaked up into her caravan. The two boys went into theirs, and sat waiting for the acrobats to come and say they were ready.

There came a tap at the door. Pedro opened it. 'Come!' said Toni's voice, and Pedro and Jack slipped like shadows out of their van. The four of them made their way in the darkness up the slope of the hill. Above them towered the great castle, its shadowy bulk looking sinister and mysterious.

They came to the bell tower. Toni and Bingo had already had a good look at it in the daylight. 'In we go,' said Pedro, in a low voice. He flashed on his torch as soon as they were safely inside.

The torch lighted up the strong wire rope that Bingo carried, and the trapeze swing that Toni held. They all looked up into the roof of the bell tower. How were they to get up by the great bell?

'There are iron rungs up the wall,' said Toni. 'I go first! Follow me!'

22

Escape!

It was not difficult to climb up the iron rungs. Toni was soon up in the roof of the tower. Kiki was first though! She flew up from Jack's shoulder, and perched on the big bell, making a slight clanging noise that startled her considerably!

The iron ladder went right above the bell, which hung from a great beam. Above it was a stone platform, with an opening in it at one side for the iron ladder to pass through. Toni climbed up to the bell, and then through the opening above it, and passed on to the stone platform. Jack came next and then Pedro. Bingo was last.

There were arched openings like windows in the top of the tower opening off the stone platform, one arch facing each way — north, south, east and west. Toni peered out of the arch that faced the window in the castle opposite.

He considered the distance carefully. Jack peered out too. It seemed a long way to him in the darkness! He shivered. He didn't at all want to go on with this idea, now that he was up so high, and could see what a drop it was to the ground.

But Toni and Bingo treated it in a very casual, matter-of-fact manner. They talked to one another, and discussed it very thoroughly and with great interest. They apparently had no doubt at all but that they could do what they had planned.

Toni said something to Pedro, and he repeated it to Jack in English. 'Toni says he is ready. He says how can we attract the attention of your friends in the room opposite? They will have to help at the beginning.'

'If we flash a torch on and off — or perhaps hoot like an owl — Philip will come,' said Jack.

'We try the owl,' said Toni, and Jack put his cupped hands to his mouth and blew virogously between his two thumbs.

'Hooo! Hoo-hoo-hoo-hoo!' came quaveringly on the night air. Jack hooted again.

They waited, their eyes on the shadowy window opposite. Then, from the window, a light flashed on and off.

'Philip's there,' said Jack, joyfully, and flashed his own torch. 'Philip!' he called, in a low voice. 'Can you hear me?'

'Yes! Where are you? Not over there, surely!' said Philip, in an amazed voice.

'Tell him Toni is coming over on a rope,' said Pedro. 'But we've got to get the rope across first – so will he look out for a stone, tied on to a bit of string – and pull on it, so that the thicker rope can come across?'

'I know a better way than that!' said Jack, suddenly excited. 'Let Kiki take the rope across – not the thick heavy wire one, of course – but the first rope – the one that's fixed to the wire! She can take it in her beak.'

'Ah – that is good!' said Toni, understanding and approving at once. 'It will save time.'

'Philip – Kiki's coming across with a rope,' called Jack, cautiously. 'Look out for her. Take the rope and pull hard. It will bring across a wire rope. Can you find something to loop it to? It has a strong ring at the end – see that it is made fast.'

'Right. But how will . . . I say, I don't understand,' said Philip, bewildered.

'Call Kiki!' said Jack. Kiki had now been given the end of the rope in her beak. She was pulling at it with interest. 'Take it to Philip,' said Jack.

'Kiki!' called Philip. 'Kiki!'

Kiki flew straight across to him, carrying the end of the rope in her strong beak. She knew she had to take it to Philip, of course, but she had no idea that behind her came a whole length, paid out quickly by Toni!

She landed on Philip's shoulder, and let go the rope to

nibble his ear. Philip just caught it in time. He wasted no time, but pulled on it hard. More and more rope came in – and then, joined to the ordinary rope, came the strong wire rope, heavy but flexible.

Philip hauled on that too until a tug warned him to stop. Now he had to fasten it securely to something. But what?

He had a lamp in his room and he lighted it, to see better. He kept it turned low, and held it up to see where he could fasten the ring that was on the end of the wire rope.

His bed had strong iron feet. Philip dragged the bed to the window, waking Gussy up with a jump as he did so, and then slipped the iron ring under one foot, pulling it up about twelve inches.

Now it should be held fast! The bed was by the window, the iron foot against the stone wall. Neither bed nor foot could move. The rope should be safe for anyone to use!

'What is it? What's happening?' said Gussy, sitting up in bed in surprise, unable to see much in the dim light of the lamp.

'Be quiet,' said Philip, who was now almost too excited to speak. 'Jack's out there. Go and wake the girls – but for goodness' sake *don't* make a noise!'

Over in the bell tower Toni pulled on his end of the wire rope. He pulled as hard as he could, and Bingo pulled with him. Was the other end quite fast – safe enough for Toni to walk across on it? He had to be quite certain of that before he tried to walk the rope.

'It's fast enough,' said Bingo, in his own language. 'It will hold you!'

Toni wasted no time. He got out of the stone archway, and stood upright on the narrow sill. Bingo held a torch to light up the wire stretching in front, from the bell tower to the window away opposite.

Toni tested the wire with his foot – and then Jack gasped in astonishment. Toni had run straight across the wire at top speed! There were his legs and feet, clearly lighted in the beam of the torch, running easily over the taut wire!

Toni reached the opposite window, and stood on the sill for a moment. Then he bent his head and climbed in, finding the bed just below the sill. Philip gripped hold of him, looking white.

'I say! What a thing to do! You might have fallen!'

The girls were now in the boys' room, having been awakened by Gussy. Kiki was with them, making a great fuss of them both. 'Who's this?' said Lucy-Ann, startled to see Toni jumping down to the bed. 'Philip – what's happening?'

'No time to talk yet,' said Philip, who wasn't really sure himself what was happening. 'We're being rescued, that's all!'

Toni was now busy pulling on a rope that he had brought across with him. he was hauling steadily on it – and along the wire, hanging neatly down from it, came a small trapeze swing – the one that Toni used each night when he swung high up in the circus tent, doing his tricks!

It clicked against the stone wall. Toni turned to Philip. 'You sit there,' he said, pointing to the swing below the rope. 'Sit still, see? And I will pull you over to Jack.'

Philip was startled. He looked at the trapeze swinging below the wire rope, running along it on a pulley wheel. So that was the idea! They were each in turn to sit on that peculiar swing, and be pulled across to the bell tower! Well!

'Hurry!' said Toni, impatiently. 'You first?'

'Yes,' said Philip, thinking perhaps that if the others saw him going across quite easily they wouldn't be afraid. He turned to Gussy and the startled girls.

'I'll go first and you watch me,' he said. 'Then Lucy-Ann – then you, Gussy – and you last, Dinah.'

He stood on the bed, and then swung himself up on the stone window sill. He held on to the rope outside, and suddenly felt Toni's strong hands under his armpits. It really wasn't very difficult to sit on the trapeze.

'I come!' said Toni, to the anxious watchers opposite, and he ran over the wire once more, pulling the trapeze back to the bell tower. Philip arrived there on the swing almost before he knew it! He was pulled off and dragged into the tower in safety. Jack found his hand and shook it hard. He found that he suddenly couldn't say a word! Neither could Philip.

Toni ran across again, pulling back the trapeze. Lucy-Ann was scared almost stiff with fright, but she was brave and managed to get on to the swing quite well, with Toni's help. Away she went, giving a little gasp as she thought of the great distance to the ground below her.

Back came Toni with the swing, and Gussy was pushed forward to get on it. He was so frightened that Toni began to wonder whether he would fall off in the middle of his trip across the wire! But Gussy held on grimly, his teeth chattering – and almost burst into tears of relief when he got safely to the bell tower.

Dinah had no trouble She wasn't afraid, and if she had been she wouldn't have shown it! She shot across easily, with Toni pulling her, as sure-footed as a cat.

Everyone suddenly felt very cheerful. Lucy-Ann hugged Jack without stopping. There was now such a crowd on the little stone platform at the top of the tower that poor Toni could hardly find room for himself!

'What about this wire rope?' said Pedro. 'How can we get it back?'

'We leave it,' said Toni. 'It is not possible to get it away. I have another.'

'Let's get down to the ground,' said Jack, half afraid that now things had gone so well, something might suddenly happen to make them go wrong. 'I'll go first.'

Soon they were all at the bottom of the tower. 'Silent, now,' whispered Jack, and they began to walk cautiously down the slope of the hill to the circus.

Lucy-Ann kept close to Jack, and he put his arm round

her. He was very glad to know that his sister was safe. Gussy stumbled along, scared and puzzled. He didn't really seem to know quite what was happening!

'The girls can have our van,' said Pedro to Jack. 'You and I and Gussy can sleep beneath it.'

But before they could get to the van, a great clamour came on the air, and startled them so much that they all stood still in panic. Whatever was that tremendous noise?

'It's a bell — it's bells!' said Jack, putting his hands to his ears. 'The bell in the bell tower — and the bell in the church — and another bell somewhere else! Whatever's happening? Have they missed Gussy already?'

The circus folk all awoke and rushed out of their vans, marvelling at the pandemonium of noise made by the bells. Clang, clang, jangle, jangle, clang, clang! It went on all the time!

And then there came shouting from the town. Lights shone out, and still the bells went on and on. 'There are some ringing from the next village too,' said Jack, marvelling. 'It's to warn the people about something. What can it be? They *can't* know yet about Gussy escaping — why, except for Count Paritolen and his sister nobody knew Gussy was a prisoner.'

No — the bells were not ringing for Gussy. They were giving other news — serious news.

'The King! The King is gone! He has disappeared! He is nowhere to be found. The King is gone!'

The townsfolk shouted the news to one another in foreboding. What had happened to their King? Had he been killed? All the bells in the country rang out the news. Enemies had taken their King! Who? Why? Clang, clang, clang, jangle, jangle!

'My word!' said Jack, when he heard the news. 'We only JUST got Gussy out in time. Only just! Another half-hour and it would have been too late.'

'Yes,' said Philip. 'And I'd like to see Count Paritolen's

face when he rushes to the tower room to get Gussy out of bed and put him on the throne – and Gussy's not there! The King gone – and no one to put in his place!'

Gussy howled. 'What's happened to my uncle?' he cried. 'Where is he? I don't want to be King!'

'Shut up!' said Jack, fiercely. 'Do you want every single person here to know you're the Prince? If someone gives you away, you'll be captured by the Count immediately! Go into that caravan and don't dare to make a sound!'

23

Beware the bears!

Jack hurried the girls and Gussy to Pedro's van. He hadn't reckoned on arriving back with them in the middle of a disturbance like this! All the circus folk were out of their vans; they were dressed in all kinds of shawls, coats and macs, hastily pulled over their night things, and were gathering together in frightened groups to talk.

It was just about the very worst time to bring Gussy to the camp. Suppose anyone recognized him? He would certainly have to be disguised at once.

Pedro realized this too. He knew, much better than Jack, what trouble the circus folk would get into if it was discovered that they were harbouring the Prince himself! They would all be clapped into prison at once. Pedro was very very worried.

'Jack! I'll have to tell Ma,' he said, desperately. 'I'll have to! She can hide Gussy better than anyone. Let me tell her. She'll help us.'

There was nothing for it but to say yes. Jack watched Pedro go up to his mother and say something urgently. Then they disappeared up the steps of Ma's caravan, and shut the door. Jack looked at Philip, who was feeling bewildered at this sudden transition from confinement in the tower room to the excited turmoil of the circus camp.

The girls and Gussy were now safely in Pedro's own caravan – trying to peer out of the windows to see what was going on. Kiki had gone with them. Lucy-Ann almost wished she was back in the peace of the tower room! She couldn't understand exactly what was happening. Where was Jack? Why didn't he come and tell her?

Pedro came out of his mother's caravan and went straight over to Jack. 'It's all right,' he said. 'Ma's taken command! She's not a bit afraid of hiding the Prince – actually she rather enjoys something like this. She'll get him some girl's clothes, put a ribbon on that long hair of his, and keep him close to her. She says she'll tell everyone he's her little granddaughter, come to stay for a few days.'

Jack gave a chuckle at the thought of Gussy as a girl. 'He'll hate it,' he said. 'He'll kick up no end of a fuss.'

'Ma won't take any notice,' said Pedro, with a grin. 'She's quite likely to give him a few hard slaps, and my word, she's got a bony hand! I'll get him and take him to her. No one will recognize Prince Aloyisus when she's finished with him.'

Pedro went off, and Jack turned to Philip, who grinned at him. 'Poor old Gussy! That's a wonderful idea though – Gussy will make a BEAUTIFUL girl!'

There came a sudden shouting from the other end of the camp – then screams. People began to stream away towards the two boys, shouting in fear.

'The bears! The bears! They're out!'

Toni came bounding up to Jack. 'Where's that friend of yours you said could manage animals? Oh, there he is. The bears are loose – they've broken three of the bars of their cage. See if your friend can help. Fank can't even get out of bed.'

Philip knew nothing about the bears, of course, and Jack

141

hurriedly told him the details as they ran to the other end of the field. 'I hope you *can* do something with them, Philip. Toni helped me to rescue you on the chance that you *could* help. It will be a terrible loss to the circus if the bears get loose and have to be shot.'

One bear was still in the broken cage, afraid to go out because of the crowds. He was making a terrible noise. No one dared to go near. In a nearby cage Feefo and Fum, the two chimpanzees, were wailing in fright. Madame Fifi made sure they were safely locked in and ran over to Jack.

'Don't go near that bear, you two boys. He's dangerous. And look out for the others. They're loose.'

'Can't someone block up those broken bars?' said Philip. 'He'll be out soon.'

'Nobody dares,' said Toni. But little Madame Fifi dared! She ran to a brilliant flaring torch, stuck in a holder nearby, plucked it out and ran back to the cage. She thrust the pointed bottom end of the torch into the ground, just in front of the cage. The bear shrank back at the bright light and crouched down in a corner. He was afraid of the brilliance.

'That settles *him*,' said Philip, pleased. 'He won't attempt to come out while that light is there. Now — where are the others?'

'Over there — sniffing round the Boss's caravan,' said Jack, pointing to two dark shapes. 'I bet the Boss is shivering in his shoes inside the van!'

'Where can I get some meat?' panted Philip as they ran across the field towards the bears. 'Or better still, can I get honey anywhere — or treacle?'

'Treacle! Yes, Ma's got a whole jar of it,' said Jack, remembering. 'I'll get it.'

He raced off to Ma's caravan, burst in and demanded the treacle. Gussy was there, standing in silken vest and pants, protesting loudly. Ma was evidently getting to work on him! She didn't seem to be at all surprised at Jack bursting in to ask for treacle.

'On the shelf,' she said, and went on brushing out Gussy's hair.

Jack found the big stone jar and fled back to Philip with it. Philip had now gone close to the bears, who turned to look at him suspiciously.

'They've already injured one man,' said Jack, in a low voice. 'Look out, won't you, Philip?'

'I'll be all right,' said Philip. 'Keep out of sight, Jack.' He took the jar of treacle, dipped his hands in it and smeared them up to the wrists with the thick, sweet syrup.

Then he walked towards the bears, pouring a little of the syrup out on the grass as he went. The bears frowled warningly. Philip turned and went back again. He sat down with the jar of treacle and waited.

By now many people were watching. Who was this boy? What was he doing, meddling with two dangerous bears? They watched in fearful curiosity, ready to run at any moment.

Jack stood out of sight – but near enough to run to Philip's help if necessary! He didn't think it *would* be necessary; he had absolute faith in Philip's ability to manage any animal.

The bears soon smelt the syrup that Philip had spilt here and there on the grass. They loved the sweetness of treacle. Fank sometimes gave it to them for a treat – and there was nothing they liked better than to have an empty syrup tin given to them, and to be allowed to lick it, and put their great paws inside.

They sniffed, and went towards the first spots of treacle on the ground. One bear found them and licked eagerly. The second bear growled at him and tried to push him aside – but suddenly smelt another few spots of treacle further on! He lumbered on clumsily and licked eagerly.

As soon as the bears realized that there was treacle about, they began to grunt excitedly. They had refused food for two days now, and they were hungry. They sniffed eagerly for more treacle.

The watching people held their breath as they saw the two

great clumsy creatures getting nearer and nearer to the boy sitting on the ground. Surely he was in danger?

'Who is he? He ought to be warned!' they said. But Toni and Bingo hushed them.

'Be quiet! He is Jack's friend, a wonder with animals! Give him a chance! He can run if the bears threaten him!'

The first bear was now quite near Philip, his head close to the ground as he sniffed about for more treacle. Philip put his hand into the jar he held, and took it out, waving it slowly in the air so that the bear could get the full scent of it.

The bear raised his head and saw Philip. He backed away a little and gave an angry grunt. Who was that sitting on the ground? His eyes gleamed an angry red in the light from a nearby lamp. A little sigh of fear went through the anxious crowd.

And then Philip spoke. He spoke in what Jack called his 'special' voice – the voice he always kept for animals. It was a low, monotonous voice, a gentle, kindly voice, but somehow it was a voice that had to be listened to. 'A sort of hypnotizing voice,' thought Jack, as he stood watching.

The bear listened. He grunted again, and backed away, bumping into the second bear. But still Philip's voice went on. What was he saying? Jack couldn't hear. How did he know how to talk to animals like this? And why did they all listen? The watching circus folk knew that most animal trainers used a special tone of voice when they petted their animals – but here was a strange boy talking to frightened and suspicious bears – and yet they listened.

The second bear came a little nearer, his ears pricked. He sniffed. He sniffed not only the treacle, but Philip's own particular smell. He liked it. It was a friendly smell. The bears always sorted out people into two kinds – those whose smell they liked and those they didn't.

He lumbered right up to Philip and sniffed at him, ready to strike if the boy moved. A little scream came from someone in the crowd, but the bear took no notice.

Philip went on talking, and now his voice was so honeyed and persuasive that even the crowd began to feel his spell. The bear licked Philip's hand, which was covered in treacle. Philip did not move. The bear went on licking, quite unafraid.

The other bear came up, and, seeing how unafraid his brother was, he took a quick lick at Philip's other hand. In two or three seconds both bears were grunting in delight at so much treacle. This boy was a friend! They didn't know who he was, but they were quite sure he was a friend.

Philip talked all the time, monotonously and kindly. He thought he could now dare to move, so he lifted one hand slowly, put it into the jar beside him, and then took it out covered with treacle again.

One bear lay down beside him to lick in comfort. Another sigh at once went through the tense crowd. Philip gave the jar to the other bear, and then with his free hand began to fondle the bear lying beside him. It grunted in pleasure.

Now the bears were happy and at peace. They had found someone they liked and trusted. Philip knew that he had them under control — if only the crowd didn't do something silly — make a sudden noise, or come surging towards him. But the circus folk knew better than that. They were used to animals.

Philip stood up, doing nothing quickly — all his movements were smooth and slow. He picked up the jar, and with his other hand on one bear's neck, began to walk to the cage. The bears followed, shambling along quietly, licking their lips.

Philip took them right to the cage, undid the door and let them shuffle in. He put the treacle jar inside, shut the door, and went quietly outside.

And then how the people cheered! 'He's a wonder! Who is he? Tell Fank the bears are safe. Who IS this boy?'

24

Morning comes!

Philip called to Jack. 'Jack – see if you can get some meat – plenty of it – and bring it to me.'

'*I'll* get some,' said Toni, and raced off. He came back with a basket containing great slabs of horse meat. Philip took it. He opened the cage door and threw in the meat, talking cheerfully to the hungry bears.

Now they were ready for their meal. They were no longer sulky, scared or angry. They were just three very hungry bears, and they fell on the meat and gulped it down.

'Let them have as much as they will eat,' said Philip. 'Then they will go to sleep. While they are asleep, someone must mend their cage bars. Keep that light in front now – none of them will venture out of the broken bars while that light is there.'

Everyone gathered round Philip. 'He's a friend of Jack,' they said to one another. 'He fetched him here because he is good with bears. He must have come from another circus. Look – the Boss wants him.'

The Boss had watched everything from his caravan window. He was most impressed and extremely thankful. Pedro told Philip that the Boss had sent for him, and he and Jack and Philip went up the steps of the Boss's big caravan.

The Boss poured out praise and thanks in a mixture of several languages. Pedro interpreted with a grin. 'He says, what can he do for you? He says you've saved the bears from being shot. He says, ask anything you like and you can have it, if he can give it to you!'

Jack answered quickly. 'There's only one thing we want. Now that there is this upset in Borken, can we all stay with the circus? Philip will be glad to look after the bears, as long

146

as Fank is ill – but he has girls with him, our sisters – can they stay too? We don't like to let them go off by themselves, in case civil war starts up in Tauri-Hessia.'

Pedro interpreted. The Boss quite thought that these 'sisters' were circus performers too. He nodded his head. 'Yes – you may let them stay. If they have tricks or shows of their own, they may get a chance here. But we must strike camp tomorrow – it will be dangerous to stay here in Borken any longer. The Count Paritolen owns this land, and as it is probably he who has something to do with the King's disappearance, it would be best for us to leave before trouble starts.'

'What does he say?' asked Jack, anxiously. Pedro translated all this into English, and the two boys were much relieved. Good! They could all stay with the circus, and would leave almost immediately with the circus folk! They would soon be out of the danger zone – and then perhaps they could get a message to Bill.

The boys went down the steps of the van with Pedro. They made their way to Pedro's own little van, feeling that they simply must have a good long talk. It was about two o'clock in the morning now, but none of the three boys felt tired – they were far too strung up with the happenings of the night.

The circus folk as they passed clapped Philip on the back. He smiled and nodded, and then at last all three were in the little van with the two girls and Kiki.

'Shut the door,' said Kiki at once. 'Wipe your feet. Fetch the King!'

'I wish we could, Kiki,' said Jack, with a laugh, as the parrot flew on to his shoulder. 'But don't you start talking about the King. Oh – Lucy-Ann – you nearly had me over! What a hug! It reminds me of the bears!'

'I can't help it!' said Lucy-Ann, and gave Philip a hug too. 'I was so anxious about you and Philip, with those bears. It all seems like a horrid dream. I was longing for you to come back to us. Gussy's gone too. Is he really going to be a girl?'

'He is,' said Jack, sitting down on the mattress. 'Now, we've got to talk and make plans. First of all, because of Philip's grand performance with the bears, the Boss has said that we can all stay with the circus. We couldn't have a better hiding place!'

'That's true,' said Dinah. 'But suppose the Count makes a search for us – and his men are sent here to look, among other places. Gussy might not be recognized if he's dressed up as a girl – but what about me and Lucy-Ann and Philip? We're all dressed in the English way – we'd soon be noticed.'

'Yes. I hadn't thought of that,' said Jack. 'I'm too English, as well. Pedro – I've got some money saved up that I made out of Kiki's performances – could you buy some Hessian clothes for us early today?'

'Ma will fix you all up,' said Pedro. 'She's a wonder with her needle! She'll get some cloth from old Lucia, the woman who's in charge of the circus clothes. And we'll borrow some grease paint from Toni and give you all tanned Tauri-Hessian faces! But don't go speaking English!'

'No, we won't. We'll talk a wonderful gibberish of our own!' said Philip, with a laugh. 'We'll come from Jabber-wocky, and talk the Jabberwock language! It goes like this – Goonalillypondicherrytapularkawoonatee!'

Everyone laughed. 'Good!' said Pedro. 'I'll tell any searchers that you are Jabberowockians, and then you can talk like that if they ask you anything. By the way, where *is* Jabberwocky?'

Kiki suddenly launched with delight into the Jabbero-wickian language. They all listened to her and roared. 'You're a very fine specimen of a Jabberwockian parrot!' said Jack, stroking her. 'Go to the top of the class!'

Dinah gave an enormous yawn, at once copied by Kiki. It made everyone begin to feel terribly sleepy. 'Come on – we'll be striking camp fairly early,' said Pedro, getting up. 'Sleep in peace, girls. We three boys will be just under the van, on a couple of rugs. As for Gussy, I expect he's snoring in Ma's extra bunk, looking like a beautiful little girl!'

Gussy was not asleep, however. He lay in the small bunk, listening to Ma's deep breathing and sudden snorts. He was very angry and very humiliated. Ma had seen to him properly! She had tried his hair this way and that, and had finally decided that he looked more like a girl with a small bow at each side rather than with one big one on top.

She had also looked out some clothes — a longish skirt, rather large, very highly coloured, and decidedly ragged — and a small red blouse with a green scarf tied skittishly round the waist. Gussy could have cried with shame.

It wasn't the slightest bit of good arguing with Ma. In fact, when Gussy refused to stand still while his bows were being tied, Ma had given him a hefty slap on a very tender place, which had given Gussy such a tremendous shock that he couldn't even yell.

'You know I'm a Prince, don't you?' he said, fiercely, under his breath.

'Pah!' said Ma. 'You're just a boy. I've no time for Princes.' And she hadn't.

Now Gussy was trying to go to sleep, his hair still tied with bows, and a peculiar sort of garment on him that looked half like a night gown and half like a long coat. He went over the exciting escape in his mind, and shuddered. No — he wouldn't think about that awful rope and the trapeze swing. He wondered about his uncle and shuddered again. Was he killed? Poor Gussy's thoughts were not pleasant ones at all.

The morning came all too soon for the five tired children. Philip went across at once to the bears' cage to see how they were. The bars had been mended and strengthened. The bears, looking extremely well fed, were half asleep — but as soon as they saw Philip they padded to the bars and grunted amiably. One bear tried to reach him with his paw.

'Good — they're quite all right,' said Philip, and gave them a little talk to which they listened entranced, as if they understood every word!

Fank was better — but still could not stand up. Philip went

149

to see him, and the little man took his hand and poured out a stream of completely unintelligible words. Philip knew what he was saying, though! Here was a grateful man if ever there was one! Fank loved his bears as if they were his brothers, and he had been almost mad with anxiety the night before, when he heard they had escaped.

'I'll take them on till you're well,' said Philip, and Fank understood, and shook Philip's hand fervently.

The next thing was clothes. The camp was to set off in three hours, so Ma had got to hurry if she was going to get the four of them clothes that would disguise the fact that they were English.

She went to Lucia, an old bent woman who kept the clothes of the circus folk in order – not the ordinary ones they wore every day, but their fine ones, worn in the ring – their glittering capes and skirts, their silken shirts and magnificent cloaks. These were valuable, and old Lucia's needle was always busy. So was her iron. Nobody could press fine clothes as well or as carefully as Lucia.

By the time the circus folk were ready to strike camp, nobody would have recognized Dinah, Lucy-Ann, Philip and Jack! Toni had lent them grease paint and each of them were tanned and looked like a Tauri-Hessian – face, neck, legs, and hands! The girls wore the Tauri-Hessian dress – long skirts and shawls, and bright ribbons in their hair.

The boys looked just like normally brought up boys of the country, and seemed to have grown older all of a sudden. Lucy-Ann stared at Jack in surprise, hardly recognizing this brown youth, whose teeth gleamed suddenly white in his tanned face.

Ma was pleased with her efforts, but most of all she was delighted with Gussy. Nobody, *nobody* could possibly think that Gussy was anything but a girl. He looked really pretty! All five of them, Pedro too, roared with laughter when poor Gussy came down Ma's caravan steps, looking very red in the face, very angry, and very ashamed.

'Dis is my little grandchild, Anna-Maria!' said Ma, with a broad smile. 'Be kind to her, plizz!'

Gussy looked as if he was about to burst into tears. 'Yes, go on, cry!' said Philip, teasing him. 'That'll show people you aren't Anna-Maria!'

Dinah gave him a punch. 'Some girls do cry!' she said. 'Oh dear – doesn't Gussy – I mean Anna-Maria – look priceless?'

'Smashing!' said Jack. 'Honestly, he's as pretty as a picture. Thank goodness for his long hair – that's what helps him look like a girl more than anything!'

'I cut it short soon, soon, *soon*,' said poor Gussy, furiously. 'Snip-snip – like that!'

'You can't. You told us that Princes of this country have to wear it long, like you do,' said Dinah.

'I will *not* be a Prince then,' said Gussy. He looked suddenly very forlorn, and gazed at Lucy-Ann beseechingly, feeling that she had the kindest heart of the lot.

'Do not tizz me,' he begged. 'I hate zis. I am full of shamefulness.'

'All right, Gussy, er – Anna-Maria,' said Jack. 'We won't tizz you. Cheer up – you'll be a Prince again before long, I'm sure.'

'If my uncle is alive, I will be,' said Gussy, soberly. 'If he is dead – I must be King!'

'God save the King,' said Kiki, devoutly, and raised her crest impressively. 'Fetch the doctor and save the King!'

25

The camp is searched

Soon a long procession of vans was going down the winding road that led away from Borken. The two girls and Gussy were in Pedro's little van, and he was driving the small skewbald horse that belonged to him.

Jack was driving Ma's van for her, and the old lady looked really happy. She loved a bit of excitement, and she roared with laughter whenever she caught sight of poor Gussy.

Philip, of course, was driving the van in which the bears' cage was built. Toni was driving Fank's little living-van, whistling cheerfully. Fank lay on his mattress inside, glad to feel better, and to know that 'that wonder boy' Philip had got his bears in charge. He felt full of gratitude to Philip – and to Toni too for so cheerfully driving his van for him. The circus folk were always ready to help one another. That was one of the nicest things about them.

The vans rumbled along the road, going very slowly, for neither the bears nor the chimpanzees liked going fast. They were all excited at being on the move again. Feefo and Fum chattered away together, looking through the window of their van.

'Where are we going?' Dinah asked Pedro, through the open window of the van. Pedro shrugged his shoulders. He had no idea.

'We must get away from Borken, where a lot of trouble may start,' he said, 'and try to find somewhere more peaceful. We shall probably make for some country road, and keep away from all the main roads. Soldiers will use those, if trouble starts.'

Dinah went back into the van. The Tauri-Hessian dress

152

suited her well, and she looked exactly right in it. 'We're making for some country road,' she told Lucy-Ann. 'It's a pity we still can't get in touch with Mother or Bill. They really will be dreadfully worried about us by now.'

'I suppose the police will have been told and will be hunting everywhere for us – but in England instead of here!' said Lucy-Ann. 'Well, anyway, we're safe for the moment, and out of that tower room. I was getting tired of that! Nothing to do all day but to play games with those funny cards they brought us!'

They all stopped for a meal at about one o'clock. The vans stood at one side of the road, and the circus folk sat beside them and ate. It was like summer, although it was only April. The sun was very hot, and masses of brilliant flowers were out everywhere.

Philip's little dormouse came out to share the meal with him. He had had it with him all the time. It was scared by the noisy talk of the circus folk, and only appeared when things were quiet. It sat on the palm of Philip's hand, enjoying a nut, its big black eyes now and again glancing up at the boy.

'I don't know what we'd have done without you, Snoozy, when we were shut up in that tower room,' said Philip, softly. 'You kept us all amused with your little games and antics, didn't you? And you told Jack where we were, the other night – you ran under the door to him!'

Soon they were on the way again. The bears settled down to sleep, happy to know that Philip was driving them. He had fed them himself again when the procession halted for a meal, and the bears grunted at him happily. Fank heard them and was happy too.

The procession wound down the road, came out into a main road, and went down that, intending to turn off at a country road about two miles on. But halfway down something happened.

Three powerful military cars swept by the procession, and drove right up to the head of it. Then they stopped, and soldiers leapt down from the cars, with a captain in command.

'Halt!' he said, to the front driver, and the whole procession came to a stop. The circus folk looked worried. What was this? Soldiers already? And why were *they* being halted? They had done nothing wrong!

They jumped down from their vans, and gathered together in little knots, waiting. Jack poked his head back into Ma's van, which he was driving. 'This is it, Ma,' he said. 'I think the vans are going to be searched. Give Gussy something to do, and scold him as if he was your grand child. Gussy, you're a girl, remember — so don't answer back, or even say a word, when the men come along. Look shy if you can.'

Pedro also knew what was about to happen. He called to the two girls, 'Come out, and mix with the circus folk. Go with Toni and Bingo. I'll come too. I'll put my arms round you both as if you were my sisters or my friends.'

Philip, however, didn't move. He decided that he was in a very good place, driving the bears' van! The men would be sure to upset the bears and he would have to pacify them. He would appear to the men to be a bear trainer!

The captain found the Boss. Pedro heard him talking to him in sharp tones.

'We are going to search your vans. We suspect you have someone here we want. It will be the worse for you, if you have. I warn you to give him up now, at once, because when we find him you will be severely punished.'

The Boss looked surprised. He was sitting in his great chair inside his van. 'I do not know what you mean,' he said. 'Search my vans! You are welcome!'

The Boss thought that the soldiers were looking for a deserter, a young man, perhaps. He did not know they were hunting for a small boy, and certainly had no idea they were after the little Prince Aloysius!

The captain gave a sharp command. His soldiers marched

down the sides of the vans, keeping a watch for anyone who might try to hide in the wayside bushes. Then they began to search carefully, probing each van, lifting up piles of rugs or clothes to see if anyone could be hidden there.

They stopped at the sight of Philip. They had been told that although they must at all costs find Gussy, there were three other children, too, to look for. Children whose presence in the camp would tell them the Prince was somewhere about too.

They came up to the bears' van, their heels clicking sharply. Their loud voices angered the three bears, and they growled and flung themselves at the bars.

Toni came up and spoke to them, telling them to keep out of sight of the bears.

'We had trouble with them yesterday,' he said, 'and this boy, who helps the trainer, only just managed to keep them under control. As you see, the bars of the cage were broken and had to be mended. Keep out of sight, please, or they will break the bars again.'

Philip didn't understand what Toni was saying, but guessed. He decided that the best thing he could do to avoid being questioned was to get inside the bears' cage, and pretend to quieten them. So in he went, and the bears fawned round him in delight.

The soldiers watched from a safe distance. The captain was satisfied. Obviously this boy belonged to the circus, and travelled as a helper with the bears. He could not be one of the boys they had been told to look out for. They went on to the next van, and Toni winked at Philip.

'Good!' he said. 'Keep there. You are safer with the bears than anywhere else!'

The soldiers went from van to van. They hardly glanced at Dinah or Lucy-Ann, who, with Pedro's arms round them, were standing watching the two chimpanzees. Madame Fifi had taken the opportunity of giving them a little airing.

The captain, however, glanced sharply at Pedro. Could he

155

be one of the boys they sought? He beckoned to him. Pedro came over, still with the girls, smiling, and at ease.

The captain snapped something at him in Tauri-Hessian. Pedro answered smoothly, pointing to his mother's van. He was saying that he travelled with his mother, and his little cousin, Anna-Maria.

'And these two girls?' said the captain, sharply.

'They are with the circus too,' said Pedro. 'They belong to the boy who manages the bears – you have seen him. They are Jabberwockians, and speak very little Hessian. But they speak French if you would like to ask them anything.'

Dinah heard Pedro say the word 'Jabberwockians' and guessed that he was saying that she and Lucy-Ann belonged to Jabberwocky! Dinah immediately poured out a string of utter gibberish to the captain, waving her hands about, and smiling broadly. Lucy nodded her head now and again as if she agreed with her sister!

'All right, all right,' said the captain, in his own language. 'It's all nonsense to me, this. I can't understand a word! What is she saying?'

Pedro grinned. He told the captain that Dinah thought him very magnificent, much grander than captains in Jabberwocky. He was pleased. He saluted the two smiling girls smartly, and went away, satisfied that they were certainly not English. He really must find out where the Land of Jabberwocky was – he didn't seem to have heard of it. These circus folk came from queer places!

And now the soldiers had reached Ma's caravan. Jack was still sitting in the driver's seat, Kiki on his shoulder. He had warned her not to talk, because he was afraid her English words might give them away. 'But you can make noises,' he told her, and Kiki understood perfectly.

She raised her crest as the men came near and coughed loudly. The soldiers looked at her in surprise.

'Powke,' said Jack, patting Kiki. 'Powke, arka powke.' He knew that this meant 'Clever parrot,' because the people who had come to marvel at Kiki when she had been on

156

show, had so often said those two words. 'Arka powke!'
Clever parrot!

Kiki gave a loud hiccup, and then another. The soldiers
were tickled, and roared with laughter. Then Kiki clucked
like a hen laying eggs, and that amused them even more.

This was the kind of thing Kiki liked. It gave her a wonderful opportunity for showing off. She put down her head,
looked wickedly at the soldiers, and gave them the full
benefit of her aeroplane-in-trouble noise.

They were extremely startled, and stepped back at once.
Kiki cackled idiotically, laughing till the soldiers and Jack
were laughing helplessly too!

A sharp voice came from hehind them. It was their
captain. They jumped to attention at once.

'Why waste time on this boy?' said the captain. 'You can
see he is a circus boy, with a parrot like that! Search the van!'

Jack knew enough of the Hessian language now to understand roughly what the captain had said. *He* wasn't suspected then – and it was obvious that none of the soldiers
suspected Philip or the girls. Now there was only Gussy left.
Would he play up and be sensible?

Two soldiers went into Ma's van. They saw Gussy at
once, sitting beside Ma. 'Who's this?' they said, sharply.
'What's her name?'

26

The pedlar's van

Gussy looked shyly up at them, and then hid his face in Ma's
lap, as if very overcome. That had been Ma's idea, of course!

'Now, now!' said Ma, in Tauri-Hessian, tapping Gussy.
'Sit up and answer the gentlemen, my little Anna-Maria!'
She turned to the soldiers.

'You must pardon her,' she said. 'She is a silly little girl, and cannot say boo to a goose! Sit up, my pet, and show these kind gentlemen what you are making.'

Gussy sat up, and held out a piece of embroidery to the two soldiers, keeping his head down as if very shy indeed. Jack, looking in through the window, was amazed at Gussy's acting. And that embroidery! How very very clever of Ma to give Gussy that to show to the soldiers! He had seen Ma working on it herself, night after night!

'She is my favourite grandchild,' Ma prattled on. 'The prettiest little thing and so good. Talk to the kind gentlemen, Anna-Maria! Say how do you do.'

'I cannot,' said Gussy, and hid his face in Ma's lap again.

'Don't bother her,' said one soldier. 'I have a little girl at home as shy as she is. It's better to have them that way than bold and cheeky. How pretty her hair is! You must be proud of her, old woman.'

'She is such a good little needlewoman,' said Ma,' proudly, and patted Gussy's head. 'Sit up, my pet – the gentlemen won't eat you!'

'We're going,' said the first soldier. 'Here, give her this to spend. She really does remind me of my little girl at home.'

He threw a coin to Ma and she caught it deftly and pocketed it at once. Jack heaved an enormous sigh of relief when he saw the two men walking away. He poked his head in at the window.

'It's all right. They've gone. Gussy, you were absolutely marvellous! Talk about an actor! Why, you're a born actor! A shy little girl to the life.'

Gussy lifted his head from Ma's lap. His eyes were bright and his face was red. He was laughing.

'It was Ma's idea, to behave like that,' he said. 'She said I must not show my face at all, I must be shy and put it into her lap.'

'A really good idea,' said Jack, and grinned at Ma's smiling face. 'Honestly, Gussy, I congratulate you – I never imagined you could act like that.'

'I like acting,' said Gussy. 'But not in girls' clothes. I feel silly. Still – it was a very good idea. Now – I am safe, is it not so?'

'I think so,' said Jack, looking up the road. 'The men are going back to their cars. They are getting into them. Yes – the first car is going off. Whew! I was in a stew when those two fellows walked into your van.'

As soon as three military cars had shot off down the road, Philip left the bears' van, and came running over to the others, grinning. They all collected round Ma's van, and heard Jack's recital of Gussy's marvellous performance.

Gussy was pleased. He was not often praised by the others, and it was very pleasant to have them admiring him for once in a way. Then he caught sight of himself in Ma's mirror, ribbons and all, and his face clouded.

'I do not like myself,' he said, staring in the mirror. 'I will now dress in my own things again.'

'Oh no – not yet!' said Jack, quickly. 'You don't know who might recognize you suddenly if you did. You'll have to be a girl until we get you to safety somewhere. Go on, now, Gussy – you like acting. You'll give a marvellous performance!'

The vans went on again. The excitement quickly died down, and everyone grew silent. They were tired with their short night and the disturbances they had had. They stopped for a snack about six o'clock and then went on again.

They were now on a lonely country road. The surface was bad, and the vans had to go slowly. Nobody minded that. Circus folk were never in a hurry except when their show was about to begin. Then everyone fell into a tremendous rush, and raced about in excitement.

They camped that night in the hills. They all slept very soundly to make up for the lack of sleep the night before. Then they set out again, jogging on slowly, not really very certain where they were going.

The Boss suddenly decided that they had taken a wrong

turning a few miles back. The vans were turned round and back they all went, grumbling hard. They passed few people on the road, for they were now in a very lonely part.

'I want shops,' grumbled Ma. 'I need to buy things. We all need to buy things. We must go to some place where there are shops. I will go to tell the Boss.'

But she didn't, because she was afraid of him. She just went on grumbling. She wanted new cotton reels. She wanted some tinned fruit. She wanted hairpins.

'Cheer up, Ma – we may meet a travelling pedlar van,' said Pedro, getting tired of Ma's grumbling.

'What's that?' asked Jack.

'Oh – a van that takes all kinds of things to lonely villages,' said Pedro. 'I don't expect we *shall* meet one – but I've got to say something to keep Ma quiet!'

The Boss gave the order to camp early that night, and everyone was thankful. Soon fires were burning by the roadside and good smells came on the air.

Just as it was getting dusk, a small van came labouring up the hill on the slope of which the camp had been pitched. Madame Fifi saw it first and gave a shout.

Everyone looked up. 'Ma! You're in luck!' called Pedro. 'Here's a pedlar's van!'

The little black van drew up at the sight of the circus camp. Two men sat in the front of it, in the usual Tauri-Hessian clothes, sunburnt fellows, one small, one big and burly.

'Better keep out of sight, Gussy,' said Jack, suddenly. 'You never know – this might be men sent to check over the camp again.'

'Oh dear!' sighed Lucy-Ann. 'Don't say they're going to search all over again.'

The small man jumped out, went to the side of the van, and swung down half the wooden side, making a kind of counter. Inside the van, on shelves, were goods of every conceivable kind! Tins of meat, sardines and fruit. Tins of salmon and milk. Skeins of wool, reels of cotton, rolls of lace, bales of cheap cotton cloth. Safety-pins and hair-pins. Combs of all kinds. Soap. Sweets. Really, it was just like a little general shop seen in so many villages.

'It sells everything!' said Pedro. 'Ma, do you want me to buy half the things for you?'

'No. I'll come myself,' said Ma, who enjoyed a bit of shopping. 'Stay here, Anna-Maria!'

'Can we go and have a look at the shop, do you think?' asked Dinah. 'You've got some Hessian money, haven't you, Jack? I do really want to buy some soap, and a few other things. Surely that van is genuine – those men can't be spies, sent to search the camp again!'

'No. I don't think they can be,' said Jack. 'The van does seem quite genuine, as you say. All right – we'll go and buy a few things. Not Gussy, though.'

So, while the others strolled off in the dusk to the little travelling shop, poor Gussy was left behind in Ma's van. He was very cross.

The small man sold all the goods. The big man merely helped, handing down this and that, and wrapping up anything that needed it. He said nothing at all. The other man was a real talker. He chattered all the time, chaffed the women, and passed on little bits of news.

'And what news have *you* got?' he asked Ma and old Lucia, as he sold them hairpins and combs. 'You've come from the direction of Borken, haven't you? Any news of the King there? He's not been found yet, you know!'

Ma gave him her news, and described the clamour of the bells in the night. Old Lucia chimed in with a few remarks too.

'Where's little Prince Aloysius?' she wanted to know. 'They say he was sent to school in England. If the King is dead, the little Prince will have to be brought back, won't he?'

'We had soldiers searching our camp today,' said

Madame Fifi. 'Though what they expected to find, I don't know. The King perhaps!'

Everyone laughed. The chattering and buying went on for some time, and the pedlars did very well. Jack went up to buy some sweets for the girls, Kiki on his shoulder.

'Good morning, good night, good gracious!' said Kiki, conversationally, to the pedlar who was serving. He laughed. But the other man didn't. He turned round and looked very sharply at Kiki indeed. Jack felt uncomfortable. Why did the second man look round like that? He tried to see what he was like, but it was now dark, and difficult to see inside the little van.

Lucy-Ann pointed to some toffee. 'I'd like some of that,' she said, in English. Jack saw the man at the back of the van stiffen. He seemed to be listening for what Lucy-Ann might say next. He reached up to a shelf, took down a tin, and then stood still again, as Lucy-Ann spoke once more.

'Let's have a tin of pineapple, Kiki likes that.'

The man swung round. Jack hurriedly pushed Lucy-Ann back into the darkness. This fellow was a spy! He was sure of it! He took another look at him, but could not make out very much. A head of black, curly hair, such as all the Tauri-Hessians had – a small black moustache – that was about all Jack could see.

'What's up, Jack?' said Lucy-Ann, in astonishment as he hurried her away from the van, pulling Dinah and Philip with him too.

He told them hurriedly what he thought and they were very worried. They rushed back to Ma's van to see if Gussy was all right. To their great relief, he was there, looking very cross. 'Though why we should think he wouldn't be there, I don't know,' said Jack. 'Gussy, get out your embroidery. We've seen somebody suspicious. He heard Lucy-Ann talking in English, and Kiki too, and he was *much* too interested!'

'Well – we'll hope he clears off soon,' said Philip. 'I'll go and watch, and tell you when they're gone.'

But the pedlar's van didn't go! The two men shut up the side of the van, safely locking up all their goods, and then sat outside with a little camp fire, cooking some kind of meal.

'They're staying the night,' reported Philip. 'Not too good, is it? And Madame Fifi told me that the small man has been asking questions about Kiki – if the boy who owns her belongs to the camp – and where his caravan is!'

'Blow!' said Jack. 'What can we do? We can't possibly run away. I've no idea at all where we are – miles away from anywhere, that's certain! Well – we can only hope for the best. We'll sleep as usual under the girls' van, and Gussy can be with Ma. After all, he's the important one – we're not really important, except that Gussy escaped with us, and presumably the Count will think that wherever we are, Gussy will be too!'

The girls went to their van and undressed to go to sleep. Gussy was safely with Ma. The three boys lay on the rugs below the girls' van as usual. Pedro soon fell asleep, but Jack and Philip were worried, and lay awake, whispering.

Suddenly Jack clutched Philip. 'I can hear someone,' he whispered, in his ear. 'Someone crawling near this van.'

Jack sat up cautiously and felt for his torch. Yes – someone *was* near the van, crawling quietly on all fours. Jack flicked on his torch at once.

A surprised face was caught in the light. A man was on hands and knees nearby. It was the big pedlar from the little van! His black hair showed up plainly in the beam of the torch.

'What do you want?' said Jack, fiercely. 'What do you mean by crawling around like this? I'll raise the camp, and have them all after you!'

27

A surprise – and a plan

'Sh!' said the man, urgently. 'I . . . '

And then, before he could say another word, a very strange thing happened! Kiki, who had been watching the man in greatest surprise, suddenly spread her wings and flew to his shoulder! She rubbed her beak against his cheek in the most loving manner, crooning like a dove.

'Kiki!' said the man, and stroked her neck.

'Silly-Bill,' said Kiki, lovingly. 'Silly-Billy, put the kettle on, send for the doctor!'

Jack was so astonished that he simply couldn't say a word. Why in the world was Kiki behaving like that – and how did this man know her? It was Philip who guessed. He suddenly rolled himself over on hands and knees, and crawled at top speed from under the wagon.

'Bill! BILL! This must be a dream! Bill, it *is* you, isn't it? Are you wearing a wig?'

With a grin, the big man stripped off the whole of his black hair – yes, he was wearing a wig! And without it he looked himself at once, in spite of the little black moustache which, of course, was merely stuck on.

'Bill, oh, Bill! I can't believe it!' said Philip. Bill put out his great hand and the two shook hands solemnly for quite a long time. Then Jack joined them, his eyes almost falling out of his head. It must be a dream! This *couldn't* be real!

But it was. It was Bill himself. He asked eagerly about the girls. 'I was so relieved to see them both looking so well,' he said. 'Though I hardly knew them in that get up they were wearing. But I knew Lucy-Ann's clear high voice all right – and I spotted Kiki too, of course. I couldn't believe it when I saw her on your shoulder, Jack. I really couldn't. Where are the girls? In this van here?'

'Yes. We heard that you had made enquiries about where our van was,' said Jack. 'And we thought you were spies! We didn't guess it was you, and that you wanted to come and find us in the night. Let's get into the van and wake the girls. We'll wake old Pedro too. He's a great friend of ours.'

Soon an extremely excited company of six people and a parrot sat in Pedro's little van. Lucy-Ann hung on to Bill and wouldn't let him move even an inch from her. Tears ran down her cheeks and she kept brushing them away.

'I can't help it, Bill, I'm not really crying, it's just because I'm so happy again, I just can't help it, Bill!' said poor Lucy-Ann, laughing through the tears that simply poured down her face.

Bill took out an enormous hanky and patted her eyes. He was very fond of Lucy-Ann. 'You make me think of Gussy,' he said, 'and the time when Philip took a kitchen table cloth to dry *his* tears! Cheer up — we're all together again — and you can give me most valuable information!'

'How's Mother?' said Philip. 'Is she very worried?'

'Very!' said Bill. 'She and I were caught and tied up the night you were kidnapped. We couldn't get free. We had to wait till Mrs Gump came along the road next morning on her way to the cottage, and call out to her. By that time, of course, all trace of you had been lost. We've had the police hunting every county in England for you! We didn't dare to say Gussy had gone too, because we didn't want the news to get to the Tauri-Hessians.'

'We went off in a plane, after a car had taken us away,' said Philip. 'Jack hid in the boot of the car and then stowed away in the plane — so he knew where we had gone. We were imprisoned in Borken Castle with Gussy — and Jack managed to rescue us!'

'I joined this circus with Kiki,' explained Jack. 'Pedro was a brick — he helped me no end. We got Toni and Bingo the acrobats to help in the rescue — phew, it was pretty dangerous!'

He told Bill all about it. Bill listened in amazement. These

165

children! The things that happened to them – the way they tackled everything that came along, and never turned a hair. And now they had got Gussy safely with them, disguised as a girl!

'But Bill – you haven't told us what *you're* doing here?' said Jack. 'Fancy you coming along in a pedlar's van – all dressed up as a Tauri-Hessian – really, it's too amazing to be true.'

'Well, it's true all right,' said Bill. 'You see, when our Government learnt that the King of Tauri-Hessia had been captured – or killed, for all we know – it was absolutely essential that we should find out whether this was true or not – and it was essential we should find Gussy too, if possible. So, as the Tauri-Hessian Government had put Gussy into my charge, as you know, it was decided that I should be the one to come out and make inquiries.'

'I see – spy round to see how the land lay,' said Philip. 'Did you think we might all be in Tauri-Hessia?'

'Yes – I came to the conclusion that wherever Gussy had been taken, you should be there too – to be held as hostages, if our own Government made any trouble about Gussy,' said Bill. 'And as soon as the news came that the King had disappeared, we felt sure that Gussy would be somewhere in Borken, Count Paritolen's own territory – and possibly the King might be held prisoner there too – so I and another man, who speaks Tauri-Hessian well, flew over straight away to do a spot of spying. Hence the pedlar's van!'

'Mother will be feeling awfully worried, with you gone too,' said Dinah.

'I'll get a message through to her sometime tomorrow,' said Bill. 'Now, I wonder if you can tell me something – have you any sort of an idea at all where the King might be hidden?'

'In Borken Castle,' said Jack, promptly. 'I'm sure of it! I'll tell you why.'

He told Bill of how he had explored the castle – and how

he had overheard the Count and Madame Tatiosa talking excitedly together. 'That was the night before the King was known to have disappeared,' said Jack. 'I think their plans were going well – probably they even had him a prisoner somewhere then. And the obvious place to take him would be the Count's own castle – he would then have Gussy there – and the King too – right under his hand! He could bargain with both, if he wanted to.'

Bill listened to this long speech with the greatest interest. 'I think you're right,' he said. 'I wish we could get into the castle and find out something. Ronald, the fellow who is with me, speaks the language fluently. I wonder if he could bluff his way in – say he's a tradesman come to do a repair, or something.'

'*I* know what he could do,' said Jack, with a sudden surge of excitement. 'I know a way in, Bill – the way I got out the first night I was there! It leads through secret passages up to the big ballroom. There's a way into the ballroom from behind a great picture. I don't know how to move the picture away, though – so as to get into the ballroom. That's the snag.'

'We'll find out!' said Bill. 'Jack, this is great! Are you game to come with me – and Ronald too, my pal – and show us the way into the castle? If only we could find out whether the King is alive or not – or whether he's a prisoner – it would be a great help. There's one thing, the plans of the plotters must be greatly upset now that Gussy has gone! No King for the country – and no Prince to set in his place! Very difficult for them!'

'I'll come, Bill,' said Jack, his face red with excitement.

'I'll come too,' said Philip.

'No – you must stay and keep an eye on the girls,' said Bill. 'I must have one of you with them. Keep an eye on Gussy too. Pedro can help there.'

'Shall we go now?' asked Jack, eagerly. 'It's a very dark night.'

'The sooner the better,' said Bill, and got up. 'Wait here. I'll fetch Ronnie. I'll have to tell him a few things first though! My word, he'll be astonished!'

Bill disappeared. For a moment the five said nothing. Kiki broke the silence. 'Ding dong bell, Billy's in the well,' she said. 'Pussy's got a cold – a-chooo!'

'Idiot!' said Jack. 'My word – what a night! Fancy BILL turning up here. It was Kiki who recognized him when he came crawling round the van. I didn't.'

'Everything will be all right now,' said Lucy-Ann. 'It always is when Bill comes.'

'Don't talk too soon,' said Dinah. 'They've not got an easy job tonight!'

Bill came back with Ronnie, who seemed rather overcome at meeting so many people at once. He had much more to say as a pedlar than with Bill in Pedro's van!

'Well – are we ready?' said Bill. 'Come on then.'

They slipped out of the caravan, and Jack followed the two men. Their van was quite near, and Jack guessed what they were going to do. They were going to drive back to Borken. It wouldn't take long, because it wasn't really very far away. The circus procession of horse-drawn vans had gone at a walking pace the last two days, and had once had to retrace their steps as well. It wouldn't take more than an hour to get to Borken.

They went off in the night, Ronnie driving. Kiki was on Jack's shoulder. She meant to be in everything, no matter what it was!

They came to Borken. The town was in utter darkness. 'Park the van in the field where the camp was,' said Jack, and guided them to it. 'The castle is only just up the steep slope of the hill then.'

They parked the van behind a big bush. Then they made their way up the steep slope to the castle. 'There's the bell tower,' said Jack, as they came nearer. 'Better go cautiously in case there are people on guard. The Count must

168

know that we escaped by means of the bell tower. We had to leave Toni's wire rope behind, stretched from tower to tower.'

Nobody seemed to be about, however. But Jack suddenly saw lights in the castle windows high above them. They blazed out of half a dozen windows – something was going on in the castle in the middle of that night, it was certain!

'We might be able to have a look in on that,' said Bill, staring at the lights. 'Must be some kind of a conference going on.'

'There's a hole in one of the walls of the conference room – at least, I think it must be a conference room,' said Jack, suddenly excited. 'I saw a round table, and chairs, and writing pads and pencils all set out. If we could get up to that room, and look through the hole, we might see something interesting – and hear something too!'

'We might,' agreed Bill. 'Come on – let's get going. Into the bell tower we go! Where's that trap door you told us about?'

They were soon in the bell tower. Jack searched about for the trap door. He found it, and Bill pulled it open. Down they went into the little cellar below. Bill pulled the trap door shut behind him.

'Lead the way, Jack,' he said, and flashed on an extremely powerful torch. With a jump Jack saw that both men now carried revolvers too. Gosh – this might be a serious business then!

'This way,' said Jack, and stepped over the junk in the underground hole. 'Better be as quiet as we can. Now – through here!'

28

To Borken Castle again!

Jack clambered through the round hole at the other end of the little cellar. He was now in the very narrow, low-roofed passage he remembered so well, because he had had to walk through it with his head well bent. He led Bill and Ronnie up the steeply sloping way, lit by Bill's powerful torch.

Jack stopped when they came to the top of the long, sloping passage. 'We're very near the room where the spy-hole is,' he whispered. 'If there is a conference being held – or some sort of meeting – we'll be able to look through the hole at it – or you will, Bill, because as far as I know there's only one hole.'

'Let me know when we come to it,' whispered Bill, and they went on again. In a short while Jack saw a little beam of light coming from the side of the right-hand wall – that must be the spyhole!

He whispered to Bill. Bill saw the beam of light and nodded. There was not room for him to get in front of Jack, so the boy went on past the little spyhole, and let Bill stand by it behind him. Ronnie was by Bill, quite silent. Kiki had been tapped on the beak, so she knew she was to be quiet too.

Bill glued his eye to the spyhole. He saw the same room that Jack had seen – a room with a round table, chairs pulled up to it, and writing materials on the table.

But now there were lights blazing in the room – and every chair at the table was filled. At the top sat Count Paritolen. Beside him sat his sister, Madame Tatiosa. On his other side sat someone else, whom Bill knew from photographs – the Prime Minister, husband of Madame Tatiosa. He looked ill at ease and grave. Men in military uniform were also round the table.

At the bottom of the table stood a tall man, with a great likeness to Gussy – his uncle, the King! Bill heaved a sigh of relief. So he hadn't been killed. Well, that was one good thing at any rate. If only he could be got away, things could be put right very quickly, and civil war would be avoided.

Bill strained his ears to hear what was going on. He could not hear very well, behind the wooden panelling, but he heard enough to know what was happening.

The King was being urged to abdicate – to leave his throne, go into retirement, and let Gussy – the Prince Aloysius – rule in his stead.

'If you will not sign this document of abdication, then it will be the worse for you,' finished Count Paritolen. 'You will, I fear, not be heard of again.'

Bill followed this with difficulty, for he did not speak Tauri-Hessian well. He had, in fact, only tried to learn it when he knew he might have to go to the country. But he had no doubt that that was what the Count was saying.

The Prime Minister said something in protest, but the Count would not listen. Madame Tatiosa made a short, angry speech and sat down. The King bowed, and then spoke in such a low voice that Bill couldn't hear a word.

'Very well,' said the Count. 'You may have tonight to make up your mind – tonight only. We will adjourn this meeting.'

He stood up and so did everyone else. The Count went out with his sister and the Prime Minister. The King followed, closely hemmed in by four men. He looked sad and worried.

The lights in the conference room dimmed, and there was silence. Bill turned to Ronnie and repeated rapidly what he had seen and what he thought had happened.

'As far as I can make out the King's got tonight to think things over. If he says no, he *won't* give up the throne, that's the end of him. I think he will say no.'

There was a silence behind the wooden panelling for a moment or two. Bill debated with himself. Could he get back to the capital of Tauri-Hessia, tell what he had seen, and bring men to rescue the King?

No – there wouldn't be time – the capital town was too far off. There was only one sure thing to do – and that was to see if he himself could get the King away.

He whispered this to Jack. The boy nodded. 'Yes. If only we knew where he was going to be tonight! He won't be put into the tower room, I'm sure. They'd be afraid he'd escape too, like Gussy. Let's go to the ballroom, where that moving picture hangs – we might be able to shove it aside and get into the room.'

He led the way again – up some very steep steps, up and up. Then round a sharp corner and into a narrow, dark passage running just inside the walls of the rooms, but a little below the level of the floor. Then came a small flight of steps, and Jack paused.

'These are the steps that lead up to that picture,' he whispered. 'You must see if you can find out how to move it away from the hole, Bill – it slides right away from it, keeping level with the wall.'

Bill and Ronnie began to feel about all over the place. Bill suddenly found a knob. Ah – this must be it! A pull at this might set the mechanism working that moved the picture away, and left a hole in its place.

He listened carefully. No noise came from the room within. Well – he'd have to risk it, anyhow. Bill pulled the knob.

Nothing happened. He twisted it. Still nothing happened. Then he pushed it – and it gave beneath his hand.

Then came a slight scraping noise, and it seemed to Bill as if part of the wall was disappearing! But it was only the picture moving to one side, leaving a hole almost as large as itself – the secret entrance to the ballroom!

There was very little light in the big room – merely a dim glow from a lamp whose wick had been turned down. Bill peered out.

'No one here,' he whispered to the others. 'We'll get into the room while we can.'

He climbed out of the hole and jumped lightly to the floor. The others followed. Their rubber shoes made no sound.

'We'd better just go and *see* if the King has been put into the tower room,' whispered Jack. 'I'll go. I know the way. You stay here – behind these curtains.'

He sped into the anteroom, and saw the spiral stairway. He stopped and listened. No sound anywhere. He ran up the steps quietly and came to the little landing. He flashed his torch on the door that led into the room where Philip and the others had been imprisoned.

It was wide open! The room beyond was dark, too, so it was plain that the King was not imprisoned there. Jack went down again.

He tiptoed to the curtains behind which Bill and Ronnie were hiding. 'No good,' he whispered. 'The door's wide open. He's not there.'

'Listen!' said Bill, suddenly. 'I can hear something!'

They They listened. It was the clump-clump of marching feet. They came nearer and nearer. It sounded like two or three people. Bill peeped round the side of the curtain when the sound had passed by.

'Two soldiers,' he whispered. 'They must have gone to relieve two others on guard somewhere – and who should they be guarding but the King? We'll wait and see if two others come back this way, then we shall know the first two have gone on guard somewhere – and we'll explore down that passage, where the first two went.'

'When I was here before, the sentry on guard kept disappearing down there,' said Jack, remembering. 'It's a kind of sentry beat, I think. Perhaps the King has been taken down there and locked into a cell.'

'Listen!' said Ronnie. Back came marching feet again and two different sentries went by smartly in the opposite direction from the others, and disappeared. The three could hear the sound of their feet for some time, and then no more.

'Now!' said Bill. 'And keep your ears open and your eyes peeled too.'

They all went down the dark passage where the two first sentries had gone. Right down to the end – round a sharp-angled turn, and down a few steps – along a narrower passage, and round another turn. But here they stopped. They could hear marching feet again – coming nearer!

There was a room opening off near where the three stood. Bill pushed open the door and the three went into it hurriedly. It was quite dark. Bill switched his torch on for a moment and they saw that it was a kind of box-room. The sentires passed right by it, went a good way up the passage and then, stamp-stamp, they turned and came back again.

Bill listened to their feet marching. They seemed to go a long way down the passage, a long, long way, before they turned to come back. 'I should think the King must be locked up somewhere about the middle of their sentry-go,' said Bill. 'We'll let them come up here once more, and when they have gone right past us, up to the other end of their beat, we'll slip down here and explore a bit. We can always go and hide beyond the other end of their walk, if we hear them coming back.'

The sentries came marching back, passed the three hidden in the little box room again, and went on to the end of their beat. Bill, Ronnie and Jack slipped quickly out of the box room and ran lightly down the passage. They turned a corner and came to a dead end. A stout door faced them, well and truly bolted – and locked too, as Bill found when he tried to open it!

'Sssst!' said Ronnie, suddenly, and pulled them back into a dark corner. Bill and Jack wondered what had scared him – then they saw!

A door was opening silently opposite to them – a door they hadn't seen because it was part of the panelling itself. Someone came through carrying a lamp. It was the Count Paritolen. Had he come to kill the King? Or to try once more to persuade him to give up his throne?

Bill saw something else. He saw what the Count was holding – a big key! The key to the King's room, no doubt!

The Count heard the sentries coming back and went back through the hidden door, closing it softly. He evidently meant to wait till the sentries had come up and then had gone back again.

'Ronnie,' said Bill, his mouth close to his friend's ear, 'we get that key, do you understand? And we get the Count too. Will you tackle him while I open the door and find out if the King's there? He mustn't make any noise.'

'He won't,' said Ronnie, grimly. The sentries came right up, and then turned, stamp-stamp, and went back again. As soon as they had turned the first corner, the hidden door opened again, and the Count stepped through swiftly, lamp in one hand, key in the other.

Everything happened so quickly then that Jack was bewildered. He heard an exclamation from the Count, and then he saw Bill running to the door with the key, and Ronnie dragging the Count hurriedly back through the hidden door. The lamp went out. There was complete silence.

Ronnie came back and switched on his torch. He saw Bill unlocking the door and pulling back bolts. 'I found a nice little cell back there,' he said, jerking his head towards the door. 'Just right for the Count. He's tied up and he can shout the place down if he likes – nobody can hear him in that room!'

'Good work,' said Bill. 'Blow these bolts – there are half a dozen of them! We'll have the sentries back here before we know where we are!'

Ronnie blew out the passage lamp that shone near the

door. 'Don't want the sentries to see the bolts are drawn!' he said. 'Buck up, Bill. They're coming back. Jack and I will wait here – just in *case* there's trouble with the sentries. Do buck up!'

29

An exciting time

Bill at last got the door open and went in. A shaft of light shone out from the room at once. Ronnie shut the door quickly. Jack found that his heart was beginning to thump again. Those sentries – would they come back before Bill had got the King?

The door opened again, but this time no shaft of light showed. Bill had turned out the lamp inside the room. Someone was with him – the King. Oh, good! thought Jack.

The sentries were coming back. Their feet could be clearly heard. Bill hurried the King across to the hidden door, opened it and pushed him through. Ronnie followed, and then Jack.

Just in time! 'Do you suppose they'll see the door is unbolted?' said Jack. 'You didn't have time to bolt it.'

'We'll soon know!' said Bill. 'I'm afraid they *will* notice it – it's their job to check up on that, I'm sure.'

Jack suddenly gave a little cry. 'Kiki! Where is she? She was on my shoulder a minute ago, now she's gone. I never felt her fly off in my excitement. Oh, Bill – she must be out there in the passage somewhere.'

She was – and she was very much annoyed to find that Jack seemed to have disappeared. Where was he? She could hear the sentries coming nearer and nearer, and the sound of their clump-clump-clumping annoyed her.

She flew up to a jutting-out stone in the wall, and when

the two men marched just below her, she hooted long and loud.

'HOOOOOO! HOOO-HOOO-HOOO!'

The sound of marching feet stopped abruptly. One of the men said something quickly to the other in a frightened voice.

Kiki yapped like a dog and then snarled. It sounded most extraordinary in that dark, echoing passage. The men looked all round. Where was the dog?

'Mee-ow-ow-ow!' wailed Kiki, like a hungry cat, and then went off into a cackle of laughter.

'Wipe your feet, blow your nose, pop goes the weasel, pop-pop-pop!'

The men didn't understand a word, of course, but that frightened them all the more. They clutched each other, feeling the hairs on their head beginning to prickle in fright.

Kiki coughed and cleared her throat in a remarkably human way. Why that should have put the two sentries into an absolute panic she couldn't guess! But it certainly did, and, casting their rifles away, they fled down the passage at top speed, howling out something in their own language.

Jack had heard all this, for he had opened the hidden door a little, feeling anxious about Kiki. He listened to her performance with a grin. Good old Kiki! He called her softly and she flew down to his shoulder in delight.

Bill wondered what would be the best thing to do now. It would be dangerous to go back the way they had come, because the scared sentries would certainly arrive back with others to probe into the mystery of the hooting and barking and mewing and coughing!

'I wonder if the passage behind this hidden door leads anywhere except to the room you put the Count in,' said Bill to Ronnie.

'We'll go and ask him,' said Ronnie, cheerfully. 'I'll poke this in his ribs and see if he'll talk.' 'This' was his revolver. Bill laughed.

'You won't need that. He'll talk all right when he sees the King here. Your Majesty, perhaps *you* would like to deal with the Count, and command him to show us the way out?'

The King could talk perfect English. Like Gussy, he had been sent to England to be educated. He nodded, his eyes gleaming. It was obvious that he would certainly enjoy a few words with the Count!

They went to the cell-like room into which Ronnie had shoved the Count, locking him in, nicely tied up. Count Paritolen was on the floor, looking furious. When he saw the King he looked so thunderstruck that Bill laughed.

'Undo his legs, Ronnie, but not his arms,' said Bill. 'He should stand up politely before the King.'

The Count's legs were untied and he stood up, his face very pale indeed. The King began to address him in vigorous Tauri-Hessian. The Count wilted – his head hung forward – and finally he fell on his knees, a picture of misery and fright. The King touched him contemptuously with his foot, and said a few more words. The Count got up again, and said, 'Ai! Ai! Ai!' eagerly, which Jack knew to mean 'Yes! Yes! Yes!'

'He's going to show us the way out,' said Bill. 'Good thing too. I seem to hear a tremendous noise starting up somewhere in the distance. No doubt our friends the sentries have brought all their buddies along – and have discovered the unbolted door and the empty room. Tell the Count to get a move on, Ronnie.'

With his arms still tied behind him the Count stumbled out of the little bare room. He led them to a door opposite and kicked it open. A small stairway led downwards. 'I'll go first,' said Ronnie, and nipped in front of the Count.

The steps led down to a little panelled room, rather like a small study. The Count said a few words, nodding his head at a panel. Ronnie stepped forward and slid the panel downwards. A hole just big enough for a man to squeeze through was now showing. Nothing could be seen the other side because something was hanging over it.

'Tapestry hangings,' said Bill, and knocked his hand against it. 'Well, well — nice lot of hidey-holes and secrets you've got here, Count. Very nice indeed. What do we do next? Get behind this tapestry?'

'He says it's tapestry hanging in one of the bedrooms,' said Ronnie. 'If we make our way behind it a bit, we'll come to an opening. Here goes!'

He went through the hole, and made his way behind endless tapestry that hung loose from ceiling to floor. At last he came to where, as the Count had said, there was an opening. It was where two different pieces of tapestry met. Ronnie poked his way between them and found himself in a bedroom. He saw beautiful furniture and carpets as he flashed his torch round. The room was quite empty.

The others came out into the room too, having made their way behind the tapestry. Jack sneezed because it was full of dust. Kiki promptly sneezed too, much to the Count's amazement. He had not met Kiki before!

'Now where?' said Ronnie, digging his revolver into the Count's ribs quite suddenly. The man gave a startled jump and almost fell over in fright.

'I hardly think that poke in the ribs was necessary,' said Bill, with a grin.

'No, not necessary — but awfully good for a nasty little double-crosser like him!' said Ronnie. 'People who threaten others with this, that and the other when they are in power deserve a bit of a fright from my gun. Now then, Count — the quickest and best way out, please!'

This last was said in Tauri-Hessian and the Count replied at once, his words tumbling over one another in his desire to please this fierce Englishman.

'It's easy now,' said Ronnie. 'We apparently go down the back stairs into the deserted kitchen quarters, and just let ourselves out of the back door. Nothing could be simpler!'

So down the back stairs they went, and into a vast

kitchen. Three cats were there, their eyes gleaming in the light of Bill's torch. Kiki yapped like a small dog, and the cats fled into corners at once.

'Kiki!' said Jack, with a laugh. 'You're irrepressible!'

Kiki tried to repeat the word and couldn't. Bill was now unlocking the great back door. They all went out into a big yard. Then down to the castle gate, a massive wrought iron affair, whose keys hung most conveniently at the side. Bill unlocked the gate and out they went, finding themselves in the main street of Borken.

'Now – where is the place we left the van?' wondered Bill. 'Jack, could you take Ronnie to it? Ronnie, we'll wait here for you.'

Jack sped off with Ronnie. He had been in the town several times and knew the way. He and Ronnie were soon in the field where they had left the van, and Ronnie started it up at once.

It was not long before the van drew up beside the other three in the dark highway. They got in. Bill was behind with the Count and Jack. The King went in front with Ronnie. It was queer to sit in the back, with all kinds of goods rattling on the shelves. The Count, however, took no notice. He was feeling extremely gloomy.

'I say – where are we going? This isn't the way back to the circus camp,' said Jack, suddenly.

'No, I know,' said Bill. 'I'm afraid we must go straight to the capital town of Tauri-Hessia, Jack – the King needs to be there at the earliest possible moment. Things are in a great turmoil, you see – nobody knows what is going to happen – no King – no Prince – the Count apparently trying to take things over – the Prime Minister a weak tool . . . '

'Yes, I see,' said Jack. 'But as soon as the King appears, everything will be all right, won't it?'

'It will certainly be all right after he has appeared to his people and spoken to them,' said Bill. 'He will have quite a lot of interesting things to tell them! I think, too, it is essential that Gussy should appear also – so that the people will be sure that he and his uncle are on good terms, and back each other up.'

'Oh, Gussy will love that!' said Jack. 'Do we go back to get him?'

'We do,' said Bill. 'And we also get the others. I'm sure the King will want to see Gussy's fellow prisoners. He has a lot to hear about, you know.'

The King certainly wanted to meet all the others when he heard the amazing story that Bill had to tell him. It was all told when they reached the Palace. Then, after a delighted and amazed welcome from a few servants on duty, the King retired to a little room with Bill, Ronnie and Jack. The Count was sent off in disgrace with four soldiers in front of him and four behind!

'Left, right, left, right!' shouted Kiki after him. 'God save the King!'

It was still dark, for the sun was not due to rise for another hour. Jack suddenly yawned. He really couldn't help it.

'You'd better have a snooze,' said Bill. 'The King is sending his State Car to fetch the others first thing in the morning. He will lend you some of Gussy's clothes, he says, if you want to look decent. The others are being sent clothes too, especially, of course, Gussy. He couldn't possibly appear in his girls' things!'

'This is going to be fun from now on,' said Jack, trying to keep awake. 'Oh, gosh, I'm sleepy. What are you going to do, Bill? Have a sleep, too?'

'No. I'm going to get in touch with your aunt by radio,' said Bill, 'and tell her you're all safe. I'll get her to fly out tomorrow, and we'll all be together again!'

Jack fell on to a sofa, feeling that he couldn't keep awake one moment longer. 'Good old Bill,' he said. 'Everything comes right when you're here. Good morning—I mean good night!'

And in half a second more he was fast asleep. What a night he had had!

30

'God Save the King!'

Jack awoke to find a pretty Tauri-Hessian maid bringing him a most magnificent breakfast. Somebody had undressed him, put silk pyjamas on him and popped him into a luxurious bed. He was amazed.

'To think they did all that and I never woke up!' he thought. 'I *must* have been tired! Gosh – what a breakfast! Kiki, look here – the biggest, juiciest grapefruit I ever did see in my life – and two halves, not one. You can have one for yourself if you don't make too much mess.'

Kiki approved of the grapefruit. She settled down to it, and for once in a way didn't say a word. Jack ate every scrap of the generous breakfast, and then lay back, thinking over the happenings of the night before.

'I bet the Count isn't eating a breakfast like this,' he told Kiki. 'What do *you* think?'

'The doctor's got a cold, fetch the King,' said Kiki, looking to see if Jack had left any of his grapefruit. 'One, two, how-do-you-do?'

'Buckle my shoe, you mean,' said Jack. '*I say* – look! Do you suppose those princely clothes are for me to put on, Kiki, old bird? Goodness, the Tauri-Hessians won't know if I'm the Prince, or Gussy.'

Bill came in, looking much smartened up. 'Oh, you're awake at last,' he said. 'My word, you don't mean to say you ate *all* that breakfast!'

'Kiki helped me,' said Jack, with a grin. 'Have the others been sent for yet, Bill?'

'Yes. I'd like to see their faces when the King's State Car rolls up, complete with clothes for them all,' said Bill. 'The King's a great sport. He's asked Pedro, Toni, Bingo and old

Ma too – and sent clothes for them all!'

'Goodness!' said Jack. 'Old Ma! She'll have the time of her life. But if it hadn't been for her looking after Gussy he'd certainly have been caught. I say – this is going to be quite a party, isn't it?'

'Oh, quite,' said Bill. 'And your aunt is arriving today too!'

'It's just like a pantomime ending!' said Jack, delighted. 'Everyone on the stage at the end!'

'You'd better get up,' said Bill. 'The King is making his speech to the people at twelve o'clock, and it's now eleven. After that there is to be a really splendid luncheon laid on – and you'll be sorry you ate so much breakfast, I can tell you!'

Jack leapt out of bed. 'Is it really eleven o'clock? Gosh, I'll never be ready. I don't know how to put all these clothes on – buckles – sashes – ruffles – good gracious, is it royal dress?'

'No. Ordinary Tauri-Hessian festival wear,' said Bill. 'I don't feel able to cope with it myself, nor does Ronnie. We feel a bit more at ease in our own things, but you and the others will look fine.'

Jack was ready at a quarter to twelve. He looked at himself in the glass. 'Gracious – I'm like a theatrical prince. I really must have my photograph taken to show the boys at school – they'll be amazed!'

There came the sound of cheering in the street below. Jack opened his window and looked out. A very grand State Car was being driven slowly up the street, followed by yet another. The people were cheering each one as it went by.

Jack nearly fell out of the window, and Kiki gave a loud screech. 'Look, Kiki – do you see who's in the first car!' cried Jack. 'Lucy-Ann, Philip, Gussy and Dinah! Did you ever see anyone looking so grand? And look in the second car – Pedro – Ma – Toni and Bingo! They look as fine as if they were just going to perform in the circus ring!'

So they did. Ma, especially, looked magnificent, and she

had a sudden unexpected dignity that made Pedro look at her with surprise and great pride. His mother! Old Ma, riding in a State Car, wearing silk clothes right down to her skin! Pedro couldn't believe it.

He looked very grand himself, and enjoyed it. He knew that nothing like this would ever happen to him again in his life and he meant to enjoy every moment of it.

Toni and Bingo looked grand but subdued. They were not in the least nervous when they went into the circus ring – but they couldn't help feeling nervous now – all this cheering and shouting when they weren't even performing!

The cars turned in at the gates, and Jack leaned out of the window and yelled, quite forgetting that he was in a King's palace.

'Lucy-Ann! I'm up here!'

Kiki squawked too. 'Hip-hip-hip-hip-hurrah! Send for the doctor!'

Twelve o'clock came. The King went out on the balcony of his palace to show himself to his people and to make a speech to explain all that had happened. There was dead silence as the loud-speakers relayed the simple, vigorous speech.

Bill thought that Tauri-Hessia had a very fine King. He was glad that the Count had not dethroned him and put Gussy up as King himself. Gussy was just a timid little boy at present – but perhaps, when he had learnt all that his good school had to teach him, at lessons and at games, he would make as fine a King as his uncle.

Gussy had a tremendous reception when his uncle called him to his side, and presented him to the people. After all the scares of the last few days, they needed to see not only the King but the little Prince too.

Gussy looked every inch a Prince, as he saluted stiffly, and then bowed in every direction. He wore magnificent clothes, and his cloak blew out in the wind, showing its scarlet lining. Jack grinned as he thought how Gussy had looked

184

when he had seen him last – dressed as a girl, with his long hair tied up in bows. Poor Gussy! Nobody must ever learn of that, or he would be teased about it for the rest of his life – and Gussy did not like teasing.

The next thing was the luncheon. The children had all been put at a table together, with Gussy and Pedro as well. Ma, Toni and Bingo were at a side table too, very conscious of their fine clothes. They used fine manners to match, and ate everything with knives, forks or spoons, instead of using only their fingers half the time as they usually did.

The six children talked eagerly together, exchanging news. 'Fank is up and about again,' said Philip. 'Thank goodness he is, or I couldn't have come. Hallo, Snoozy, do you want to join us at last? He's seen those almonds, Dinah – do look at him, holding one and nibbling it!'

'I don't like him on the table,' said Dinah, but she was much too happy to make a fuss. She told Jack of the excitement when the message came that they were all to dress in State clothes and be driven to the Palace. 'We just couldn't believe it!' she said. 'Tell us again about last night, Jack, and how you rescued the King and caught the Count.'

Gussy was tremendously excited. His eyes sparkled, and he talked nineteen to the dozen. He felt in his element now – he was a Prince, the heir to the throne, Prince Aloysius Gramondie – not a timid little boy with a lot of long hair!

'Here's Aunt Allie!' cried Lucy-Ann, suddenly. She threw down her table-napkin and flew across the luncheon room, thinking of nothing but welcoming the person she loved so much. 'Aunt Allie! You've come!'

Mrs Cunningham was being ushered into the great room by two servants, who called out her name. Bill went to her at once, and Dinah, Philip and Jack joined Lucy-Ann in her rush across the room. This was all that was needed to make things perfect!

Bill's eyes were shining as he took his wife to introduce her to the King. A place had been left for her on his other side, for her aeroplane had been expected for the last half hour. She was quite bewildered by everything, for she knew only half the story, of course.

Gussy waited till the others had made enough fuss of her and then went up himself. She held out her hand to him, and he bowed over it, and kissed it politely, just as his uncle had done. Somehow it seemed right in Tauri-Hessia – quite a natural thing to do, and none of the children even thought of laughing.

After the grand lunch the children went to see over the Palace. 'My word – you're lucky to be able to spend the rest of your hols here, Gussy,' said Jack. 'It's a wonderful place. Not that I'd like to *live* here, of course – but to stay for a few weeks as you'll be able to do – you're jolly luck!'

'We shall miss you, Gussy,' said Lucy-Ann. 'I suppose we'll be leaving tomorrow, or sometime soon. I'm quite sorry this adventure is over.'

'But it *isn't*,' said Gussy, his face beaming all over. 'It isn't! I have asked my uncle to let me have you here as my guests. You will stay? Or do you not like me well enough? You have so often tizzed me – like when my finger blidded.'

'Oh, Gussy – it doesn't mean we don't like people when we tease them!' said Lucy-Ann. 'Do you *really* mean that your uncle wants us to stay? All of us? I don't want to stay without Bill and Aunt Allie.'

'All of you',' said Gussy, beaming again. 'Kiki and Snoozy too. But not Pedro and the others because they must go with the circus, they say. Then you will stay with me till we go back to school togezzer?'

'We'd love to,' said Jack. 'I could do with a couple of weeks in a Palace. I'll take some pictures back to show the boys. They'll think I'm telling them fairy-tales if I don't!'

Pedro, Ma, Toni and Bingo said goodbye to the five children that evening. They were still wearing their splendid clothes. 'We've been told we can keep them,' said Pedro, grinning. 'I shall fancy myself when I go into the ring to help

Toni and Bingo set up their wires now – the Great and Only Pedro the Magnificent.'

He bowed himself almost to the ground. Ma gave him a resounding slap. 'Ha! You will peel potatoes for your old Ma tonight!' she said, and laughed loudly. Kiki imitated her and made her laugh all the more.

The children were sorry when the circus folk had gone. They had been such good friends. 'I hope we'll see them sometime again,' said Lucy-Ann. 'I liked them all.'

'You will now come to my uncle and tell him you will stay, plizz?' begged Gussy, who seemed to think they might change their minds. 'And I have to ask him something. You must help me with it.'

He dragged them off to his uncle's room. They all bowed politely. 'Well, Aloysius,' said the King, looking amused. 'Have you persuaded your friends to put up with you and stay for the rest of the holidays?'

'They will stay,' said Gussy. 'And, sir, I have something else to beg of you – BEG of you, sir. These boys, they will tell you it is very, very important. You will grant it to me, sir?'

'I might, as I feel quite pleased with you at the moment,' said his uncle, smiling. 'But tell me what it is first.'

'It is my *hair*,' said Gussy. 'I want it short – snip snip – like Philip's and Jack's. I will not look like a girl, I WILL NOT.'

'You're not supposed to wear it short, Aloysius,' said his uncle, 'but I know how you feel. I felt the same when I was a Prince and went to school in England. Very well – you shall have it cut short!'

Gussy's face was a study. Nothing in the world could have pleased him more. 'I go tomorrow,' he said. 'I go tomorrow at seven o'clock in the morning. Ha – it will be so short that never will a ribbon sit on it again!'

'Thank you for asking us to stay, Your Majesty,' said Jack, speaking for all the others. 'We shall love it, and it's nice of Gussy to want us.'

'Fussy-Gussy!' cried Kiki, saying quite the wrong thing.

'Fussy-Gussy! Your Majesty! Majesty, Majesty! Send for the doctor, Blow your nose.'

'*Kiki!*' said Jack, shocked.

Kiki looked at the King. She raised her crest to its fullest height, and gave a little bow. 'Your Majesty!' she said. 'God save the King!'

The River of
Adventure

Contents

1

Four miserable invalids

'Poor Polly!' said a small sad voice outside the bedroom door. 'Poor Polly! Blow your nose, poor Polly!'

There was the sound of loud sniffs, and after that came a hacking cough. Then there was a silence, as if the person outside the door was listening to see if there was any answer.

Jack sat up in bed and looked across at Philip in the opposite bed.

'Philip – do you feel you can bear to let Kiki come in? She sounds so miserable.'

Philip nodded. 'All right. So long as she doesn't screech or make too much noise. My head's better, thank goodness!'

Jack got out of bed and went rather unsteadily to the door. He and Philip, and the two girls as well, had had influenza quite badly, and were still feeling rather weak. Philip had had it worst, and hadn't been able to bear Kiki the parrot in the bedroom. She imitated their coughs and sneezes and sniffs, and poor Philip, much as he loved birds and animals, felt as if he could throw slippers and books and anything handy at the puzzled parrot.

Kiki came sidling in at the door, her crest well down. 'Poor thing,' said Jack, and she flew up to his shoulder at once. 'You've never been kept out before, have you? Well, nobody likes your kind of noises when their head is splitting, Kiki, old thing. You nearly drove Philip mad when you gave your imitation of an aeroplane in trouble!'

'Don't!' said Philip, shuddering to think of it. 'I feel as if I'll never laugh at Kiki's noises again.' He coughed and felt for his handkerchief under the pillow.

Kiki coughed too, but very discreetly. Jack smiled. 'It's no good, Kiki,' he said. 'You haven't got the flu, so it's no use pretending you have.'

'Flue, flue, sweep the flue,' said Kiki at once, and gave a small cackle of laughter.

'No, we're not quite ready yet to laugh at your idiotic remarks, Kiki,' said Jack, getting back into bed. 'Can't you produce a nice bedside manner – quiet voice, and sympathetic nods and all that?'

'Poor Polly,' said Kiki, and nestled as close to Jack's neck as she could. She gave a tremendous sigh.

'Don't – not down my neck, please,' said Jack. 'You *are* feeling sorry for yourself, Kiki! Cheer up. We're all better today and our temperatures are down. We'll soon be up and about, and I bet Aunt Allie will be glad. Four wretched invalids must have kept her hands full.'

The door opened cautiously, and Aunt Allie looked in. 'Ah – you're both awake,' she said. 'How do you feel? Would you like some more lime juice?'

'No, thanks,' said Jack. 'I tell you what I suddenly – quite suddenly – feel like, Aunt Allie – and that's a boiled egg with bread-and-butter! It came over me all at once that that was what I wanted more than anything else in the world!'

Aunt Allie laughed. 'Oh – you *are* better then. Do *you* want an egg too, Philip?'

'No, thanks,' said Philip. 'Nothing for me.'

'Poor boy, poor boy,' said Kiki, raising her head to look at Philip. She gave a small cackle.

'Shut up,' said Philip. 'I'm not ready to be laughed at yet, Kiki. You'll be turned out of the room again if you talk too much.'

'Silence, Kiki!' said Jack and gave the parrot a small tap on the beak. She sank down into his neck at once. She didn't mind being silent, if only she were allowed to stay with her beloved Jack.

'How are the two girls?' asked Jack.

'Oh, *much* better,' said Aunt Allie. 'Better than you two are. They are playing a game of cards together. They wanted to know if they could come into your room this evening and talk.'

'I'd like that,' said Jack. 'But Philip wouldn't, would you, Phil?'

'I'll see,' said Philip, grumpily. 'I still feel awfully bad-tempered. Sorry.'

'It's all right, Philip,' said his mother. 'You're on the mend – you'll feel yourself tomorrow!'

She was right. By the evening of the next day Philip was very lively, and Kiki was allowed to chatter and sing as much as she liked. She was even allowed to make her noise of an express train racing through a tunnel, which brought Mrs Cunningham up the stairs at once.

'Oh *no!*' she said. 'Not *that* noise in the house, please, Kiki! I can't bear it!'

Dinah looked at her mother, and reached out her hand to her. 'Mother, you've had an awful time looking after the four of us. I'm glad you didn't get the flu too. You look very pale. You don't think you're going to have it, do you?'

'No, of course not,' said her mother. 'I'm only just a bit tired racing up and down the stairs for the four of you. But you'll soon be up and about – and off to school!'

Four groans sounded at once – and then a fifth as Kiki joined in delightedly, adding the biggest groan of the lot.

'School!' said Jack, in disgust. 'Why did you remind us of that, Aunt Allie? Anyway I hate going back after the term's begun – everyone has settled down and knows what's what, and you feel almost like a new boy.'

'You *are* sorry for yourselves!' said Mrs Cunningham, with a laugh. 'Well, go on with your game – but do NOT let Kiki imitate aeroplanes, trains, cars or lawn-mowers.'

'Right,' said Jack, and addressed himself sternly to Kiki. 'Hear that, old thing? Behave yourself – if you can.'

'Mother does look a bit off-colour, doesn't she?' said Philip, dealing out the cards. 'I hope Bill will take her for a holiday when he comes back from wherever he is.'

'Where *is* he? And hasn't anyone heard from him lately?' asked Dinah, picking up her cards.

'Well, you know what old Bill is – always on some secret

hush-hush job for the Government,' said Philip. 'I think Mother *always* knows where he is, but nobody else does. He'll pop up out of the blue sooner or later.'

Bill was Mrs Cunningham's husband. He had married her not so very long ago, when she was the widowed Mrs Mannering, and had taken on Dinah and Philip, her own children, and the other two, Jack and Lucy-Ann, who had always looked on her as an aunt. They had no parents of their own. All of them were very fond of the clever, determined Bill, whose job so often took him into danger of all kinds.

'I hope Bill will come back before we return to school,' said Jack. 'We haven't seen him for ages. Let's see – it's almost October now – and he went off into the blue at the beginning of September.'

'Disguised!' said Lucy-Ann, remembering. 'Disguised as an old man, do you remember? I couldn't think who the old, bent fellow was who was sitting with Mother that night he left. Even his hair was different.'

'He had a wig,' said Jack. 'Buck up, Dinah – it's your turn. Have you got the king or have you not?'

Dinah played her card, and then turned to the radio nearby. 'Let's have the radio on, shall we?' she said. 'I feel as if I'd like to hear it tonight. Philip, can you bear it?'

'Yes,' said Philip. 'Don't pity me any more. I'm as right as rain now. Gosh – when I think how miserable I was I really feel ashamed. I wouldn't have been surprised if I'd burst into tears at any time!'

'You did once,' said Jack, unfeelingly. 'I saw you. You looked most peculiar.'

'Shut up,' said Philip, in a fierce voice. 'And don't tell fibs. Dinah, that set's not tuned properly. Here, let me do it – you're never any good at that sort of thing! Dinah – let *me* do it, I said. Blow you!'

'Aha! Our Philip is quite himself again!' said Jack, seeing one of the familiar brother-and-sister quarrels beginning to spring up once more. 'You've got it, now, Philip – it's bang on the station. Ah – it's a skit on a burglary with John Jordans in it. It should be funny. Let's listen.'

It *was* funny, and Aunt Allie, having a quiet rest downstairs, was pleased to hear sudden roars of laughter upstairs. Then she heard a loud and prolonged whistle and frowned. That tiresome parrot!

But it wasn't Kiki. It was John Jordans in the comical play. He was the policeman, and was blowing his police whistle – pheeeeeeee! Then someone yelled 'Police! Police!' and the whistle blew again.

'Police, police!' yelled Kiki too, and produced a marvellous imitation of the whistle. 'PHEEEEEEEE! Police! Police! PHEEEEEEEEEEEE!'

'Shut up, Kiki! If you shout and whistle as loudly as that you'll have the *real* police here!' said Jack. 'Oh, my goodness! – I hope Kiki doesn't start doing this police-whistle business. She'll get us into no end of trouble! Kiki – if you shout "Police" *once* more, I'll put you down at the very bottom of the bed.'

Before Kiki could make any reply, a knock came on the bedroom door – a most imperious knock that made them all jump. A loud voice came through the door.

'Who wants the police? They're here. Open in the name of the law!'

The door opened slowly, and the startled children watched in amazement. What did this mean? Had the police really come?

A face came round the door, a smiling face, round and ruddy and twinkling, one that the children knew well and loved.

'BILL!' cried four voices, and the children leapt out of bed at once, and ran to the tall, sturdy man at the door. 'Oh, Bill – you've come back! We never heard you come home. Good old Bill!'

2

What a surprise!

Bill came right into the room and sat down on Jack's bed. Kiki gave a loud cackle of pleasure and flew to his shoulder, nipping the lobe of his ear gently. Aunt Allie came in too, smiling happily, looking quite different now that Bill had arrived.

'Well, what's this I hear about four miserable invalids?' said Bill, putting an arm round each of the two girls. 'You'll have to get up now I'm back, you know. Can't have you lazing in bed like this!'

'We're getting up tomorrow at teatime,' said Lucy-Ann. 'Bill, where have you been? Tell us!'

'Sorry, old thing. Can't say a word,' said Bill.

'Oh – *very* hush-hush then!' said Dinah, disappointed. 'Are you going to stay at home now?'

'As far as I know,' said Bill. 'I sincerely hope so. It looks to me as if somebody ought to look after your mother now. She's gone thin. WHY did you all have to have flu together, so that she couldn't have any of you to help her?'

'It was very selfish of us!' said Jack. 'And even you were away too, Bill. Never mind – everything seems all right when you're here – doesn't it, Aunt Allie?'

Mrs Cunningham nodded. 'Yes. Everything!' she said. 'Shall we all have a picnic meal up here in the bedroom, children, so that we can have a good old talk with Bill?'

It was a very hilarious meal, with Kiki more ridiculous than usual, blowing her police-whistle whenever she felt like it. Everyone got tired of this new trick very quickly, even Bill.

'Bill! Bill, pay the bill, silly-billy, silly-bill!' shouted Kiki. She got a sharp tap on the beak from Jack.

'No rudery,' said Jack. 'Behave yourself, Kiki.'

Kiki flew down to the floor, very hurt. 'Poor Kiki, poor, poor,' she muttered to herself and disappeared under the bed, where she found an old slipper and spent a pleasant half-hour pecking off a button.

Everyone talked, asked questions, laughed and felt happy. The flu was quite forgotten. But about half-past nine Lucy-Ann suddenly went pale and flopped down on the bed.

'We've overdone it!' said Bill. 'I forgot they'd all had a pretty bad time. Come on, Lucy-Ann, I'll carry you to bed! Dinah, can you walk to your room?'

Next day the doctor came as usual, and was pleased with all four. 'Up to tea today – up after breakfast tomorrow,' he said. 'Then up the same time as usual.'

'When can they go back to school, Doctor?' asked Mrs Cunningham.

'Not yet,' said the doctor, much to the children's surprise. 'They *must* go somewhere for convalescence – ten days or a fortnight, say. Somewhere warm and sunny. This flu they've had is a bad kind – they will feel very down all winter if they don't go away somewhere. Can you manage that, Mrs Cunningham?'

'We'll see about it all right,' said Bill. 'But I'm not letting my wife go with them, Doctor. She needs a holiday herself now after so much illness in the house – and it wouldn't be much of a holiday for her to be with these four live wires. Leave it to me.'

'Right,' said the doctor. 'Well, I'll be in on Saturday, just to see that everything goes well. Goodbye!'

'A holiday!' said Dinah, as soon as the door had closed. 'I say! What a bit of luck! I thought we'd have to go straight back to school!'

There was a conference about what was best to be done. 'It's October tomorrow,' said Bill, 'and the weather forecast isn't too good. Rain and wind and fog! What a climate we have! It's a pity they can't go abroad, Allie.'

'They can't go abroad without anyone responsible in charge,' said his wife. 'We'll have to find somewhere on the south coast, and send them there.'

But all the plans were altered very suddenly and dramatically. On Friday night, very late, the telephone-bell shrilled through the house, and awoke Bill and his wife, and also Kiki, whose ears were sharper than anyone's. She imitated the bell under her breath, but didn't wake the boys. She cocked up her crest and listened. She could hear Bill speaking in a low voice on the telephone extension in his bedroom along the landing. Then there was a clink, and the little ping that sounded whenever the telephone receiver was put back into place.

'Ping!' muttered Kiki. 'Ping pong! Ping!' She put her head under her wing again, and went to sleep, perched comfortably on the edge of the mantelpiece. The children all slept peacefully, not guessing what changes in their plans that telephone call was going to mean!

In the morning Bill was not at breakfast. All the children were down, and Lucy-Ann had even got down early enough to help to lay the table. They were pale, and rather languid, but very cheerful, and looking forward now to their holiday, even though the place chosen did not seem at all exciting – a quiet little village by the sea.

'Where's Bill?' asked Dinah, in surprise at his empty place. 'I didn't hear him whistling while he was shaving. Has he gone out for an early-morning walk or something?'

'No, dear – he had to leave hurriedly in the middle of the night,' said her mother, looking depressed. 'He had a telephone call – didn't the bell wake you? Something urgent again, and Bill's advice badly needed, of course! So he took the car and shot off. He'll be back about eleven, I expect. I only hope it doesn't mean that he'll have to race off again somehwere, and disappear for weeks. It would be too bad so soon after he had come back!'

Bill returned about half-past eleven, and put the car away.

He came whistling in at the side door, to be met by an avalanche of children.

'Bill! Where have you been? You haven't got to go away again, have you?' cried Dinah.

'Let me go, you limpets!' said Bill, shaking them off. 'Where's your mother, Dinah?'

'In the sitting-room,' said Dinah. 'Hurry up and talk to her. *We* want to hear your news too.'

Bill went into the sitting-room and shut the door firmly. The four children looked at one another.

'I bet he'll be sent off on another hush-hush affair,' said Jack, gloomily. 'Poor Aunt Allie – just when she was looking forward to having him on a little holiday all to herself!'

Half an hour went by and the talking was still going on in the sitting-room, very low and earnest. Then the door was flung open and Bill yelled for the children.

'Where are you, kids? Come along in – we've finished our talk.'

They all trooped in, Kiki on Jack's shoulder as usual, murmuring something about 'One-two, buckle my shoe, one-shoe, buckle my two!'

'Shut up, Kiki,' said Jack. 'No interruptions, now!'

'Listen,' said Bill, when the children were all in the room and sitting down. 'I've got to go off again.'

Everyone groaned. 'Oh, *Bill*!' said Lucy-Ann. 'We were afraid of that. And you've only just come back.'

'Where are you going?' asked Jack.

'That I'm not quite sure about,' said Bill. 'But briefly – and in strict confidence, mind – I've got to go and cast an eye on a man our Government are a bit suspicious of – they don't quite know what he's up to. It may not be anything, of course – but we just want to be sure. And they want me to fly out and spend a few days round about where he is and glean a few facts.'

'Oh! So you may not be long?' said Philip.

'I don't know. Maybe three or four days, maybe a fort-

201

night,' said Bill. 'But two things are important – one, that nobody suspects I'm out there for any Government purpose – and two, that as the climate where I'm going is warm and summery, I feel you'd better all come too!'

There was a dead silence as this sank in – then a perfect chorus of shrieks and exclamations. Lucy-Ann flung herself on Bill.

'*All* of us! Aunt Allie too! Oh, how marvellous! But how can you take us as well?'

'Well, as I told you – nobody must suspect I'm a lone investigator snooping about on my own,' said Bill. 'And therefore if I go as a family man, complete with a string of children recovering from illness, and a wife who needs a holiday, it will seem quite obvious that I can't be what I really am – someone sent out on a secret mission.'

The children gazed at him in delight. A holiday somewhere abroad – with Bill *and* his wife! Could anything be better? 'Wizard!' thought Lucy-Ann. 'I hope it's not a dream!'

'Where did you say it was? Oh, you didn't say! Do we go to a hotel? What will there be to do? It's not dangerous, is it, Bill – dangerous for *you*?'

Questions poured out, and Bill shook his head and put his hands over his ears.

'It's no good asking me anything at the moment. I've only heard the outline of the affair myself – but I did say that as a kind of camouflage I could take you all with me, and pose as a family man – and it seemed to click, so I left the High-Ups to arrange everything. Honestly, that's all I know at the moment. And don't you dare to talk about this except in whispers.'

'We won't, Bill,' Lucy-Ann assured him earnestly. 'It shall be a dead secret.'

'Secret!' yelled Kiki, catching the general excitement and dancing up and down on the table. 'Secret! High-up secret! High, high, up in the sky, wipe your feet, blow the secret!'

'Well, if anyone's going to give it away, it's Kiki!' said Bill, laughing. 'Kiki, can't you ever hold your tongue?'

Kiki couldn't, but the others could, as Bill very well knew! They hurried out of the room and up the stairs and into a little boxroom. They shut the door, and looked at each other in excitement.

'Whew!' said Philip, letting out an enormous breath. 'What a THRILL! Thank goodness for the flu! Now – let's talk about it – in whispers, please!'

3
Away they go!

That weekend was full of excitement. The telephone went continually, and finally a small, discreet car drew up in the drive on Monday night, and three men got out; they went, as instructed, to the garden door, where Bill let them in. He called to the boys.

'Philip! Jack! Go and sit in that little car out there and keep watch. I don't think anyone is likely to be about, but you never know. These are important visitors, and although we don't think anyone knows of their visit here, you may as well keep watch.'

The boys were thrilled. They crept out to the car, and sat there, hardly breathing! They kept a very sharp look-out indeed, scrutinizing every moving shadow, and stiffening every time a car came up the quiet road. The girls watched them enviously from an upstairs window, wishing they were hidden in the car too.

But nothing exciting happened at all. It was very disappointing. In fact, the boys got very tired of keeping watch, when two or three hours had gone by. They were very thankful indeed when they heard the garden door opening quietly and footsteps coming to the car.

'Nothing to report, Bill,' whispered Jack, and was just about to slip away with Philip when Kiki decided that the time had come to open her beak again. She had not been allowed to make a single sound in the car, and had sulked. Now she really let herself go!

'Police! Fetch the police! PHEEEEEEEEE!' She whistled exactly like a real police-whistle being blown, and everyone was electrified at once. Bill hadn't heard Kiki's newest achievement, and he clutched at one of the three men in alarm. All of them stood stock still and looked round in amazement.

Jack's voice came penitently out of the darkness. 'Sorry, Bill. It's only Kiki's latest. I'm awfully sorry!'

He fled indoors with Philip. Kiki, sensing his annoyance, flew off his shoulder and disappeared. She let herself down into the big waste-paper basket in the sitting-room, and sat there very quietly indeed. Outside there was the sound of an engine being revved up, and the car moved quietly out of the gateway and disappeared into the night. Bill came back indoors.

'Well!' he said, coming into the sitting-room and blinking at the bright light. 'What came over Kiki to yell for the police like that? It nearly startled us out of our wits! My word, that whistle – it went clean through my head. Where is she? I've a few straight words to say to her!'

'She's hiding somewhere,' said Jack. 'She knows she shouldn't have done that. She heard it on the radio the other night, and she keeps *on* calling for the police and doing that awful whistling. Bill, any news?'

'Yes,' said Bill, filling his pipe. 'Quite a lot. Rather nice news, too – we're going to have some fun, children!'

'Really, Bill?' said his wife. 'How?'

'Well – the place we are going to – which I am not going to mention at present, in case Kiki is anywhere about, and shouts it all over the place – is quite a long way off, but as we are going by plane that won't matter. And, my dears, the Powers-That-Be have decided that they will put a small river-launch at our disposal, so that we can go on a nice little trip and see the country – enabling me to make quite a lot of enquiries on our journey!'

'It sounds great!' said Philip, his eyes shining. 'Absolutely tops! A river-launch of our own! My word, what a super holiday!'

'It does sound good,' said his mother. 'When do we go, Bill? I'll have to look out summer clothes again, you know.'

'We have to catch the plane on Wednesday night,' said Bill. 'Can you manage to be ready by then? Everything will be arranged for us at the other end – you won't have to bother about a thing.'

Everyone was in a great state of excitement at once, and began to talk nineteen to the dozen, the words almost falling over themselves. In the midst of a little pause for breath, a loud hiccup was heard.

'That's Kiki!' said Jack, at once. 'She always does that when she's ashamed or embarrassed – and I bet she was horrified at her outburst in the dark garden. Where is she?'

A search began, but Kiki was not behind the thick curtains, nor under the chairs or tables. Another hiccup made everyone look about them, puzzled. 'Where *is* she? We've looked absolutely everywhere. Kiki – come out, you fat-head. You haven't got hiccups – you're putting them on.'

A sad and forlorn voice spoke from the depths of the waste-paper basket. 'Poor Polly! Polly-Wolly-Olly all the day, poor Polly!' There followed a tremendous sigh.

'She's in the waste-paper basket!' cried Lucy-Ann, and ruffled all the papers there. Yes – Kiki was at the very bottom! She climbed out, her head hanging down, and walked awkwardly over the floor to Jack, climbed all the way up his foot and leg, up his body, to his shoulder.

'I suppose you've forgotten how to fly!' said Jack, amused. 'All right, you idiot – put up your crest and stop behaving like this. And DON'T shout for the police and blow that whistle any more!'

'You're going on a trip, Kiki,' said Dinah. But the parrot was still pretending to be very upset, and hid her head in Jack's collar. Nobody took any more notice of her, so she soon recovered, and began to enter into the conversation as usual.

After a while Mrs Cunningham gave a horrified exclamation. 'Do you know what the time is? Almost midnight – and these children only just recovered from being ill! What am I thinking of? They'll all be in bed again if we're not careful! Go to bed at once, children.'

They went upstairs, laughing. They had quite thrown off the miserable feeling they had had with the flu – and now that this exciting trip lay in front of them, they all felt on top of the world.

'I wonder where we're going to,' said Jack to Philip. 'Bill didn't tell us even when he thought Kiki wasn't there.'

'Bill's always cagey about everything till we're really off,' said Philip. 'It's no use badgering him – and anyway, what does it matter? It's wonderful to go off into the blue like this – literally into the blue, because we're going to fly – instead of straight back to school.'

'Lucy-Ann wouldn't like to hear me say so – but it's quite an adventure!' said Jack. 'Come on, get into bed. You must have brushed each of your teeth a hundred times.'

The next two days were very busy indeed. Summer clothes were taken from drawers and chests, canvas aeroplane-cases were thrown down from the loft by the boys, everyone hunted as usual for lost keys, and there was such a hubbub that Mrs Cunningham nearly went mad.

'Hubbub!' said Kiki, pleased with the new word, when she heard Bill complaining about it. 'Hubbub, hip-hip-hubbub! Fetch the doctor, Hubbub!'

'Oh, Kiki – I can't help laughing at you, even though I'm so busy,' said Mrs Cunningham. 'You and your hubbubs! You're a hubbub on your own.'

206

By Wednesday night all the bags were more or less neatly packed, the keys put safely in Bill's wallet, and arrangements made for someone to come in and air the house, and dust it each day. Bill went to get the car from the garage, and at last it was time to start.

Bill drove to the airport. It was exciting to arrive there at night, for the place was full of lights of all kinds. A loud amplifier was giving directions.

'Plane now arriving from Rome. Rome plane coming in.'

'The plane for Geneva will leave ten minutes late.'

'Plane arriving from Paris. Two minutes early.'

The little company, with Kiki on Jack's shoulder, sat in the waiting-room, for they were early. They began to feel sleepy in the warm room and Lucy-Ann felt her head nodding. Bill suddenly stood up.

'Here's our plane. Come on. We'll have to keep together, now. Don't let Kiki fly off your shoulder or scream or anything, Jack. Put her under your coat.'

Kiki grumbled away under Jack's coat, but as she felt a little overcome by the constant roar of arriving and departing planes, she said nothing out loud. Soon all six of them, and Kiki too, were safely in their plane-seats.

They were exceedingly comfortable, and the air hostess plied them with food and drink at once, which pleased the children immensely.

There was nothing to be seen outside the plane as it flew steadily through the night. The weather was good, the skies were clear and calm. All the children slept soundly in their tipped-back seats. Kiki, rather astonished at everything, settled under Jack's coat and went to sleep too.

The plane flew on and on. Stars faded in the sky. Dawn crept in from the east, and the sky became silver and then golden. The sun showed over the far horizon and the children awoke one by one, wondering at first where they were.

'Another two or three hours and we're there,' said Bill. 'Anyone want anything to eat? Here's our kind air hostess again.'

'I wish I *lived* on an aeroplane,' said Jack, when the air hostess brought them a tray full of most delicious food. 'Why is food always so super on a plane? Look at these enormous peaches – and I don't think I've *ever* tasted such delicious sandwiches!'

'This is fun!' said Lucy-Ann, taking her fourth sandwich. 'Jack, stop Kiki – that's her second peach, and she's spilling juice all over me!'

Yes, it was fun! *What* a bit of luck that Bill had to go on this trip!

4

What part of the world is this?

The children spent a good bit of time after that looking out of the windows and seeing the earth below. They were flying high, and very often wide stretches of white cloud, looking like fields of dazzling snow, lay below them. Then came gaps in the clouds and far down they could see hills and rivers and tiny towns or villages.

There was a great bustle when the plane at last landed on a long runway. Many men ran up, steps were wheeled here and there, luggage was unloaded, passengers streamed out of the plane and were soon greeted by friends.

A big car was waiting for Bill and his family. They were soon seated comfortably in it, and a very brown-skinned man drove them away.

'Everything laid on, you see,' said Bill. 'We are going to a fairly small place called Barira, where there is a very comfortable hotel. I don't want to stay in a large place, where someone might possibly recognize me. In fact, from now on I'm going to wear dark glasses.'

The 'small place' was a long way away, and it took the

car three hours to get there. The road was very bumpy in parts, and ran through country that was sometimes very well wooded and sometimes bare and desert-like. But at last they arrived, and the big car stopped outside a rambling hotel, white-washed from top to bottom.

The hotel manager himself came to receive them, small and plump, with a very big nose. He bowed himself almost to the ground, and then barked out very sharp orders in a language the children did not understand. Porters came up and unpacked the luggage from the car, perspiring in the hot sun.

'You wish to wash, Madame?' said the hotel manager. 'Everything is most ready, and we speak a hearty welcome to you.'

He bowed them into the hotel and took them to their rooms. These were spacious and airy, and very simply furnished. The children were delighted to find a shower bath in their rooms. Jack promptly stripped and stood underneath the tepid shower.

'Any idea where we've come to, Philip?' he called. 'I know Bill said it was somewhere called Barira, but I've never heard of it in my life.'

Bill came into their room just then. 'Well, everything all right?' he said. 'Where are the girls? Oh, is that their room next to yours? Good! Ours is just across the landing if you want us. We're to have a meal in about a quarter of an hour's time. Come and bang on our door when you're ready.'

'Hey, Bill – what part of the world are we in?' called Jack. 'The men we've seen look like Arabs.'

Bill laughed. 'Don't you know where we are? Well, we're some way from the borders of Syria – a very old part of the world indeed! Tell the girls to join you as soon as they can, will you?'

The small hotel proved to be extremely comfortable. Even Kiki was made welcome, after the manager had got over the shock of seeing the parrot perched on Jack's shoulder.

'Ha – what you call him – parrot!' said the little manager. 'Pretty Poll, eh?'

'Wipe your feet,' said Kiki, much to the man's surprise. 'Shut the door!'

The small man was not sure whether to obey or not. 'Funny bird!' he said. 'He is so much clever! He spiks good. Polly, polly!'

'Polly put the kettle on,' said Kiki, and gave a screech that made the man hurry out of the room at once.

There were no other guests at the hotel. The children sat in the shade on a verandah overhung with clusters of brilliant red flowers. Enormous butterflies fluttered among them. Kiki watched these with much interest. She knew butterflies at home, but these didn't seem at all the same. She talked to herself, and the waiters going to and fro regarded her with awe. When one of them coughed, and Kiki imitated him exactly, he looked very scared and ran off quickly.

'Don't show off, Kiki,' said Jack, sleepily. 'And for goodness' sake keep still. You've been dancing about on my shoulder for the last ten minutes.'

Next day plans were made for the river-trip, which was to last at least a week. Bill produced a map which showed the winding course of a river, and pointed to various places.

'We start here – that's where our launch will be. We go here first – see? And then down to this town – I don't know how you pronounce it – Ala-ou-iya – something like that. I leave you there and have a snoop round for my man – though, as I said, I might take you boys with me.'

'What's his name?' asked Jack.

'He calls himself Raya Uma,' said Bill. 'No one knows whether that is his real name or not, or exactly what nationality he is – but we do know he's a trouble-maker who wants watching. What he's out here for we simply can't imagine. It may be something that is perfectly innocent, but, knowing his record, I don't think so. Anyway, all I have to do is to spot him, find out what he's doing, and report back.

Nothing more – so there's no danger attached, or I wouldn't have brought you with me.'

'We wouldn't have minded if there *had* been!' said Philip. 'A spot of danger makes an adventure, you know, Bill!'

Bill laughed. 'You and your adventures! Now listen – this fellow Uma doesn't know me personally, and has never met me – but he may have been warned that his doings are being enquired about, so he may be on the look-out for a snooper. If anyone questions any of you, answer candidly at once. Say you've been ill, and this is a trip to give you sunshine, and so on – which is perfectly true as far as you're concerned.'

'Right,' said Jack. 'What's this man Uma like?'

'Here are some photographs of him,' said Bill, and he spread out five or six prints. The children looked at them, astonished.

'But – they're all of different men,' said Dinah.

'Looks like it – but they're all our friend Uma,' said Bill. 'He's a master of disguises, as you see. The only thing he cannot very well disguise is a long white scar on his right forearm, which looks very like a thin curving snake. But it's easy enough to cover that up, of course, with the sleeve of his shirt or coat, or whatever garment he happens to be wearing.'

He gathered up the prints and put them back into his wallet. 'You're not likely to recognize him at all,' he said. 'So don't go suspecting everyone you meet – you'll spoil your holiday! I know where to find people who know him, and I may get word of him. On the other hand, he may not be anywhere about now – he may have flown to America or Australia. He gads about all over the place – a most extraordinary fellow.'

Something long and sinuous suddenly glided by Bill, disappearing into the bushes nearby. He jumped, and then put out a restraining hand as Philip darted by him. 'No, Philip – that might be a *poisonous* snake – don't try any tricks with animals here.'

Dinah gave a small shriek. 'Was that a snake? Oh, how

211

horrible! Bill, you didn't tell us there were snakes here. I hate snakes. Philip, don't you dare to catch one, else I'll scream the place down.'

'Fathead,' said Philip, sitting down again. 'All right, Bill. I won't keep a poisonous snake, I promise you. That was rather a pretty one. What was it?'

'I don't know,' said Bill. 'I'm not over keen on snakes myself. And be careful of some of the insects here too, Philip. They can give you nasty nips. Don't carry too many about in your pockets!'

Dinah was not so happy now that she knew there were snakes about. She kept her eyes on the ground wherever she walked, and jumped at the least waving of a leaf. The little hotel manager saw her and came to comfort her.

'Many snakes here, yes – beeg, beeg ones that do not bite – and little, little ones, which are much poison. The little bargua snake is the worst. Do not touch him.'

'Oh dear – what's it like?' asked poor Dinah.

'He is green with spottings,' said the manager.

'Oh! What sort of spottings?' asked Dinah.

'Red and yellow,' said the little man. 'And he is fast with his head when he strikes – so!' He struck out with his hand as if it were a snake darting at Dinah, and she gave a small scream and drew back.

'Ah – I fright you!' said the plump manager, filled with dismay. 'No, no, do not be fright. See, I have somethings for you!'

He scuttled off to fetch the 'somethings' and brought back a dish of extremely rich-looking sweetmeats.

'I give you my apologizings,' he said. 'And my beggings for pardon.'

Dinah couldn't help laughing. 'It's all right,' she said. 'I wasn't really frightened – you just made me jump. But thanks awfully for these sweets.'

The little man disappeared and the children tried the sweets. They were very rich, very sticky, and very sweet.

After one each they all felt slightly sick. Kiki, however, helped herself generously, and then began to hiccup loudly, much to the delight of a passing waiter.

'Shut up, Kiki,' said Jack. 'That's enough. Be quiet now.'

But this time Kiki really *did* have hiccups, and was rather astonished to find that she couldn't stop. 'Pardon,' she kept saying, in a surprised tone that sent the children into gales of laughter.

'That'll teach you not to be so greedy!' said Jack. 'I say — we're starting on the river-trip tomorrow! Bags I drive the launch sometimes!'

'Bags I, bags I!' repeated Kiki at once, dancing up and down. 'Three bags full! Bags I! Oh — pardon!'

Tomorrow! Away on an unknown river to mysterious places in a strange land — what could be more exciting?

5
Away down the river

Next day they all drove down to the river. The white road wound here and there, and the people they met ran to the side of the road to keep out of the way of the big car.

'They look like people out of the Bible,' said Lucy-Ann.

'Well, many of the people in the Bible came from these parts!' said Bill. 'And in some ways the people *and* their villages too have not changed a great deal, except for modern amenities that have crept in — the radio, for instance, and wrist-watches, and modern sanitation *some-times*. And cinemas, of course — you find them everywhere.'

'Bill — in the picture-Bible I had years ago Abraham looked *exactly* like that man!' said Lucy-Ann, nodding towards a dignified, white-robed man walking by the road-side. 'And look at that woman with a pot on her head —

pitcher, I mean. She's like the picture I had of Rebecca going to the well.'

'Hey, look – camels!' shouted Philip, suddenly excited. 'Oh, there's a baby one. I've never in my life seen a baby one before. Oh, I wish I had it for a pet.'

'Well, at least you couldn't keep it in your pocket, like a snake or a mouse,' said Dinah. 'Don't those camels look cross!'

'Yes,' said Bill. 'Camels always look annoyed. That one over there is looking down his nose at us as if he really couldn't bear the sight of our car.'

'He probably can't!' said Dinah. 'It must smell horrible to him. Yes, he does look down his nose, doesn't he? Cheer up, camel!'

They saw patient donkeys too, loaded down with such heavy pannier-baskets that it was a marvel they could walk at all. Philip was interested in the birds too, almost as much as Jack was.

'I wish I'd brought my big world-bird book,' mourned Jack. 'I'd be able to look up all these brilliant birds then. I did put it out to bring, but I left it on my dressing-table.'

'You wouldn't have been allowed in the aeroplane with that monster book,' said Bill. 'I see you brought your field-glasses, however. You'll find plenty to look at with those.'

'Is that the river?' said Dinah, suddenly, as she caught sight of a flash of blue through the trees. 'Yes, it is! I say – it's very wide here, isn't it!'

So it was. The farther shore seemed quite a distance away. Their launch was waiting for them, a trim little vessel with a boatman on board looking very spry and neat. He saluted them when they came over from the car.

The launch was beside a little jetty, and Bill looked at it with approval. He nodded to the man.

'I Tala,' said the man, and bowed. 'Tala look after ship, and look after you, Sir.'

Tala showed them over the launch. It was small but quite

big enough for them all. The cabin was stuffy and hot, but nobody planned to be there very much! The bunks down below looked stuffy and hot too, but, as Bill said, they could sleep on deck, providing they rigged up a mosquito net over them. A little breeze blew every now and again, which was very pleasant.

'You start now, this minute, at once?' enquired Tala, his black eyes taking them all in. He had remarkably white teeth and a twinkle in his eyes that the children liked immediately. Bill nodded.

'Yes. Off we go. You can show me any gadgets there are, and I'll take the wheel if I want to. Cast off.'

The launch went off smoothly, her engine making very little noise. At once it seemed cooler, for the breeze was now in their faces. The children sat on the deck and watched the banks slide by on either side.

Mrs Cunningham went down into the lower part of the launch to see what kind of food was stored away there. She called to Bill.

'Just look here!' she said. 'They've done you proud again, Bill – there's enough for an army here – and such *nice* food too! And there's a fridge packed with butter and milk. You must be quite an important person, Bill, to have all this done for you!'

Bill laughed. 'You come along up on deck and get some colour into your cheeks!' he said. 'Hallo, what are the children excited about?'

The launch was passing a small village and the village children had come out to watch it go by. They shouted and waved, and Jack and the others waved back.

'What's this river called, Tala?' asked Philip.

'It is called River of Abencha,' answered Tala, his eyes on the water ahead.

'I say, you others!' called Philip. 'He says this river's called the River of Adventure – sounds exciting, doesn't it?'

'Abencha, Abencha,' repeated Tala, but Philip thought he

was trying to say 'Adventure' and not pronouncing it correctly. Tala found many English words difficult to say!

'All right, Tala – we heard you,' said Philip. 'It's a lovely name for a river, I think – the River of Adventure. Well, this is certainly an adventure for us!'

It was a quiet, peaceful trip that day, gliding along hour after hour. Bill took the wheel when Tala went down below to prepare a meal. The children wondered what kind of a meal it would be. They were all extremely hungry.

Tala came up with a marvellous repast. As Dinah said, it was much too grand to be called just a 'meal' – it was nothing less than a 'repast', or perhaps even a 'feast'!

Tala had apparently opened a good many tins, and concocted some dishes of his own, garnished with pickles and sauces of many kinds. There were fresh rolls to go with the meal, and to follow there was fresh or tinned fruit. Lucy-Ann pounced on a big peach and put it to her lips.

'No, don't eat the skin of that peach, Lucy-Ann,' said Bill. 'All fruit eaten out here must be peeled before being eaten. Don't forget that, please.'

Mrs Cunningham really enjoyed that peaceful day, hearing the lap-lap of the water against the bows of the boat, seeing the villages slip by on the banks, and sometimes meeting other boats on the blue-green water.

The sun and wind tired them all out, and each of them fell asleep at once when they had bedded down on deck. Tala tied up the boat safely, and went to his own shake-down in the stern.

Jack just had time to think that the stars seemed amazingly large and bright before he fell fast asleep. Nobody heard a sound that night, not even the cry of a night-bird, whose voice seemed half a hoot and half a shriek. Kiki opened one eye and considered whether to answer back in her own language of squawk-and-scream – but decided that Bill might not like it!

The river was beautiful in the early morning. It was a pale

milky blue, and Jack was thrilled to watch a whole covey of tiny water-birds swimming round the yacht. 'What are they?' he asked Tala, pointing to the little blue and yellow things. Tala shrugged his shoulders.

'Tala not know,' he said. Jack soon found that Tala knew absolutely nothing about birds, insects or flowers. He could not put a name to a single one. His whole interest was in the launch's engine and in the care of it.

'We come to big, big place soon,' said Tala, early that evening. He looked rather excited. 'Place name Sinny-Town.'

'Sinny-Town?' said Bill, puzzled. 'I don't think so, Tala. There is no big town along this river-side – only small ones. I've never heard of Sinny-Town. It isn't on my map.'

Tala nodded his head vigorously up and down. 'Yes, Sinny-Town. Tala know. Tala been. Half an hour and we see Sinny-Town.'

Bill took out his map, and looked down the river as it was shown there. He shook his head again, and showed the map to Tala.

'You're wrong,' he said. 'There is no Sinny-Town marked here. See.'

Tala put his finger on a place where the river shown on the map curved a little.

'Sinny-Town there,' he said. 'You will see, Sir. Tala right. Tala been there. Big big town. Many peoples. Big big towers, tall as the sky.'

This was most astonishing. Bill couldn't understand it. Why wasn't this 'big big place' shown on the map? Even small places were shown there. In fact, the little place he had planned to go to was marked as being very near the curve of the river where Tala said Sinny-Town was.

He shrugged his shoulders. Tala must be mistaken. Towers as tall as the sky – what nonsense!

The darkness came suddenly, as it always does in southern countries. Stars shone out, large and mysterious, and very very bright. The river turned black and silver, and held as many stars as were in the sky.

'Bend of river, Sir – then Sinny-Town,' said Tala, in an excited voice. 'You will see!'

The launch glided smoothly round the bend – and then Bill and the others saw a most astonishing sight!

A great city lay there, on the west bank of the river. A city of lights and noise. A city with towers that went up to the sky, just as Tala had said!

Bill stared in the utmost astonishment. He simply could not understand it! Here was a big place not even marked on the map – and the map was a modern one, not a year old! A city could not be built in a year. Bill was more puzzled than he had ever been in his life. He stood and stared as if he could not believe his eyes.

'Tala go Sinny-Town tonight?' said Tala, beseechingly. 'Tala like Sinny-Town. Tala go, Sir? Boat be all right with you, Sir.'

'Yes, yes – you go,' said Bill, finding his voice. 'Bless my soul, this is a most extraordinary thing. A large, lively town, with great buildings – and it's not marked on the map, and no one in London told me a word about it. What *can* it mean?'

'Let's visit it, Bill,' said Jack.

'Not tonight,' said Bill. 'We'll see what it looks like in the daylight. But what a brilliantly lighted place – and what enormous buildings! I simply don't understand it. It's very – very – strange!'

6

Sinny-Town

Everyone slept very well that night. They had stayed up fairly late looking at the lights of the surprising Sinny-Town. Tala had gone off in glee, leaping from the launch to the shore with one lithe spring. He had not come back by the time the others had bedded down on the cool deck, and Bill was rather uneasy, wondering if he *would* return.

But in the morning the sound of someone tinkering with the engine of the launch awoke Jack – and there was Tala, looking rather the worse for wear after his late night, at work on the plugs. He grinned at Jack when the boy stood up and stretched.

'Tala go to Sinny-Town,' he said, and nodded towards the bank. Jack remembered their surprise of the night before and ran to the other side of the launch to gaze at the mysterious Sinny-Town.

It was so extraordinary that he called to Bill. 'Bill! I say, Bill – do come and look.'

Bill awoke and joined Jack. The two of them looked at the sprawling town. Bill was astonished.

'There's something odd about it,' he said. 'Look at those towers – somehow they don't look real – and what's that over there – a palace or something? There's something peculiar about that too. Isn't one side missing? Where are your field-glasses, Jack? Lend them to me.'

Jack handed them to him and Bill gazed through them. 'No – I don't understand this,' he said, lowering them. 'The town is a most peculiar mixture of buildings – there are shacks and sheds, ancient houses, towers, that palace, and something that looks remarkably like an old temple – and here and there are crowds of people milling round, and droves of camels, and . . . no, I don't understand it.'

'Do let's go and look at it after breakfast,' said Jack.

'Yes, we certainly will,' said Bill. 'Sinny-Town is no village – it's quite a big place – but WHY isn't it marked on my map? I had a look at another map last night, but it's not shown there either. Wake the others, Jack.'

Soon they were all having breakfast. Mrs Cunningham was as surprised as the rest of them to see such a strange mixture of a town on the bank of the river.

'That palace looks quite *new*,' said Lucy-Ann, staring at it. 'And yet it must be thousands of years old and ought to be in ruins.'

After breakfast they all went ashore, leaving Tala in charge of the launch. Kiki was on Jack's shoulder as usual, and very talkative, much to the amusement of the people they met.

'Shut the door,' she ordered imperiously. 'Fetch the doctor, Polly's got a cold. A-HOO-CHOO!'

Her sneeze was so realistic that Lucy-Ann almost offered her a hanky. Soon Jack had to make the parrot stop talking, for, on looking behind him, he found a group of small, excited children following, pointing at Kiki in delight.

They came near to the town – and then Bill gave an exclamation. 'It's not a real town! It's a fake! All these towers and temples are imitation! Look at this one – it is only a front – there's no back to it.'

They stared in wonder. Bill was right. It was just a flimsy false front, which, from a distance, looked exactly like a real temple – but behind it was nothing but boards and canvas, with joists of timber holding the whole thing up.

They went on, coming to well-built sheds, stored with masses of peculiar things, jerry-built shacks that served all sorts of purposes – one sold cigarettes, one sold soft drinks, and others sold groceries and so on.

The people were a curiously mixed lot. Men and women walked or ran here and there, mostly dressed in sloppy-

220

looking European clothes – and others, dressed in flowing robes, went on their way too. Small children with hardly anthing on darted everywhere.

And then, round a corner, they came upon a curious sight. It was a procession of magnificently dressed men, walking slowly, and chanting as they went. In the midst of the procession was a space, and here, surrounded by women dressed in the robes of long, long ago, was a kind of bed on which lay a very beautiful woman, carried by four slaves, tall, strong and dark-skinned.

Bill and the others stood and stared – and then Bill heard a curious whirring noise. He looked to see what was making it – and gave an exclamation.

The others looked at him. Bill grinned at them. 'I've got it!' he said. 'I see it all now, and I can't think why it didn't dawn on me before. The reason why Sinny-Town isn't shown on the map is because it probably wasn't here when the map was drawn a year ago! See those enormous cameras? They're ciné-cameras – they're taking pictures for a film, and . . . '

Then everyone exclaimed, too, and began to talk excitedly.

'Of course! It's a town specially built for the making of a film of long-ago days!'

'Why didn't we think of it before! That's why that temple is only a front and nothing else!'

'And why there is such a mixture of people here!'

'*And*, of course, it's *Ciné*-Town, *not* Sinny-Town as we all imagined!' said Jack. 'A town of cinema cameras taking pictures – Ciné-Town.'

'It's jolly interesting!' said Philip. 'Bill, can we wander round on our own? Look, there's a fellow doing acrobatics over there – look at him bending over backwards and catching hold of the back of his ankles with his hands!'

Bill laughed. 'All right. You can go and have a good look round. I expect this place attracts a lot of show-people, who

221

think they can make a bit of money by their tricks. You may see something interesting. But keep together, please. Boys, see that the girls don't get separated from you. I'll go off alone with your mother, Philip – I might pick up some useful information.'

The children knew what *that* meant! Bill hoped to find out something about Mr Raya Uma. Well, it was quite likely that he had come to Ciné-Town!

They set off by themselves, followed by a little tail of interested noisy children. Beggars·called to them as they passed by, holding out all kinds of wares – trays of sticky sweetmeats, covered with flies, that made the two girls shudder in disgust. Fresh fruit in baskets. Little gimcrack objects such as might be found in fairs at home. Pictures of the stars who were, presumably, acting in the film being made in the town. There were all kinds of goods, none of which the children wished to buy.

Even the babies seemed to speak English – or, rather, English with a pronounced American accent, for the company making the film was one of the biggest ones from America. It was easy to pick out the Americans and Europeans, not only by their dress but by their bustling walk and loud voices.

The four children wandered round the false temples and towers, wondering what the film was that was being made – it was obviously a story taken from the Old Testament. Then they made their way to a large group of huts where a little crowd sat watching a man who was performing a most peculiar trick. He was walking up a ladder of knives!

A weird chant went up from two of his attendants as he climbed up the edges of the blades, setting his bare feet on them without flinching. Someone began to play a kind of tom-tom, and the children stood there, fascinated.

The man leapt down, grinning. He turned up the soles of his feet to show that they were not in the least cut. He invited the audience to come and test the sharpness of the knife-edges with their hands, and some of them did.

222

He beckoned to the four children and they went to the strange ladder of knives and felt the edges too – yes, they were certainly sharp! They gazed at the man in respect, and put a little money into his bag. It was English money, but he didn't seem to mind at all. He could probably change it into his own coinage at any of the ramshackle shops around.

'What a way to earn your living – climbing up sharp knives with bare feet!' said Lucy-Ann. 'Oh, look – there's a juggler!'

The juggler was extremely clever. He had six glittering balls and sent them up and down, to and fro, as fast as he could, so that it was almost impossible for the eye to see them. He caught them so deftly that the children stood lost in admiration. Then he took six plates and juggled with those, throwing them over his shoulder and between his legs, one after the other, without dropping or breaking a single one.

Just as the children were clapping him, Jack felt a hand sliding into his shorts pocket and turned quickly. He grabbed at a small, skinny boy, but the child wriggled away quickly.

'Hey, you! Don't you dare to do that again!' yelled Jack, indignantly, feeling in his pocket. As far as he could tell, nothing had been taken – he had been too quick for the little thief. Still, it was a lesson to him and to all the others too.

We obviously mustn't get so engrossed in watching things that we forget to guard our pockets,' said Jack. 'Why didn't *you* see that little monkey of a fellow, Kiki? You could have yelled out "Stop thief!" '

'Stopthief, stopthief, stopthief!' shouted Kiki immediately, thinking that it was all one word. This astonished all the passers-by so much that they stood and stared. One small girl darted away at once.

'She thinks Kiki is addressing *her*,' said Philip, with a grin. 'I expect she had just planned to pinch your little bag, Lucy-Ann.'

Just then a queer, thin music floated over to them, and

they stopped. 'I say – that sounds like snake-music!' said
Philip, suddenly excited. 'Come on, quick – I've always
wanted to see a snake-charmer at work. Quick!'

7

A surprising morning

Jack, Philip and Lucy-Ann hurried towards the sound, but
Dinah hung back.

'Ugh! Snakes! *I* don't want to see them,' she said. 'I hate
snakes. I'm not coming.'

'Dinah, you've got to keep with us,' said Philip, impatiently. 'Bill said so. You don't need to watch, you can
turn your back. But you *must* keep with us.'

'All right, all right,' said Dinah, crossly. 'But why you
want to go and gloat over snakes I cannot imagine. Horrible
things!'

She dawdled behind, but kept within reach, and then,
when they came to the little crowd surrounding the snake-
charmer, she turned her back. She felt rather sick, for she
had caught sight of a snake rising up from a basket, wavering to and fro. She swallowed once or twice, and felt better,
but she did not dare to turn round again. She stared out over
the strangely mixed crowd.

The other three were in the little crowd round the snake-
charmer. He was a rather tough-looking man, with a turban
wound round his head, and a wide cloth round his middle.
He had only one eye. The other was closed – but his one eye
looked round piercingly, and Lucy-Ann decided that she
didn't like it at all. It was as unblinking as a snake's!

Beside the man stood his attendant, a small boy, quite
naked except for a cloth round his middle. He was painfully
thin, and Lucy-Ann could easily count all his bony little ribs.

His eyes were sharp and bright – not like a snake's, thought Lucy-Ann, but like a robin's. He was talking at top speed about the snakes in the basket.

He spoke a curious mixture of his own language and American. The children could not follow half of it, but they gathered enough to know that the snakes in the basket were dangerous ones, with a bite so poisonous that it could kill even a grown man in twelve hours.

'He dart like this,' chanted the little fellow, and made a snake-like movement with his arm, 'he bite quick, quick, quick . . . '

The man sitting by the round basket began to play again the strange, tuneless music that the children had heard a few minutes before. The snake that Dinah had seen had disappeared back into its basket – but now it arose again and everyone gasped at its wicked-looking head.

Lucy-Ann whispered to Jack. 'Jack – it's the snake that the hotel manager told us about – green with red and yellow spots – look! What was its name now?'

'Er – bargua, I think,' said Jack, watching the snake. 'My word, it's a little beauty, but wicked-looking, isn't it? See it wavering about as if it's looking round at everyone. My goodness, here's another!'

A second snake had now uncoiled itself and was rising up slowly, seeming to look round from side to side. Some of the crowd came a little closer to the snake-charmer, and at once the small boy cried out sharply, 'Back, back, back! You want to be bit? He bite quick, quick, quick!'

The crowd at once surged back, frightened. The snake-charmer went on with his weird music, blowing interminably on his little flute, his one eye following all the movements of the crowd. A third snake arose and swayed from side to side as if in time to the music.

The small boy tapped it on the head with a stick and it sank down again.

'He very bad snake, he not safe,' explained the boy,

earnestly. The other two snakes still wavered about, and then, quite suddenly, the man changed his music, and it became louder and more insistent. One of the snakes swayed more quickly, and the little boy held a stick over its head as if to stop it.

The snake struck at it, and then, before anyone could stop it, slithered right out of the basket towards the crowd.

At once there were screams and howls, and everyone surged back. The small boy ran at the snake and picked it up. He threw it back into the basket, and a cry of admiration went up at once. Shouts and claps and cheers filled the air, and the snake-charmer stood up slowly, and patted the small boy on the head.

'He save you all!' he said, and then added a few rapid words in his own language. 'He brave. Snake might bite him. He brave,' he finished.

'What a kid!' said an American voice, warm with admiration. 'Here, boy – take a hold of this!' and he threw a dollar bill on the ground. The little boy darted on it as quickly as a snake, and nodded his thanks.

That was the signal for other people in the crowd to throw down money for the boy too, and he picked it all up, stuffing it into a fold of his waist-cloth.

The snake-charmer took no notice. He was busy putting the lid on the snake-basket, preparing to leave.

Jack put his hand into his pocket to throw down a coin, but to his surprise Philip stopped him. 'No, don't,' said Philip. 'It's all a fake.'

Jack looked at him in enormous surprise. 'A fake? How? That kid's as brave as can be! You heard the hotel manager tell us how poisonous those barguas are.'

'I tell you, it's a fake!' said Philip, in a low voice. 'I agree – they are barguas, and dangerous – but not one of those snakes could hurt a fly.'

'What do you mean?' asked Lucy-Ann, astonished.

'Come away and I'll tell you,' said Philip. They joined

Dinah and went a little way away. Jack looked at Philip impatiently.

'Come on, then – tell us how it was a fake.'

'Did you notice that when those snakes were swaying about in the basket they kept their mouths shut all the time?' said Philip. 'They didn't open them at all, or show their forked tongues, not even when one of them was tapped on the head – which would usually anger a snake and make him get ready to bite.'

'Yes – now I come to think of it, they *did* keep their mouths shut,' said Jack. 'But what does that matter? The one that escaped might easily have opened his to strike if he had had a chance. I wonder he didn't pounce at that small boy.'

'Do listen,' said Philip. 'I was a bit suspicious when I saw that those snakes didn't open their mouths at all – so that when one snake escaped – though it's my firm opinion that that "escape" was all arranged, part of the trick, you know – well, when that snake escaped and came writhing near us I took a jolly good look at him. And believe it or not, the poor thing's mouth was *sewn up*!'

The others gazed at him in horror. 'Sewn up!' said Lucy-Ann. 'Oh, how cruel! That means, of course, that the snake-charmer is perfectly safe – he can't be bitten because the snakes can't open their mouths to strike.'

'Exactly,' said Philip. 'I never knew before how the snake-charmer's trick was done. The snake that "escaped" had its mouth well and truly sewn up – I saw the stitches. The snake was probably doped somehow, and then, while it was doped, the man sewed up its mouth.'

'But it can't eat or drink then,' said Lucy-Ann, feeling sick. 'It's cruel. Why doesn't someone do something about it?'

'That boy wasn't brave after all then,' said Jack.

'No. That's what I told you,' said Philip. 'He had been trained to put on that little bit of spectacular courage. You

227

saw how it pulled in the money, didn't you? My word, talk about a hard-hearted swindle! To sew up snakes' mouths and use them for a living – ugh, horrible!'

'I'm jolly glad I didn't throw down any money,' said Jack.

'And I'm jolly glad I didn't watch,' said Dinah.

'I'm sorry for those snakes,' said Lucy-Ann. 'I hate to think of them.'

'So do I,' said Philip. 'Such pretty things too – that lovely bright green, and those glittering red and yellow spots. I'd like one for a pet.'

Dinah stared at him in horror. 'Philip! Don't you dare to keep a snake for a pet – especially a poisonous one.'

'Don't fly off the handle, Di,' said Jack, amused. 'You know jolly well that Bill would never allow him to keep a poisonous bargua. Cheer up!'

'Do you suppose we could buy ice-creams here?' said Lucy-Ann, suddenly feeling that she could eat at least three. 'My mouth feels so hot and dry.'

'We'll find a decent place,' said Jack. 'What about that one over there?'

They walked over to it and looked inside. It was clean and bright, and at the little tables sat many Americans and two or three actors and actresses still in costume.

'This should be all right,' said Philip, and they went in. People stared at the children, and especially at Jack, who, of course, had Kiki on his shoulder as usual.

A little bell was on each table, so that customers could ring if they wanted anything. Jack picked up the one on his table and rang it.

'Ding dong bell,' remarked Kiki. 'Pussy's in the well. Fetch the doctor!' She went off into one of her cackles of laughter, and then began again. 'Pussy's in the well, me-ow, me-ow, puss, puss, puss! Ding dong bell!'

There was a sudden silence, and everyone stared in amazement at the parrot, who now proceeded to cough like an old sheep. Jack tapped her on the beak.

'Now then, Kiki – don't show off!'

'Great snakes!' drawled an American voice nearby. 'That's a *ree*markable parrot, young fellow! Like to sell him?'

'Of course not!' said Jack, quite indignantly. 'Shut up, Kiki. You're not giving a concert!'

But Kiki was! Delighted at all the sudden attention, she gave a most remarkable performance – and was just in the middle of it when something happened. A man came in and sat down at the children's table!

'Hallo!' he said. 'Surely I know you! Don't you belong to old Bill? Is he here with you?'

8
The snake-charmer again

The four children stared at the man in surprise. He was dressed well, and his face looked brown and healthy. He smiled at them, showing very fine teeth.

Nobody answered for a moment. Then Kiki cocked her head on one side, and spoke to the man.

'Bill! Silly-bill! Pay the bill, silly-billy, pay the billy!'

'What a wonderful parrot!' said the man, and put out his hand to ruffle Kiki's crest. She gave him a quick nip with her beak, and he scowled at once, making his face completely different.

'Well?' he said, nursing his finger and smiling again at the children. 'Have you lost your tongues? I asked you who you were with? Is it old Bill, my good old friend?'

Both girls got a quiet kick on the leg from Jack and Philip. Everyone had remembered what Bill had said. They were not to give away any information if they were asked questions!

'We're here with my mother,' said Philip. 'We've all been ill, so this is a sort of convalescence trip. We're just having a short river-trip on a launch.'

'I see,' said the man. 'You don't know anyone called Bill then?'

'Oh yes,' said Dinah, to the horror of the two boys. 'We know Bill Hilton – is he the one you mean?'

'No,' said the man.

'Then there's Bill Jordans,' said Dinah, and by the glint in her eye the boys knew that she was making all this up. They joined in heartily.

'He may mean Bill Ponga – do you, sir?'

'Or Bill Tipps – he's the fellow who had four big cars and two small ones – is he the Bill you mean?'

'Perhaps he means Bill Kent. *You* know, Jack, the chimney-sweep Mother always has.'

'Or do you mean Bill Plonk, sir? You might know him – he's a biscuit-manufacturer, and his biscuits are . . . '

'No. I do *not* mean him – or any of the others!' said the man shortly. 'Isn't anyone called Bill with you?'

'No. As you can see, we're all alone,' said Jack.

'Where's your launch?' asked the man. This was getting awkward and Jack cast about in his mind for a way to bring the conversation to a natural end. He glanced suddenly at Lucy-Ann and spoke urgently.

'I say, old girl! Do you feel sick? Better go out, if so.'

Lucy-Ann took the cue at once and stood up, looking as ill as she could.

'Yes. Take me out,' she said, in a suitably faint voice. The others led her down the room and out into the open air.

'Scoot!' said Philip as soon as they were outside. 'I don't *think* he'll come after us – but he might. Jolly good idea of yours, Jack, to pretend Lucy-Ann felt sick.'

They disappeared at top speed round the building and went into an empty shed. There was a dirty window there and they peered through it, keeping a watch for the over-friendly man. Lucy-Ann made a peculiar noise.

'I think I *am* going to be sick', she said. 'Jack was right!' But she wasn't sick after all, and soon began to feel better.

'Here comes our friend,' said Jack, gazing through the dirty window. 'He's standing still, looking this way and that. Now he's got into a car – he's driving off at top speed. Goodo!'

'Do you think he was Raya Uma himself?' asked Dinah.

'Shouldn't think so,' said Jack. 'Though he did have very white teeth – did you notice? And Bill said that Raya Uma had *remarkably* white teeth. I couldn't see if he had a scar on his arm, because his coat-sleeves were long.'

'We told him about plenty of Bills,' said Dinah with a laugh.

'Bill! Pay the bill!' said Kiki, joining in as usual.

'We did, old thing!' said Jack. 'We paid for the ice-creams when they were brought to us. Didn't you notice? You're as blind as a bat!'

'Batty,' said Kiki, jigging up and down. 'Batty, batty, batty!'

'Quite right. You are!' said Philip, and everyone laughed. They went to the door of the shed. 'Is it safe to go now, do you think?' asked Dinah. Jack nodded.

'Oh yes. He won't try and get anything more out of us. He knows we were fooling with him – but he doesn't know if it was because we were being cautious, or were just plain rude. We'll have to tell Bill about it and see what he says. I think there's no doubt but that the man has got wind that someone's coming out to snoop, and has been looking out for newcomers.'

They went out of the shed and wandered round. They came to a collection of tumbledown wooden huts, which looked as if they might have been built for years, not merely for the film outfit.

'A bit too far,' said Jack. 'Let's go back. I say, though – what's that?'

231

A sudden cry had come to his sharp ears. He stood still and then the others heard a cry too. They also heard something even worse – the sound of a cane or stick being used as a weapon!

Every time that the sound of a blow came, there followed immediately a high-pitched scream of pain and terror.

'That's a child yelling!' said Philip. 'He sounds as if he's being half killed. Come on – I can't bear this. We've got to do something about it!'

They raced round the huts, and came to a bare space, where old boxes and crates lay about. At the back stood a man, thrashing a child with a thick stick. One or two other people were there, but nobody made the slightest attempt to stop the whipping.

'Gosh – it's that snake-charmer!' cried Jack. 'And that's the little boy who picked up the money – look, the fellow has got him on the ground!'

All four of them raced over to the angry man. Philip caught hold of his arm, and Jack wrenched the stick from his hand. The man swung round in fury.

He shouted something they didn't understand, and tried to catch at the stick. But Philip put it out of reach. 'No you don't! You're a cruel beast, lashing out at that little kid like that! What's he done?'

The man shouted again, and his one eye glittered dangerously. The small boy raised his head, and sobbed out a few words.

'He say I keep money. He say I rob. But see, I have none!'

He opened his folded waist-cloth and shook it. He pointed at the snake-charmer. 'I give him all, all! He say I spend some. He beat me. Ai, ai!'

The small boy put his thin arms across his face and wept again. The man made a move towards him as if to strike him with his bare fist, but Philip jumped forward with the stick.

'Don't you touch him again! You let him be! I shall report you for this!'

Philip had no idea to whom he should report the man, but he was determined not to let him hit the child again. The snake-charmer glared at him in fury out of his one eye. Then he made a sudden move towards his snake-basket, which lay on the ground nearby. He kicked off the lid and at once the snakes rose up, scared and angered.

'Run! Run!' he shouted, in English. 'I tell my snakes bite, bite, bite!'

Dinah turned and ran at once, but the others kept their ground. If Philip was right, and the snakes' mouths were sewn up, they were harmless, and there was no need to run. Two of the snakes came gliding rapidly over the ground towards them. Then Philip did something surprising. He threw the stick to Jack, and then knelt down on the ground. He made a curious hissing noise, the same noise that he used in his own country when he wanted to tame grass snakes.

The snakes stopped immediately. They raised their heads and looked towards the boy. Then they glided right up to Philip and ran their mouths over his hands. One snake writhed up his arm and hung itself round his neck.

The snake-charmer stared in the utmost amazement. Why – the snakes had never done that to him! They had avoided him whenever they could, for they hated him. Never, never had he seen wild snakes go to anyone as they went to this quietly hissing boy! He wasn't even afraid!

'Snakes bite – bite, bite, bite!' he said, and stamped on the ground to frighten them and make them strike with their shut mouths.

'They can't,' said Philip, scornfully, and ran his hand gently along the sides of their mouths. 'You have sewn them up. In my country you would be sent to prison for such a cruel deed.'

The man fell into a rage and yelled loudly in his own language. The small boy ran to Philip. 'Go, go! He call friends, they hurt you. Go!'

Philip put down the snakes promptly, thinking of the two

girls. They must go at once if there was any danger of this fellow's friends coming and making themselves a nuisance. 'We'd better scoot,' he said to Jack. But it was too late!

Three youths had come running at the snake-charmer's call, and they surrounded the four children, pushing Dinah close to the others. Philip put on a bold face. He walked forward.

'Make way!' he said. 'Make way, or we'll get the police.'

But the youths closed in even more, and the boys felt their hearts sink. They couldn't take on these three and the angry snake-charmer too!

But Kiki was not going to stand this kind of thing. She danced up and down on Jack's shoulder in anger, and screamed out at the top of her voice.

'Police! Police! Fetch the police!' she screeched, and then whistled like a police-whistle. 'PHEEEEEEEEE! PHEEEEEEEEEE! PHEEEEEEEEEEEEEEEEE!'

9

At lunch time

Kiki's shouts for the police and her marvellous imitation of a police whistle terrified all the youths. They stood aghast, staring at this extraordinary parrot. Then, with one accord, they and the snake-charmer took to their heels and fled. The snake-charmer snatched up his basket of snakes as he went— all three were in it again, which was a pity.

The four children stood gazing after the runaways, most relieved. Kiki gave an enormous chuckle, and then such a cackle of laughter that the children couldn't help joining in.

'Kiki! Thanks very much!' said Jack, scratching the delighted parrot on her head. 'I suppose you heard Philip say the word "police" and that reminded you of your police-whistle performance. Very very lucky for us!'

'No police came, though,' said Lucy-Ann. 'Good old Kiki! That was the best whistling you've ever done – better even than your train-whistle.'

'We'd better get back to the launch, I think,' said Philip. 'I don't like us getting mixed up in anything like this. Bill would row us like fury if something serious happened.'

They were just setting off, when a small figure ran out from behind a hut. It was the little boy. He ran to Philip and took his hand. He knelt down before him.

'Take me with you, boss! Bula has gone with snakes, and I have no money. He bad man, I no like him. Take me with you.'

'I can't,' said Philip, gently undoing the boy's hands from his. 'I will give you money, though.'

'Not money. Take me with you, take Oola with you!' said the boy, beseechingly.

'No, Oola, we can't,' said Philip.

'Yes, boss! Oola be yours, Oola work for you!' said the boy, clutching at Philip's hand again. 'You like snakes, boss? Oola bring you some!'

'Listen, Oola – I do like snakes – but not those with their poor mouths sewn up,' said Philip. 'And it would be dangerous to have one that could bite. Have you no family to look after you?'

'Only Bula, who my uncle is,' said Oola, still clutching Philip's hand. The boy felt really embarrassed. 'Bula bad man, Bula hit, see, see!'

He showed bruises and weals all over his body. Lucy-Ann gave a sudden little sob.

'Poor little Oola!' she said. 'Can't we take him, Philip?'

'No, Lucy-Ann, we can't,' said Philip. 'We can't collect all the poor, ill-used animals or children we see here – that mangy dog over there, the poor donkey I saw today, with sores all over it – the little baby, so thin and tiny, that we saw lying on an old rug, don't you remember? They each want

235

help and friends — but we can't collect them all and take them to the launch. No, Oola — we cannot take you.'

'What I do? What I do?' said Oola in despair.

'We'll take you to the First Aid Tent,' said Philip. 'I saw one somewhere about. They will look after you and help you, Oola. They will bathe your bruises for you.'

Oola went with them disconsolately, dragging his bare feet, his head hanging down — but as soon as they came to the immaculately white tent, with its nurse at the door in a starched apron, Oola fled! They heard him wailing as he went, and both Dinah and Lucy-Ann had tears in their eyes as they watched the half-naked little figure running behind a shack.

'Blow!' said Jack. 'I feel awful about this. I feel as if we've let Oola down very badly — But I don't see what else we can do.'

'Come on,' said Philip. 'Let's go back to the launch. We're supposed to be back by one, and it's almost that now.'

They made their way back to the river, none of them feeling very happy. Philip kept a watch for the man who had questioned them, but there was no sign of him. They arrived safely at the launch, and were greeted with pleasure by Tala. They all jumped aboard, and heard Bill's voice calling to them.

'You're rather late. We were getting a bit worried about you. Go and wash and we'll all have a meal.'

Over the meal they exchanged news with Bill. 'Did you find out anything about that fellow Raya Uma?' asked Philip, dropping his voice so that Tala could not hear.

'Not a thing,' said Bill. 'But perhaps I shall when I get to Ala-ou-iya. Your mother and I just wandered about, found out about this film, saw a friend we knew, and came back here. Very dull. What about you? What did you do?'

Bill sat up straight when the children began to tell him about the man in the ice-cream shop who had come up and questioned them. 'He didn't say your surname, Bill,' said

Jack. 'He just kept on saying "Bill". Wouldn't he know your surname?'

'No. But he might know my Christian name,' said Bill. 'You didn't by any chance say what my surname *was*, did you?'

'Of *course* not,' said both boys, indignantly. 'But we told him a whole lot more Bills, and asked him if he meant *them*,' added Jack, with a chuckle.

'What do you mean?' said Bill, puzzled.

'Well – we asked him if he meant Bill Hilton – or Bill Jordans – or Bill Ponga – or Bill Tipps, who has four big cars and two small ones,' said Jack.

'Or Bill Kent the chimney-sweep – or Bill Plonk who makes biscuits,' went on Dinah.

Bill threw back his head and laughed. 'You little monkeys! All make-believe Bills, I gather. Well, what happened next?'

'Oh – he asked where our launch was – we'd told him about the river-trip for our convalescence,' said Philip, 'and we realized things might get a bit awkward – so Jack decided that Lucy-Ann looked as if she was going to be sick, and we shot out with her, and hid.'

Bill roared again. 'I'd rather have you kids on my side than against me,' he said. 'You're too smart for words! Well – it rather looks as if that fellow was a spy of Raya Uma's. What was he like?'

They told Bill. 'It doesn't somehow sound like Uma,' said Bill. 'Except for the teeth. No, I don't think it was Uma. If he's going about openly like that he couldn't be up to anything serious. He could be too easily watched. Still, it looks as if Uma *is* out here, if he has a friend who spots you and asks you leading questions about someone called Bill. Thanks for keeping my surname secret!'

'Any other news' asked Mrs Cunningham. 'What else did you do?'

'Oh – the snakes!' said Dinah, remembering. 'You tell

237

about them, Philip.'

Philip related the whole story, right down to where Kiki had yelled for the police and whistled. Bill frowned.

'Now this kind of thing won't do, you know,' he said. 'You might have got yourselves into serious trouble. You must never go wandering about in back streets again.'

'Yes, but Bill — we couldn't let that fellow go on hitting Oola without doing something about it, surely?' said Jack.

'You two boys could have gone to stop the man, and have sent the girls away for help — they would have been quite safe then,' said Bill. 'Even if your feelings run away with you, you have ALWAYS got to think of your sisters first. If you want to jump into a brawl, do it when you're alone. Understand?'

'Yes, sir,' said both boys, rather red in the face. 'Sorry, Bill!'

'Sorry, Bill,' echoed Kiki. 'Sorry, sorry, Bill.'

Everyone laughed, and Bill changed the subject. 'That's an extraordinary place,' he said, nodding his head towards Ciné-Town. 'Scores of all kinds of buildings put up just for six months! Did you see the fair they've got there?'

'No,' said the children, surprised. 'We missed that.'

'Oh yes — hoopla stalls, gambling games, dancing girls, shooting acts and goodness knows what,' said Bill. 'I've no doubt your snake-charmer came from there. Whether he will venture back again after Kiki's alarming call for the police I very much doubt. They've even got a fire-eater there.'

'A fire-eater!' said Philip. 'I'd like to see him do his act. Take us, Bill!'

'No, I think not,' said Bill. 'I'd better be getting on to Ala-ou-iya. That's where I *really* hope to get news of Uma. You'll have to hope to see a fire-eater another time. By the way, did you see the fellow climbing a ladder of knives? We saw him just as we came back.'

'Yes, we saw him too,' said Jack. 'I do wish we had more

time to spend at Ciné-Town – it's ugly and queer, but it's quite fascinating!'

Bill got up, filling his pipe. He called to Tala. 'We've finished, Tala. Start for Ala-ou-iya in an hour's time, please. We should be there about six o'clock. We'll spend the night there, off-shore, of course.'

'Good, Sir!' called back Tala, and came to collect the trays. The children settled down under an awning to read. Bill had given them some books about the countryside nearby, telling them that it was extremely interesting, and that civilisations thousands of years old had lived in the countryside they passed on their way down the river.

It was a pleasant trip on the water that afternoon. Ciné-Town was soon left behind as the launch glided slowly and smoothly along. Tala called to them just before six o'clock.

'We come to Ala-ou-iya!' he chanted, making the name sing on his tongue. 'You know old town, Sir? It called Ala-ou-iya, Gateway of Kings!'

10

That night

Tala took the launch deftly to a mooring-post by a small wooden jetty. One or two fishing-boats were there already. Trees came right down to the water, but beyond them the children could see the outlines of small houses, low and whitewashed. Smoke rose on the evening air, rising straight up, for there was no breeze away from the river.

'What did Tala mean – that Ala-ou-iya is the Gateway of Kings?' asked Dinah. 'It says that too in the books you gave us to read, Bill – but it doesn't explain it.'

'I don't expect it means anything much,' said Bill. 'Unless it is a name handed down from old times, when much of this country was the site of civilisations thousands of years old.'

'As old as Ur, the town in the Bible?' asked Lucy-Ann.

'Yes – as old as Ur – and probably much older!' said Bill, with a laugh. 'There must have been great palaces and temples here in this country even before the Great Flood, when Noah sailed off in his Ark.'

'Oh, "The Gateway of Kings" might *really* have meant something then,' said Dinah. 'There might have been a golden gateway leading to a palace – or to a temple. I wish this book explained more. Bill, it's strange, isn't it, to think that perhaps seven or eight thousand years ago, if we had sailed down this river, we might have passed the most wonderful buildings on the way! All towering high and glittering in the sun!'

'We might have seen the Tower of Babel, that reached to the sky,' said Lucy-Ann. 'Should we, Bill?'

'Not from this river. Babylon is miles away,' said Bill. 'Look – here comes nightfall – and out come the stars!'

'And we can see the gleam of the fires now, outside the huts, through the trees,' said Dinah. 'I love the evenings here. That little group of village houses looks most picturesque now – but I know if we went and sat near them they wouldn't look so nice. It's a pity.'

'Spitty!' said Kiki, at once. 'Spitty, spitty, spitty.'

'I didn't say that, Kiki,' said Dinah. 'I said "It's a pity." Don't be rude!'

'Spitty,' said Kiki, working herself up in a crescendo. 'Spitty, spitty, SPITTY . . . '

'Be quiet,' said Jack, and tapped her on the head.

'Spitty!' repeated Kiki at once, and went off into a shriek of laughter. Tala burst into laughter too, and his huge guffaw made them all jump. He thought Kiki was the funniest thing he had ever met, and was always bringing her titbits. He brough her one now – a piece of pineapple out of a tin. She took it in one foot, and shook the juice from it.

240

'Don't!' said Dinah. 'I don't like pineapple juice down my neck, Kiki. Do be good.'

'Good, good, goody good,' said Kiki and nibbled daintily at the pineapple. 'Good boy, goodbye, good morning, good afternoon, good . . .'

Tala roared again, and Bill motioned him away. He would have stood all evening watching Kiki if he had been allowed to.

'Are you going ashore tomorrow or tonight, Bill?' asked Mrs Cunningham.

'Tonight, I think,' said Bill. 'The man I want to talk to may be out all day— and anyway I'd rather talk to him at night, with no one about.'

Bill went off about nine o'clock, slipping like a shadow through the trees. He had been told how to find the man he wanted, and any villager would direct him to the house, which was built alongside a big store.

'I think I'll turn in,' said Mrs Cunningham, after a while. 'I don't know why this air makes me feel so sleepy, but it does. You turn in too, children – and remember your mosquito-nets!'

Dinah was already yawning. She and Lucy put up their net not far from Mrs Cunningham, arranging it over their mattress on the deck. The boys were not sleepy and hung over the side of the launch, talking in whispers. Tala could be heard snoring at the other end of the boat.

'Wonder how Bill's getting on,' said Jack, in a low tone. 'Shall we wait up for him?'

'No. Better not. He may be pretty late,' said Philip. 'Let's turn in now. It must be about half-past ten. Where's our net? Oh, you've got it. Good. Come on then.'

They lay down on their mattress, glad to feel cool after the heat of the day. It was very peaceful lying there, hearing the small lappings of the river, and a night-bird calling out suddenly, or a fish jumping in the darkness.

Jack went drifting off to sleep, and began to dream of enormous palaces and golden gates, and vast store-houses of treasure. Philip tossed and turned, listening for Bill.

Ah! There he was! Philip heard a noise as if someone were creeping on to the launch, trying to keep as quiet as possible. He listened for Bill to pour a glass of lime-juice for a last drink as he always did. But no sound came. Bill must have decided to turn in at once.

Another small sound made him sit up suddenly. *Was* that Bill? Somehow it didn't sound like him. Bill was big and heavy, and no matter how quiet he tried to be, he always made *some* noise. Surely he would have made more noise than this? If it wasn't Bill – then who was it?

Philip rolled quietly off his mattress and pushed aside the mosquito-net. He sat on the bare floor of the deck and listened again. Yes – someone *was* creeping about! Someone in bare feet.

It couldn't be Tala. He had bare feet – but Philip could quite well hear his snores at the other end of the boat. Was it – was it that man who had asked them questions about Bill, come to snoop about? Or could it possibly be the snake-charmer, come for a revenge of some sort? No – that was impossible, surely!

Philip listened once more. A small sound came to him again, this time down in the cabin of the launch. He crept silently over the deck, only the stars showing him the way.

He came to the top of the hatchway steps that led down to the cabin, and listened again. Yes, someone was down there – and it sounded as if the someone was helping himself to food. And drink too! There was a noise exactly like someone drinking!

Philip thought it was probably some person from the group of houses beyond the trees. What should he do? Wake Tala? That might be a bit of a job, and Tala would probably wake up in a fright and yell, which might give the intruder time to get away!

Then a bright thought came to Philip. Of course – he could close the hatchway and catch the thief that way! So he tried to shut it down, but it was tightly fastened back, and he couldn't move it. He decided to creep back to Jack and wake him. Together they would be a match for any native.

He crept back very quietly, stopping every now and again to listen for any other sounds from the intruder. He half thought he heard one behind him and listened again. No. Nothing.

On he went, and rounded the corner that led to his mattress, coming out of the shadow into the starlight.

And then he saw a black shadow standing in front of him! A shadow that seemed to look at him and recognize him. It flung itself on him, and held him tightly, while he struggled to shake it off.

'Boss!' said the shadow. 'Boss, Oola follow you. Oola here, boss. Oola here!'

The sound of Oola's voice woke everyone up – everyone, that is, except the snoring Tala. Mrs Cunningham sat up at once. Jack leapt off his mattress and found himself entangled in his mosquito-net. The girls sat up with hearts thumping loudly. What was happening?

Jack switched on a torch, and Dinah felt about for hers. Mrs Cunningham threw aside her net, and flashed her own torch in the direction of the noise. It lighted up a queer sight!

Philip was standing on the deck, and little Oola was kneeling in front of him, his arms clasping Philip's knees so tightly that the boy couldn't move!

'Let go!' said Philip. 'You're waking everyone up. What on *earth* have you come here for?'

'Oola yours, boss,' said the small voice. 'Oola belong you. Not send Oola away.'

'Philip! What *is* all this?' called Mrs Cunningham. 'Where's Bill? Isn't he back yet?'

'No, Mother!' said Philip. 'This is the kid we rescued from that snake-charmer we told you about – the one who was beating him. He's followed us all the way here!'

'Oola follow boat, all way, all way, Oola run,' said Oola.

'Good gracious! Fancy running all the way down the banks of the river!' said Jack. 'Poor little creature! He seems determined to be near you, Philip. Oola, are you hungry?'

'Oola eat down there,' said the little boy, pointing towards the hatchway. 'Oola no food two, three days.'

Mrs Cunningham examined him by the light of her torch, and exclaimed in horror. 'Why, he's absolutely *covered* in bruises and weals – and he's as thin as a rake. Poor little thing! Has he *really* run all the way after the boat to find you, Philip?'

'Seems so,' said Philip, finding his heart suddenly full of pity and affection for this strange little creature. He couldn't bear to think of him clambering through the bushes by the riverside all day long, trying to follow the boat – hungry, thirsty, tired and sore. All because Philip had rescued him from his hateful uncle! Perhaps nobody had ever been kind to him before.

Suddenly a voice came from the bank. 'Hallo! Are you all still up? I hope you didn't wait for me.'

It was Bill. He leapt on to the launch, saw Oola kneeling on the deck, and stopped in amazement.

'Whatever's all this? What's happening?' he demanded. 'Who's this come to visit us in the middle of the night?'

11

Oola and his present

Oola crouched down at the sound of Bill's loud voice. Philip felt him trembling against his knees. He pulled him up. 'It's all right,' he said. 'Don't be frightened. Bill, this is that kid we rescued this morning from the snake-charmer. He's followed us all the way here, running along the banks.'

Bill stared in astonishment. 'But – he can't do this!' he said. 'Climbing on board someone else's boat in the middle of the night! Has he stolen anything? Some small kids are taught to steal as soon as they can walk.'

'He took some food from the cabin. He says he hasn't had any for two or three days,' said Lucy-Ann. 'Bill, he seems to think he wants to be Philip's servant. Whatever are we to do?'

'He'll have to go,' said Bill. 'It's just a trick to get on the boat. No doubt his snake-charmer uncle has put him up to this, and is waiting for his share of the goods! Clear off, now, boy! Quick!'

Oola was so scared that he could hardly walk. He left Philip and stumbled over the deck towards the jetty. As he passed Mrs Cunningham, she put out her hand to the stumbling boy, and caught him, so that he came to a standstill. She turned him round gently so that he stood in the light of her torch, with his back towards Bill.

'Bill – look!' she said. And Bill looked, and saw the poor thin little body, with the bruises all over it. He gave an exclamation.

'Good heavens! Who did that? Poor little creature, he looks half-starved. Come here, Oola.'

Oola came, half reassured by the kinder tone in Bill's voice. Bill shone his torch on him, and the boy blinked. 'Why did you come, Oola?' asked Bill, still stern. 'Tell me the truth and nothing will harm you.'

'I come to find *him*,' said Oola, and pointed to Philip. 'I make him my boss. Oola his servant. Oola bring present for boss.'

Bill looked him over. Except for the dirty cloth round his waist, Oola had nothing to bring!

'You bring no present,' said Bill. 'Why do you lie, Oola?'

'Oola spik truth,' said the boy. 'My boss, he say he like snake. Very much like snake. So Oola bring one. Bargua snake!'

And, to everyone's horror, Oola slid his hand into his

245

waist-cloth and brought out a slim, wriggling green snake, spotted with bright red and yellow!

'Its mouth isn't sewn up!' yelled Jack. 'Look out, everybody! Look out, Oola, you fathead! It's a poisonous snake. Its bite will kill you!'

Dinah shot to the hatchway, ran down and locked herself into a cupboard, trembling all over. A *bargua*! One of the most poisonous snakes there were! How COULD Oola wear it round him like a belt! She felt quite sick.

Oola still held the snake, which writhed about in his hand, opening its mouth and showing its forked tongue.

'Throw it overboard, Oola!' shouted Bill. 'For goodness' sake, throw it overboard! Are you mad?'

'Oola bring present for boss,' said Oola, obstinately. He lifted the snake towards Philip, who retreated at once. He liked snakes. He was not afraid of them. But to take hold of a poisonous one which was already frightened and full of anger would be a crazy thing to do!

'THROW IT OVERBOARD!' yelled Bill, terribly afraid that somebody would get bitten. 'You silly little idiot!'

'Snake not bite,' said Oola. 'All poison gone. See!'

To everyone's horror he forced open the snake's mouth. Philip bent down and looked inside, suddenly feeling that the snake might not be dangerous after all. He looked for the poison-gland and the duct that led down to the hollow tooth out of which poison pours when a snake bites.

He looked up again in the midst of a dead silence. 'The snake's *not* poisonous,' he said, and he calmly took it from Oola. 'Someone has cut the ducts that take the poison from the poison-glands to the teeth. It's a horrible trick, because it usually means that the snake dies in three or four weeks' time. Oola – who did this?'

'Old woman,' said Oola. 'Oola tell her my boss wants bargua snake, and she give Oola this one. Safe snake, boss, not like snake-mouth sewn up. You like this one?'

Philip was now talking to the snake in his special 'animal'

voice, and it was attending, lying quite still in his hands.

'Poor thing!' said Philip. 'All because of me you have been injured! You have no poison in you now, but you will die because of that. You shall live with me and be happy till then. Oola, you must never have such a thing done to snakes again! It's cruel!'

'Yes, boss,' said Oola, humbly. He looked round fearfully at Bill. 'Oola stay?' he enquired. 'Oola boss's man. Belong him,' and he pointed at Philip.

'All right – you can stay for the night anyhow,' said Bill, feeling quite exhausted with all this. 'Come with me. I'll wake Tala and you can sleep with him.'

'Go, Oola,' said Philip, seeing the boy hesitate, and Oola went.

'I wanted to put some ointment on his back,' said Mrs Cunningham. 'Poor little mite! Oh, Philip – have we *got* to have that snake living with us now?'

'I'll keep it in my pocket,' said Philip. 'I won't let it out unless I'm alone, or with Jack. It's quite harmless, Mother. Mother, can we let Oola stay with us? He can help Tala and I'll see that he's not a nuisance. I can't imagine why he has attached himself to me.'

'Well, you rescued him from that awful uncle of his, didn't you!' said Lucy-Ann.

'We'll see what Bill says,' said Mrs Cunningham. 'He'll do what he can for him, I know. Where's Dinah?'

'Probably locked in the broom cupboard!' said Jack. 'I'll go and see.'

Dinah was still in the cupboard, feeling rather ashamed of herself now, but not daring to come out till someone fetched her. She was most relieved to see Jack.

Jack decided not to tell her yet that Philip had the snake. She might kick up a terrible fuss and have a violent quarrel with Philip. Better have all that in the morning, not now, when everyone was tired and upset.

'Come on out, Di,' he said, opening the door. 'Don't

worry! The snake wasn't even poisonous! The poor thing has had its poison-ducts cut, so no poison can run down to the hollow fangs. We had all that fright for nothing.'

'I don't believe it,' said Dinah. 'It's still poisonous. You're just making that up to get me out!'

'No. It's true, Dinah!' said Jack. 'Do come out. Everybody wants to go to bed now. Oola has gone to sleep with Tala. He's absolutely determined to be Philip's servant, poor little boy!'

Dinah imagined that the snake had also gone with Oola, and she consented to come up on deck again. Soon everyone had settled under their mosquito-nets and were soon asleep. What an extraordinary evening!

In about half an hour, when Tala was snoring loudly again, a small figure crept over the launch to where the boys slept. It was Oola. He had come to be near his 'boss'! He curled himself up on the bare deck at Philip's feet, and closed his eyes, perfectly happy and at peace. He was with his 'boss'. He was guarding him! No one could come near Philip without waking Oola.

In the morning Tala, as usual, awoke first. He remembered the episodes of the night and looked for Oola. The boy was gone. He nodded his head in satisfaction. Had he not told Mister Bill that boys like that were no good? But Mister Bill had said, 'He sleeps with you, he will stay here.' And now the boy was gone, and Tala was right.

He prepared breakfast, planning what to say to Bill. 'Sir, Tala right. Tala spoke true. Boy gone.'

Tala was therefore extremely surprised and disappointed to see Oola curled up at Philip's feet. He gave him a push with his foot and Oola was up on his feet at once, ready to defend Philip.

'You go back there,' said Tala, fiercely, in his own language, but under his breath so as not to wake anyone. He nodded towards his own quarters. Oola shook his head and sat down by Philip again. Tala raised his hand as if to strike him and Oola slid away deftly, running to hide.

But as soon as Tala went away Oola came back to Philip again, and sat looking down at the sleeping boy with so much pride and admiration in his face that Philip would have been quite embarrassed to see it.

The snake was safely in a little basket beside him. Oola scratched his finger against the basket and whistled very softly. The snake hissed and tried to get out.

'You are my boss's snake,' Oola told it in his own language. 'You belong him, Oola belong him!'

What a to-do at breakfast when Dinah realized that the snake now belonged to Philip, and he was going to keep it. She gave such a shriek when its head peeped out of his pocket that everyone jumped. 'Philip! I won't have you keep that snake. You know how I hate snakes. Bill, tell him he mustn't. Bill, I do so hate them. I shan't stay a minute longer on this boat if you say he can keep it. I'll go back to the hotel!'

'All right, Dinah,' said Bill, mildly. 'There's no need to go up in smoke. I shan't stop you from going back to the hotel if you are so distressed. I'll get Tala to run you back with a note to the hotel manager. You should be quite all right there, especially as he has two nice old English ladies coming to stay at his hotel this week to do some painting. They'll look after you.'

Dinah couldn't believe her ears. What! Bill would actually let her go back – all alone – instead of ordering Philip not to keep the snake?

'I'll call Tala now, shall I?' said Bill.

Dinah went brilliant red, and looked at him with tears in her eyes. 'No,' she said. 'I'd – I'd rather put up with the snake than leave you all. You know that. You win, Bill.'

'Good girl, Dinah,' said Bill with a sudden smile. 'Now – what are our plans for today? And WHAT are we going to do with Oola?'

12

Good news for Oola

Oola had been sent to have breakfast with Tala. Tala was very offhand with him, and kept him strictly in his place. He liked children, but this boy had no business here, on *his* boat, thought Tala.

Oola did his best to please Tala. He listened to all that he had to say, only spoke when he was spoken to, and put himself at the man's beck and call, running here and there at top speed for him.

When Tala was tinkering with the engine, Oola crept away to see Philip. He sat down in a corner and feasted his eyes on the boy, noting the tuft of hair in front, just like Dinah's, the loud, merry laugh, and the way he waited on his mother.

Oola nodded in satisfaction. This was his 'boss'; never before had he met anyone to whom he wanted to give such utter loyalty or love. He had never known his mother, who had died when he was born, and he had hated his father, who was as cruel as Bula, his uncle. When his father had gone away he had given the boy to Bula, to be of use to him in his snake-charming.

And then had begun a miserable life for Oola, which had become steadily worse. But now – ah, now he had *chosen* a master, his 'boss' Philip, the boy who sat over yonder, listening to big Mister Bill. Oola patted his full stomach contentedly, and thought about the present he had given to his 'boss.' Philip had the snake in his pocket – or somewhere about him – yes, under his shirt. Oola could see the boy put his hand there at times as if he were caressing something.

He heard his name being spoken by Bill, who was just then saying, 'And WHAT are we going to do with Oola?'

Oola's heart nearly stopped beating. To do with him? What did Big Mister Bill mean? Would they throw him overboard – or give him to the police? He bent forward anxiously to listen – and just at that moment a strong brown hand came down, and yanked him upright by the neck.

It was Tala! 'What are you doing here?' he said, in his own language. 'Sitting here half asleep in the morning! You come and help me, you lazy little son of a tortoise!'

Oola gazed at him fiercely, but did not dare to disobey. The words Bill had said rang in his ears still. '*What* are we to do with Oola?'

Bill and the others were discussing everything. Bill was all for putting the boy ashore, giving him some money, and letting him go off to some relative. How could they bother with a boy like that on the boat?

Mrs Cunningham wanted him to have a chance. 'At least let him stay till we've fed him up a bit and put some flesh on him,' she said. 'He's such a miserable little specimen. And when he looks up at me with those big frightened eyes as if all he expects is a blow, I just can't bear it.'

'He'd be an awful nuisance to Philip,' said Bill. 'I know what it is when one of these kids takes a fancy to anyone. Philip would find him underfoot all the time!'

'I could deal with him,' said Philip, quietly. 'I wouldn't mind.'

'What do you others think?' asked Mrs Cunningham, looking round.

'We'd like him,' said Lucy-Ann, and everyone nodded. 'We'll keep him busy – and so will Tala! Once Tala has got used to him he'll like him, I know he will. Don't send him away, Bill.'

Dinah was sitting as far away from Philip as she could, trying not to think of the snake he had somewhere about his person. She still felt very upset but she was doing her best to be sensible. Bill felt pleased with her. He turned to her.

'You agree too, Dinah?'

She nodded. 'Yes. I wish he was cleaner and not so skinny, but I like him.'

'Oh, well – we can soon get rid of the dirt and the bones, said Bill. 'I'll give him a trial, and tell Tala to see that Oola washes himself, and has a clean bit of cloth to wind round his middle. I'll call Oola. OOLA! OOLA!'

Oola dropped the piece of wire he had been holding while Tala tinkered with the engine and ran forward immediately, his heart thumping. Was he to be turned away?

He stood before Bill, eyes downcast. 'Oola,' said Bill, 'we are going to give you a chance and let you stay with us while we are on this ship. You will do everything that Tala tells you. I am Big Mister Bill, he is Little Mister Tala. Understand?'

'Big Mister kind, Big Mister good!' said Oola, his eyes shining. 'Oola glad. Oola be good worker!'

He looked at Philip, his face one big smile. 'I be with my boss!' he said to him. 'Oola boss's servant! Oola work for him!'

Bill called Tala. 'Tala! Come here a minute!' Tala came so quickly that it was quite obvious he had been listening. He saluted and stood waiting, his face rather stern.

'Tala – Oola is to stay with us while we are on the ship. See that he washes himself and eats properly. See that he does not steal. Give him work to do. Tell me if he is good or bad.'

Tala saluted again but said nothing. He sent a quick look at Oola, who was now standing as close to Philip as possible, his head bowed, listening.

'That's all, Tala,' said Bill. 'Today we go on down the river, and I will tell you where to stop.'

'Very good, Sir,' said Tala, and went off, still looking rather grim. He heard his name called again.

'Tala! Tala, Tala, Tala!' He went running back at once. But this time the caller was Kiki, who felt that she could not keep silent any longer!

'Tala! Wipe your feet! One, two, four, seven, three, quick march! PHEEEEEEEEEEEE!'

The police-whistle ending startled everybody, especially Oola, who almost threw himself overboard in his fright. Tala forgot his gloom and burst into one of his enormous guffaws, staggering about the deck in delight at the parrot's ridiculous talk.

'Stop that whistling, Kiki,' ordered Mrs Cunningham. 'It goes right through my head. What a din!'

'Din-din-din-dinner!' chanted Kiki, enjoying the interest she had created. 'Din-din-din . . . '

But a sharp tap on her beak from Jack silenced her, and she flew to a corner and muttered rude things all to herself.

'Tala, take Oola with you and deal with him,' said Bill. 'See that he gets clean from top to toe first of all. He's dirty.'

This was news to Tala. He hadn't realized that Oola was dirty from his journey. He looked in his direction at once and pretended that he could see something horrid. He wrinkled up his nose in disdain.

'Bad,' he said, scornfully. 'Bad dirt. Pooh!'

'Pooh!' repeated Kiki in delight, waddling out of her corner. 'Pooh! Boo! Bad dirt, pooh!'

Tala roared, grabbed Oola by the hand, and went off with him, Oola protesting all the way.

When they were safely out of hearing, Jack turned to Bill.

'Did anything interesting happen last night?' he asked. 'At Ala-ou-iya, I mean. You were jolly late back, weren't you?'

'Yes. I don't know that I found out much,' said Bill. 'The man I had to contact didn't come home to his house till fairly late, and I had to wait for him. He knows Raya Uma, of course, and he thinks he is up to something, because he keeps disappearing, but nobody knows where he goes.'

'What is Uma supposed to be doing when he isn't disappearing?' asked Mrs Cunningham.

'Well, apparently he is interested in Ciné-Town,' said Bill. 'He goes there quite a lot – has a bedroom in the big hotel they've run up there. He says he was an actor himself once, and is extremely interested in films – that may be just a tale, of course, to cover other activities.'

'Yes – but I can quite well believe that he *was* once an actor,' said Mrs Cunningham. 'Those photographs you have of him – they might all be of different men! I am sure he could put on different voices and ways with each change of costume!'

'You're right,' said Bill. 'Well, granted that he *was* once an actor, and *is* interested in films, where does he disappear to for a week or ten days every now and again? He's up to mischief of some kind, I'm sure!'

There was a pause. 'What *sort* of mischief, Bill?' said Jack.

'Well – here is a list of some of his past activities,' said Bill, taking out a notebook. 'Gun-running on a big scale – that means supplying guns illegally to those who will pay a big price for them. Spying – he's clever at that, but no Government will use him now, because they can't trust him – he's quite likely to go over to the other side if they offer him a bit more.'

'What a charming fellow!' said Jack, stroking Kiki, who was now on his knee.

'And smuggling,' said Bill. 'That's another thing he is very successful at. He did it on such a big scale once that he almost made himself a millionaire – then someone gave him away, and in spite of big bribes he offered to others to take the blame, he had to go to prison. Well – those are just a few things he has done. Now it's said that he has very little money indeed, not many friends, and is determined to pull off something big.'

'And you think that that something big might be hatched out here?' said Philip. 'How can you stop him?'

'It isn't my job to stop him – only to report back to head-quarters,' said Bill. 'If it's nothing that will harm our own country or its trade, they won't do anything, but if he's stirring up trouble somewhere – arming some group or other that will start a small war and plunge us all into danger once more, then we *shall* have something to say.'

'And you found out nothing much last night?' said Mrs Cunningham. 'Well, maybe you'll track down something at the next place – what was its name?'

'A place called Ullabaid,' said Bill. 'The man I saw yesterday says that Uma has a small motor-boat himself, and uses this river quite a bit – so it's clear that the places he goes to are somewhere on or near the river. Well – we'd better start. Go and see if Tala is ready, Jack. Tell him we'll go slowly – it's a lovely day, and we're in no hurry!'

Jack hurried off to the other end of the boat.

'Can you start again now, Tala?' he called. 'You can? Good! Off we go, then!'

13

After tea

It was a lovely trip that day. The sun as usual shone all day long, and Tala kept near to the left bank on which tall trees grew, in order to have a little shade when possible. They passed many villages on the banks, and whenever the natives saw the boat gliding along, out they came and shouted and waved.

Oola was kept busy by Tala, and Philip saw little of him till the afternoon rest. The sun was so hot then that the boat was run in under the shade of trees, and moored. Everyone puffed and blew, and Bill ordered a general rest.

Then it was that Oola crept forward to where the boys lay in a shady corner, and curled up not far off, his eyes on Philip.

Philip saw him and grinned at him, and Oola was happy at once. 'Boss,' he whispered, 'Oola is here to guard you. Sleep in peace!'

And, although everyone else on board, including Tala, slept soundly, Oola was awake, his eyes darting about at any sound, but always coming back to rest adoringly on Philip's flushed face. Once he saw the wicked-looking head of the bargua snake peeping out of the boy's shirt, and smiled proudly. Ah – his lord had his present safely. He even kept it close to his heart.

Tea was a very pleasant meal. Everyone felt refreshed after their sleep, and was ready for biscuits and something to drink. Mrs Cunningham was the only one who wanted a cup of tea – the others all demanded lime juice.

Oola had disappeared as soon as he heard Tala calling for him in a fierce whisper. Tala was actually quite pleased with the small boy – but he was jealous of the way he went to sit near the children when he had a chance. Tala would not have dared to do that.

Oola had become extremely interested in the launch's motor. Tala was already amazed at the way the boy grasped all the details. 'Oola drive boat!' said the boy, after tea. 'Oola know how!'

'Oh no you don't,' said Tala, at once. 'No monkey tricks from you, Oola, or I go straight to Big Mister Bill and say "Throw this boy overboard, he no good, Sir!" You hear, Oola?'

'I hear, Little Master,' said Oola at once, terrified that Tala might complain of him. 'Oola clean up oil for you? Oola polish?'

Yes – Oola was welcome to do any of the dirty work, certainly. The only thing that Tala regretted about that was that the boy would become filthy dirty again – and Tala had taken great pride in getting him spotlessly clean that morning. He had rubbed far too hard, and the boy had cried out when his bruises had been roughly scrubbed.

'Ah – no filth, now, no dirt!' said Tala, when he had

finished. 'You had much dirt, Oola, very very bad.'

Oola certainly looked better now – clean, his mass of black hair smoothed back, and a new, brilliant blue cloth round his middle, of which he was extremely proud.

They came to Ullabaid, a pleasant-looking village set a little back from the bank of the river. There was quite a fleet of small boats tied to the fairly big jetty.

'I'm going ashore,' said Bill. 'Like to come with me? We'll leave your mother in peace, I think. We're a noisy lot, you know!'

The children leapt to the jetty with Bill and ran ashore, leaving Tala, Oola and Mrs Cunningham behind. Tala was annoyed, because he would have liked to stretch his legs ashore too, and because he could not go he would not let Oola go, either, and set him a long job to do. Oola scowled, determined to slip off as soon as Tala's back was turned – or, as was most likely, the man fell asleep. He had the unusual gift of being able to sleep at any moment, and in any place, no matter how uncomfortable.

The village of Ullabaid was quite a big one. There were the usual low, whitewashed houses, with sleeping-roofs, and the usual hearths outside for cooking. There were also the crowds of almost-naked small village children, first half afraid and shy, then bold and curious.

Bill went to the biggest house in the place, which turned out to be a school. The teacher was friendly, with a fine face, intelligent and kind. He seemed surprised to see Bill, but when Bill showed him a card, and spoke a few words in a low tone, he asked him in at once.

The four were left to wander round. Kiki was quite silent for once in a way, staring round at the big-eyed children of the village.

A boy about twelve came up with a packet of post-cards in his hands. He showed one to Jack, and pointed away in the distance, nodding his head vigorously, and saying something over and over again.

The four children crowded round to look at the card. It

was a picture of a ruin – an old old temple which had apparently been discovered and excavated some years before when a famous archaeologist had brought along a big digging-party.

'The Temple of the Goddess Hannar,' read Philip. 'Looks interesting. Shall we go and see it while Bill is busy? Here, boy – how far is it? How – far?'

The boy could not speak any English, but he guessed what Philip was saying, and gestured that he would take them.

They followed the boy between the trees and then through some cultivated fields, and were themselves followed by a rabble of excited children, who could see that a tip would soon be forthcoming.

And behind the rabble came a small figure, keeping out of sight – Oola! He had waited till Tala had fallen asleep, and had left the launch immediately. He had asked where his friends had gone, and been told – and now he was keeping them in sight, not daring to join them.

The rabble of children began to push close to the four friends, and Jack looked round impatiently. 'Keep back!' he said. 'Do you hear me? – keep back!'

But after a moment or two the little crowd was on their heels again – and this time Kiki took a hand.

'Back!' she ordered. 'Back, back, quack, quack, BACK!' And then she gave her famous imitation of an aeroplane about to crash, which alarmed the little crowd behind so much that they at once kept a very long distance away.

Philip laughed. 'Good old Kiki!' he said. 'I don't know what we'd do without you!'

They came to the temple at last. It was rather disappointing – much more of a ruin than the picture appeared to show. 'It's like one of those buildings in Ciné-Town,' said Lucy-Ann. 'All front but not much at the back!'

'Look here,' said Philip, suddenly. 'See these funny little insects, basking in the sun – I think my snake would like those. He's probably hungry by now.'

And, to Dinah's horror, Philip slid the bargua snake from beneath his shirt, and let him loose on the ground, not far from the insects.

Dina screamed, of course, and ran back. Her scream startled the local children – and when they saw the snake, which they all knew to be deadly poisonous, they too screamed in terror and fled.

'Bargua!' they shouted. 'Bargua!' The big ones dragged along the little ones, and even the big boy who was the guide fled too, after one look at the gliding snake.

'Good gracious!' said Philip, quite as startled as the other children. 'They've all gone – just because I took my snake out for a meal. What a to-do!'

'I don't blame them,' said Dinah, from a distance. 'We know the snake's safe – but they don't! Honestly, Philip, that was a mad thing to do. Anyway, you'll lose the snake now, thank goodness! It won't come back to you now you've let it loose.'

'Well, if it doesn't, it can go,' said Philip. 'But I bet it'll come back!'

The snakes snapped at the insects, and had a very good meal. It also glided into some undergrowth and caught a small frog, which it swallowed whole. Then it came back to Philip! The others watched in amazement as it glided over to him, and, without any hesitation at all, wriggled up his leg, made its way between two buttons of his shirt, and disappeared.

'Ugh! It makes me feel sick,' said Dinah, watching in fascinated horror.

'Don't watch then, silly,' said Philip. Then he looked round, alarmed.

'I say – I believe it's going to get dark pretty soon – what's the time? Whew, yes, we've let the time slip by without noticing it. We must get back to the launch at once. Come on.'

But after about ten minutes the children knew they had

gone wrong. They stopped and looked round.

'We didn't pass that tree struck by lightning before, did we?' said Jack, doubtfully. 'Anyone remember it?'

Nobody did. 'Better go back a bit,' said Philip, feeling anxious. 'Buck up. Darkness may come at any moment and none of us has a torch.'

They went back for a hundred yards or so, and then took another path. But this one led them into a wood and they knew *that* was wrong. They went back again, all of them in rather a panic.

'I'll shout and see if those local children will come back,' said Jack. So he called in a stentorian voice: 'Hey, you kids! Come back! Come back, I say!'

'Come back, I say!' echoed Kiki, and ended with a screech that could surely have been heard half a mile away.

But no little band of local children came running up. Except for a bird that went on and on singing without a stop, there was hardly a sound to be heard.

'What are we to do?' said Jack, anxiously. 'There isn't even a house in sight. Gosh, this is awful, Philip!'

'What I'm afraid of is that darkness will fall suddenly, as it always does here,' said Philip.

And, just as he said that, darkness did fall, like a black curtain! Now they were truly lost, and Lucy-Ann caught hold of Jack's hand in fright.

'What are we to do?' she said. 'What are we to do?'

14

Back to the boat

The four children stood in the darkness, hoping to see the stars shine out bright and clear. Then they might be able to see a little. But for once in a way it was a cloudy night, and only when the clouds parted could a few stars be seen.

Their eyes got used to the darkness in a little while, and they made a few steps forward. Then Jack thought he caught sight of something moving cautiously a short distance away.

'Who's there?' he called at once. 'Don't come any nearer. Who is it?'

The shadow moved quickly forward, and knelt down at Philip's feet. He felt two hands grasping his knees. It was Oola!

'Oola here, boss,' said a voice. 'Oola follow, follow. Tala say no, not come, but Oola come. Oola guard you, boss.'

Such a wave of relief went over all four children that they could hardly speak!

'*Oola*! Good gracious, you're the last person we expected,' said Philip, gladly. He patted the boy's head as he knelt. 'Get up. We're VERY glad to see you. We're lost. Do you know the way back to the launch!'

'Yes, boss,' said Oola, delighted at the pat on his head. 'Oola take you now. Follow Oola.'

'Have you been behind us all the time, Oola?' asked Lucy-Ann, astonished.

'Yes, Missy, all time Oola follow, follow,' said Oola, walking on ahead. 'Oola guard his boss.'

Oola seemed to have cat's eyes. He went forward without any hesitation, taking this path and that, and at last they came to the village, which now had fires alight, and looked rather mysterious.

The band of children came running up when they saw strangers walking through their village – but when they saw that it was the same children who had had the terrible snake, they ran away in fear, crying out loudly, 'Bargua! Bargua!'

Philip stopped. He had seen the big boy who had acted as guide. He was standing some distance away, peering at them, lighted by the flames from a fire.

'Oola – see that boy over there?' said Philip, pointing. 'Go give him this money.'

'No! Boy not good!' said Oola, indignantly.

'Oola, yes!' said Philip in a commanding voice, and Oola at once took the money and sped off to the boy. Judging by his angry voice, he was ticking the boy off well and truly – but he gave him the money all the same. The boy was delighted and ran into his house at once, calling out something in an excited voice.

'After all, the kid *did* take us all the way to the old temple,' said Philip, and the others agreed. 'Whew! What a stir the snake made! I never dreamed that those kids would be so frightened.'

'We're going to get into a frightful row with Bill when we get back to the launch,' said Jack, gloomily. 'He won't like us being out in the dark like this.'

'Let's hope he won't be back,' said Dinah, who had no wish to make Bill annoyed again.

They made their way quickly to the river, and went on board the launch. Mrs Cunningham was sitting reading down in the cabin, for it was unexpectedly cool that evening. She was most relieved to see them.

'Oh – you had Oola with you – that's all right then,' she said, as she saw Oola's face peering down the hatch with the others. 'Bill's not back yet. Are you hungry? Because if so, tell Tala, and we'll have supper.'

'We're always hungry,' said Jack. 'You never really need to ask us that, Aunt Allie. But we'd better wait for Bill.'

Bill came back ten minutes later. 'Had supper yet?' he asked. 'Good, tell Tala we'll have it. I'm famished. Well, what did you four do?'

'Nothing much – just went to see an old temple, but there wasn't much to look at when we got there,' said Jack.

'There was a lot of digging round about this district some years ago,' said Bill. 'I've been hearing about it from that teacher you saw – a very fine and intelligent fellow. Made me wish I could do a litttle digging myself!'

'Did you hear anything about Raya Uma?' asked Jack,

very much relieved that Bill had shown so little interest in their own doings that evening. He was determined to keep Bill on some safe subject now.

'Yes. The teacher knows him quite well, and likes him. Says he is a most interesting man and can talk on any subject under the sun! Even archaeology, which is rather a learned subject – the study of old buildings and other remains. He appears to think that Uma is here to study the old temples and so on that have already been excavated – but he's not, of course. That's just a cover for something *else* he's doing!'

Jack suddenly sniffed hard. A most delicious smell was coming from Tala's quarters. Fried fish!

'Yes,' said Mrs Cunningham with a laugh. 'Tala has been fishing – and we're having his catch for supper. Doesn't it smell *good*!'

'My word, yes,' said Philip. 'We've been having so many cold meals that I didn't even guess that Tala could cook. I bet Oola is pleased – he'll enjoy a meal like that.'

'That reminds me – Tala was very angry because Oola slipped off this evening, after you had all gone,' said his mother. 'He came to me in quite a rage. But as Oola had apparently done all the work Tala had set him to do, I didn't take much notice. I suppose he went after you, didn't he?'

'Yes,' said Jack. 'He came to guard his lord! He's cracked about Philip. I simply can't understand it!' He looked at Philip and grinned.

'I can't understand it either,' said Dinah, at once. 'I mean – I could understand him having an admiration for Jack, because of Kiki – but why Philip?'

The conversation was cut short by Oola and Tala bringing trays. The big dish of fried fish, garnished with some strange greenery, and surrounded by most succulent vegetables, was hailed with enormous enthusiasm, and Tala grinned in pleasure as he saw the smiling faces that greeted him.

Oola was a little subdued. He had been well scolded by

Tala, who had threatened to tell Bill how he had left his work and run off.

But when Oola had related to Tala how the children had been lost in the darkness, and how he, Oola, had rescued them and brought them safely back, Tala said no more. He did not praise Oola, for secretly he was jealous of what the boy had done, but at least he ceased to scold him.

Oola was very much hoping that Tala would let him share in this delicious meal, and so he was most attentive and obedient. Tala could not hold his anger for long, and had already made up his mind to give the boy a big helping as soon as he could.

Everyone set to and ate heartily, even Mrs Cunningham, who usually had a very small appetite. 'Tala would make his fortune in a restaurant as a chef,' she remarked. 'What *is* this sauce? I've never tasted anything so delicious in my life.'

Better not ask,' said Bill, mischievously. 'It might be a score or so of some peculiar insects mashed up – or . . . '

Dinah gave a small moan, and spat out a mouthful of the sauce at once.

'Don't, Dinah!' said Mrs Cunningham. 'Do remember your manners. Bill, don't say things like that. You've rather spoilt the sauce for me too.'

'Sorry,' said Bill, contritely. 'It was just a bit of fun. I do agree that this sauce is marvellous. Ah, here's Tala. Tala, this sauce is fine. What is it made of?'

Dinah put her hands over her ears at once. She felt sure that it was mashed-up insects, as Bill had said, or water-snails, or something equally horrible.

'Sir, it is milk and onion, and bark of a tree called in our language Mollia,' said Tala, pleased at the praise. 'Also some mashed-up – mashed-up – how you call it? – er . . . '

'Insects,' supplied Jack, helpfully.

Tala looked hurt. 'Tala not use insects. Tala use – yes – it is mashed-up potato – a very very little.'

Everyone roared. It seemed so ordinary after what Bill

had been suggesting. Tala smiled. He liked to make people laugh, though he certainly had no idea what the present joke was.

'Take your hands from your ears, Dinah,' said Jack. 'It was only mashed up POTATO – very very little!'

Dinah took down her hands, very much relieved to be told that the sauce was so harmless. The dish was soon completely empty, and everyone felt much better.

Oola was sent with a dish of fresh fruit, bought by Tala at one of the villages that day. It was about all that anyone could manage after the very rich fish.

When the meal had been cleared away, Tala and Oola sat down to theirs. Oola was very happy. Here he was, with the most marvellous meal in front of him, and the evening's adventure to gloat over. He had guarded his boss, and brought him safely back to the boat!

He began to tell Tala about it all over again, but Tala had no wish to hear such an epic twice. He told Oola to take the dishes and scrape them over the side of the launch.

'Fish eat pieces, fish grow fat, Tala catch fish, we eat again,' he explained to Oola, who saw the point at once.

Oola went to scrape the dishes, and suddenly caught sight of another boat gliding up through the darkness, its prow set with a single light. He stared at it. Would it pass by without hailing their own boat?

It slid into the bank, and stopped by the jetty. Bill had heard the motor, and was already looking over the side.

A man jumped out of the motor-boat and walked to where the launch was tied. He called up loudly.

'Anyone there?'

'Yes. Who's that?' Bill shouted back.

'Someone to see you!' came an answering shout. 'Can I come aboard?'

'What's your name?' asked Bill.

'RAYA UMA!' came the answer, and everyone on board sat up at once. Goodness – Raya Uma!

15

Mr Raya Uma

Bill was enormously surprised. He was so nonplussed that he didn't say a word.

'Hey – can I come on board or not?' said the voice impatiently. 'I heard there was an English family on the river, and I thought I'd like a chat.'

Bill recovered himself. 'Yes – come on up,' he shouted back. 'You took me by surprise. I wasn't expecting to hear an English voice here, I must say!'

'Shall we go away, Bill?' said Jack, in a low voice. Bill shook his head.

'No. Better stay with me. I don't know if he guesses who I am or not. Anyway, it's better if he sees a whole family aboard. Here he is!'

Tala had gone to light the man up to the launch. Now he was bringing him to where Bill and the others sat under an awning draped with mosquito-netting, lighted by a big lantern. Everyone gazed at him in interest.

They saw a medium-sized man, dressed in ordinary summer clothes – flannel trousers, shirt and thin pullover. He wore a white linen hat, and had a beard and thin little moustache. He wore dark glasses like Bill.

He smiled down and the children saw that he had very white teeth. He bowed to Mrs Cunningham, and, as Tala held back the mosquito-net, he put out his hand. She shook it, and then he shook hands with Bill. He nodded at the four children.

'Ah – you've got your family with you, I see!'

'Yes – the children all had flu very badly, and the doctor said they should go somewhere warm – abroad if possible – so we decided to come out here,' said Mrs Cunningham,

266

politely. 'I must say it's doing them a great deal of good.'

'Ah – and what are the children's names?' asked Mr Uma, smiling down and showing a lot of teeth.

Philip answered for all of them. 'I'm Philip – that's Jack – Lucy-Ann – and Dinah.'

'And what is the parrot's name? What an unusual pet!' said Mr Uma.

'Her name's Kiki,' said Jack. 'Kiki, this is Mr Uma.'

'Wipe your feet, blow your nose, fetch the doctor,' said Kiki, politely, spoiling the whole effect by giving a terrible screech at the end.

'Don't, Kiki,' said Mrs Cunningham. 'Not when we have visitors!'

'How did you hear of us?' asked Bill, offering Mr Uma a seat.

'Oh, news soon gets round, you know,' said Mr Uma. He gave Bill a straight look. 'I've no doubt you've heard *my* name too,' he said.

'Er – yes,' said Bill, frowning as if he was trying to remember where. 'Someone told me of a Mr Uma who was interested in films at Ciné-Town.'

'Oh, that's only a side-show for me,' said Mr Uma, puffing at his cigarette. 'My great hobby is archaeology.' He looked at the four children and made what they considered to be a very feeble joke. 'That's the study of arks, you know!'

The children ha-ha-ed politely. How old did he think they were, making feeble jokes like that? Lucy-Ann tried to see if he had the snake-like scar on his arm, but his shirt-sleeves were long, and she couldn't.

'We went to see an old temple outside Ullabaid this afternoon,' said Jack. 'Very disappointing. All front and no back – like the one at Ciné-Town.'

Mr Uma took this as a joke and laughed too much. 'Ah, yes,' he said. 'Well, of course, archaeology *is* disappointing. Like the story of old Brer Rabbit, you know – "he diggy-diggy-dig but no meat dar".'

'I suppose it's very very expensive to do a lot of excavating for old towns and so on, isn't it?' asked Mrs Cunningham, seeing that the children did not appreciate Mr Uma very much.

'Yes, Ma'am! You can pay out thousands of pounds doing that!' said Mr Uma. 'I've given it up, it's too expensive. You don't make any money out of it, either – your only reward is the excitement of – er – uncovering ages-old civilisations. All the same, it's a wonderful hobby. I've decided to combine an interest in films with my hobby – make a bit of money in films, and spend it wandering about this old, old country, making maps and plans of the last excavations and so on. And what about *you* sir – are *you* interested in that kind of thing?'

'About as much as the average man,' said Bill, cautiously, knowing that he was being sounded about his own mysterious work. 'But any new experience is of interest to me. I write articles, you know, and one of these days I'm going to write a book – plenty of interesting things to put into it!'

The children smiled quietly to themselves. Bill did write articles. That was true – but this was the first time they had heard of a book. Bill *could* write a marvellous book if he were allowed to! The things he had seen and done were quite unbelievable. They felt proud at having shared in so many of his adventures.

'Ah – a writer! A man of leisure,' said Mr Uma. 'It's only you writers and you painters that can afford to dispense with an office and go all over the world to look for material for your brush or your pen.'

The children began to feel bored. It was quite obvious now that Mr Uma did not know for certain who Bill was, nor whether he had come out merely for a holiday or on some other mission. He and Bill had been 'crossing swords' so to speak, testing each other out. They felt that Bill was winning. He had persuaded Mr Uma that he was a writer, they were sure of it.

'Where are you going to next?' asked Mr Uma. 'May I offer you any hospitality? I have a little shack farther down the river — I'm on my way there now, actually. I would be pleased to give you dinner — such as it is — if you and your wife would care to come?'

Bill considered this invitation quickly. Should he accept? It would look queer if he didn't. Well — he might conceivably find out a little more if he went to Uma's house. So he nodded and thanked him.

'Well, thank you, that's kind of you. We'll be pleased to come. When? Tomorrow?'

'Certainly,' said Mr Uma, and got up to go. 'Tomorrow night at seven o'clock, shall we say? Your man will know the landing jetty at Chaldo, I'm sure. I will be there to meet you and take you to my house.'

'Stay and have a drink,' said Bill. 'I'll call Tala.'

But Mr Uma would not stay. He bowed very politely, and raised the mosquito-net. Then he almost fell over somebody crouching on the floor just outside.

He kicked out and there was a yell.

'Now then — who's this? Get out of the way there, lying ready to trip me up!' roared Mr Uma, losing his temper suddenly and surprisingly. He kicked out again.

Philip was up in a trice, guessing it was Oola who had crept up as usual to be near him.

'Mr Uma — it's only the little boy who helps our man,' he said, angrily, and at once felt Bill's hand pressing his shoulder warningly.

'Sorry, Mr Uma,' said Bill. 'I hope you haven't hurt your foot, kicking out like that.'

Mr Uma didn't quite know how to take that. He recovered himself immediately, said good-night quite heartily, and was led off by Tala with a lantern.

'Oola! It serves you right if people fall over you, if you hide in corners like that!' said Bill.

'Bad man that,' said Oola. 'Bad bad man. Oola come to guard boss from bad man.'

269

'Don't be silly,' said Bill. 'You don't know anything about him. Or do you?'

Oola shook his head. 'Oola know he bad man, Oola say so. Oola not seen bad man before.'

'Go behind with Tala,' said Bill. 'And don't come over to us again till we call you. Understand?'

Oola disappeared, and Bill went under the mosquito-net to the others. Uma's motor-boat had now been started up, and had gone down the river, disturbing all the stars reflected in the water.

'Well?' said Bill to his wife. 'What do you think of our friend Uma?'

'I don't trust him a scrap,' said Mrs Cunningham. 'He's, he's ...'

'Slimy,' said Dinah, and everyone nodded. It was just the right word.

'What do you suppose he *is* up to?' said Bill. 'Anything?'

Mrs Cunningham considered. 'No,' she said. 'I think he's got a bad reputation and knows it, and he's nervous in case anyone *should* think he's up to anything and spy on him. I think he's probably hard-up, and making a bit of money in Ciné-Town somewhere. He was so insistent on his love for old buildings that I feel his *real* interest must be in something else.'

'You mean he may be using this archaeology hobby of his to camouflage the business he's doing in Ciné-Town?' asked Bill.

'Yes,' said Mrs Cunningham.

'Well, I bet whatever he's doing in Ciné-Town is something underhand,' said Jack. 'Probably backing a shady little fair or something – or a string of shops – and having an interest in the film too. Plenty of irons in the fire.'

'Well, if that's the kind of thing he's doing, it's pretty harmless from my point of view,' said Bill. 'I am after bigger stuff than that – the kind of things I told you he had done before! If it's no more than messing about in Ciné-Town, well, he's of no interest to the High-Ups!'

'Good,' said Mrs Cunningham, heaving a sigh of relief. 'I don't want you mixed up in anything dangerous, Bill – and I somehow think that Raya Uma could be very dangerous and very ruthless.'

'You're quite right, my dear!' said Bill. 'Now, what about bed? I'll just go and stand by the rail. The stars are out beautifully now, and I shall enjoy a quiet ten minutes looking down the river.'

They all said good night. They were tired, and fell asleep immediately their heads were on the pillows. Bill stood silently gazing out, thinking of the strange Mr Uma. Then he saw a small figure creeping over the deck and settling down at the foot of Philip's mattress. Oola had come to guard his boss!

Oola sat up in fright when Bill came over, on his way to his own mattress.

'You may stay, Oola,' said Bill, softly, and Oola sank down again happily. His lord was asleep – and he, Oola, was guarding him!

16

Next day

Next day Tala took the boat farther on down the river. They went very slowly, for Chaldo was only half a day's run, and they did not want to get there too soon. They passed some desolate country on the way, almost desert-like.

'Some of Mr Uma's beloved excavations must have been going on here!' said Jack. 'Bill, it certainly must cost an awful lot of money to dig over this enormous expanse – look!'

'It does,' said Bill. 'But there are rewards, you know. It's not only old ruined cities that are found lying beneath the mud and dust of centuries, it's treasure too.'

'Treasure!' said Philip, surprised. 'What treasure?'

'Well, much of this country held age-old buildings that housed the tombs of rich kings,' said Bill. 'Don't ask me their names, I've forgotten them.'

'Nebuchadnezzar?' suggested Lucy-Ann.

Bill laughed. 'You certainly know your Bible, Lucy-Ann. Yes – probably even Nebuchadnezzar might have lived in a palace not many miles from here, or the great King Sargon! I really don't know. Anyway, when they died, they were buried in magnificent tombs, surrounded by their jewels and their other treasures, such as jewelled shields, wonderful swords, and so on.'

'My word!' said Jack, thrilled. 'And do you mean to say that things like that have been dug up – things thousands of years old?'

'Oh yes,' said Bill. 'They are in museums all over the world – bought gladly because of their historic value. They are valuable in themselves too, of course. I have seen one beautifully carved gold bowl, with bulls all the way round it, that must have been worth thousands of pounds. It was set with wonderful precious stones.'

'Well, then,' said Jack, 'I'm not so sure that Mr Uma's hobby isn't just the right one for him. Picking up priceless treasures for nothing!'

'That's where you're wrong,' said Bill. 'They can't be picked up for nothing – as I told you, a digging outfit, composed perhaps of fifty or so workmen, and a good sprinkling of white experts, may cost thousands of pounds. And we should certainly know if Mr Uma had an outfit like that!'

'Yes – I suppose you would,' said Jack. 'I mean – you can't *help* seeing wholesale excavations going on, can you? It would be in the papers too, of course.'

'Look – there are some ruins, over there!' cried Lucy-Ann, pointing to the opposite bank. 'They look fairly recent. Would Tala know about them, do you think?'

'Go and ask him, if you like,' said Bill. 'I don't expect he can tell you much.'

The children went off to ask Tala. He nodded his head. 'Tala know. Tala's father, he dig there. Dig for treasure, much, much treasure. But no find any. All gone.'

That seemed to be all Tala knew. The children went back to Bill and repeated what Tala had told them. He nodded.

'Yes – he meant that whatever expert was in charge of the digging probably had a plan showing that royal tombs were to be found at a certain depth below – tombs possibly with much treasure. But when they got down to them, the graves were probably already despoiled and robbed.'

'But who did *that*?' said Lucy-Ann.

'Maybe robbers three or four thousand years ago,' said Bill, and smiled at Lucy-Ann's surprised face. 'I told you that this is an old, old land, that goes back thousands of years. Under the dust archaeologists may find ruins of city upon city, one built above the other.'

This was almost impossible for Lucy-Ann to grasp – city upon city! She tried to send her mind back through the centuries and to imagine the years passing over the land on which she was now gazing – cities rising, falling into ruin, other cities rising on the ruins and themselves falling into dust, only to have yet more towns built upon them.

She gave a little shiver. 'I don't much like thinking about it,' she said. 'Let's talk about something else, Bill.'

Bill gave her a hug. 'Well – what about lime-juice?' he said. 'Shall we talk about that, Lucy-Ann? It seems a very suitable subject for this hot day.'

'Oh, Bill – what you mean is that you want me to *fetch* you some,' said Lucy-Ann, who knew Bill's little ways very well. 'Jack – Philip – do you want some lime-juice?'

'Juice!' echoed Kiki. 'Juicy, juicy, juicy! Juicy Lucy! Send for the juice! Blow the juice!'

Philip was giving his snake an airing, and it was slithering round and about his feet. Lucy-Ann did not mind it, but

273

Dinah did, so the boys usually chose a moment when Dinah was down below, doing something there.

'Isn't it a lovely creature?' said Philip, admiring the bright green of its skin, and the brilliant markings, or 'spottings' as the hotel manager had called them. 'It's a shame it's had its poison-ducts cut, isn't it, Jack?'

'Well, personally, at the moment, I'm glad it can't give me a poisonous bite,' said Jack.

The lime-juice arrived, Oola carrying the tray proudly. He was pleased to see the snake gliding round – his present to his lord! Dinah stopped dead when she saw it, and Philip picked it up at once.

The day went pleasantly enough, especially as, for the first time, they came to a little cove where the water was clean and clear enough to bathe.

'You come in too, Oola,' said Jack. 'Do you good!'

But nothing would persuade the small boy to get into the tepid water. He touched it with his toe, yelped loudly and drew it back as if something had bitten him. He gazed in wonder and admiration as all four children swam and dived and kicked about under water. He had been deputed to hold the bargua while Philip bathed, and he was very proud to hang it round his neck and keep it there.

Kiki was not very pleased with the way in which everyone deserted her for the pool. She flew to an overhanging branch and screamed at them.

Philip splashed her. 'Stop that row, Kiki! You sound as if you're being killed!'

Kiki flew high in the air, angry at being splashed. She flew down to the deck and waddled up to Oola for sympathy. But when she saw the snake hanging round his neck she backed away, hissing exactly like a snake herself. Mrs Cunningham smiled to see her, and made her come to her shoulder.

'Poor Polly,' said Kiki, into her ear. 'Poor poor Polly. Jolly Polly, jolly Polly.'

'Well, which are you, poor or jolly?' said Mrs Cunningham, laughing. 'Now don't sulk, the others will soon be out of the water!'

'I wish we hadn't got to go out to dinner tonight,' said Bill, a little later. 'It's a nuisance, Allie. I wish I hadn't said we would. I do so enjoy the quiet evenings on the boat.'

'So do I,' said his wife. 'Never mind – we don't need to stay long – and we *might* learn something; you never know!'

The boat glided on down to Chaldo and arrived about half-past six. Bill and his wife got ready and waited for Mr Uma to fetch them. 'You children have your supper,' said Mrs Cunningham, 'and then read and go to bed as usual. We shan't be late. Tala will look after you.'

'Here comes Mr Uma,' said Jack, spotting someone coming along in the dark, with a lantern. 'Goodbye – and keep your eyes and ears open! Mr Uma may not be as innocent as he seems.'

Mr Uma called up to the launch.

'Good evening! If you are ready I will guide you to my house. It is not very far. I am wondering if the four children would like to watch a dance in the next little village. There has been a wedding there, and the dancing is amusing to watch. My man here can take them.'

'Oh yes – do let us!' cried Lucy-Ann, and the others joined in.

'No, I don't think I want them to go,' said Bill, firmly. 'I'd rather they stayed on the boat.'

'Oh, blow!' said Jack. 'Be a sport, Bill. We'll be all right, and we won't do anything silly, I promise you.'

'I think not,' said Bill. 'I'd rather you didn't go. Village wedding dances are not always safe to watch – your presence might be resented!'

There was no more to be said, but the four children were very disappointed. They called a subdued goodbye, and watched the lantern held by Uma's servant bobbing away through the trees.

'I wish we could have gone,' said Dinah. 'What harm

could we come to, with Uma's man beside us? Blow!'

'Oh, well – it's no good thinking about it,' said Jack. 'I wonder what's for supper?'

Tala produced a fine meal, and when they were in the middle of it, the children heard him talking to a man who had come to the side of the launch.

'Who is it, Tala?' called Philip, at once.

'It is Jallie, Mr Uma's servant,' said Tala. 'He say Master send him tell you go watch dancing. He say he change mind, you go.'

'Oh, good, good, good!' cried Dinah, delighted, and the others exclaimed in pleasure too. They finished their supper hurriedly, and called out to Tala.

'Tell the man we're ready. We're just getting our cardigans. It's a bit chilly tonight.'

'Oola go too?' said a small voice. But Tala overheard and called him roughly.

'No! You have work to do. Mister Bill send word you not go. You stay with Tala.'

Oola was bitterly disappointed. He made up his mind to do his work quickly and then go to meet the others. He would soon find out where that village was.

'Goodbye!' called Lucy-Ann to the disappointed boy. 'We won't be long. Look after the boat, Oola.'

Oola stood looking after them in the darkness. A curious dread had come over his heart. Something was going to happen – something bad, bad, bad! Oola knew!

17

Extraordinary happenings

It seemed quite a long way to the village. The children stumbled along, and suddenly, for no real reason, Jack felt uneasy.

'How far is the village now?' he asked Jallie, the man with the lantern.

'It quite near,' answered the man, in a surly tone.

Ten minutes later there was still no sign of the village, and Jack spoke to Philip in a whisper.

'Philip, I don't like this. I don't feel easy in my mind. Ask him about the village again.'

'What about this village?' demanded Philip, tapping the man on the arm.

'It quite near,' answered Jallie again.

Philip stopped. He too now had a very uneasy feeling. He began to wonder if the message about going to the village dance was genuine. Suppose it was a way to get them off the boat – so that Uma could send someone to search it? It wasn't really at all like Bill to change his mind about a thing – especially when he had been so determined that they were *not* to go.

'Come!' said the man, and held the lantern high to see why they had stopped.

'Lucy-Ann – pretend you feel ill – cry, and say you want to go back!' whispered Jack. Lucy-Ann obeyed at once.

'J-J-Jack!' she cried, pretending to weep. 'I don't feel w-w-well. Take me b-b-back! Oooooooh!'

'Oooooooh!' said Kiki, in sympathy.

'Oh, poor Lucy-Ann!' said all the other three, and began to pat her on the back. 'Yes, you shall go back.'

Jack went to Jallie. 'My sister must go back to the boat,'

he said. 'She isn't well, as you can see. We must return at once.'

'No,' said the man. 'Come.'

'Don't be silly!' said Jack, angrily. 'You heard what I said. Lead us back.'

'No,' said the man. 'I have orders. Come.'

'Look here – what's all this?' said Philip, joining in. 'There's something queer here. I don't believe you're going to take us to any wedding dance! Anyway, *my* orders are that we go back. Understand?'

Jallie glared at them. It was obvious that he did not quite know what to do. He could not make four children come with him by main force. On the other hand he certainly did not mean to take them to the launch.

The children glared back, Lucy-Ann giving sobs that were now becoming real, for she felt frightened.

'You *will* take us back,' said Philip, slowly. 'See – I have someone here who will *make* you take us back!'

He slipped his hand under his cardigan and shirt, and pulled gently at the snake coiled there, fast asleep. The gentle pressure awoke the sleepy creature and it wriggled in pleasure at feeling Philip's hand on it.

The boy slid out the snake, and the man saw it suddenly in the light of the lantern. He stared at it as if he could not believe his eyes.

'Bargua,' he gasped, backing away. 'Bargua!'

'Yes, Bargua! My bargua! He does what I say,' said Philip. 'Shall I tell him to bite you?'

The man fell on his knees, trembling, as Philip held the writhing snake between his hands. He pointed it at Jallie, and the snake darted its forked tongue in and out.

'Sir, I take you back,' said the man, in a shaking voice. 'Mercy, sir. Put your snake away.'

'No,' said Philip. 'I hold him near you, see, like this!' And he thrust the snake nearer to the man, who at once fell over backwards in utter fear.

'I send my snake after you if you leave us and run,' went on Philip, quite determined that he and the others were not going to be left in an unknown place in the darkness of the night.

'Sir, I take you,' whimpered the man.

'Well, get up and go, then,' said Philip, cradling the snake against him. It ran its forked tongue caressingly over the boy's wrist. The man shuddered – and for the thousandth time Lucy-Ann admired Philip, and the way he could tame all creatures and make them love him.

The man picked up the lantern and set off, his legs trembling as he walked along, thinking of the snake behind him, that very poisonous snake. What manner of boy was this that could harbour deadly snakes in his bosom?

He went along, taking the same path as he had gone before, though the children could not know this for certain, and just hoped for the best. The two boys were extremely worried.

'If Uma sent this fellow to take us goodness knows where, with orders to leave us stranded somewhere, whatever is he doing to Bill and Mother?' thought Philip, desperately.

On and on they went, and at last through the trees came the welcome glint of silver water – the river.

'The River of Adventure!' thought Jack suddenly. 'My word – it's living up to its name.'

Jallie pointed with a trembling hand to the river. 'I bring you back,' he said. 'I go now, please.'

'Yes. Go,' said Philip, and thankfully the man fled with his lantern, stumbling in haste.

Someone came from the trees and flung himself down by Philip. It was Oola!

He moaned as he laid his head against Philip's knees. 'Bad men come,' he said. 'Bad men. What I do, what I do?'

In alarm Philip jerked him to his feet. 'Oola! Tell me quick – what's happened?'

Oola pulled them through the trees to the jetty. He

pointed through the starlit night, and the others looked in astonishment and fear.

The launch was gone!

'Oola – what's happened?' asked Philip, shaking him.

'Bad men come. Bad men put Big Mister Bill and Missus on launch. Bad men get Tala and tie him up, and throw him on ground. Bad men take launch away, away, down river!' said Oola, sounding as if he were going to burst into tears.

'Whew!' said Jack, and flopped down on the grass, quite knocked out by all this news. The rest sat down too.

'How do you know all this, Oola?' said Jack, at last. 'Why didn't they tie you up too?'

'Oola just going after his boss,' said Oola. 'Oola creep away from boat – and then see bad men. Bad men no see Oola. Oola watch. Oola hide.'

'Well, we've now got a pretty good picture of what has happened,' said Philip, grimly. 'Uma suspected old Bill of knowing too much – and so he's captured him very neatly. But what a pity Mother had to be captured too! *We* were going to be neatly put out of the way as well. Thank goodness for Oola!'

'And Tala,' said Jack. 'Tala's about too, apparently – all tied up. We must get him. What in the world are we going to do?'

They got up and walked down to the edge of the water. Oola pointed to a dark shadow close by the bank, away from the jetty.

'Bad man's boat,' he said. 'Why he no take that?'

'I suppose because he wanted to hide away all evidence of us and *our* boat,' said Jack. 'I wish he *had* taken his own boat. Hallo – that sounds like Tala.'

- Groans could now be heard somewhere near by. Oola disappeared and then they heard him calling.

'Tala here!'

They all hurried over to him and there was Tala, so securely tied up that it was very difficult to free him! He was in two different states of mind at once – he felt extremely sorry for himself, and also extremely angry. He wriggled impatiently as the boys tried to untie him. In the end they cut the ropes and he rolled free.

Tala poured out his version of the happenings, pausing to bang his chest in anguish when he related how he saw Big Mister Bill and Little Missus being dragged away, and then yelled out in anger at the idea of him, Tala, being bound and thrown out like a sack of rubbish.

'Tala, listen,' said Philip. 'Was it Uma who came?'

'No. Other men,' said Tala. 'Servants. Bad men. Tala spit on them!'

'Where have they taken Big Mister Bill and Missus?' asked Jack.

'Down river,' said Tala, pointing. 'I hear them say Wooti. Tala not know Wooti. Tala very angry!'

'What *are* we going to do?' said Dinah. 'We can't spend the night out here – but where can we go? We don't know the way to anywhere.'

'Oola know,' said Oola's eager voice. 'Oola show you,' and he pulled at Philip's sleeve.

He took the boy away from the jetty, to the corner where Uma's motor-boat was tied. 'See – bad man's boat. We take, yes?'

'Oola! What a brain-wave!' said Philip, delighted. 'Of course! Tit for tat. We'll go off in it now, straight away – back up the river!'

'No – let's go down to Wooti,' said Jack. 'It's probably just as near as the last village we visited. Let's hope it's a big place and we can get word about this to someone in authority. We can get news of our own launch there too.'

'Yes – that's the best idea, I think,' said Philip. 'Tala, can you manage this motor-boat?'

'Yes, yes, Tala know,' said Tala, eagerly. 'We chase bad men, yes?'

'I don't quite know *what's* going to happen!' said Jack.

'But we're certainly not going to stay here and let Uma catch us in the morning! Come on – in we all get!'

And one by one they clambered into the motor-boat, while Tala tinkered with the engine. Now where were they off to? Wooti? And what would happen there?

18

Away through the night

They were all in the motor-boat very quickly indeed, half afraid that someone might come out of the shadows to stop them. Jallie might have gone to tell his friends that after all he had been compelled to bring back the children, instead of abandoning them far off in the darkness – and three or four of Uma's men might have come to look for them, and taken them captive.

But nobody came. Nothing stirred except the murmuring river, and the only other noises were the little sounds made by Tala as he tried to start up the engine. Oola patiently held a torch for him to see by.

'Click-click! Click-click!' The engine was coming to life – good! There – it was going!

'Buck up, Tala!' whispered Philip, urgently, for the noise now sounded very loud in the stillness of the night. 'We may get some unpleasant callers if we don't go off soon.'

With a sudden roar the boat went off into mid-stream, and the children heaved sighs of relief. It steadied, and then, keeping in the starlit centre of the river, it headed downstream.

There were no angry shouts behind them. Nobody seemed to know that they had gone in Uma's own motor-boat. Jack spoke to Tala.

'You said you didn't know Wooti. Do you know how far down the river it is?'

'Yes, Tala hear about Wooti,' said Tala. 'It is far down. Oola know Wooti?'

Oola didn't, but he remembered that another village was near to Wooti.

'Village name Hoa,' he said. 'We come to Hoa, Oola go there, ask about Wooti, yes?'

'Right,' said Jack. 'We don't particularly want to arrive at Wooti all set to be captured! We must tie up somewhere some distance away, and then go in cautiously and see what we can learn.'

'Tala – will you keep going for an hour, say, then tie up somewhere so that we can sleep?' asked Philip. 'If we sail through the night we shall probably miss Wooti – we'd far better bed down for a few hours, as soon as we feel safely out of reach of Uma's men.'

'Well, as far as we know there were no more boats at Uma's place, so no one *could* chase us,' said Jack. 'Still, it's no good taking risks. Yes, drive the boat for an hour, Tala, and then we'll tie up somewhere.'

Tala steered on through the starlit night, and the children talked quietly among themselves. Oola was contentedly sitting close to Philip, perfectly happy. Why should he worry? Were these children not clever enough to do anything, clever enough even to defeat bad man Uma? And anyway, he had the thrill of being near Philip all the time now, because the motor-boat was much smaller than the launch.

After about an hour Jack called to Tala. 'All right, Tala. We'll tie up somewhere. We don't seem to have passed any villages at all. This must be a deserted part of the river. Tie up anywhere.'

Tala's trained eye picked out a straight young tree on the edge of the left bank. He steered towards it, and it came to rest by the tree with a gentle bump. The engine stopped, and the quiet night closed in round them.

'Good, Tala,' said Jack. 'I'll help you to tie up. Then we'll all curl up and sleep.'

In five minutes' time everyone was fast asleep, though, like a dog on guard, Oola slept with one ear open! The two girls were huddled together, and the boys lay beside them, with Oola at Philip's feet. Tala slept by the wheel in a most uncomfortable attitude, snoring loudly at intervals. Kiki sat on Jack's leg and slept, head under wing.

They slept on and on. Dawn came and silvered the water. The sun rose and a pleasant warmth fell on the six sleepers. The bargua snake felt it, and slid silently out of Philip's shirt, to lie on his shoulder, basking in the sun.

Dinah awoke first, wondering why she felt so stiff. She lay still, remembering the events of the night before. She moved a little to look round at the others – and she saw, quite close beside her, Philip's snake, lying on his shoulder, enjoying the sun.

She gave a scream before she could stop herself. Everyone awoke immediately, and Tala reached automatically for a knife he had somewhere about him. Oola leapt to his feet in front of Philip, ready to protect him to the death!

'Who screamed?' demanded Jack. 'What's up?'

'*I* screamed,' said Dinah, penitently. 'I'm sorry – but the first thing I saw when I woke was Philip's snake looking at me. I just couldn't help it. I'm *so* sorry.'

'*So* sorry, *so* sorry!' chanted Kiki, and then gave a scream like Dinah's.

'Now don't *you* make a habit of screaming!' said Lucy-Ann. The snake had now slid into hiding somewhere about Philip, and Dinah felt better. They all rubbed their eyes and took a good look round.

There was nothing of much interest as far as the river was concerned. It ran on as smoothly as ever, lined on each side with trees that came down to the water's edge. What *was* of interest to the children was the motor-boat!

Was there any food or drink in it? Was it merely a boat that ran Uma here and there, as a car would run him about on roads?

'Let's see if there's any food,' said Philip, and they hunted round at once.

'Look at this!' said Jack, swinging open the door of a cupboard set under a seat in the bows.

They looked. It was full of tins! They read the names – there was tinned ham, bacon, sardines, fruit of many kinds, and even soup.

'Funny!' said Philip. 'Why does Uma want to take food about in a motor-boat like this? He must have gone off sometimes on queer little jaunts, and stayed away long enough to need food – and yet not near enough to villages to get any.'

'Well, I don't care *why* he takes food about with him,' said Dinah. 'All I care is that he conveniently left some for *us*! And drink too – look, there are tins of lime-juice and orange-juice – they'll be very strong so we shall need water with those.'

Tala nodded his head towards a small enclosed tank. 'Water there,' he said.

But he was wrong. It was empty. So if the children wanted anything to drink it would have to be very strong undiluted orange or lime-juice.

In another cupboard were ropes, powerful torches, and big strong hooks. 'Whatever are these hooks for?' said Lucy-Ann, in surprise.

'They're grappling hooks – often used for climbing,' said Jack. 'Now why did Uma want those?'

'I know! For his hobby – archaeology,' said Dinah. 'Don't you remember? Well, if he goes about exploring all the old, deep-hidden places here, I suppose he *would* use these. Anything else of interest?'

'Some spades,' said Jack, 'and a small pick. Well, if Uma uses his hobby of studying old buildings as a camouflage for his other dirty work, whatever it is, I must say he seems to take it pretty seriously. Look – there are books about it here too.'

He pulled out books, some new, some old, all evidently well-read, for there were small notes written here and there on certain pages.

'I'll have a snoop into these when I've had something to eat!' said Jack. 'I'm beginning to feel hungry now!'

So were the others. They found two tin-openers hanging on a nail in the cupboard. Jack promptly put one into his pocket for safety! They opened a tin of ham and two tins of pineapple, feeling that these might go quite well together. They drank the juice in the tins, but still felt rather thirsty.

'We ought to try and fill this water-tank,' said Philip, peering into it. 'It looks perfectly clean.'

'Tala and Oola fetch water next village,' proposed Tala. 'And bread.'

'Right. But we'll have to make sure it's not Wooti before we go boldly into it,' said Jack. 'Look at Kiki! That's her fifth bit of pineapple! Hey, Kiki, are you enjoying it?'

Kiki swallowed the last bit and flew over to the tin again. It was empty. She gave a squawk of disappointment. 'All gone!' she said, in a sing-song voice. 'All gone. Send for the doctor!'

'Fathead,' said Jack. 'Tala, are you ready to start? Stop at a village that you think is safe.'

Tala untied the boat and set the engine going. They chugged into midstream and set off. The sun was lovely and warm now, and everyone felt more cheerful — though nagging at their minds all the time was the worry of what had happened to Bill and his wife.

They came to a small village whose huts ran right down to the edge of the water. At once eager children ran to watch the boat. Tala swung in towards shore, where there was a small jetty for boats.

He conversed rapidly with a boy standing near. Then he turned to the others.

'He say this Hoa village. Wooti long way on. Two-three hours. He say will give Tala waterbag and bread. Yes?'

'Right,' said Jack. 'We'll come ashore and stretch our legs too. You and Oola go and see what the water's like. It must be drawn straight from the well. Draw it yourself, Tala. Come on, you others – it seems quite safe here, but all the same, we'll keep near the boat!'

19

The river is very peculiar

It was good to stretch their legs. Kiki as usual was on Jack's shoulder and created great interest among the excited children. They crowded round, pointing and chattering. Philip kept his snake hidden – he knew what a stampede it would cause if it so much as showed its head!

Tala and Oola had fortunately discovered a couple of large pails in the boat and had taken those to fetch the water. The children were glad – none of them liked the big skin bags, made of animal-hide, that water was so often carried in by the villagers.

Tala and Oola were a long time coming back, and the children began to feel worried.

'Why don't they come?' said Jack. 'I do hope nothing has happened to them. We *should* be in a fix without Tala.'

However, at last the two came, each carrying a heavy pail of water, and with loaves of bread strapped over their bare shoulders. Fortunately Tala knew enough of the ways of this family to know that they liked their bread wrapped and he had managed to get some cloths to wrap it in.

'You've been too long, Tala,' said Jack, not at all pleased.

'He talk and talk,' said Oola. 'Oola want to come back, but Tala talk.'

Tala glared at him, and then drew himself up to his full height. 'Yes, Tala talk. Tala find out much things. All

287

peoples know Uma. He diggy-diggy-dig. Much much dig. Peoples say Uma know where is big treasure. Much gold.'

Jack laughed. 'You've been gossiping. Uma likes to make people *think* he's digging for lost, long-ago things – but that's not what he's really doing. He's got something else up his sleeve – and I wish I knew what it was.'

Tala didn't understand this. 'What he got up sleeve?' he enquired. 'Big knife?'

'Come on,' said Philip impatiently. 'Let's put the water in the tank. I'd like a drink of orangeade straight away. I'm jolly thirsty.'

They all were. As the water splashed into the tank Jack considered it. It didn't really look very much for six people!

'Let's go on,' he said to Tala. 'We can look out for Wooti after two hours, if it's really two or three hours away.'

Tala started up the engine and on they went again. They passed quite a few small villages, and then came a larger one. Could this be Wooti? Jack glanced at his watch. No – they had only been going for an hour and a half, and Tala had been told that Wooti was two or three hours away.

'Tala stop?' called Tala. 'Tala ask name of village?'

'No. It can't be Wooti yet,' said Jack, and on they went. And then, quite suddenly, the river became very wide! The children were most astonished as the banks receded farther and farther away. It almost seemed as if the river had become a lake!

'Goodness! If the river gets much wider we shan't be able even to *see* the banks!' said Dinah.

Lucy-Ann stared out in amazement. 'Jack,' she said, 'we – we're not out at *sea*, are we?'

Everyone roared. Even Tala smiled. Lucy-Ann went red, and Jack clapped her on the back.

'Never mind! It certainly *looks* as if we're all at sea! I expect the river will narrow soon. Maybe the river bed is very shallow here, so the water has spread itself out well and made itself wide.'

Philip called to Tala.

'Tala! Better keep to one or other of the banks, or we'll lose our sense of direction. I can hardly see the right-hand one as it is!'

Tala swung over to the left to find the bank there. It was quite a long way away!

'I wish we had a map of the river here,' said Jack. 'Like the one Bill had, do you remember? It showed every village on it, and it would have shown us where Wooti came, and what happens to the river here — why it gets so wide, and if it narrows again!'

They were now close to the left bank instead of in midstream. The opposite bank could not be seen. The water seemed to stretch away interminably on their right, giving the impression that they were on the edge of the sea, sailing close to the shore — just as Lucy-Ann had imagined!

Tala was surprised, and a little afraid. 'The river's very wide here,' he said to Oola in his own language. 'We shan't see Wooti if it's on the other bank.'

This had also occurred to Philip. He pulled at Jack's sleeve. 'Jack — suppose Wooti is on the other bank? We'd miss it!'

'Gosh, yes,' said Jack. 'We can't even *see* the bank, let alone any village on it. Well — let's see — we'll get Tala to stop at the next little village on the left here, and ask about Wooti. If it *is* on the opposite bank we'll have to chug over there and look for it! Let's hope we haven't gone right past it!'

They looked out for the next little village, but the undergrowth was thick and grew right down to the water's edge, so that even if any village *had* been on the left-hand side, they could not have seen it. An hour passed, and the children grew uneasy.

'I *wish* we had a map!' said Jack. 'Blow Uma! Why didn't he keep maps on his boat! They would have been such a help. Hallo — I can see something on the right — yes, it's the

289

righthand bank come back into view at last!'

Sure enough a line of brown could be seen over to the right. It seemed rapidly to come nearer, which meant, of course, that the river was narrowing again, so that both its banks could be seen.

In fact, it narrowed so much that the banks were far nearer to one another than they had ever been before!

'This is extraordinary!' said Philip, suddenly. 'The river flows in the direction we're going, as you know – we've been taking advantage of the current the whole time. Well – rivers usually keep either more or less the same width as they flow to the sea, or they get *wider* as other streams feed them by joining them. And they are at their widest as a rule when they flow into the sea.'

Jack stared at him. 'Yes. I know. Then – how is it this river has suddenly gone so small and narrow? Especially after being so wide! I know we're nowhere near the sea, and I can't imagine why it went so wide – just as I can't imagine now why it's gone so narrow!'

'It must have split into two streams – or perhaps more,' said Philip. 'Maybe it made itself into two separate rivers, some way back – one wide, one narrow – and we're in the narrow one. That's the only thing I can think of.'

'Tala! Stop the boat a minute,' commanded Jack. 'We must talk.'

Tala stopped the boat gladly. He was feeling extremely worried. What had happened to the river? Where was Wooti? What was the best thing to do?

They all talked together in the middle of the boat. It was a very serious conference and even Kiki did not dare to interrupt.

'Tala – what do you think has happened? Why has the river gone small? Do you think it split into two or three separate streams some way back?' asked Jack.

'Tala not know. Tala frighted,' said the man. 'Tala say, go back. This bad river now.'

'Well, *you're* not much help, Tala,' said Philip. 'We must have missed Wooti altogether. I bet it was on the right-hand bank – and we couldn't spot it because we were too far away. Blow! This looks like being serious.'

'Let's go on,' said Dinah. 'We're *bound* to come to some place soon, absolutely bound to.'

Jack looked over the side of the boat, to the left bank and then to the right.

'It all looks pretty desolate to me,' he said. 'Just a few trees only – and some mouldy-looking bushes – and then nothing but sand or dust in hillocks and mounds. Well – we'll go on for half an hour and then if nothing turns up – no village or anything where we can ask for advice, we'll go back – and cruise along the *right*-hand bank of the river. Maybe we'll find Wooti then.'

'Tala say, go back,' said Tala, obstinately. 'This bad river now. Deep deep water, see!' He got up and pointed downwards over the side.

'You can't tell how deep it is,' said Jack, looking down into the water, which was now murky instead of clear.

'Tala know. Boat sound different on deep water,' said Tala, confidently. 'Bad river now.'

'All right. We'll sail on bad river for another half-hour,' said Philip firmly. 'Then if there is no village anywhere we'll turn back. Start up the motor, Tala, please.'

But Tala stood there obstinately, and the boys' hearts sank. Surely Tala was not going to be difficult at this important moment? They could not give way to him. He would consider himself on top then, and any other decision they made might also be put aside by Tala.

'Tala! Do as you're told!' said Philip, sternly, imitating Bill's voice exactly. Still Tala sat there, mutinous and obstinate.

And then, to everyone's astonishment, the motor of the boat suddenly started up, and the boat shook and quivered as it shot forward and sent everyone almost on their faces!

A voice came from behind them. 'Oola obey you! Oola drive boat for boss!'

With a fierce yell Tala leapt over to Oola. He rained blows on him and took the wheel from him at once. He shouted a long string of unintelligible words at the grinning Oola, and then, still with a very fierce expression on his face, he guided the boat down the narrow river.

Oola scrambled back, not seeming to have felt Tala's blows at all. He was smiling all over his face. 'Oola make Tala obey you!' he said, and was delighted at the grins he got.

'Jolly good, Oola,' said Philip. 'But don't do that kind of thing too often. You gave us all a frightful shock!'

20

Whatever happened?

Tala drove the boat rather fast, to show that he was still angry. Philip signalled to him.

'Slower, Tala!'

And Tala slowed down, afraid that Oola might come and show him how to drive more slowly. The boat went on between the banks, which were now narrowing even more. And then, as well as narrowing, the banks began to grow higher!

'Why — we seem to be going between cliffs now!' said Jack, in wonder. 'Tala! Don't go so fast!'

'Tala *not* go fast!' called back the man, looking puzzled. '*River* go fast — very fast! Take boat along. Tala stop motor, and you see!'

He stopped the motor, and the children did indeed see what he meant! The current was racing along at top speed, and the boat needed no motor to take it along — it was carried by the current!

The cliff-like banks rose even higher, and the children felt alarmed.

'We're in a kind of gorge now,' said Philip. 'A gorge that must be dropping down in level all the time, and making the water rush along. Hey, Tala, stop! This is getting dangerous.'

Tala called back at once. 'Tala no can stop! Boat must go on, on, on. River take boat all the time.'

'Whew! He's right!' said Jack. 'How *can* we stop? And if we did, where? There are only these high cliffs of rocks on each side now – nowhere to stop at all! We'll be dashed to pieces if Tala doesn't keep the boat straight.'

The children were very pale. Kiki was terrified and put her head under her wing. The boys looked up at the rocky cliffs on each side. Yes – they were now getting so high that they could see only a strip of sky. No wonder it seemed dim now, down here in the boat.

The water raced along, no longer smooth, but churned-up and frothy. 'It's pouring down a rocky channel, a channel that goes downwards all the time, and makes the water race along,' said Jack, raising his voice a little, for the water was now very loud.

'We must be going down into the depths of the earth,' said Philip, staring ahead. 'Jack – listen, what's that noise?'

They all listened, and Tala himself went pale.

'Water fall down, water fall down!' he called, above the roar of the river.

Jack clutched at Philip, panic-stricken. 'He's right. We're coming to a cataract! A gigantic underground waterfall! We're pretty well underground now, it's so dark. Gosh, Philip, the boat will swing over the top of the fall, and we'll be dashed to pieces. It sounds an *enormous* cataract!'

The noise became louder and louder, and entirely filled the rocky gorge. It seemed to be the loudest noise in the world, and the girls pressed their hands to their ears, terrified.

Tala, too, was terrified, but he still had his hand on the

wheel, trying to prevent the boat from crashing into the rocky sides. He suddenly gave a shout.

'We come to waterfalling!'

The children could not hear anything now but the roar of the waterfall ahead. Nor could they see anything, for the gorge was now too deep to admit much daylight. They could only clutch at the boat-seats and each other.

And then – and then – the boat swung violently to the left, almost turned over, rocked dangerously to and fro, and came to a shuddering stop!

All round was the sound of the giant cataract, but the noise had diminished. What had happened? Wonderingly the children raised their frightened faces and peered round. They were in darkness and could see nothing.

Philip felt something clutching his knees – a pair of hands. That must be Oola at his feet.

'Is boss safe?' said Oola's voice, sounding over the noise of waters.

'Quite safe, Oola,' said Philip, finding his voice trembling as he spoke. 'You all right, girls?'

'Yes,' they answered, but that was the only word they could manage to say. They were still clutching each other tightly.

'I'm safe too,' said Jack's voice, sounding unexpectedly cheerful. 'Hey, Tala! Are you all right?'

The sound of moaning reached the children, a doleful regular moan. Jack felt his way across the boat to Tala.

'Are you hurt?' he asked, feeling the man all over. He felt for his torch in his pocket and flicked it on. Tala was at the wheel, bent over it, which his hands over his head. He moaned all the time.

Jack could not see that he was hurt. He shook Tala, and at last the man looked up. He was shaking violently.

'ARE YOU HURT?' shouted Jack, thinking that Tala must have suddenly gone deaf.

Tala seemed to come to himself. He blinked at the torch

and rubbed his eyes. He felt himself all over very carefully.

'Tala not hurt,' he announced. 'Tala good.'

Jack flashed his torch around to see where they were. They appeared to be in a quiet pool surrounded by walls of rock. How extraordinary! How did they get here, out of the raging torrent? Only just in time too, for the waterfall could not be far away.

He went back to the others, who were now recovering. 'Well, we seem to be safe for the moment,' said the cheerful Jack. 'I vote we have something to eat. Nothing like something in our tummies to make us feel better. Where's Kiki?'

'In that cupboard,' said Dinah. 'I heard a little unhappy squawk from there just now.'

Jack flashed his torch at the cupboard. The door was a little ajar, burst open by the tins that had rolled about violently. Kiki had gone there to hide in peace, away from the roar of waters.

'Kiki! You can come out now,' called Jack. And Kiki waddled out, her crest down, looking very old and bent and sorry for herself! She climbed all the way up Jack, as if her wings couldn't possibly fly, and was at last on his shoulder. She settled there, grumbling away, angry at all the disturbance she had been through.

'Get out a few tins, Dinah — you're nearest to the cupboard,' said Jack. 'Cheer up, Lucy-Ann. Philip, reach over to that lamp and light it, will you? It's the one used for the prow of the boat and ought to be bright. Buck up!'

It was a good thing that Jack took charge. He made everyone brighten up, even Tala, whose moaning still went on for a while. Soon they were all sitting together, munching sandwiches made of bread and ham, with orangeade to drink.

'Fun this, isn't it?' said the indomitable Jack, looking round at the little company, lighted quite brightly by the boat's lamp.

Lucy-Ann managed a weak smile, though she felt that

nothing could possibly be fun at the moment.

'Don't be silly,' said Philip. 'Let's enjoy our misery before we say it's fun! Gosh – I feel as if I'm in a peculiarly unpleasant dream. Anyone know what happened yet?'

Nobody did. It seemed an utter mystery. There they had been, whirling onwards to what must be an enormous cataract by the sound of it – and yet, all of a sudden, they had shot round to the left – into safety.

The food loosened their tongues, and soon they were talking much as usual. Tala condescended to take a sandwich, and he soon felt better too. He astonished the company by suddenly beaming round at them with the broadest smile on his face that the children had ever seen.

'What's up, Tala?' said Jack, amused. 'You look as if you've lost a penny and found a shilling!'

Tala looked puzzled. 'Tala not lost penny,' he said.

'All right, all right – forget it!' said Jack. 'What are you suddenly so happy about?'

'Tala brave man. Tala save everybody,' said Tala, beaming round again.

There was an astonished silence. Whatever did Tala mean? He sounded slightly mad, and certainly looked odd, sitting there in the light of the lamp, nodding his head up and down like a mandarin.

'I don't get it,' said Jack. '*How* did you save everybody?'

'Tala just now remember,' said Tala, still beaming. 'Boat go fast, fast, fast – big noise come – waterfalling near. Then Tala sees where cliff break – Tala swing boat round – bump-bump – boat nearly over. Now we here!'

There was another astonished silence. All the children stared at Tala, and even Kiki peered at him round Jack's face.

'But, Tala – you *couldn't* see a break in the cliff – it was too dark!' said Jack at last.

'Yes, yes,' said Oola's voice from beside Philip. '*Oola* see big hole too – big hole in cliff. Have good eyes for dark, Tala too.'

'Well, I'm blessed!' said Philip. 'I never saw a thing. But I suppose Tala must have been deliberately looking out for some break in the cliff, and caught sight of one just in time. He must have eyes like a cat!'

'Tala eyes good, very good,' agreed Tala, pleased at the interest he had caused. 'Tala see much, much. Tala save everybody. Tala good man.'

Tala looked as if he would burst with pride at being such a 'good man'. Jack reached over and patted him on the back.

'Tala, you're a marvel!' he said. 'Shake hands!'

This idea delighted Tala enormously. He shook hands very solemnly with everyone, including Oola – and was most gratified when Kiki too bent down and offered him her foot.

'God save the Queen,' said Kiki, in her most pompous voice, and gave a hollow cough, feeling sure this must be a solemn occasion.

'So *that's* what happened!' said Jack, handing round more sandwiches. 'Well, whether this is a dream or not – and I'm not really certain about it yet! – it's pretty exciting. Let's finish our meal and then do a spot of exploring. We may be out of the frying-pan and into the fire, of course!'

'Gosh – I hope not!' said Philip, looking round. 'But I can't say that I feel awfully hopeful!'

21

Much excitement

In about ten minutes' time they all felt cheerful enough to want to get out of the boat and explore round the cavern they were in. It was not part of the gorge, that was quite clear, for the rocky roof closed over their heads about ten feet above them. The torches showed this clearly.

'It's a big cave opening into the cliff from the gorge

outside that takes the river to the waterfall,' said Jack. 'That much is clear, anyway.'

'Tala see one, two, three others,' said Tala, nodding his head. 'Boat go by fast. Tala no stop.'

'I see. Yes, I daresay there are quite a lot of caverns in the sides of the gorge,' said Jack. 'The thing is – are they just caves – or do they lead anywhere?'

'We'll have to find out,' said Philip. 'Now, before any of us step out of this boat on to any ledge nearby, please see that you each have your TORCH. We'll leave the lamp burning on the boat – then we can all see it and come back to it safely. But for goodness' sake keep together if possible.'

Tala had put the boat near to a ledge on the left-hand side of the cavern. He had managed to find a jutting rock nearby and had tied a rope round it. He was terrified that the boat might swing over the pool, and be drawn by the current into the river again.

Soon all six were out on the ledge. Tala had a powerful torch that he had found in the boat, and proudly flashed it all around. As far as they could see, the cavern stretched a good way back, ending in darkness.

'Perhaps this quiet pool runs right back, and becomes a kind of underground stream,' suggested Jack, hopefully.

'What a hope!' said Philip. 'Why, we can't even see a way out for ourselves, let alone the boat. You're too cheerful, Jack. Pipe down a bit, or you'll be raising false hopes all the time!'

'Let him say what he likes,' said Lucy-Ann, flashing her own torch round. 'I feel as if I want to hear all the cheerfulness possible in this horrible place!'

Oola was well in front of everyone, scrambling about with a torch that was very faint indeed. But he seemed quite literally to be able to see in the dark! Jack called out to him.

'You be careful, Oola! You'll fall into the water and you know you can't swim.'

'Boss pull Oola out,' called back Oola cheerfully. 'Brave boss save Oola.'

That made everyone laugh. They scrambled about, flashing their torches here and there, getting farther and farther towards the back of the cavern.

The water ran back in a wide channel, a rocky ledge beside it on each side. The cavern narrowed at the end. Oola, who was first, shouted back.

'Ai! Ai! Here is tunnel!'

At once everyone felt excited. A tunnel? Then surely it must lead somewhere.

They clambered over beside Oola. He was right. In the centre of the back of the cavern the water stretched away into a narrow tunnel, pitch-black, and most mysterious!

'Could we get the boat along here, Tala?' asked Philip, excited.

Tala shook his head. 'Much dangerous,' he said. 'Boat get stuck? Water stop? Boat get hole? No, no. We go on. We see more.'

'Oh well – come on, then,' said Philip, who had had wonderful visions of taking the boat along this underground tunnel and coming out into daylight somewhere else. He knew Tala was right, of course. They must explore much farther before they could plan to move the boat.

The tunnel ran on and on, curving at times to right or left. It sometimes widened, sometimes narrowed. At times the roof grew so high that it could not be seen; at others it came down low, so that it seemed only an inch or two above their heads.

'We could bring the boat along as far as here, anyway,' said Jack to Philip. 'Hallo – what's the matter with Oola? He's away in front there, yelling like anything!'

Oola was shouting in excitement. 'Come! Come see, boss!'

Jack and Philip made what haste they could, though it

was not easy in this rocky, slippery tunnel, with the dark water waiting beside them.

They found Oola in a great state of excitement. He was peering through an uneven hole in the side of the tunnel wall.

'What's up?' asked Philip, pushing him aside.

'Bricks,' said Oola. 'Old bricks!'

Philip pushed his torch through the hole and gazed at something that was certainly a very peculiar thing to see just there!

His torch lighted up what seemed like part of a brick wall! But surely that could not be so? Who would build with bricks under the earth like this – and why?

'It looks as if someone built them on the other side of this hole to hide it,' said Philip.

'Or perhaps it's part of a *wall* built along some passage underground!' said Jack. 'Maybe the wall went past this hole – and wasn't meant specially to hide it.'

'Yes – but why should a wall be built *here*?' said Philip. 'It's most peculiar. Tala, come here – what do you make of this?'

Tala came thrusting forward. He shone his very powerful torch through the hole and on to the bricks. 'Ha!' he said. 'Old bricks. Very very old. Tala see bricks like this before. Tala's father dig them deep deep down.'

'Whew!' said Jack, startled. 'It looks as if this, then, might be a place where people long long ago built tombs for their kings or queens. They were big places, weren't they? – deep underground – with passages leading to them.'

'We'd better read a few pages of those books of Mr Uma's, in the boat,' said Philip. 'Let's go back and see if we can't find out something about this place – surely that great waterfall must be marked, for instance.'

Tala squeezed into the hole, and struck the nearby bricks hard with the flat of his hand. To the boys' utter amazement they collapsed into dust!

'Tala clever! Tala see father do same, Tala remember!'

said Tala triumphantly. 'Ai, Ai! *Now* what you do, Oola, son of a monkey!'

Oola had pushed Tala roughly aside and had squeezed past him, taking Tala's breath away. He leapt through the broken wall and stood beyond, flashing Tala's powerful torch.

'Here, here! A road is here!' he called, in excitement. 'Oola go!'

'Come back, you idiot!' yelled Philip. 'Don't get separated from us. OOLA, come back!'

Oola had already disappeared, but came back at once. 'Oola here, boss,' he said, in a subdued voice. Philip looked at him sternly, and then he and Jack also got through the hole in the wall, followed by the others.

Yes. Oola was right. Here was an underground way. Was it a passage made down to some old tombs? Had anyone else found it? Perhaps it was an underground cellar to some temple — or palace?

'Come on — let's go down it,' said Jack. 'This is too exciting for words. Keep together, everyone. Kiki, stop dancing about on my shoulder. Your feathers tickle. Keep still!'

'Keep still!' repeated Kiki at the top of her voice. 'KEEP STILL!'

Then everyone suddenly stopped in fright. An enormous giant-like voice echoed all round them. 'Keepstillkeepstill-KEEPSTILLKEEPSTILL'

Lucy-Ann clutched at Dinah and made her still more scared. Jack was startled at first and then laughed — and immediately his laugh ran round and round, and came back to him, eerie and scornful. 'Ha-ha-ha-ha-ha-ha . . . '

'Oh dear — it's only an echo,' said Jack, lowering his voice so that the echo could not so easily catch it. 'It made me jump out of my skin. It's shut Kiki up all right!'

But at that moment Kiki lifted her head and let out one of her cackles of laughter — and immediately everyone closed their ears in horror. The echo came at once, sounding like a hundred jeering giants laughing together.

'For goodness' sake, Kiki!' said Lucy-Ann. 'Don't do that any more!'

'Come on,' said Jack. 'Are we all here? Where's Oola?'

But Oola had gone. There was no sign of him.

'Blow him!' said Jack. 'Where is he? We simply *must* keep together!'

'Together!' shouted the echo. 'Together!'

'Oh, shut up,' said Jack, angrily, and back came the echo. 'Shutupshutupshutup.'

Oola came into sight behind a rock. He was terribly scared of the echo, for he had never in his life heard one before. 'Come on, Oola,' said Philip, not unkindly. 'Keep close to me. I won't let the echo eat you!'

They made their way down the sloping passage. It was quite empty. The walls were of brick, and here and there an archway of brick had also been made.

'Mud bricks,' said Jack. 'Not quite the same shape as ours — more the shape of long loaves of bread with rounded tops. Hallo — here's a big door. Can we get through? I expect it is locked.'

Thousands of years ago it had not only been locked but sealed, too, for the old seal still hung there, waiting to fall into dust. Jack pushed the great carved door gently — and to his horror it fell into fragments, giving a little sigh as it went. It was absolutely rotten!

What was beyond? Philip flashed his torch and saw only a blank wall of rock. Then the light picked out something else — a flight of steps going down into the earth — down, down, down!

By this time the little company was so excited that nothing could stop them continuing their way underground! 'Come on — let's go down!' said Philip, and put his foot on the first step. 'Everybody here? Follow carefully — it's jolly steep. Talk about an adventure — this is the best one we've ever had!'

22

The mystery is solved

Before Philip could go down to the second step, someone pushed roughly past him, almost making him fall. Oola's voice cried out loudly.

'No, boss, no. Danger here, boss. Oola go first, boss. Oola go first!'

And Oola began to climb down before Philip could even grab at him. 'Come back!' yelled Philip, really angry. 'You hear me, Oola? Come back! What do you think you're doing.'

'Ai! Ai!' came a doleful yell, and there was suddenly the sound of a series of thuds. 'Ai! Ai!'

'He's fallen,' said Jack, in alarm. 'Gosh, isn't he a little idiot! These steps may be as rotten as that gate! Now what are we to do?'

Tala called out. 'Tala go get rope. Rope in boat. Tala go now.'

There didn't seem anything else to be done about it. Philip yelled down to Oola.

'Are you hurt?'

'Oola not hurt. Bump-bump-bump! Oola climb up again, boss!'

'Don't try! You may fall even farther next time!' shouted Philip.

'Gosh – he certainly saved *you* from falling, Philip,' said Jack. 'You'd have gone down with a crash. We were idiots not to think of that.'

'Let's sit down while we wait for Tala,' said Dinah. 'Poor Kiki – you don't like all this, do you? You've lost your tongue!'

They talked as they waited for Tala. They were all quite

determined to go on. For one thing, they had to find a way out, that was certain. Jack wanted to go back *up* the passage to see if it led to the open air far above them. But Philip firmly said *no*.

'That would be idiotic just now,' he said. 'We'd be properly separated then . . . Oola down there – Tala gone to the boat – and us exploring somewhere else. The main thing at the moment is not to lose touch with one another. Ah – is this Tala? Good old Tala, he deserves a medal!'

It was Tala, with a rope from the boat. He had also brought a grappling hook, which was very sensible of him.

'Rope coming down now, Oola!' shouted Philip. Tala forced the great hook into a jutting-out piece of rock. He tied the rope to it, and he and Philip let the thin, very strong rope run down the old steps. Oola, down below, felt it slithering against him, and caught the rope in his two hands. With Tala and Philip pulling, and his own efforts at climbing, he was soon at the top.

'Well, thanks for falling down instead of me,' said Philip, clapping him on the back. 'But don't do it again.'

'Oola guard boss,' was all that the small boy had to say. Philip turned and spoke to the others.

'Well, now that we've talked over everything, we are all agreed that the best thing to do is to go back to the boat and have a meal and a rest. What's the time? Half-past six – gosh, no, it's half-past eight! Would you believe it!'

'Half-past eight at *night*?' said Lucy-Ann, and she looked at her own watch to make sure. 'Yes, so it is. Well, when it's as dark as this all the time, it's difficult to know *what* the time is!'

'We'd better have a meal, and a night's *sleep*, not just a rest,' said Jack. 'We'll all feel fresh in the morning. Then what do we do, Philip?'

'We have a good breakfast – we study the books up there in the boat, in case we can find out anything about this place, and get some idea whereabouts we are,' said Philip.

'Then we tie ropes round our waists, we each make up a fat parcel of food, and we start off.'

'Right, boss,' said Jack, and made everyone laugh.

'Anyone think of anything else?' asked Philip. Nobody did, so the little party started off back to the boat. Through the hole in the wall, back through the watery tunnel, and lo and behold, there was the boat, rocking very gently on the big pool just off the gorge.

They all had a meal, and Kiki ate so much that she began to hiccup.

'Hiccup! Pardon! Hiccup! Pardon! Go in the corner!'

'Yes, that's where you ought to go,' said Jack. 'Greedy bird. You ought to be ashamed of yourself!'

'Let's get those books now and have a look at them,' said Dinah, when they had finished their meal. 'I'm not a bit sleepy. I feel awfully excited, really. I just wish we could be sure that Mother and Bill are all right.'

'I don't think we need worry too much, seeing that Bill is there,' said Jack. 'He's come through tougher spots than this. I think Uma has put them both carefully in hiding somewhere while he finishes whatever hush-hush affair he's on – something away in Ciné-town, I've no doubt.'

'Do you remember how he tried to pretend he was so interested in archaeology and old buildings and things like that?' said Dinah. 'He thought he would put Bill off the scent!'

'Well, pretence or not, he's got some jolly interesting books here,' said Philip, who now had them all out on the deck, in front of him. 'Here, take one each – and see if you can track down this River of Adventure in any map, if you can find one – it will be called River of *Abencha*, don't forget.'

Neither Tala nor Oola took up a book. They did not feel confident about reading scholarly books of that sort – in fact, Oola could hardly read at all. They sat and lazed, feeling pleasantly full.

'Here's a map!' said Dinah, suddenly. 'Oooh – a good one too. Look, it unfolds out of the inside cover of this big book. No wonder we didn't find it before!'

They all looked at it. Jack gave an exclamation. 'It shows the river – see – going all the way down the page. This is fine. "River of Abencha" – that's the one. Now, let's trace the villages we've called at.'

'Here's Ala-ou-iya,' said Lucy-Ann. 'It's such a pretty name, I think. And I like its meaning too – the Gateway of Kings!'

'Yes – and here's Ullabaid, where we went to see that temple, and the children were frightened by Philip's snake,' said Dinah, pointing.

'And Chaldo, see – where that horrible Mr Uma kidnapped Bill and Mother,' said Philip. 'And where we took his motor-boat. And here's Hoa, where we got the water and bread.'

They traced the river down the page, their fingers passing over the names of villages they did not know. They were looking for the village of Wooti, to which Uma had probably taken Bill and his wife.

'Here it is,' said Jack. 'We *did* pass it, then – look, it's where the river begins to widen. We were in midstream then, and didn't see it. Blow! We went right by it. Now see how the river widens in the map!'

They were following the curving river line with great interest. Philip gave an exclamation.

'It *does* divide – look! I thought it did. See, it actually divides into three. One bit flows to the east, one goes on to the south – and the third one is only just a tiny line – that must be the one that narrows into the gorge we went into. Yes, it is.'

They all looked. The third leg of the river was called, quite simply, 'Teo gra', which, Tala explained, meant Deep Gorge, or Tunnel. It came to a very sudden end on the map. That seemed strange!

'Funny! Where does the gorge water go to eventually?' wondered Philip.

'Underground, I should think,' said Jack. 'After all, it was pretty well underground already when we shot off into this cavern. After the waterfall it might be *right* underground. My word – I'm glad we didn't go with it! We certainly should be right off the map too!'

'Well, we've solved the mystery of the dividing river,' said Philip, pleased. 'Now let's try and find out what underground cities or temples or tombs are near here. Are there any marked on this map?'

'There aren't,' said Jack. 'I tell you what – let's look up Ala-ou-iya, Gateway of Kings, in some of these books. They might tell us something about the district round this curious gorge.'

They looked up Ala-ou-iya. Most of the books said exactly the same thing, to the effect that this part of the country was very rich in buried palaces and temples, and that only part had been excavated.

'Listen to this,' said Jack, suddenly, and began to quote. ' "It is known that in the land around the strange and mysterious Deep Gorge there was once a most magnificent temple, far exceeding in beauty any other temple of that day (about seven thousand years ago). Excavations have continually been made, as it is likely that some of the greatest finds in the history of archaeology will be found here, and treasures beyond price. The temple was erected in honour of a well-loved goddess, and to her were brought gifts from kings and noblemen for many many generations. These were probably placed in the underground compartments of the temple, and securely sealed. Whether robbers have been at work during the thousands of years since history lost sight of the temple is not known." '

'I *say*!' said Philip and Dinah together. 'Is it true, do you think?'

'Well – this is a very serious, *solemn* sort of book,' said

Jack. 'I expect it doesn't go in for fairy-tales – only for what is true, or what is *likely* to be true.'

'What about that queer passage we found – and those steps leading downwards, through that old door?' said Lucy-Ann, sounding quite out of breath with excitement. 'Could we – could we possibly have found the way to some sort of old temple or palace, do you think – with the dust of thousands of years burying its ruins?'

'It's *possible*,' said Jack. 'After all – the entrance we found is not the usual one! I don't expect anyone has ever gone into this cavern before – how could they? Nobody in their senses would ever go into the gorge in a boat. We wouldn't have, either, if we'd studied a map and seen it marked.'

'And another thing,' said Dinah. 'I bet this gorge wasn't as deep as it is now, all those centuries ago. It must have been quite shallow then – it takes hundreds of years to make a deep gorge, cut right down into rock, like this one. I expect that all those thousands of years ago the gorge was quite shallow – perhaps not a gorge at all – and therefore our cavern entrance wouldn't be almost above water, as it is now – it would be far away below it. Nobody could possibly get into it then.'

'Dinah's right,' said Philip. 'The river-bed would be higher than this cavern, in those far-off days. That means that *we* have found a way underground to any old ruined cities there are here, that nobody else has *ever* found!'

This was a very startling thought. They stared at one another, deeply excited. And then a loud noise made them jump. It was poor Tala, so tired that he was fast asleep and snoring, even in the midst of this truly exciting talk.

'We'd better try to go to sleep too,' said Jack, laughing. 'Do you know it's midnight now? Leave the ship's lamp on, Philip. You can turn it down to a glimmer – but I'm sure we'd all feel happier if we had a night-light tonight!'

It wasn't long before everyone was sound asleep, and the tiny glimmer of a light showed no movement at all in the boat, except when Philip's snake slid out of his shirt and went scouting round to find something to eat.

It found nothing at all and had to return to the warmth of Philip's shirt, still hungry. It settled down again – and after that there was nothing to be heard except quiet breathing – and the constant, menacing roar of the torrent outside the cavern.

23

An astounding sight

Dinah woke first and switched on her torch. A quarter to eight! Goodness! She awoke the others at once and they all sat up, yawning and stiff. Tala turned up the light in the ship's lamp. He glanced round to see that everyone was all right.

'Ai! Ai!' he cried. 'Oola is gone!'

'Gone! He can't have gone!' cried Philip – and, at that very moment, Oola came into the cavern from outside, dripping wet!

'Where have you been?' asked Philip, sternly. 'You are wet. Did you fall into the water? You cannot swim!'

'No, boss. Oola not fall,' said the boy. 'Oola go to see waterfalling! Oola go to see wonderful thing.'

'Well, I'm blessed!' said Philip. 'You little scamp! You might have been killed! How did you go?'

'Oola show boss,' said the boy eagerly. 'Wonderful, wonderful! Boss come? Quite safe, boss!'

He ran along the ledge beside the water in the cavern, and stood at the opening. He turned and beckoned, his face shining. 'Come, boss. Oola show you.'

'Well, we'll see what he means,' said Jack, feeling a sudden surge of excitement. What a thing to see – that waterfall pouring down from the gorge, hurling itself over, and disappearing underground!

Oola had his torch, for although it was day very little light penetrated down between the tall narrow cliffs. Tala unhitched the ship's lamp and took that along too, feeling the same excitement.

The roar of the waters increased tremendously as they came to the entrance. Outside was a broad rocky ledge, just above the level of the tumultuous water.

'Follow Oola!' cried the boy. 'Safe, quite safe! Go higher soon.'

The spray from the water about three feet below them soon soaked them through. The ledge went steadily higher and was certainly broad enough to be quite safe.

Soon it had risen to about twelve feet above the water, and now the daylight was much stronger. The children snapped off their torches, and put them into their pockets.

The roar became louder and louder and beat painfully on their ear-drums. Oola led them onwards and up, and then stopped dramatically.

'Here, boss!' he shouted, his voice quite unheard in the din of waters. 'River gone!'

The six gathered together on a little natural platform, and gazed down. The floor of the gorge came to an abrupt end just below them, and dropped in a sheer cliff of rock hundreds of feet down. Over this edge poured the swirling, tumultuous water in a mass of foam and froth and spray. It plunged down, and down, and down – nobody could see where it ended, for it went into utter darkness.

Far down below, strange lights danced and played, like little specks of rainbow, brilliant and glowing. It was a strange and magnificent sight, and nobody spoke a word as they stood and looked.

The spray flew so high that it fell on the platform of rock on which they stood, drenching them time and again. But nobody even felt it. They were nothing but eyes and ears, revelling in what must surely be one of the most astounding sights in the world!

The gorge itself went on and on – but there was no water in it beyond this spot – all the great torrent of river fell into this enormous fathomless hole, disappearing endlessly into the heart of the earth. That was the end of the river that ran through Teo Gra, the Deep Gorge.

'Where does it go to?' wondered Lucy-Ann, more awed than she had ever been in her life.

'To think that our boat might have gone over this, if Tala hadn't seen the cavern!' thought Philip, and shivered to his very soul.

'How beautiful!' thought Dinah. 'Those broken rainbows down there – I shall never forget them all my life long!'

'Unbelievable!' though Jack. 'Absolutely unbelievable!'

Tala thought it was time to go back. How long would these children stare and stare? He Tala, was hungry, and water did not make a meal. He pulled gently at Jack's sleeve.

Jack turned, startled. Tala put his mouth to Jack's ear. 'We go back? Yes?'

'I suppose so,' said Jack, though he could quite well have stayed there all day. He nudged Philip, and together they all made their way along the sloping ledge, back to the cavern.

They were silent for quite a while. 'I feel as if I'd been to church,' said Lucy-Ann, voicing what they were all feeling. 'It was so – awe-inspiring, wasn't it?'

Kiki had not liked the continual drenching spray, and had not seen anything of the waterfall at all. She had hidden herself under Jack's cardigan, afraid of the noise and afraid of the spray. Now she was very glad indeed to be back in the boat, with a tin of pineapple being opened in front of her very eyes!

Breakfast was an unexpectedly hilarious meal. Everyone laughed a great deal, and Oola surpassed himself by laughing so much at Kiki that he actually fell over the side of the boat. Fortunately he fell on to the rocky ledge beside it.

They packed up as much food as possible when they had finished, and tied string round it, after wrapping it in old papers. Tala hung two tins of lime-juice round his neck, and Oola was also very well laden.

'Now then – everybody got their torches? Everybody got their parcel of food? Everybody quite sure they will keep in touch with the one in front?' said Jack.

'Yes,' answered everybody, Kiki too.

'Got the ropes round your waist, Tala?'

'Tala have rope,' said Tala. 'And hook. And Tala have trowel and fork!'

So he had, all tied with string somewhere about his person. He had wanted to take a spade too, but all the spades were heavy, and it didn't seem possible to drag one about all the time, strong though Tala was.

'You're carrying as much as a camel,' said Philip, with a laugh.

'Oola carry like camel too,' said Oola at once, jealous of any praise of Tala from his boss.

'Oh, Oola carry like *two* camels!' said Philip, and the plucky little boy was happy at once.

'Well, I suppose it's goodbye to this boat,' said Philip, looking round it. He stopped and picked up something.

'What's that?' asked Dinah.

'Oh, just an idea of mine,' said Philip. He tore a page or two out of one of Uma's books and stuffed them into his pocket.

'It's some pages that Uma marked,' he said. 'If he thought them important enough to mark, we may as well take them. You never know – they might come in useful!'

They set off along the little ledge that ran alongside the water in the cavern. They came to the hole that had once been backed by the old brick wall, which Tala's hand had touched and crumbled into dust.

They went through it and stood in the passageway. It was dark all around them, save for their torches.

'We'd better just explore this passage upwards and make sure that we *can* get out that way, before we explore that exciting-looking flight of steps we found,' said Jack. 'I expect the passage leads to ground-level.'

'I sincerely hope so!' said Philip. 'Though I have my doubts. Surely if there were a way out up there, other people would have found it and come in by it? Yet that sealed door that fell into bits was still in place.'

'Yes — and that looks as if nobody *had* come down here since it was put there,' said Dinah. 'Well — let's go on up!'

They went upwards, shining their torches into the darkness — but some way up the passage they came to a full stop. A wall of stone greeted them, built right across the passage.

This wall was not made of mud bricks that crumbled at a touch! It was made of solid blocks of stone, set in rows, one above the other. Now it was plain why no one had ever come that way! At some time someone must have ordered the stone wall to be built, to block up completely the entrance to whatever was below.

'No good,' said Philip, a little cold feeling gripping his heart. 'No way out here. We'd better go downwards again — to that old flight of steps. *They* may lead us somewhere!'

24

A strange and wonderful find

Jack looked at Philip in the light of the torches. Philip pursed up his lips and put on a grim look — they were certainly up against things now! He nodded his head towards the girls, warning Jack not to frighten them. Jack nodded back.

They went down the passage to where the rotten old gate had been. They came to the flight of steps. Although these were of stone, the edges had crumbled badly, which was why Oola had slipped and fallen. Even so, he had not fallen right to the bottom!

'Tala, you and Jack hold the end of the rope,' said Philip, who had now taken command. 'Send the other end down the steps – that's right. Now, I'll take hold of it and go down carefully, examining the steps, and counting them – and if I come to a rotten one I'll shout up what number it is, so that when we all go down we can be extra careful when we come to that step.'

'Good idea,' said Jack. He and Tala held the rope firmly and Philip began to go down. Oola was prevented by Tala from pushing in front and going down first, or he would have done exactly the same as he had done before. He was very angry, but it was no good – he had to stay behind.

Philip went slowly and carefully down the steps, counting as he went. 'One, two, three, four – number four is crumbling, Jack – five, six, seven, eight, nine – number nine is almost gone – ten, eleven . . .'

'One, two, six five, ten!' shouted Kiki, thinking this was a number game. 'One, two, good fat shoe, nine ten, buckle my hen, three four . . .'

'Number fifteen is gone – and number sixteen,' called Philip.

'Four, nine, fifteen, sixteen,' repeated Jack. 'Shout louder, Philip – it's difficult to hear you now you're going down ow.'

'Right,' yelled back Philip, holding tightly to the rope, afraid of missing his footing. 'These steps are jolly steep. You'll all have to be careful!' He went on calling up the numbers, but when he came to number 39 they could hardly hear his voice. There had been so many missing or crumbling steps that Lucy-Ann had had to find a pencil in Jack's pocket and scribble them down in his notebook.

'I'm at the bottom now,' yelled Philip.

'WHAT?' yelled Jack.

'I'M – AT – THE – BOTTOM!' yelled back Philip. 'Let Dinah come next. BE CAREFUL!'

Dinah set off down the steps. The others heard her counting them, and when she came to a bad one they shouted a warning to her. But Dinah had them all in her memory. She managed very well indeed, holding hard on the rope. At last she was standing beside Philip.

Then came Lucy-Ann. She was more afraid than Dinah, and slipped at the fifteenth step. But her hold on the rope saved her, and she soon recovered her balance.

Then Jack came, steady and sure of foot. It seemed a very long way down. The steps were very steep at times, and the hole down which they went was not very wide.

'Now that's us four here,' said Philip, shining his torch. 'Tala, send Oola down!' he shouted.

But Tala came next instead. He explained that Oola wanted to come down last of all, and didn't need the rope. He had sent it slithering down the steps after Tala had reached the bottom.

'He'll fall and break his leg,' said Jack, vexed. 'He's a fathead!'

But even as he spoke Oola was beside them, grinning in the light of the torches. Now that he knew that so many steps were rotten, he had been careful. He was as sure-footed as a cat in his bare feet.

'Oola here, boss,' he announced to Philip.

'Now – where do we go from here?' wondered Philip. He shone his torch in front of him. There was another passage there, narrower than the one above the steps. Its walls were made of the same kind of bricks they had seen before. The children did not dare to touch them in case they too fell into dust. There was something rather horrible about that!

They went along the passage, which sloped quite steeply downwards, and came to an archway, also built of bricks.

'I suppose they kept making these archways in order to strengthen the roof of the passages,' said Jack. 'It's amazing that some of them haven't fallen in.'

'I bet a lot of them have,' said Dinah. 'I hope nobody sneezes while we're down here – I feel as if it might bring the roof crashing in on top of us.'

'Don't,' said Lucy-Ann, sharply. 'I'm afraid of that too.'

The passage led them to a kind of room, almost round, with a great door at the farther end. The children stopped and flashed their torches round. In one corner was a curious heap of many things, and they went over to them.

But even as they came near, the sound of their footsteps disturbed the air enough to make the little heap crumble into dust! With small sighs it settled into a much smaller heap – but one thing still stood, solid and bright.

'What is it?' said Dinah, not daring to touch it. Very carefully Jack picked it up. It shone brightly.

'A bowl!' he said. 'A golden bowl! Set with stones, look, all round the edge. Gold is one of the things that never perishes, or loses its colour – and this bowl has lasted all through the centuries! Isn't it lovely!'

They all looked at it in awe. How old was it? Three, four, five thousand years old? Who had used it? Who had carved these camels round it? It was beautiful!

'This must be priceless,' said Philip, in wonder. 'It must have contained offerings to some god or goddess that the people of those days worshipped. My word – this is wonderful!'

'Philip – do you think – is it *possible* that we're near the lost temple of that well-loved goddess you read about in Uma's book?' asked Lucy-Ann.

'I should think it's *quite* possible,' said Philip, running his hand round the bowl. 'We may even now be getting near to the temple itself – or perhaps we are under it – and coming to the compartments beneath it where gifts were stored! My word – no, surely such a thing couldn't really happen!'

'It might – it *might*!' said Dinah, excitement almost choking her voice.

Oola and Tala were most interested in the bowl, particularly Tala. 'Gold!' he said, tapping the bowl. 'Tala know gold. This gold!'

'Carry it, Tala,' said Philip, 'and don't dare to drop it! Now, what about this door? It is sealed.'

Oola ran to it, and shook the great seal. It dropped into his hands! Philip went to the door and pushed at it. It suddenly sagged on its hinges and then fell away from them, hanging oddly sideways, leaving a gap big enough for everyone to climb through.

And now it was quite obvious that they were in some old and mighty building! Here were great rooms, stretching one into the other, some with doors that had crumbled, some with no doors at all.

'They're rather like great cellars,' said Jack, as their torches shone down square compartments built of stone, and then on oblong ones, then on communicating passages. It was a vast labyrinth, and piled everywhere were strang heaps of unrecognisable things. Everything had perished except what was made of metal or stone.

'Look — here's a tiny statue, standing in a niche of its own,' said Lucy-Ann, and she picked it up. It was carved out of some curious stone — most beautifully done, with every fold of the robes lovingly wrought. They all looked at it. How old was it? How many many centuries ago had some craftsman toiled over it in delight for weeks or months? Who had brought it to the temple to give to the goddess? They would never know!

They began to examine some of the things set in heaps. Gold always stood out well, for its colour was unchanged — and there was much gold! Gold statues, gold bowls, gold combs, gold ear-rings, gold ornaments . . .

In one small square room there were swords, their hilts set with precious stones. What stones? Nobody knew! Jack picked up a dagger whose hilt was carved and ornamented with gold. 'I'd like this!' he said.

'We can't take anything!' said Philip. 'Except what we need in order to show the value of our discovery.'

'Right. Then I'll take this dagger,' said Jack, and stuck it into his belt.

'I'll take this gold comb,' said Dinah. 'I'll wear it in my hair!'

'I'll have this tiny statue,' said Lucy-Ann. 'I wish it really *could* be mine – it's beautiful. But of course, these things can never belong to any one person – they belong to the whole world, because they are bits of real, long-ago history.'

'You've said exactly what I was thinking myself, Lucy-Ann,' said Philip. 'I'm taking along this cup – at least, I think it's a cup. It's gold – and look at the carvings of bulls all round it! Marvellous!'

They went on until at last they came to the end of the store-rooms. They felt quite bemused by the thousands of things they had seen! No robbers had been here, that was certain. Here were treasures that had been undisturbed through all the ages that had passed since they had been given to the goddess of the temple!

'Boss, Oola wants sun,' said Oola to Philip. 'Oola doesn't like dark. Doesn't like this place.'

'Well – I expect we all feel that we want a bit of sun,' said Philip. 'But has anyone seen a way upwards, a way out of these underground cellars? *I* haven't!'

25

Is there a way out?

They had all been so interested and absorbed in the treasure they had found that they had quite forgotten their danger. Jack sat down on a stone seat. He sat down gingerly, half afraid it might crumble as did so many things in these store-rooms. But it was of stone, and bore his weight safely.

'There must have been *some* way down to these store-rooms,' he said. 'Two or three ways, I should have thought, because they're so vast in extent. Anyone see any steps downwards?'

'Only those we came in by,' said Philip. 'Maybe that was the only entrance.'

'No. I should think that was a secret entrance, used by the priests,' said Jack. 'There must have been some more usual way into this place. I imagine that the temple itself was immediately overhead — it must have been an enormous place!'

'Yes — but don't run away with the idea that it's there still, rising magnificently into the air!' said Philip. 'It was in ruins thousands of years ago, and other buildings may have been set above it, and yet others above them! We may be far down under the earth — and probably are. You read bits of those books in Uma's boat, didn't you? We are in a long-ago, lost, forgotten place, which we have happened on by chance.'

Everyone listened to this in silence. Lucy-Ann gave a little shiver. Long-ago — lost — forgotten — they were somehow sad, frightening words. It was strange too, to think that above their heads might be ruins of several other temples, also lost and forgotten.

'I want to get out of here,' said Lucy-Ann, suddenly. 'I feel frightened now.'

'Let's have something to eat,' said Jack at once. Everyone always felt better after a meal, he had noticed — including Lucy-Ann, whose imagination was more vivid and sensitive than that of the others!

So they sat down in one of the temple store-rooms and enlivened the centuries-old silence by chatter and even laughter, for Kiki decided to join in the meal and the chattering too.

'Where's your hanky?' she demanded of the surprised Tala. 'Blow your nose! One, two, how do you do? Wipe your feet, knock-knock, who's at the door? A-whoooooo-shoo!'

Her sneeze was so realistic that Tala and Oola stared in

wonder. Then Kiki practised various kinds of hiccups, and Tala gave one of his guffaws, which echoed round and round the little stone chamber in a most remarkable way, quite silencing Kiki. It also disturbed a small, mouldering heap of things in a nearby corner, and they subsided with one of the odd little sighs that the children now knew so well.

'There, Tala – see what your laugh has done,' said Jack, pointing. 'You'll have the whole place down on our heads if you laugh as loudly as that!'

Tala was quite horrified. He gazed at the roof by the light of his torch as if he really thought it might be coming down. Oola gazed too. He was very silent, and obviously scared and unhappy. He kept very near to Philip.

Tala threw down the wrapping from his sandwiches. 'No, don't do that, Tala!' said Jack, at once. 'Please pick that up! It's a shame to litter up a place like this with modern newspapers!'

Tala picked up the paper, looking as if he thought that Jack was quite crazy. Philip felt about in his pocket, and pulled out the two or three pages he had torn out of one of Uma's books – the ones on which Uma had made notes.

'I'll just have a look at these,' he said. 'I don't expect they'll be of any help, but they might. I have an idea that this place we're in is the one that interests Uma – and, knowing what is here through seeing it with our own eyes, I am beginning to feel that we've made a big mistake about Uma.'

'How do you mean?' asked Jack. 'We were more or less certain that he was using his "hobby" of archaeology to cover up his real affairs in Ciné-Town, weren't we? Do you mean that we were wrong?'

'Yes. I think his *real* business *is* archaeology!' said Philip. 'But not because he is interested in history or old buildings – oh no! All that Uma is interested in is getting at the priceless treasure that he thinks may be here! He's just a mean, ordinary robber – all his digging is merely to find and steal the kind of treasure we can see around us this very minute! He is after such things as that gold bowl we gave Tala to carry, and . . . '

'Yes! You're right!' cried Jack. 'And probably just as he is feeling that his excavating is almost at an end, and he'll soon be able to take what he wants, along comes Bill! And Uma's afraid, because he knows Bill's reputation, and is certain he's come out here to watch him!'

'That's it!' said Philip. 'And he makes his plans carefully – kidnaps Bill and Mother – plans to get *us* out of the way too – and to finish his digging and clear off with the spoils!'

'Whew!' said Dinah, quite overcome by all this explanation. 'I think you're right! And what happens is that we go off in Uma's boat, and actually find the treasure chambers ourselves!'

'Yes – but we're up against a very big snag,' said Philip, soberly. 'We don't know how to get out of here!'

'Have a look at those notes of Uma's. See if there's anything in them to help us,' said Lucy-Ann. 'He was looking for this place, wasn't he? – and you said that you thought he had almost finished his excavations – so his digging must have brought him very near these treasure chambers! Look at his notes!'

Philip spread out the marked pages on the floor, and Tala shone his powerful torch on them. The children knelt down to examine them.

On one page was a list of the buildings that were known to have been built over the site of the great temple. Uma had put ticks beside them, and also the word 'Trouvé'.

'Trouvé! That's French for found,' said Jack. 'That means that in his digging he has come across some of these other remains and has dug through them. Yes – he's done well. He must be very near here in his digging. I wonder how many men he's got on the job. It's usually a very long job, isn't it, Philip?'

'Not if you're merely a *robber* and not an archaeologist!'

said Philip. 'A man really interested in old things would not dig straight through them, destroying all kinds of interesting bits of history – he would go carefully, bit by bit – sifting the soil, examining everything. But Uma . . . '

'Yes – Uma's only a robber! All he'd do is to pay workers to dig, and tell them where – and to dig fast!' said Jack, interrupting. 'Gosh – he's clever!'

'Not clever,' said Dinah. 'Just smart! Horrible man! Do you suppose his men are digging over our heads this very minute?'

'Maybe!' said Philip. 'Hallo, look – here's a little map he's drawn. Is that any use to us?'

They pored over it, but could not make out what it was meant to be. Philip sighed. 'Well – except that they give us an idea of Uma's real business, these papers aren't much help. Come on – let's *really* hunt for an exit. There simply must be some way out of these underground chambers into the temple that was above.'

They wandered all over the store-rooms again, becoming very tired of the darkness and the mustiness, which seemed to be more 'smellable' now, as Dinah kept pointing out. Oola was frankly miserable, and trailed along after Philip, dragging his bare feet dejectedly.

They sat down again at last in the biggest store-room of all. 'The only thing I can think of is to climb up those steps again, and go all the way back to the boat,' said Philip at last. 'I honestly don't see any sense in staying here any longer – there doesn't seem to be ANY way out!'

'What's the good of going back to the boat?' said Jack, gloomily. 'There's no way of escape from that cavern!'

'I don't know about that,' said Philip. 'You remember that rocky platform that Oola took us to – where we looked down and saw the river disappearing far below? Well, there *might* be a chance of climbing up and up the sides of the cliff at the side of the gorge, and getting to the top.'

'Impossible!' said Jack. 'I had a jolly good look when we

were there. Still – we'll go back and see. I agree that it's no good sitting here. Nobody's likely to rescue us!'

Most dispiritedly they made their way back through the vast range of store-chambers. They came to the door that still hung partly on its hinges, and climbed past it into the room where they had found the beautiful golden bowl, and then through that and into the narrow passage beyond, that led to the steep steps.

'Oola – go up first, you climb like a cat,' said Philip. 'Tala, give him the rope to take up, and the grappling hook. Oola, need help. You must run up the steps carefully – CARE-FULLY – with rope and hook. Do you understand?'

Oola was a different being at once, now that he thought they were leaving the great rooms down below. He nodded eagerly and took the rope. Ah – he was doing something for his boss – something important. He, Oola, and not Tala! Very proudly he began to climb the steps, feeling each with his hands before he trod on it. He slipped once, but managed not to fall.

At last he was at the top, and yelled down.

'Oola here! Oola safe! Here comes rope!'

Oola let the rope slither down the steps, carefully holding the other end himself. He had tied it to the big hook, which he now stuck firmly into a jutting-out rock as he had seen Tala do before.

The rope tightened in his hands and he knew that some-one was climbing. Perhaps his boss? Oola held on tightly, bracing himself behind a rock, in case Philip slipped and had to pull on the rope to save himself.

And then Oola heard something that scared him almost to death! It was a knocking sound away up the passage behind him! Knock-knock – thud, thud, thud! Oola's heart turned over and he fell to the ground in fright, letting the rope go slack.

At once he heard Philip's voice. 'Tighten the rope, Oola – it's slack! Hey, what are you doing?'

Knock-knock-thud-thud! Was it the old gods and goddesses coming back, angry because people had been in their temple? Oola screamed loudly, and Philip almost fell down the steps in alarm.

'The gods! They come!' screamed Oola. 'They come!'

26
'The gods! They come!'

Philip couldn't hear what the boy was screaming and he was most alarmed. He hurriedly climbed the rest of the steps, trying to be extra careful, for Oola had forgotten all about holding the rope tight, he was so terrified.

'Oola! What's up? What are you screaming for?' demanded Philip, as soon as he had reached the top.

'The gods!' cried Oola, pointing up the passage. 'They come. Listen, boss!'

Philip had heard nothing but Oola's screaming when he was climbing the steps — but now to his startled ears came the sound of the knocking that Oola had heard!

Knock-knock-knock-knock! Thud!

Philip stared up the dark passage, his heart beating. For one wild moment Oola's terror infected him, and he imagined angry gods demanding entry. What *was* that noise?

He turned and called down. 'Come up, quickly! Something's happening!'

His hands trembling, he held the rope as tightly as he could, with Oola clinging to his knees, quite weak with fright. Dinah came up, alarmed at Philip's shout. As soon as she stood beside him she heard the knocking too and was very scared, especially as she heard Oola's continual plaintive moans.

'The gods! They come! They come!'

The others climbed up, Tala last. As soon as he heard the knocking he turned in fright to go down the steps again, missed his footing and rolled cursing to the bottom. He too thought that the gods had come to revenge themselves on the little company of people who had dared to wander through their temple rooms!

Philip had no time to think of the terrified Tala, nor even to wonder if he were hurt. He had to decide what to do about the knocking. Where exactly did it come from?

'It's somewhere up the passage – and we know there's no way in, because we've been there and seen the wall of stone that is built right across!' said Philip. 'Jack – do you think it is Uma and his men?'

'Can't be anyone else,' said Jack. 'Do shut up, Oola. I can't hear myself speak.'

Knock-knock-knock!

'They come, they come!' moaned Oola, still clinging to Philip's knees.

'Uma must have found a plan or map that somehow enabled him to dig down to this passage,' said Philip, thinking hard. 'But instead of coming in at *this* side of that stone wall, they dug down just behind it. They must be trying to break the wall down. What a hope!'

'They'll do it, though,' said Jack, listening. 'They've got some powerful tools. Quick, Philip, what's our plan?'

'Can't think of one. It's all so sudden!' groaned Philip. 'Gosh, I'm glad to know that at any rate we'll be able to get out of here!'

'Uma won't be pleased to see us, if it's really him and his men,' said Jack, soberly. 'Well, we can't do anything but wait. Philip, I'm afraid Uma is going to rifle those temple store-chambers now – and take away things that are of absolutely priceless value. I don't see how we can prevent that.'

'I wish we could!' said Philip, and the girls echoed his wish. It was shocking to think of Uma and his gang of robbers stripping those old rooms of the marvellous treasures there. The knocking went on and on, and they all stood and listened. Obviously the stone wall was very strong!

Then suddenly part of the wall gave way, and one of the big stones fell into the passage with a crash. The children heard it, though they were not near enough to see what had happened.

'The wall's giving way,' said Jack. 'They'll soon be through. Just stand here quietly and wait. Oola, stop that awful row. These are not gods who are coming, but men.'

'No, no – *Oola* say gods! *Tala* say gods!' moaned Oola. Tala had now climbed up the steps again, feeling his bruises with horror, and quite determined that, gods or no gods, he was not going to fall down those steps again. But as soon as he heard the knocking he almost repeated his performance, and only just clutched the rope in time. Fortunately the grappling hook held and he pulled himself to safety.

Another crash. That would be the stone next to the first one. Now it would be easy for the men to prise out two more and then creep in through the hole.

Crash! Thud! Then came shouts, echoing down the passage. Tala listened in astonishment. Why – these gods were speaking in his own language! He began seriously to doubt whether they *could* be gods! Oola listened too and stood up. Who were these gods who talked as men – who spoke the same words as he and Tala?

A light shone far away up the passage. 'One of the men is through,' said Philip. 'Ah – there's another light. Two men are through. Here they come!'

Two men, carrying torches, came down the passage cautiously, flashing the light here and there to see what kind of place they were in. They came suddenly upon the silent group of children, with Tala behind, and stared as if they could not believe their eyes. Philip stepped forward, about to speak.

But, in absolute panic, the men fled at top speed back to the broken wall, shouting in terror.

'Men frightened,' said Oola, in great satisfaction. 'Men go.'

'Come on – let's go to the wall and get through it ourselves,' said Philip. 'I'm longing for some good clean air and the sun on my shoulders. I daresay it's a long long way up to the sun, but however long the climb it will be worth it!'

They all moved up the passage, and came to the stone wall. Tala shone his big torch on it, and they saw that four great stones had been prised out and had fallen into the passage. 'Come on,' said Philip. 'You go first, Jack, and we'll follow.'

But at that moment a man looked through the hole, and shone a torch right on them. He whistled.

'So the men were right. There *is* someone here – and surely – surely it's Bill's little lot! Well, I'm blessed – is this a dream? How did *you* get here?'

'Never mind that,' said Philip, coldly. 'We have plenty of questions to ask *you*, Mr Uma! Where are Bill and my mother? Are they safe?'

Mr Uma didn't answer. He ran his torch quickly over the little group to see how many there were. 'Was it you who took my motor-boat?' he asked, abruptly. 'Where is it?'

'Never mind that,' repeated Philip. 'Tell me about my mother and Bill. You're going to get into trouble about all this, Mr Uma. We know all about your plans – you're nothing but a robber!'

'You hold your tongue!' shouted Mr Uma, suddenly losing his temper. 'How did you get here? There's no way in except this.'

'Oh yes there is,' said Philip. 'But it isn't one you are ever likely to find! Now, let us out of this hole, and tell us where to find Bill.'

Mr Uma then addressed Tala in his own language, and by his angry tone and fierce expression he was threatening Tala with all sorts of things. Tala listened stolidly to the questions and threats thrown at him.

'Tala not know, Tala not know,' he kept answering, in English, which really infuriated Mr Uma.

'What's he saying, Tala?' asked Philip.

'He say, how come we here? He say he catch us all, not let us go. He say many bad things. He bad man.' Tala suddenly spat at Mr Uma, who immediately flung his torch at him, hitting him on the cheek. Tala laughed, bent down, picked up the torch, and put it into his waist-cloth. Then he stood gazing stolidly at the angry Mr Uma.

Mr Uma shook his fist and then disappeared. They heard him shouting for his men.

'He send men to tie us up,' said Tala, listening. 'Mr Uma bad man, very bad man.'

'Will he really have us tied up?' asked Dinah, fearfully.

'I shouldn't be surprised,' said Jack. 'He needs us out of the way while he steals what he wants from those treasure-chambers. Then, when he has taken all the best and most valuable things, he'll be off, and we'll be set free – I hope!'

'Beast!' said Dinah, fiercely. 'I suppose he's got Mother and Bill tied up somewhere too.'

'Yes. Probably in his house at Chaldo,' said Philip. 'What are we to do? We can't fight a whole lot of men!'

'Let's climb through that hole in the cavern wall, and get back to the boat,' said Jack, suddenly.

'Quite a good idea,' said Philip. 'Except that it leaves Uma free to rifle all through those store-rooms, and take what he pleases – and I've been hoping somehow we might be able to stop him.'

'We're too late,' said Lucy-Ann. 'Here come the men!'

She was right. A man came through the hole in the wall, and then another and another. It was too late now to run, for the men would follow them and see where they went. So the children stood their ground. Kiki, who had been silent for some time, was very excited when she saw the men squeezing through the hole. She jigged up and down on Jack's shoulder and gave a loud screech, which startled the men considerably.

There were now six men through the wall, and they came menacingly towards the children.

'Keep off,' said Philip, commandingly. 'Don't lay hands on us, or you will get into serious trouble with the police!'

'Police!' screamed Kiki at once. 'Police! Fetch the police! PHEEEEEEEEEEEE! PHEEEEEEEEEEEE!'

The men stopped abruptly, startled almost out of their wits. The shrill whistle that Kiki gave echoed round and round the passage in a very terrifying manner. 'PHEEE-EEEEE, PHEEEEEEEE, PHEEEEEEEE.' It went on and on – and then, to crown everything, Kiki added her noise of a motor-car back-firing. 'Pop! Crack! Crack!' These joined the whistling echoes, and alarmed the men so much that they turned and ran for the wall, adding their own screams to the crazy chorus of echoes!

The children laughed as they watched the men scramble through the wall in a panic.

'Thanks, Kiki,' said Jack, stroking the parrot's feathers. 'For once in a way I shall not say "Be quiet!" You just came in at the right moment!'

27

What now?

Tala laughed heartily as he saw the men scrambling to get away from the mysterious noises. His enormous guffaws filled the passage too. Oola danced about and clapped his hands in glee. Both appeared to think that now that they had put the men to flight all their troubles were over.

But the children knew better. They turned gravely to one

another. 'Should we try to get through the hole ourselves, now there's a chance?' said Philip.

'I don't know. We are comparatively safe here, now that the men have been so frightened,' said Jack. 'What do you think, Tala? Will those men come back?'

'Men frighted, very frighted,' said Tala, showing all his white teeth. 'Men not come back. Never come back. We go, then?'

'No. Wait a bit,' said Jack. 'We don't want to walk out of the frying-pan into the fire. The men will go to Uma, and tell him what happened – and he'll perhaps lie in wait for us, hoping to catch us as we climb through the wall.'

Tala nodded. 'That good talk. We wait. Uma much bad man.'

They sat down and waited. Nothing happened for a while, and then a man came to the hole in the wall. He wore a turban and white robes.

'I would speak with you,' he called, in a voice that was not quite English. Philip thought he might be a messenger of Uma's, and waited to see what he would say.

'I would come through the wall. I would speak with you,' repeated the man.

'Come through, then,' said Philip, wondering who the man was.

The man squeezed through the hole and came over to the children. He had a very polite manner, and bowed gravely to them all.

'May I sit with you?'

'You may,' said Philip, on his guard. 'Why do you come?'

'I come to tell you that my friend, Mr Raya Uma, is sad that he has frightened you,' said the man. 'He was – how do you say it? – *startled* – at your being here. He said things that he is sorry for.'

Nobody said a word. Jack and Philip were all ears. What was Mr Uma's little game now?

'His men have been to him to say that they will not work

330

for him any more,' went on the man, in his soft voice. 'They are too afraid. That is bad news for him. He must get others. So he has sent me to say that you may go unmolested. He will see that you are set on the right road, and he will lend you his biggest car, so that you may go back to Chaldo in safety.'

'Why Chaldo?' asked Philip, at once.

'Because it is there that he has Mr Bill and his wife,' said the soft-spoken man. 'You will join them and can then do what you will. Is this agreeable to you?'

'Who are *you*?' asked Jack, bluntly.

'I am his friend,' said the man. 'But I am not so hasty as he. I said he was wrong to frighten you, you are but children. He listens to me, as you see. Now – will you accept his generous offer? He is sincerely sorry for his foolishness.'

'Go and tell him we will think it over,' said Jack. 'We need to talk about it. We do not trust Mr Uma, your friend.'

'That is sad,' said the man, and he stood up. 'I go to wait outside the wall, and you will come to tell me when you have talked together. We are agreed?'

The man suddenly saw the golden bowl beside Tala, and stared at it in surprise.

'Where did you get that?' he asked. 'May I see it?' He bent down to pick it up, but Tala snatched it away, standing up with it held high in his hands. Uma's friend reached up for it, his white sleeves falling back over his bare arms. But Tala would not release his hold on the bowl. He said something rude in his own language, and the man looked as if he were about to strike him. But he recovered himself, bowed and walked off to the hole in the wall. He squeezed through it and stood waiting on the other side.

'Well – what about it?' said Philip.

Jack shook his head vehemently. 'No, no, no! Didn't you notice something when he reached up to get the bowl from Tala? He's no friend of Mr Uma's!'

'Who is he, then?' said everyone, astonished.

331

'He's Mr Uma *himself*!' said Jack. 'Didn't you see his right fore-a. m when he reached up for that bowl? His sleeve fell back – and there, on his arm, was the white scar of an old wound – just like a curving snake!'

There was a dead silence. Then Philip whistled. 'My word!' he said. 'The daring of it – coming to us like that – the cunning! It never once occurred to me that it was Mr Uma himself – dressed like the ordinary people – speaking the same kind of broken English. My, he's a cunning fellow! No wonder all those photos of him looked as if they were of different men!'

'Well!' said Dinah, astounded. 'Fancy having the *nerve* to come and talk to us like that! Trying to persuade us to walk right into a clever little trap. Good thing you saw that snake-like scar, Jack!'

'Good thing Bill *told* us about it!' said Jack. 'Well – what do we do now? Go and tell him it's no go, we know who he is?'

'Yes,' said Philip, getting up. 'Come on, we'll tell him now, Jack. You others stay here.'

The boys walked up the passage to the wall. Mr Uma, his hands folded inside his robes, waited impassively, looking for all the world like a distinguished man.

'Mr Uma,' said Philip, boldly, 'we say no to your little trap.'

'What do you mean?' said the man. 'I am not Mr Uma! I am his friend. Do not be insolent, boy.'

'You *are* Mr Uma,' said Philip. 'We saw the snake-like scar on your right arm – your mark, Mr Uma, and a good one too – for your ways are surely as cunning as a snake's!'

Mr Uma cast away his soft voice and polite manners. He screamed at them, both his fists in the air.

'You bring it upon yourselves! I will teach you a lesson! You think you will walk out of here and up to the sun. You will not! You will not! I will block up this hole and you shall not come this way!'

'We'll go out the way we came, then,' said Jack, boldly. 'This is not the only way in.'

'Ah, you cannot go out the way you came in!' said Mr Uma. 'If you could, you would have left by now. I am not so foolish as you think. You need a lesson, and you shall have it!'

He called loudly, leaning away from the stone. 'Come here, men. Come! I have work for you to do!'

The children and Tala and Oola were now all beside the wall, listening. No men came in answer to Mr Uma's call. He shouted again in a language the children could not follow, and this time two men came, very reluctantly.

'Bring bricks! Block up this hole!' commanded Uma. The men stared at him sullenly, looking fearfully in through the hole, remembering what their comrades had said when they had come back from the passage beyond.

Uma began to talk very fast to them, and the men listened with sudden interest.

'What's he saying, Tala?' asked Jack.

'He promise gold,' said Tala. 'He say they rich men if they obey. Much, much gold.'

The men looked at one another and nodded. They went off and came back with a pile of bricks. A third man brought mortar, and the blocking up of the hole began.

The little company inside were in despair. They knew that they could go back to the boat and find plenty of food, and could get fresh air outside the cavern – but for how long was Uma going to imprison them? They would *have* to give in sooner or later. They watched the gradual filling-in of the hole – and then Philip suddenly had an idea!

He put his hand inside his shirt and gently eased out the bargua snake he still cherished. He slide the bright green creature on to the edge of the small hole still left in the wall, and held it there.

'Mr Uma!' he called. 'Mr Uma – are you there? Here is something for you!'

Uma came at once to the wall, and put his face near to the hole, shining his torch into it. He saw the writhing bargua snake at once. He gave a scream of real panic as the snake came gliding out. The three men outside saw it too, dropped their tools and fled, shouting in terror.

'Bargua! Bargua!'

Nobody could see what happened next, for the other side of the hole was now in complete darkness. The children could hear nothing, after the cries had died away in the distance.

'Tala break wall,' said Tala, suddenly. He took the little trowel he still had hanging round his neck and attacked the wall vigorously, Oola helping him with his bare hands. The mortar was still soft and it was not very difficult to force out the roughly-set bricks and make the hole as big as it was before.

'Good, Tala – good, Oola!' said Philip. 'Now, out we all get as quickly as possible, while the bargua is still scaring everyone. Ready?'

They squeezed out one by one and found themselves in a very narrow passage, evidently quite newly excavated. They went along it and came to what looked like a shaft going straight up. Rough steps were cut in the side and a rope hung down as a handhold.

'Well – up we go!' said Philip, shining his torch upwards. 'Good luck, everybody – this is our only chance of escape!'

28
Uma is in trouble

It was a long and difficult way up the deep shaft. Philip reached the top first, feeling quite worn out, for the footholds were none too good, and it was tiring work climbing,

climbing, climbing, with only a thin rope to pull on.

He found himself still in darkness at the top, in a small narrow tunnel that sloped upwards. He stood at the top of the shaft to help Lucy-Ann out and then went to see where the passage led. It led to another shaft, but a much shorter one, for Philip could see daylight at the top. His heart leapt. Daylight again! What a wonderful thing!

Soon all the others had arrived safely up the shaft, though Tala was complaining bitterly. 'Tala slip,' he said. 'Tala hold rope, Tala burn hand, see!'

Poor Tala! He had slipped, and had slid down the rope so fast that he had scorched his hands on it. Philip handed him his handkerchief.

'Here you are. Bind it round,' he said. 'There is no time to make a fuss. I wish I could see my bargua snake somewhere, but I can't.'

'You surely didn't expect it to climb the shaft, Philip!' said Dinah.

'Snakes can wriggle anywhere,' said Philip. 'Come on! There's another shaft to climb – then daylight!'

Everyone was delighted to hear that. They were soon climbing the next shaft, which was very much easier because it had a rope ladder hanging down the side. They were soon at the top.

'It's heaven to stand in the daylight again!' said Lucy-Ann, blinking at the brightness around. 'And doesn't this sun feel good, Dinah! Oh, Philip – you're surely not looking for the bargua up *here*. It *couldn't* climb two shafts, poor thing!'

Dinah was secretly very glad indeed that the spotted bargua had gone, but she didn't dare to say so, for it had been the cause of their sudden freedom. She stood looking round eagerly, delighting in the sunshine.

They were in a most desolate spot. 'Like a builder's yard in the middle of a dusty, sandy desert!' she said, and they all agreed.

'Where is everyone?' wondered Jack. 'Oh – there are the men over there. What are they doing – bending down over something.'

The men heard the voices and looked round. Then one of them came running at top speed, leaping over the mounds of dug-up earth. He signalled urgently to Philip and Jack, calling out something in his own language.

'What does he say?' asked Philip, turning to Oola and Tala, puzzled at the man's urgency.

Oola laughed triumphantly. 'He say bargua snake bite his master. He say master very frighted, will die, because bargua poison-snake. He say Mr Uma want to speak with you.'

The children looked at each other, and smiled small, secret smiles. They knew that the bargua snake had no poison, but it had bitten Mr Uma and now he thought he was certain to die – unless he was taken to a doctor at once and treated for snake-bite!

'*Could* your bargua bite?' asked Dinah, in a low voice. 'Even though it has no poison?'

Philip nodded. 'Oh yes – but its bite is now harmless. Well – this is rather funny. Let's go and talk to Mr Uma. He's evidently feeling very sorry for himself.'

They went over to where he was lying on the ground, so frightened that his brown face was almost white. He was holding his right arm and groaning.

'That snake – it bit me,' he said to Philip. 'You'll have caused my death unless you help to take me to Ciné-Town at once. There are good doctors there – they may save me.'

'Your man Jallie told us that you had taken Bill and my mother to Wooti,' said Philip, sternly. 'Answer me. Is that so? Are they there?'

'Yes. And the motor-launch too,' said Mr Uma, feebly. 'We will go there at once. Mr Bill can take me in his launch to Ciné-Town, away up the river – he shall find me a doctor. Help me, boy. I may not have long to live. Have mercy – it was *your* snake that bit me!'

Philip turned away, scorning this man who now cried for mercy and for help, although a short while back he had given orders to his men to brick them into the underground passage. He spoke to Tala.

'Please arrange this, Tala. There is a lorry over there, and a van. Tell the men to put Mr Uma into the van, and we will come in the lorry. Mr Uma will know the way. You drive the lorry, Tala, then if there is any trickery you can put your foot down hard and race us to safety.'

But there was no trickery this time. Mr Uma was in such a panic over the snake-bite that all he wanted to do was to get to Wooti and beg Bill to take him to Ciné-Town as soon as possible.

They set off, the van leading the way and Tala following after in the lorry. Both were exceedingly well-sprung, strong vehicles, and this was just as well, for there was no real road to speak of. The lorry and van jerked and jolted over hills and mounds, and poor Mr Uma, lying in the van, cried out in misery as he rolled from side to side. He was not really ill, but he was so certain that his whole body was being poisoned by the snake-bite that he was sure he had aches and pains all over!

It was a long way to Wooti, but they got there at last. Mr Uma gave his driver a few directions when they arrived, and both lorry and van stopped outside a shack set by itself beside a desolate cart-track.

The driver got down and took some keys from Mr Uma. He unlocked the door of the shack and out came Bill at once, looking more furious than the children had ever seen him look before.

'Now then!' shouted Bill. 'Where's that fellow Uma?'

The van-driver gesticulated and said a good deal. Evidently he was telling Bill about the snake-bite. Bill however, was not at all sympathetic. Jack and Philip judged it time to say a few words themselves and they leapt out and ran over to Bill.

He stared at them as if he were dreaming. 'Jack! Philip!

What on earth – good heavens, what *is* all this? Explain quickly, Philip.'

Philip explained a little, enough to make Bill understand what was happening at the moment.

'Uma's back in the van,' he said. 'He thinks he's been bitten by a poisonous snake – but he hasn't really, it was only my own bargua – and you know how harmless *that* was! He's so anxious to get to a doctor at Ciné-Town up the river that he agreed to take us here and free *you*, so that you could take him in your launch to find a doctor. That's briefly what's happening now, Bill.'

'Well, I'm blessed,' said Bill again. 'So our friend Uma thinks he's been fatally bitten, does he? Then perhaps he would like to confess a few things and clear his conscience! Right – find out where the launch is, boys, tell Uma I'm coming, and I'll just go and fetch my wife.'

Bill ran off to the shack, and Philip, anxious to see his mother, went with him. Jack went to tell Uma that Bill was coming, and to ask where the launch was.

Uma was still very pale. He groaned. 'Good boy,' he said. 'Ah, this is a punishment for all my sins. I have been a wicked man, boy.'

'It sounds like it,' agreed Jack, hard-heartedly. 'Bill wants to know where the launch is.'

'By the riverside,' groaned Mr Uma. 'The poison's working in my veins, I know it is! We shall have to hurry!'

Bill came out with his wife, who certainly looked none the worse for being locked up in the shack for a few days. She seemed quite cheerful, and had been told a little of the children's adventures by Philip. She and Bill had had no idea, of course, that the children had been through so much excitement.

They drove off to the river. Bill went in the van with Uma, who poured out such a lot of confessions that Bill was almost embarrassed. The things that Mr Uma had done in his life! His sins had certainly been very many.

The launch was by the river as Uma had said. By the time

338

they reached it Mrs Cunningham had heard more of the children's news from everyone in the lorry, and had been greeted joyfully by Kiki, who insisted on shaking hands with her at least a dozen times.

'Pleasedtomeetyou,' said Kiki, running all the words together. 'Pleasedtomeetyou, good morning, goodbye!'

'Oh, Kiki — it's so nice to see you all again,' said Mrs Cunningham. 'We imagined that Tala would look after you, and that he would raise the alarm and bring help to us as soon as possible. I never realized you had been through a bad time like this! Poor Mr Uma — he must be in a terrible panic over this snake-bite.'

'Don't say "*poor* Mr Uma", Mother!' said Dinah. 'He's wicked. You wait till you hear *all* our story. It's hair-raising, really it is!'

The lorry and the van were left at Wooti, and the launch took everyone to Ciné-Town, with Mr Uma tossing and groaning all the time. It seemed remarkable that he could simulate all the symptoms of snake-bite like this, and Bill half wondered if Philip's bargua had been as harmless as they had imagined!

He frowned as he thought of all the things that the scared Mr Uma had blurted out to him — and this latest plan to rob the old, forgotten temple of its priceless treasures for the sake of mere greed sickened Bill. Mr Uma was *not*, of course, being taken to see a doctor — no, he was being taken to see some very high-up police!

It was a really terrible shock to Mr Uma to be handed over to the police at Ciné-Town, when they arrived there. Bill had ordered two cars as soon as the launch had reached Ciné-Town, and he and his wife and Uma had gone in the first one, and the other six, with Kiki, in the second — and they had all driven to police headquarters. Mr Uma could hardly believe his eyes when he was half led, half carried into a bare police-station, instead of into the pleasant private room of a hospital that he had expected.

'What's this?' he cried. 'Is this a kind trick to play on a

man dying of snake-bite – a poisonous snake bite?'

'You're quite all right, Uma,' said Bill with a laugh. 'It *wasn't* a poisonous bite – the snake had unfortunately had its poison-ducts cut, and was no longer poisonous. So cheer up – you're not going to die – but you've got a tremendous lot of things to explain to the police, haven't you?'

29

End of the adventure

It wasn't only Uma who had to explain a great many things – it was the children too, who had so much to tell Bill and his wife that they felt it would take a week to finish their tale!

After Uma had been taken charge of by some much-amused police officers, who had heard the whole story from Bill and the others, they had been allowed to depart for the launch.

'The police seem to find it very funny that Uma is so disappointed not to have had a poisonous bite after all,' said Bill, as they left. 'Of course – it *is* bad luck when one's sins find one out – but they always have a nasty little habit of doing that. Crime simply does NOT pay!'

'Well, Uma's learnt that now – or do you think he hasn't?' asked Philip. 'Will he start his bad ways all over again, now he knows he *hasn't* been bitten by a poisonous bargua, Bill?'

'I fear he will have to disappear from public life for quite a time!' said Bill. 'Long enough to get over any snake-bite, real *or* imaginary. I must say that snake of yours repaid you well for your kindness to him, Philip.'

Yes. But I wish I could have got him back,' said Philip. 'I liked him.'

'Don't say that in front of Oola or he'll produce a few more barguas,' said Dinah, in a panic.

It was wonderful to laze on the launch again, and talk and talk. Bill was amazed at the children's adventures.

'There were we, cooped up in a silly shack with barred windows and a locked door and nothing whatever happening – and you four having the time of your lives,' he said. 'Rushing down gorges, almost shooting over cataracts, crawling through holes, exploring age-old treasures . . . '

'It was pretty tough at times,' said Jack. 'The girls were marvellous. And so were Tala and Oola!'

This was such an unusual compliment from Jack that both the girls stared in surprise.

'Kiki did *her* bit too,' said Jack. Bill laughed.

'She certainly did, from all you've told me!' he said. 'She seems to react marvellously to the word "police".'

'Police!' called Kiki at once. 'Fetch the police! PHEEEEEEEEEEEEEEE!'

Some people stopped beside the launch at once, eyes round with fright.

'It's all right,' called Jack. 'It's only the parrot. Don't do that too often, Kiki, or one of these fine days you'll find a policeman will come along and lock you up!'

'PHEEEEEEEEEEEE!' began Kiki again, and got a tap on the beak.

'Bad boy!' she grumbled at Jack. 'Bad boy! Fetch your nose, blow the doctor!'

'It's nice to hear her again,' said Mrs Cunningham. 'Bill and I could have done with a bit of Kiki's fun those long dull days in that shack.'

'I suppose you know, you youngsters, that you have made the find of the century?' said Bill, after a while. 'I know that Uma was also on the mark, but he's a bit discredited, at the moment – finding a place like that wonderful old temple merely to rob it is rather different from discovering it by accident as you did, and doing your best to keep off those who wanted to despoil it.'

'What do you think of the things we brought back, Bill?'

asked Dinah, eagerly. 'That gold bowl – it *is* gold, isn't it? – and the cup – and the little statue – and the dagger. Don't you think they are marvellous? I wish we could keep them, but I know we can't.'

'No, you can't. They belong to the whole world,' said Bill, 'not only to our own generation, but to all those who follow us. They are wonderful relics of the history of man – and I am prouder than I can say that you have had a hand in bringing them to light.'

'What will happen about the temple, Bill?' asked Jack. 'And what is going to happen to the things we brought back? – we had to leave them at the police station, you know.'

'Yes – well, they are being shown to some of the finest experts in the world,' said Bill. 'The police say that when the news gets round that this long-lost temple has been found, there will be many famous archaeologists flying here, anxious to see that any excavating is now done properly.'

'Shall we meet them?' asked Philip, eagerly.

'No. You'll be at school', said Bill, hard-heartedly.

'*School*! Oh, Bill, you're *mean*!' said Dinah, who had imagined herself having a wonderful time talking learnedly to famous men. 'Aren't we going to stay on and see it all being dug out?'

'Good gracious, no!' said Mrs Cunningham. 'It may take five or six years – even more – to excavate that wonderful temple. It's not done in the haphazard way that Mr Uma did it, you know. Why, practically every piece of earth will be sifted!'

'Oh! How disappointing that we can't stay for the excitement!' sighed Lucy-Ann.

'My dear Lucy-Ann – haven't you had *enough* excitement already?' asked Bill, astonished. 'I should have thought that you four had had enough adventures to last the ordinary person for the rest of his life!'

'Well – perhaps we're not ordinary persons?' suggested

Philip, with a twinkle in his eye.

'*You're* not an ordinary person, Philip!' said Dinah. 'I wish you were! No *ordinary* person would take a snake about with him. I expect you'll adopt a camel next!'

'Well, that reminds me – Bill, I *did* see a baby camel today that didn't look too happy,' said Philip, hopefully. 'I thought that if any prizes were going for brilliance in finding a long-forgotten temple, perhaps mine might be something like a baby camel.'

'Certainly not,' said Mrs Cunningham, sitting up straight. 'You can't be serious, Philip! What – take one *home*, do you mean!'

'Well, this was a very *little* one,' said Philip, earnestly. 'Wasn't it, Lucy-Ann? Not more than two days old. It was absol . . . '

'Philip – do you or do you *not* know that camels grow very big – and that they do *not* like a cold climate like ours?' said his mother. 'And that I would *not* dream of having a camel sitting in the middle of my rose-beds, and . . . '

'All right, Mother, all right,' said Philip, hurriedly. 'It was only just an *idea* of mine – and you both seemed so pleased with us that – well . . . '

'That you thought you'd make hay while the sun shone and cash in on a camel?' said Bill with a grin. 'No go, Philip, old son. Try something else.'

'I hope we're not going back to school *immediately*,' said Jack. 'I did rather want to show you that waterfall hurling itself over the edge of the gorge, Aunt Allie. Can't we go and explore a bit down in the old temple – wouldn't we be allowed to, seeing that we found it? Then you could creep through that hole in the cavern wall and crawl out on to the ledge and go and stand on the platform, and see what Oola calls the "waterfalling" – it's unbelievable!'

'Oola find waterfalling, Oola show kind Missus?' said Oola's voice, and his small black head appeared round a corner.

'Oh! So there you are!' said Philip. 'Come here, Oola. Sit with us and tell how you went out all by yourself to find the waterfalling.'

Oola was very proud to tell his story. He would not sit down to tell it, but stood there, a small, lithe figure, still with the marks of bruises and weals on his back, his eyes sparkling as he told his tale.

Mrs Cunningham drew him to her when he had finished. 'You're a good little boy and a brave one, Oola,' she said. 'We shall never forget you.'

'My boss remember Oola too?' asked Oola, looking at Philip with love in his eyes.

'Always,' said Philip. 'And when we come back here, sometime in the future, to see the temple when it is all dug out, and its treasures on show, you must be here to guide us round, Oola. Promise?'

'Oola promise. Oola keep clean, Oola go to school, Oola do all things like boss say,' said the small boy, valiantly. He gave an unexpected salute and disappeared, his eyes shining with proud tears.

There was a little pause after he had gone. 'I like him very much indeed,' said Lucy-Ann, emphatically. 'Don't you, Jack?'

Everyone nodded vigorously. Yes – Oola had been as astonishing a find as any of the treasures in the temple. Would they ever see him again? Yes, of course!

'Well, we've talked so much that I really feel my tongue is wearing out,' said Mrs Cunningham. 'But I must tell you one thing to relieve your minds. We are not going to *fly* back home – we are going by sea, and we shan't be home for a week or more.'

'Oh – super!' cried Dinah, and the others agreed in delight. Another whole week – what luck!

'Do you think we shall have had enough convalescence by then?' asked Lucy-Ann. 'Shall we be *fit* to go back to school?'

'Good gracious – you're all as fit as fiddles!' cried Mrs Cunningham.

'Fiddles! Fiddle-de-dee!' shouted Kiki. 'Diddly-fiddly, cat and spoon!'

'You're getting a bit mixed, old thing,' said Jack. 'Sign of old age! Now, don't peck my ear off, please!'

They all sat silent for a while, and listened to the river flowing past, lapping gently against the boat.

'The River of Adventure,' said Lucy-Ann. 'We couldn't have given it a better name. We ran into adventure all the way along its banks.'

'And *what* adventures!' said Jack. 'Oh, *don't* keep nibbling my ear, Kiki, *pleeeeeeeeeeese!*'

'Pleeeeeece! Fetch the pleeeeeece!' shouted Kiki, and whistled. 'PHEEEEEEEEEEEEEEE!'

Goodbye, Kiki. You *always* have the last word!

The Island of Adventure

For Philip, Dinah, Lucy-Ann and Jack, the holiday in Cornwall is everything they'd hoped for – until they begin to realize that something very sinister is taking place on the mysterious Isle of Gloom.

But they're not prepared for the dangerous adventure that awaits them in the abandoned copper mines and secret tunnels beneath the sea.

The Castle of Adventure

What was the secret of the old castle on the hill, and why were the locals so afraid of it?

When flashing lights are seen in a distant tower, Philip, Dinah, Lucy-Ann and Jack decide to investigate – and discover a very sinister plot concealed within its hidden rooms and gloomy underground passages.

Enid Blyton's ADVENTURE Series

The prices shown below are correct at the time of going to press. However, Macmillan Publishers reserves the right to show new retail prices on covers which may differ from those previously advertised.

ENID BLYTON

The Island of Adventure	0 330 30175 6	£4.99
The Castle of Adventure	0 330 30178 0	£4.99
The Valley of Adventure	0 330 30171 3	£4.99
The Sea of Adventure	0 330 30173 X	£4.99
The Mountain of Adventure	0 330 30177 2	£4.99
The Ship of Adventure	0 330 30172 1	£4.99
The Circus of Adventure	0 330 30174 8	£4.99
The River of Adventure	0 330 30176 4	£4.99

All Pan Macmillan titles can be ordered from our website, www.panmacmillan.com, or from your local bookshop and are also available by post from:

**Bookpost
PO Box 29, Douglas, Isle of Man IM99 1BQ**

Credit cards accepted. For details:
Telephone: 01624 677237
Fax: 01624 670923
E-mail: bookshop@enterprise.net
www.bookpost.co.uk

Free postage and packing in the UK.